SERPENTS IN THE GARDEN

On a muggy August day in 2002, Alexandra Lind was unexpectedly thrown backwards in time, landing in the year of Our Lord 1658. Catapulted into an unfamiliar and frightening new existence, Alex could do nothing but adapt. After all, while time travelling itself is a most rare occurrence, time travelling with a return ticket is even rarer.

This is the fifth book about Alex, her husband Matthew and their continued adventures in the second half of the seventeenth century.

ANNA BELFRAGE

Serpents in the Garden

SilverWood

Published in 2014 by the author
using SilverWood Books Empowered Publishing®

SilverWood Books
30 Queen Charlotte Street, Bristol, BS1 4HJ
www.silverwoodbooks.co.uk

ISBN 978-1-78132-173-7 (paperback)
ISBN 978-1-78132-174-4 (ebook)

British Library Cataloguing in Publication Data
A CIP catalogue record for this book is available from the British Library

Set in Bembo by SilverWood Books
Printed on responsibly sourced paper

This book is dedicated to my mother, who very early on introduced me to the magical world of books

Chapter 1

"Are you sure?" Betty Hancock trembled with agitation. "What if you don't come back? Ships are wrecked, and—"

Jacob Graham scoffed and went on stuffing his few belongings into the canvas sack he had procured a day or so ago. "I know the man. Captain Miles is a wily sailor. He's been sailing the seas longer than most – he'll keep me safe."

"But—" Betty protested, only to find her mouth covered by his. For some minutes, all other activity came to a halt as they concentrated on exploring this new found pleasure. His tongue flicked against her lips, and she opened her mouth under his, keeping her eyes wide open.

He pulled back with a pleased grin. "You like it, don't you?"

Betty's face heated. It was wrong to lust for someone not yet your husband, and still… She smiled and nodded, going back to helping him pack his clothes.

She peeked at Jacob from under her lashes. Four years he'd lived with them, and the boy she had once regarded as a brother had in the last few months changed into a man – a very young man, but definitely a man. Well over six feet tall, with fair hair that hung straight and thick down to his shoulders, and startling light hazel eyes, Jacob Graham was a lad that turned more than his fair share of feminine heads on the street, and not only among his contemporaries.

"Why?" Betty asked for the hundredth time.

Jacob exhaled and sat back on his heels. "You know I've always wanted to."

She gave a grudging nod. As long as she'd known him, he'd spoken of his desire to see the world, and these last few years living so close to the sea had increased that itch. Still, all of this made her feel inconsequential, discarded.

"But what about me?"

"I'll come back, and the pre-contracts are already signed."

Betty made a sound halfway between a sob and a chuckle. "The pre-contracts? You know as well as I do, that they can easily be broken. Our fathers may decide to not uphold them, and in particular my father might be tempted not to." She was not for nothing the daughter of the single man of law in town, had grown up in a household where deeds were drawn up and amended on a daily basis, and had seen far too many contracts for marriage being declared null and void by one or both contracting parties. "He'll be very disappointed."

Jacob nodded, cheeks colouring. "I don't want that. But this isn't for me; I can't spend my life drawing up papers."

"My father will never allow me to wed a seaman. So what will you do, Jacob? Once you come back from your journeys?" She'd touched upon a sensitive subject, she could see.

He twisted, muttering something about becoming a merchant, mayhap a farmer like his da. A farmer? She couldn't quite see herself as a homesteader's wife.

Jacob raised a hand to her cheek. "A healer, I think. That's what I would like to be." He pulled out his three books from where he kept them under his bed, and opened the heaviest of them. "I know this almost by heart."

So did she, what with the time they'd spent perusing the Culpeper herbal he'd inherited from his grandfather.

Jacob's finger traced the detailed drawings of a foxglove. "We grow this at home. My Offa brought the seeds with him."

She leaned against him to look over his shoulder.

"You're tickling me," he said.

No she wasn't, it was her hair. Betty hated it: wild, exuberant, impossible to tame into anything resembling a neat hairdo, and on top of that a reddish brown, not a bright gold like her sisters'.

Jacob rubbed his head against hers, let the book slide to lie on the floor, and kissed her.

"How long?" she said much later. "How many years must I wait for you?"

"I don't know. Two? Three?"

Betty shook her head. "My father won't let me wait. I'll be wed elsewhere before you come back." Around them, the house was quiet, everyone but them asleep. She'd never been in his room at night before, and never in only her chemise and a shawl. She was very aware of her breasts pushing against the thin cloth, of how his eyes kept returning to them time and time again. Jacob moved closer. She shifted away and he followed after.

"If…" He broke off and took her hand, playing with her fingers.

"If what?" Betty asked, breathing heavily.

"If we bed…"

She scooted away from him. Bed with him? His fingers grazed her arm, the side of her neck, and she had no idea what to do with the responding flickers of heat that coursed through her.

"We can handfast," he suggested, "and then…"

Betty looked at him with trepidation. According to her father, handfasting was a custom best eradicated, as it left the woman vulnerable to misuse. But in their case, the betrothal was already formalised, the contracts drawn up and signed. Except that the contracts called for Jacob to be eighteen, and that was more than two years away.

For a long time, they sat on the bed, eyes locked together. Scarcely able to breathe, Betty nodded and placed her hand in his much bigger one. What was she contemplating? She tried to reclaim her hand, but his fingers had already closed round hers, a warm, strong grip. Her pulse was swift, like the fluttering of a bird's wing, and beads of sweat formed along her hairline and behind her knees.

"I, Jacob Graham, take you, Betty Hancock, as my truly wedded wife, and to you I pledge myself," Jacob said, eyes huge in his pale face.

"I…" Betty licked her upper lip, feeling somewhat faint. "I, Betty Hancock, take you, Jacob Graham, as my truly wedded husband, and to you I pledge myself." A nervous gust of laughter escaped her. She wasn't entirely sure she wanted to do this.

Their clasped hands were slippery with sweat. Jacob leaned forward and brushed his lips against her cheek. His hot breath tickled her skin, and she shivered. He kissed her again, his hand came up to rest lightly on her breast, and Betty felt the oddest sensation, like miniature feet pattering over her skin. She panicked when he pressed her down on her back, a quick instinctive struggle that made him freeze, his eyes never leaving hers. He waited, his hand heavy on her breast. She could feel her heart begin to race. He slipped his leg between hers, and she fell back against the pillows. He tugged at the drawstring of her shift, and she crossed her arms to hold the cloth to her. Gently, he loosened her hold, and she let him, allowing him to bare her chest.

"You're very pretty," he said, raising a finger to one of her nipples. She held her breath as he touched her, closing her eyes when his hand inched the shift up her legs. She liked the warmth of his fingers on her skin, and she relaxed, her whole body softening. Jacob kicked off his breeches and lay on top of her. She opened her eyes wide when she felt his member pressing into the skin of her belly. So big? Jacob slid down to lie between her legs, and then he was inside of her and it was all over. Betty Hancock was now officially a married woman, and she still didn't know if she wanted to be.

When the time came for him to leave, they had managed a couple of times more, and Betty was left strangely disappointed and sore, with the dawning realisation that this night might lead to a child. Jacob kissed her one last time, stroked her over her undone hair, and smiled.

"My wife." He clambered out of the window and dropped to the ground below. A few moments later, he was gone, swallowed up into the night.

Jacob moved stealthily through the sleeping port. *Regina Anne* was due to sail at daybreak, and he had but an hour to make it on board without being noticed. He hadn't been entirely honest with Betty. Captain Miles hadn't offered him a place on board, would never offer him a place unless it was with parental consent. Jacob hefted his bag higher onto his shoulder and slunk along the shadows in the direction of the furthest end of the wharf.

For some minutes, he stood studying the *Regina Anne*, trying to assess how to best get on board. He sighed. He'd have to swim and clamber up her sides. Not that much of a trial this balmy August night, and a while later Jacob curled into a tight sodden ball in his chosen hiding place. He used his damp bag as a rudimentary pillow and closed his eyes, reliving the night. Not yet sixteen and already a man...

In his head, he saw Betty's coppery eyes as they stared up at him. He felt a flash of guilt at leaving her to face their parents alone, but consoled himself with the thought that Mama would be there for her. He was almost asleep when an unsettling thought struck him, and he sat up so abruptly he banged his head against the low ceiling. Nay, he decided, they were too young for there to be issue; of course they were.

Some hours later, rough hands closed on Jacob. He was dragged from his makeshift bed by a sailor the size of a giant and frogmarched over to where the captain was waiting, looking anything but pleased.

"Jacob Graham." He sighed. "And what am I to do with you? Whip you and set you ashore?"

Jacob grinned. The coast was dwindling fast behind him, and as to the whipping – no, he didn't much believe in it.

"I want to see the world," Jacob said, "now, before I grow too old."

Captain Miles huffed with exasperation. "And do your parents know where you've gone?"

Jacob hitched his shoulders. "I left them a letter," he replied in a tone far more relaxed than he was.

"You left them a letter? Daft lad! Matthew Graham is not going to like this, is he?"

Jacob ducked his head. A pit yawned inside of him at the thought of Da's reaction.

"Besides, aren't you under apprenticeship?"

"Aye, but I don't want to be a man of law."

"An absconded apprentice…" Captain Miles scratched at his cheek, all the while studying Jacob. "As I recall it, you're contracted to…" He broke off and gave Jacob a compassionate look. "Ah, I see. You don't like her."

Jacob blinked, confused. "Like who?"

"The lass – Betty, isn't it?"

"Oh, I like her very well. Once I'm back, we'll wed properly." Jacob stretched. A man, he was a married man.

"Wed properly? What have you done, lad?" Under the captain's disapproving eyes, Jacob squirmed, but mumbled that handfasting was a recognised tradition.

"Handfasting?" The captain's voice was incredulous. "You handfasted with a lawyer's lass, and you think that will be binding?"

"Not in itself, but we…" Jacob made an unequivocal gesture, all of him swelling with pride.

Captain Miles seemed mightily unimpressed, two parallel furrows forming between his brows. "You're a wee fool, Jacob Graham. What have you done? What have you left the lass to face alone?"

Jacob felt most of his bravado dissipate at the expression on the captain's face. What had until now seemed a romantic gesture paled into unappetising tawdriness, and his ears heated at the thought of what they might all think of him. Bed with her and then be off, and Betty would be branded at a minimum a fool, at worst a slut. He squeezed his eyes shut and tried to block out the sudden clear images of William Hancock and his wife Esther, and the way they stared at their youngest daughter.

"Maybe I should go back." Jacob looked at the faint shoreline.

"Och aye? How? Are you a fish?" The first mate, Smith, laughed at his own joke.

"I can swim." But not that far; even he realised that.

Captain Miles clapped Jacob on his shoulder. "Too late, son. We can't turn back now. But you'll be off this ship the

12

moment we get to Edinburgh, and there I will turn you over into the hands of your uncle. And let us hope the wee wench isn't too harshly whipped."

Jacob's guts wrenched at his words. No, he told himself, Mr Hancock wouldn't do that. Surely he wouldn't.

Betty couldn't move. Her back, her thighs, but mostly her buttocks were one huge burning pain. When her father had discovered Jacob was gone, he had been most upset, but when he threatened to tear up the pre-contracts, she had defiantly told him it was too late, because she was a wife in all ways that counted. The silence that had fallen had been absolute. She'd heard her mother gasp an "oh, Betty" before her father's hand had closed on her. He had dragged her upstairs and commanded her to undress down to her shift.

She hadn't understood what was about to happen until her father had yelled for her one remaining unwed sister to come, and for Doris, the serving girl, to come up with his horsewhip. Still she hadn't fully believed he would do it, because she had never seen him hit anyone before. Curtly, he'd told her to turn around and grab the bedpost, and to her surprise, he had tied her hands to it. She had yanked at her bindings, looking with brimming eyes at her mother.

The household had stood silent while her father explained that his daughter had shamed him, acting the whore to his erstwhile apprentice. When she protested, he had yelled at her to be quiet, to hold her tongue, depraved child that she was, and then he had raised his hand and brought the whip down for the first time.

Once he stopped, she was no longer crying: she was mute with pain and shock. When he had undone the ropes around her wrists, she had fallen neatly to her knees before her bed. A hand on her elbow helped her to stand; someone had eased her out of her bloodied shift, washed her and dressed her in cool linen before leaving her alone to meditate upon her sin and seek forgiveness from Our Lord.

★

Two days later, the door to her room was unlocked, and Betty was told to come downstairs. She dressed slowly, barely capable of moving without pain, and when she finally made her way down to the parlour, her father told her she was coming with him to break the news about Jacob to his parents. At his instructions, she returned upstairs to pack some clothes together. Her mother came to help, but Betty shook her head, turning her back until she left the room. If she was shocked by her father's anger, she felt betrayed by her mother, and she vowed she would never speak to her again – at all.

To sit a horse was torture. Betty spent a considerable amount of time padding her backside with her skirts. Her father's eyes burned into her back, and she hoped he was at least slightly ashamed of what he'd done to her. She was never going to forgive him for it, ever. She adjusted her straw hat so that her face and particularly her eyes were fully shaded, and sat waiting while her father kissed his family farewell. She had kissed her brother and sister, but had stood cold and unresponsive in her mother's embrace, ignoring the look of hurt that flashed across her mother's face.

Not once did Betty look back. Her spine was stiff with defiant pride, but inside she was crying for her mother.

Chapter 2

Matthew Graham was not given to romantic gestures, but on this, his wife's birthday, he wandered for some time through the woods surrounding their home to pick her a posy, something he had done but rarely before. Forty-seven... It made him want to shake his head in astonishment because, to his eyes, Alex looked not many years older than when he had first met her, twenty-one years ago.

He stopped to scratch his head, flapping his hat in a feeble attempt to create a cooling breeze. Maryland in the last week of August of 1679 was a hot place, distinctly different from the Scotland they had left behind, and on days like this he longed for the cool of a Scottish glen, the softness of a northern summer, so different from this browbeating, constant heat.

He swore when his thumb caught on a thorn, but gave a determined yank to add a pink briar rose to his little bouquet, and turned at the sound of young voices, one repeating a shrill "wait for me, wait for me".

A late three clover in sons, he smiled, seeing David and Samuel rush across the yard with Adam tagging at their heels, his smock billowing in the wind. From the stable came Daniel, as always in a heated discussion with Ruth, and where Ruth was, there, inevitably, was Sarah.

He scrutinised his daughters from a distance: one tall and willowy, with hair of such a dark red that it at times looked almost purple and his own hazel eyes to match; the other sturdier and rounder, with inquisitive eyes and fair hair that fell in a thick curtain well down to her waist. Or would have, had their mother allowed the girls to go unbraided. Of all their children, only two had inherited their mother's blue eyes: Daniel and Sarah. All the rest were clearly stamped with his own hazel green, and, according to Alex, the likeness between him and his sons was at times risible. Matthew didn't agree; he was secretly proud to have fathered children so unmistakably his.

He took a step back into the shade when his wife appeared at the kitchen door, not wanting her to see him standing like this, more or less spying on them all. She clapped her straw hat onto her head and strode off towards the kitchen garden, her full skirts swaying as she moved. He smiled when he recalled the first time he'd met her: how she had stared at him, not fully comprehending what had happened to her! Well, who would? An undulating crossroad, a rift in the fabric of time, and Alex tumbled from 2002 to land at his feet, badly burnt by lightning and concussed. His wife… Matthew's chest expanded with warmth. His magical lass, God's gift to him.

God's gift was in a black mood. It was too hot, far too humid, and why did all the flies within a three-mile radius seem to hover round her hat? She hitched her skirts up and frowned down at her dirty feet. A bath, she decided, a long solitary swim in the river later on, with no children, no sounds but that of her own breathing and pulse. She slapped at a bug on her arm, glared at her empty basket and the overflowing vegetable garden. This was one of those days when she longed for very strange things from her former life, chief among them an ice-cold bottle of Coca-Cola – the retro kind with its bulging shape. Or a 99 flake, with the soft ice swirling round and round inside the little cone… She sighed and went back to her digging.

"For you."

Alex sat back and raised her face to Matthew, squishing her eyes shut when the sun hit them.

"For me?" The black mood evaporated and she stretched out her hand to the wilting little bouquet. "Thank you." She stood and smiled at her man. Not exactly ice cream, but still. She studied the little posy and stuck her hand into his. "This needs water, and so do I." She led the way down to the house, set her flowers in a stone jar, and grabbed her basket. He took her hand, and they strolled off towards the cool of the river.

"Alone!" Alex barked at her children when they seemed to be on the point of joining them. "We want to be alone, okay?" She suppressed the twinge of guilt she felt at the crestfallen expression on Adam's face — after all, it was her birthday and if she wanted to have quality time with her husband, well then…

"Okay, okay." Daniel grabbed at his youngest brother to keep him back. "We'll go down later," he promised Adam.

"Later." Adam nodded, eyes hanging off Alex. Nope, she wasn't about to give in. Beside her, Matthew chuckled, tightened his hold on her hand, and led them in under the trees.

A few moments later, they were both in the water. Alex floated on her back, her hair flowing round her head like strands of dark seaweed. Her breasts bobbed in the water, the nipples puckering with the cold. Matthew took hold of her feet and towed her after him towards the deep.

"Eleven years since we came here," she said.

Matthew didn't reply. He let go of her feet and dove below her, coming up just beside her head.

"It seems longer," she went on. "Much, much longer."

"You think?" He waded over to fetch the scented soap she bought down in Providence, and settled down to lather both of them thoroughly. "To me, it's but a blink of the eye."

"Blink of the eye?" She held her nose and dipped her head under the surface to rinse off. "That just goes to show that you're not the one who's been pregnant four times since we got here," she said when she resurfaced.

He smiled. "Nay, that would have caused a raised eyebrow or two."

He liked how she got out of the water without self-consciousness, standing for a moment fully revealed. With the exception of her forearms and feet, all of her was a startling pinkish white, her skin glittering with water droplets. A possessive pride surged through him at the sight of his wife, his eyes sliding over the slope of her hips to her bottom. A right bonny sight she was; a sight reserved for his eyes only – as it should be.

She was aging well, her body firm and strong, her skin taut and unmarked by wrinkles, except for those round her eyes and mouth that showed just how often she laughed. He knew that when she turned, he'd see a belly marked by all her pregnancies, and where he found the resulting roundness attractive, she most certainly did not, now and then nipping at the slight excess of flesh with an irritated scowl. Today though, she twirled, a languidness to her movements that had him wading towards the shore. She picked up a linen towel and dried herself with leisurely movements, lifting limbs this way and that.

"I can do that," he said, coming out of the water.

"Do what? This?" The towel stroked her flank, continued down towards her pubic mound. "Or this?" She dried her breasts, one at a time. Two swift steps, and he was by her side.

"Aye, I dare say I can manage." He took the towel from her. Her thighs, the cheeks of her bottom, the curve of her back, and she stood stock-still under his touch, eyes never leaving his.

"There," he murmured, patting at her hair, "all nice and dry." He drew her into his embrace, scraping his nails ever so lightly down her spine. It made her shiver and lean against him. Her warm body was a perfect fit to his, soft curves against his larger frame.

"And now I'll have to dry myself all over," she said, kissing his wet shoulder. He didn't reply, concentrating on her round arse in his hands. She exhaled, slipping her arms round his waist, and shifted that much closer, her thighs against his, her full breasts squished against his chest. He was considering just how to love her when he felt her tense in his arms.

"What?" He leaned back to see her face.

"Angus. I swear that young man does it on purpose! Sneaking up like that…"

Matthew straightened up and swept the surrounding woods with narrowed eyes. He enjoyed loving his wife outdoors, and resented the intrusion. Angus in general was somewhat of a problem, a taciturn worker that spent far too much of his free time alone, and who, with the exception of his sister, never really spoke to anyone above the age of fourteen.

"Not anymore," he said.

"No, but it sort of kills the mood to know he might be out there peeking."

He grunted and hunted about for a towel.

Where she had no self-consciousness, Matthew definitely did. It was only with Alex, and on occasion with his bairns, that he was ever fully naked, far too aware of how scarred he was. His back was a criss-cross of welts, sword slashes had over the years decorated his torso, and the latest addition, a wide puckered scar on his thigh, was due to a blow with an axe. He made a discreet inspection of himself: still tall, still broad in chest and shoulders, and with a full head of wavy dark hair – even if there was some grey in it.

Alex approached him with her flask of oil and stopped for an instant to cock her head at him.

"Gorgeous," she said, making him laugh. "Eye candy, all of you."

He liked that, preened under her eyes, and adopted one pose after the other to show off his physique.

"Yes, yes," she grinned, "you already know I consider you the most beautiful man alive, don't you?" She patted at her spread petticoats. "Lie down, and I'll see to your back."

He did as she said, pillowing his head on his arms. He loved this: the strength and warmth of her hands, the intimacy of her touch, and the relief that flooded through his aching back when she massaged blood back into permanently tensed muscles. He was not as enthused when she went on to dig her fingers into his buttocks, yelping in protest when she found a particularly tender spot.

"No pain, no gain," she reminded him, and finished up by covering all of him with oil. "There, as good as new," she said, handing him his shirt.

Matthew decided to remain where he was. The sun warmed his skin, grasses tickled his nose, and he closed his eyes, drifting into an agreeable doze. Alex patted him on the rump and moved off.

It was nice down here by the river, a welcome breather after more than a month of strenuous harvest work. Alex reclined against her arms and stuck her nose up towards the sun. Vaguely, she could hear the sounds of her children, the piercing voices of the younger boys carrying through the quarter-mile of distance.

Nine children…no, ten, she corrected herself. There was Isaac as well, but he was somewhere in the distant future, by now a man she couldn't even envision apart from being sure he had dark hair and eyes. She firmly relegated her 21st century son to the outer fringes of her consciousness, turning her thoughts instead to those children she had around her. Children was something of a misnomer when it came to Ian and Mark, both of them married men. Jacob was down in Providence, detained by his work from coming home for the harvest, while the remaining six were most hale and hearty, at least to judge from the noise they were making.

"Peter Leslie's had yet another son." Matthew came to sit beside her and rummaged in the basket for something to eat.

"A boy? How do you know?" Alex shook her head at the offered bun and hunted about for her comb.

"Ian told me. Peter sent word to them this morning."

"I wonder what they talk about," she mused, tugging the comb through her wet hair. He took it from her, settling down to untangle her curls.

"I imagine they don't. He hasn't married Constance for her conversation, has he?"

Too right he hadn't. Their closest neighbour, Peter, was well over fifty, and his young wife was thirty years younger than him.

"And not because he needs more children either." After all, Peter already had ten children by his first wife. No, eight, because the youngest boy had died of smallpox together

20

with his wife, Elizabeth, and one of the girls – Amy? – had recently died in childbirth.

"Two lads in two years. I dare say he's pleased with her fecundity." Matthew pulled his brows together, and Alex knew exactly what he was thinking: Peter's daughter, Ian's wife, had so far presented her husband with only one son in six years' marriage, and that was not for want of trying – at least not according to Ian.

Alex patted Matthew on the arm. "They have one. In time, they'll have more." She had said the same thing repeatedly to Ian, comforting her stepson as well as she could.

"You think?"

"I hope so." She shared a quick look with him. Both of them had noticed the increased strain in Ian and Jenny's relationship.

While Ian was a frequent visitor, coming over on a daily basis for a quick word with his father, or to borrow the mules, leave a cheese, collect a ham, Jenny rarely came with him, preferring to remain at home with her cows. It probably didn't help that Naomi, Mark's wife, was pregnant with her second child – her firstborn, Hannah, was only a year old. Alex smiled at the thought of her granddaughter. Sturdy and serious, Hannah was a biddable child with hair that grew in interesting wisps, and eyes that clearly marked her as a Graham.

On top of this, there was Adam. From the way Jenny would at times eye Alex's youngest son, it was obvious she resented Alex for having produced yet another baby when Jenny seemed incapable of conceiving again. Alex blew out her cheeks: she'd been terrified at finding herself pregnant again, Samuel's protracted birth still too fresh in memory. She glanced at Matthew. If she'd been scared silly, he'd been frantic, berating himself for being an inconsiderate fool until she'd told him to shut up – it wasn't as if she'd wanted him to be careful at the time, was it?

"Jenny should come over more often," Alex said. "It does her no good to sit all alone and brood."

"Aye, and she doesn't go to Leslie's Crossing either. The whole place is overrun by weans."

"Plus there is the matter of Constance. Imagine having a stepmother who is five years your junior. Ugh!"

"Aye, that must be difficult, and wee Constance doesn't really help, intimidated as she is by all her stepchildren."

Alex made a disparaging sound: anyone less intimidated than Constance she couldn't imagine, however frail she looked. Behind those fluttering eyelashes lived a hard-nosed young lady, frustrated by her restricted role in the Leslie household.

"A bed warmer," Alex muttered. "Poor woman, that's all she's there for."

Matthew rose to his full height, tightened his belt, and waited while Alex pulled on her skirts. They walked barefooted towards their home. Around them stood fields of ripe wheat, fringed by the high trees of the forest, and where ten years ago there had been nothing but a small cabin, there now stood a two-storey building, its roof made out of larch shingles, its outer walls beginning to acquire the soft grey of weathered wood. It snuggled into the hillside behind it, sun glinted off the precious glass windows, and two chimneys protruded from the roof, one at each end. To the side of the main house stood a large barn; opposite to the barn were the elongated stables and a collection of small sheds. Together, the buildings created a haphazard 'U' round the central yard which was dominated by an impressive white oak.

Matthew did as he always did when he saw his house: he stopped and let his eyes run over it, puffed with pride. Alex smiled and sneaked her hand into his. It was a fine home he'd built them, a house that would stand for generations. She rested her head against his shoulder, and they remained like that for a long time, content just to stand like this, close together.

The peace and quiet was disrupted by their boys. Matthew winked at her, disengaged his hand and rushed at them, sending his sons squealing in pretend fear when he chased after them.

"Mama?" Ruth appeared by Alex's side.

"Yes?" Alex turned to face her, still laughing at the antics of her man who was now pretending to be a lion.

"Look." Ruth pointed in the direction of the lane.

William Hancock? What was he doing here? And why was Betty with him, looking as if she'd seen a ghost? Alex uttered a strangled sound.

"Alex?" Matthew hurried over to her.

"Jacob, oh God, Matthew, something has happened to Jacob!" And then she was off, running towards the horses.

Chapter 3

William Hancock dismounted stiffly and nodded in the direction of Matthew. He turned to bow to Alex, and for an instant, his eyes widened, his mouth falling open before he regained control over his features. Matthew glanced at his wife, noting just how visible her body was through the sheer cloth of the linen chemise she wore with neither stays nor bodice. Her uncovered hair hung in damp curls well down her back, and beneath her skirts peeked her bare toes – no doubt in themselves something of an affront to a man as strict as William.

"Jacob?" Alex sounded hoarse. "Is he dead?"

William averted his face from her and shook his head, lips pressed together.

"Then what—" Alex began.

"Get dressed," Matthew interrupted in an undertone, handing her the discarded bodice from her basket. She went a most becoming shade of pink, and with a mumbled apology disappeared inside the house, calling for Agnes, the maid, to serve their guests something to drink.

She reappeared in less than five minutes, the dark hair now pinned up below a cap and her curves constrained by stays and bodice. Much better, Matthew decided, even if he saw William's eyes lock on her feet – still bare, if now in her sandals. Well, he wasn't about to force his wife into stockings on a day as hot as this.

He offered William some more beer. Alex's eyes drifted over to Betty, a thoughtful expression appearing on her face when she studied Betty's careful movements. Aye, it would seem the lass had paid dearly for helping Jacob abscond.

A wave of hot anger tinged with shame rose up Matthew's gullet. By rights, it should be Jacob, not wee

Betty, who wandered the world with a striped and sore arse.

"Jacob?" Alex said.

"He isn't injured, Alex, not even seriously ill."

Her shoulders dropped; she unclasped her hands and sat down beside him. "So what is it?"

"He has chosen to leave," William said. "It seems your son has a yearning for the adventures of the high seas."

"Jacob?" Alex sounded so surprised William smiled.

"Apparently. Aboard the *Regina Anne*."

"I'm going to have a wee word or two with Captain Miles next time I see him. To take on our lad without our consent!"

Alex gave Matthew a long look. "Captain Miles wouldn't do that."

Nay, Matthew agreed silently. Damned Jacob! Not only had he decided to do some travelling, but he had also chosen to go as a stowaway.

"Well, at least we know where Jacob will end up. Captain Miles will take him back home to Edinburgh and turn him over to Simon." Alex sounded relieved, a feeling Matthew fully reciprocated. His brother-in-law would take good care of their lad.

"His uncle Simon will give him quite the warm welcome, no?" Mrs Parson put in, shaking her head. "The lad deserves to be whipped." She set a heaped platter before William: hot griddle cakes dripping with butter and honey that had the children converging like hopeful flies around them. With a grunt, Mrs Parson sat down beside Alex. The old woman was a formidable housekeeper, but first and foremost she was a family member, no matter that she was no blood relation to either Matthew or Alex.

"I'm afraid there's a further complication." William nodded in the direction of Betty. He licked some honey off his finger and wiped at the crumbs stuck in the corner of his mouth.

"You want to annul the betrothal," Matthew said.

"Oh yes! If only it were that simple." William wrinkled his long nose into an expression of disgust. "You have a devious son, and a son rudimentarily versed in the law as well. It would seem he has convinced my daughter to consent to marriage and seal that verbal vow by consummating it."

Matthew bit back on a curse, tightening his hold on the earthenware mug to the point he feared it might break. How could Jacob shame him so?

"But…" Alex shook her head. "They're children!"

"Not anymore. Now they're married adults." William pulled at his lip, deep in thought. "We can handle this together. Once we've ensured she isn't with child, we can annul the contracts, and I'll find her another husband. I have contacts both in Boston and Jamestown, and a lost maidenhead can be compensated in other ways." He grimaced.

"Or we let the marriage stand," Matthew said, making Mrs Parson nod in agreement.

Alex gave him an exasperated look. "They're kids. And, as such, they've sworn to love each other forever and slept with each other without comprehending what it is they've committed themselves to."

"How do you know? And seeing as it's a match we have already considered as being a good one, why call it off?"

"Because I have no wish to wed my daughter to an absconding apprentice," William said coldly. "My daughter will wed a man that can support her decently, not a man who roams the seven seas, only occasionally putting in at port."

Matthew regarded both of them in silence and finally shook his head. "In Scotland, such a marriage as they've made is legal, and I won't be party to unravelling it."

"It isn't legal here," William snapped.

Matthew raised a brow: that wasn't true. The church frowned on clandestine marriages but generally accepted them after the fact. "Mayhap not, but I suspect you don't wish to have your daughter branded a harlot, do you? Besides, my lad has bedded your lass, and he'll stand by her. Had I caught them at it, I would've belted the wee idiot to an inch of his life, and then it would have been directly to the minister with both of them." He bowed stiffly in the direction of William. "My son has dishonoured you, Brother William, and I can but offer my deepest regrets for that. But the lass is now my daughter-in-law, and I'll see her cared for, that I promise you."

For all that William was a lawyer, he was not very good at disguising his thoughts. Clear as a day Matthew could read them: how hurt he was by Jacob's defection, how worried he was for his daughter, and how humiliated he was by this whole matter.

William did some more lip pulling and inclined his head in grudging assent. "I would leave her with you for some months – until we know if she's with child or not."

"Of course," Matthew replied. "We will gladly have the care of her. But you'll stay the night with us at least."

"No," William said. "I must be starting back as soon as possible."

It was a stilted and formal farewell, William standing before Betty, who kept her eyes firmly on the ground. The lass was punishing her father as best she could, and Matthew felt quite sorry for William, who tried repeatedly to catch his daughter's eyes.

William attempted a hug, Betty stood stiff in his arms, and with a sigh William let go of her. "I will convey your regards to your mother." He sat up on his horse. For an instant, Betty's eyes flashed into his.

"I have no regards to convey to her," Betty said in a heartbroken voice. She curtsied and sidled over to stand beside Matthew, a silent disowning of her father that cut William to the quick, at least to judge from how his mouth settled into a thin line. Without a further word, he wheeled his horse and set off up the lane, his servant at his back.

"Come, lass," Matthew said once William had dropped out of sight. "Let me show you where you'll be sleeping."

"He's whipped her!" Alex said later that evening. "The poor girl can barely sit, and it hasn't exactly helped to spend days in a saddle."

"He was within his rights," Matthew said. "The lass forced his hand."

"Would you do that?" She looked straight at him. "Would you lash your girl to the bedpost and whip her until you drew blood?"

Matthew ducked his head to hide his face from her. Not perhaps quite as savagely as that but, aye, he might, had one of his daughters dishonoured him so.

"Right now it's Jacob I wish to lay my hands on," he sidestepped. "Not only has he shamed me by absconding from his master, but to that he has added the effrontery of bedding a lass and leaving her to face the consequences alone."

"How could he? And what possessed him to leave in the first place?"

In response, Matthew handed Alex the letter their son had written them, and waited while she read it.

"Adventure?" Alex folded the letter together. "He takes off in search of adventure?"

From her customary position by the kitchen hearth, Mrs Parson snorted. "That lad has been dreaming of seeing the world for as long as I've known him, and it hasn't helped to have his head filled with pictures of foreign places, has it? It's you, Alex, telling him of the wonders of London, of how Venice is built on pillars of stone in an endless marsh, of Rome and the ruins of the old empire, that have woken all that in him." She went back to her knitting, ignoring Alex's irritated look.

"How was I to know he was going to do something like this?" Alex protested.

"You should know," Mrs Parson said. "He's your son, no?"

"And mine, so the blame is ours to share." Matthew exhaled, looking down at his hands. What had they done wrong for Jacob to behave as he had done? His fingers tightened around each other. May you be safe, laddie, for all that I want to stripe your back. May you be alright and come back to us, safe and sound.

★

"Rue, tansy and pennyroyal." Mrs Parson placed the herbs in a linen sachet.

Alex frowned. "You think? Pennyroyal is—"

"No more than a pinch," Mrs Parson said, "just in case."

Alex considered this for some seconds before nodding. After some consultation, Mrs Parson and Alex had decided that Betty was too young to become a mother, and so they'd spent most of the morning amicably arguing over what to give her to ensure this potential pregnancy ended before it became anything more than potential.

"Do we tell her why?" Alex asked Mrs Parson, receiving a pitying look in return.

"The lass bedded Jacob to commit herself to him for life. A wean would, in her present state of mind, just strengthen the bond, no?"

"So then why are we asking her to drink this?" Alex grimaced at the bitter scent.

"For her broken skin. We'll make poultices as well."

"I'll have to tell Matthew."

Mrs Parson shrugged, muttering that in her opinion men were best left out of women's problems, but after having had Matthew present at Alex's last three birthings, she'd given up when it came to him. "He might not approve."

"Of course he won't," Alex said, "but I have to tell him all the same."

"Is it dangerous?" Matthew asked once he had heard her out.

"Mrs Parson knows her business. She's been a midwife for fifty years or so by now. Old like the hills, she is." Alex smiled: she loved that old woman like a mother.

Matthew looked down at her with a deep crease between his brows. "You know she helped Jenny when she was dallying with yon Jochum."

"And it seems to have worked, right?" She suppressed a grin at his scowl. Matthew had issues with Jenny's amorous adventures prior to marrying Ian.

"Perhaps it worked too well."

Alex laughed. "Seriously! If Jenny drank rue tea for some weeks seven years ago, how can it possibly have an effect on her fertility now?"

His frown deepened. "You never know, do you?" He thought about it and then acquiesced. "The lass is too young to face motherhood alone." He kissed her on the brow, called for his three eldest sons and his servants, and told her they'd be late getting back – he wanted to harvest the last of his fields while the weather still held.

A tired Matthew returned well after dusk, trailed by his sons.

"All of it." Daniel yawned, blinked and yawned again. "We've done all of the wheat and most of the barley."

Alex gave him a quick hug, served them all a gigantic late supper, and sent them off to bed. She closed down the house, banked the fire, whispered a goodnight to Mrs Parson, and went upstairs to their room.

Matthew was already in bed, clothes left in a heap on the floor. Well, at least he'd washed, a wet and dirty linen towel left beside the basin.

"The day I get hold of Jacob Graham I'm going to chew his ear off," Alex said as she went about the room, hanging up his clothes. "What was he thinking of?" She was still upset after applying poultices on Betty's inflamed skin, cursing both William and Jacob to hell.

"You mean thinking with, and you know the answer to that as well as I do." Matthew cupped his privates and winked, making her laugh.

"Do you really think that's all it was?" She sat down in front of her little looking glass to undo her hair.

Matthew stretched out on the bed and propped himself up on one arm. "He's not yet sixteen and, aye, he's a lad of much heart – we both know that – but he's also of an age when your member is beginning to itch, when at times there's no blood left in your head on account of it all being down below your waist." He fondled himself, his eyes meeting hers in the mirror. "Jacob has known for several months that he and Betty were to wed eventually, and there's a fondness

30

between them. He wouldn't have done it unless he cared for her. Unfortunately, he didn't care enough for her not to."

"Or he was too young to understand that."

"Aye, not quite sixteen is a wee bit too young." He caught her eye in the mirror. "Forty-nine, however, is not too young."

"Not too old either, I can see." She smiled and set the brush down. Fluidly, she stood, drew the shift over her head, and came over to the bed.

She basked in the glow of his admiring eyes. She loved the warmth of his hands, the words he murmured in her ear. Even more, she loved how he groaned at her touch, how his thighs tensed, how the muscles of his abdomen hardened. His hot exhalations tickled her skin, his kisses left trails of searing heat on her body. She kissed him back; she slid her hands over his shoulders, down his belly to his groin. Matthew quivered and closed his eyes, his buttocks bunching.

"No more, Alex." He lifted his head off the pillow to throw her a burning look, gripped her shoulders, and lifted her upwards. "I don't want your hands, I want—" Whatever he wanted, she drowned in a kiss.

With a grunt, he rolled her over. He filled her, and she widened her legs to accommodate him. He rose on his arms, she clung to his hips, relishing the size of him, the sensation of being possessed by her man.

"I love you." He held still and she groaned out loud. "Don't you love me?" he asked, and she could hear the laughter in his voice.

"Oh, for God's sake," she panted. "You know I do, you stupid man! Now will you please... ah!" There, at last! He drove into her with exquisite force until all she could think of was him, him, him.

"Definitely not too old," she stated some minutes later. Her pulse had reverted to a more normal pace, but her body was covered in sweat.

He smoothed at her hair. "I don't think I'll ever be – not for this."

"I sincerely hope not," she said.

Chapter 4

"Not again," Alex muttered, throwing an irritated glance up the lane.

"Long time since the last one." Mrs Parson shrugged before bustling off to prepare something to drink and eat for their unbidden guests.

Alex made a face. Mrs Parson was right: the impromptu visits from militia troops were, thank heavens, becoming rarer now that some kind of peace had been re-established between colonists and Indians. In Alex's opinion, the men who still rode in militia companies were the scavengers of this world, more out to feather their own nests than to uphold any kind of peace, but the rules of common courtesy prevailed, and so Alex stepped into her yard to welcome the dozen or so men who were riding down their lane.

It was years since Alex had laid eyes on Philip Burley, but she knew him immediately. Older, gaunter, but still with that lock of hair that fell forward over his face, giving him an air of mischievousness belied by the coldness of his light grey eyes. He bowed, his mouth curling into an amused smile at what she assumed to be her aghast expression. With an effort, she closed her mouth.

"Did you hope I had died?" he asked, dismounting.

"Yes, but at least I wished you a quick and painless death – you know, falling off your horse and breaking your neck or something."

Philip Burley laughed, eyes doing a quick up and down before returning to her face. "Alas, here I am."

"But looking quite worn round the edges." Alex took in his threadbare coat, his downtrodden boots.

"I don't dress up for riding through the woods."

"No, none of you have, have you?" Alex nodded to the

32

man who seemed to be in charge, swept her hand towards the bench under the oak. "Beer?"

"And food," the older man said, patting at his rumbling stomach.

"I'll get you some bread, and then there's some leftover stew from yesterday," Alex said.

Philip Burley sniffed the air. "What? No chicken?"

"No, they're meant for our dinner. Besides, they're not done."

"But we can wait." Philip smirked.

No way! She'd rather have a cobra at her feet than him in her yard. "Stew and bread. Take it or leave it." Alex directed herself to the leader.

"We take it," the man said, "however ungraciously offered."

"That's because of him." Alex pointed at Philip. "For some reason, he gives me severe indigestion – it must be the general look of him. Quite repulsive." Not entirely true, as the man exuded some sort of animal magnetism, as graceful and dangerous as a starving panther.

Some of Burley's companions broke out in laughter, quickly quenched when he glared at them.

Alex and Mrs Parson served the men, helped by Agnes. For all that they looked dishevelled and stank like hell, the men were relatively polite, taking the time to thank them before falling on their food. Alex retreated indoors, keeping a worried look not only on their guests but also on the barn and the path beyond.

"He's over on the other side of the river," Mrs Parson said, no doubt to calm her. "He won't be coming in for dinner – you know that. Besides, it's not as if that Burley can do anything at present, is it? However unkempt and wild, I doubt his companions will help him do Matthew harm."

Alex relaxed at the irrefutable logic in this. "At least it's only him. I wonder where his brothers are."

"We know where one of them is: in hell, there to burn in eternal agony." Mrs Parson replenished her pitcher and stepped outside to serve the men some more to drink.

"Yeah, thanks to Matthew."

"Good riddance," Mrs Parson said over her shoulder. "And we both know why, no?"

Alex nodded. Will Burley had died while attempting to kill her Matthew, and for that the remaining Burley brothers intended to make Matthew Graham pay. Alex swallowed, smoothed down her skirts, ensured not one single lock of hair peeped from under her cap, and grabbed the bread basket.

"So many children," the officer, who by now had introduced himself as Elijah Carey, said. "All yours?"

"No, but most of them are." She was made nervous by the way Philip Burley kept on staring at her girls, in particular at Sarah.

"Not that young anymore," Philip said. "Soon old enough to bed."

"Absolutely not!" Alex bristled.

Philip laughed, tilting his head at her daughters. "I don't agree, Mrs Graham, but then I like them young."

"Burley…" Carey warned with a little sigh. The younger man raised those strange, almost colourless irises in his direction and just stared, nailing his eyes into the officer until Carey muttered something about needing the privy and, with a hasty nod in Alex's direction, disappeared.

"My, my, what have you done to him? Sneaked up on him at night and kicked him in the back? That's how you do it, isn't it? Under cover of the dark—" In a movement so swift Alex had no time to back away, Philip was on her, crowding her against the oak.

"You don't take me seriously, do you, Mrs Graham?" he said, in a voice so low only she could hear him. "Most women – and men for that matter – know better than to taunt me."

"You don't scare me." Her knees shivered with her lie.

He looked at her for a long time. "Oh yes, I do, Mrs Graham. Only a fool wouldn't be frightened of me, and that you are not."

Alex shoved at him, creating some space between them.

34

"I suppose I must take that as a compliment," she said, mentally patting herself on her back for how casual she succeeded in keeping her tone.

Philip Burley laughed, an admiring look in his eyes. "Take it as you will, Mrs Graham. But never commit the mistake of thinking we have forgotten the blood debt your husband owes us. However long it takes, we will have revenge for what he did to our Will."

Alex tried to say something, but her tongue had glued itself to the roof of her mouth, and to her shame she could hear her breathing become ragged, a slight whistling accompanying each inhalation.

"I was right: I do scare you." With an ironic little bow, Philip Burley walked off, and Alex wasn't quite sure how she made it from the tree to her kitchen door.

By the time Matthew came in for supper, the militia company was long gone. In silence, he listened to Alex's brief recap of her meeting with Philip Burley, and once she was done, he shoved the plate away – most of the food uneaten.

"Damn!" Matthew drove his fist hard into the wall, cursed again, and sucked at his broken knuckles. "Where were they headed?"

"To Virginia," Mrs Parson said. "At least, that's what they said. Up for disbandment, they reckoned."

"And his brothers?" Alex was as always amazed by how much information Mrs Parson was able to gather in a matter of minutes.

"Ah, his brothers... Well, that Walter fell foul of his commanding officer some months back, and is kicking his heels down in Jamestown, while Stephen, he was wounded, struck down by an arrow."

"Serve him right," Alex said. "I hope it leaves him permanently incapacitated."

"It near killed him," Mrs Parson said with a shrug. "They won't be back this way."

"For now," Matthew corrected. "We all know that, sooner or later, they will be."

"Three Burleys are no match for us, Da," Ian said.

"You think?" Matthew shook his head. "They're lethal, Ian."

"We're all good shots," Mark protested. "They won't make it down the lane."

"They won't come down the lane," Matthew said. "They'll come at night, from the direction we least expect them to."

Blood rushed so quickly out of her head, Alex felt faint, no matter she was sitting down.

Matthew leaned forward to clasp her hand. "I'll think of something, lass."

"Of course you will," she replied with a false smile.

It took Alex several days to regain some kind of equilibrium, but when one day after the other passed without any incidents, she managed to shove the Burley bogeymen into a dark and rarely visited corner of her brain, submerging herself in the demanding day to day instead. Foremost on her mind was Daniel's imminent departure for Boston, and when she saw her son making for the river, she called for him to wait and hurried over to join him.

"Are you nervous?" Alex fell into step with Daniel, extending her stride to match his. At thirteen, Daniel already overtopped her, and now he smiled at her and shortened his steps.

"Aye, but not in a bad way." He stared off across the harvested fields, shifting his shoulders.

Alex patted him on his cheek. Thirteen and already on his way out into the world... For the last year, he'd been living down in Providence, with Minister Walker, and Alex was secretly very impressed by how much he had learnt in such a short period of time. She liked Walker, and had tried to imprint in Daniel that there was a minister to emulate, a man that combined a deep knowledge and love of the Bible with huge quantities of compassion and humility.

Matthew had howled with laughter when she'd shared this view of Minister Walker with him, saying that, aye, the minister was a right godly man in many ways, but he was no paragon of human virtues – what with his frequent and regular visits to Mrs Malone's little establishment. That had stumped Alex. She'd forgotten about the minister's visits to the brothel. Should they really have Daniel staying with him in that case? Matthew had laughed yet again, assuring her he had no fears whatsoever on that count – the minister partook of beer, no more, and Mrs Walker would ensure their son was kept well away from the seedier parts of Providence.

"I suppose it's a comfort for you that the Walkers will be in Boston the first few months." It was a huge relief for Alex, making it much easier for her to relinquish him, and he'd be living with Harriet Leslie and her husband, which was almost like family. Almost… Neither she nor Matthew had ever met Naomi's elder sister.

"Aye."

She threw Daniel a look. One more year of school, and next year he'd begin to study divinities. She took a deep breath. Matthew wouldn't like her for asking him, but she had to. "Do you want to become a minister?"

He turned blue eyes her way, and it tugged at her heart to see the uncertainty in them. "Da wants me to." He gnawed at his lip, muttered something about not wanting to disappoint Da, not now with Jacob— He interrupted himself abruptly.

"It's your life, and if you don't want it, I'll talk to him, okay?" But she could see he wasn't about to take issue with his father's decision – at least, not yet.

"Will you come and visit, do you think?" Daniel asked.

"No, I don't think so – we simply can't afford it. But you'll be coming down once a year to visit us."

Daniel nodded, his whole face brightening. She smiled at him, patted his cheek, and detoured to their little graveyard, with Daniel following.

Alex brushed off some dry leaves from her father's headstone and placed a freshly cut rose on the stone. Stupid man, she thought as she traced his name, to decide to go time-travelling with a brain tumour.

She'd never forget the total surprise – no, that went no way to describe her feelings – the utter, terrified shock, when she found him hanging in a thorn thicket after his fall from their time to this time.

For the first year or so he'd been fine, but then the brain cancer had come back, and so he'd died, centuries before he was born. She swallowed, her insides churning – they always did when she thought about the stranger aspects of her life, and this definitely included the reappearance of her father in her life, just as it included her own free fall through time and her strange time-travelling mother. Nope, don't go there.

"You never talk of your mother," Daniel said from behind her. What was he: some sort of mind-reader?

"I don't?" Alex turned to face him with a strained smile. "That's probably on account of her being Catholic and long dead." And a witch – a reluctant witch, to be sure, cursed with the ability of painting portals through time, small squares of whirling blues and greens that somehow trapped your eyes and sent you flying from one age to another.

Poor Mercedes: she'd had no true control over the magical powers that lived in her fingers, and so she'd been flung out of her age, desperately trying to paint her way home with zero success. As a consequence, she'd littered the world with these goddamn dangerous scraps of art.

"A Catholic?" Daniel's voice quavered. Alex gave him an irritated look.

"I've been raised a Protestant," she said, even if that was a huge lie. Until she met Matthew, she'd been at best agnostic, at times an atheist, and every now and then she wondered if perhaps God looked down at her and laughed His head off. She could live with that, because after all she owed Him big time, didn't she? Without divine intervention, she would never have met Matthew, of that she was sure.

"So you are of the faith," Daniel said, sounding relieved.

"Faith? I would argue Catholics are of the faith as well, as are Anglicans and Protestants, and to some extent even Muslims and Jews."

Daniel gaped at her.

Alex watched him with some amusement, but with substantially more exasperation.

"You know this, don't you? The People of the Book, that's all of us who believe in the single God. Muslims do, Jews definitely do – they've been doing it for far longer than anyone else – and all Christians do."

"You can't say such, Mama. Muslims and Jews don't go to heaven, and nor do any but those of the faith. And then only if you're accorded grace and have lived a life of virtue."

"Oh, really? And what's a life of virtue?"

"For you, it's being a dutiful wife to Da, a good mother to your bairns. A righteous woman is man's foremost helpmeet, bending to his stronger will and better sense."

He sounded so prim she nearly laughed him in the face: her thirteen-year-old son telling her she was subservient to her husband – unfortunately an opinion he shared with most men, and a large majority of the women, living in the here and now.

Alex gave him a long look. "Tell me, would you say Ruth or yourself is better at ciphering?"

"Ruth," Daniel mumbled.

"And who would you say is best read – you or Ruth?"

"Ruth," he repeated, colouring slightly.

"And if one day you were to marry a woman as smart as Ruth is, would you bend her to your stronger will, or would you take decisions together with her?"

Daniel was silent for some time. "I would take decisions together with her," he finally said, sounding as if he didn't mean it.

"Like your father and I do."

"You do?"

Alex laughed at his surprise and stood on her toes to ruffle his dark hair. "That's what defines a smart woman. She makes sure everyone thinks it's her husband who decides everything. And a smart husband, he makes sure he involves his wife – if nothing else because it makes his home life so much nicer." With a quick wave, she hurried off in the direction of her kitchen garden.

"Da?" Daniel sat down on the workbench.

Matthew chipped off yet another piece of wood from the table leg he was making before looking at him.

"Aye?" He held up the leg to measure it against the others, swearing under his breath when he noted a minor disparity. Well, he could disguise that with some woodworking. A clambering vine would look nice up the legs, and maybe he could somehow work that into the tabletop.

"Do you always talk to Mama before taking decisions?"

Matthew bit back on a smile. "Not always. There are things I decide on my own." He saw Daniel nod with satisfaction. "Just as she does," he said, making his son's face shift into an expression of surprise.

"You let her?"

Matthew grinned. "Son, who do you think decides what to sew, when to launder, what to grow in the kitchen garden? Who do you think orders the accounts, decides what to sell at the markets?"

"You?" Daniel tried.

Matthew shook his head. "A good wife is a woman with a head on her shoulders, and it is a foolish man who doesn't let her use it." He looked down at his son with a small smile. "You wed a woman for many reasons. You wed her to keep you warm at night, to give you bairns and care for you. But first and foremost, you wed her that she be a good companion to you through life, and that includes discussing all decisions with her." He went back to his table leg. "And if you don't, you might find yourself very cold at night," he added as an afterthought, his eyes on Betty who was sitting by herself on the rope swing.

Solitude was a precious commodity in the Graham family, Betty reflected, using her bare toes to set the swing in lazy motion. Wherever she went, she was surrounded by people – sometimes very small people like Adam, who would stick his hand into hers and not say much, at times the constantly talking Sarah, who wanted to know everything about

Providence, this tantalising town that she had never seen, despite being all of ten.

Having grown up without brothers except for sweet little Willie, she watched with fascination when David, Samuel, Adam and Ian's son, Malcolm, rolled together in wild games that very often resulted in one or the other of them crying. A lot of time Betty spent with Naomi, three years her senior and already showing with her second child. It made Betty jealous to see Naomi and Mark, and she longed for Jacob, for him to hold her hand and help her over stiles like Mark did with his wife. Betty inhaled, held her breath and exhaled, eyes on the sky.

This was a strange household: the women went about with their heads uncovered – well, not Mrs Parson or Agnes, and not, thank the Lord, when there were visitors – meals consisted to a large extent of raw vegetables, and Betty had been horrified when Alex had told her that bathing in the Graham household meant undressing and getting into the cold water of the river there to wash yourself.

"Naked?" she had squeaked, watching with apprehension as Agnes, Ruth and Sarah undressed and hurried into the water, apparently enjoying what to Betty seemed a most excessive way of keeping clean.

"It helps," Alex informed her before shedding her clothes and leaping in after the girls.

Betty sat back on the swing and increased her speed, bending and extending her legs until it seemed to her she was flying. If she were to let go at the highest point, she would be sent hurtling into space, and maybe the speed would be enough for her to fly all the way to where Jacob might be. Jacob... She suppressed a little sob. What if the *Regina Anne* had met with disaster and was now a wreck at the bottom of the sea? How would she ever know?

She increased the speed even more, and all around her the trees were blurring. At the highest point, she let go. For an instant, she soared, before the earth came rushing towards her, and she landed hard on her knees and hands. Betty Hancock – or was it Graham? – hid her face in her arms and cried.

★

From a distance, Alex watched and ached. Pretty bubbly Betty retreated into silences and escaped them as much as she could, her beautiful carnelian eyes mostly shielded by her long reddish lashes, her gorgeous hair braided and hidden from view under a huge lace cap. God damn you, Jacob. How could you do this to her?

"Do you think he'll come back to her?" Alex asked Matthew later that evening. To us, she meant, her head filling with images of her Jacob.

"Oh, he will. He has given the lass his word, and I'll hold him to it."

"You're forgetting her father."

Matthew looked down at her, lying pillowed against his chest. "You think he'll wed her elsewhere?"

"Don't you?" Alex fiddled with his chest hair, tugging at the brindle curls.

"Aye, probably, and there's not much I can do to stop him."

"I think the main question is if you should."

"You think I shouldn't?"

"To me, it all seems very rash." Alex fiddled some more, circling his nipples. "But for her sake, Matthew. Because it would break her heart to be forced into marriage with another."

"Aye, she loves him."

"Hmm." In Alex's opinion, no sixteen-year-old was mature enough to know what they wanted out of life, but then she thought back to Mark and Naomi, contracted at thirteen at Mark's insistence, betrothed at sixteen, and wed just after he turned eighteen. "They're all in such a hurry to become adults."

His chest vibrated beneath her cheek. "That's on account of them not knowing what it's like."

Alex propped herself up to look at him. "But with Jacob there's a real problem, isn't there? Ian and Mark could marry as young as they did, because they're already set up – both of them will inherit land. But how is Jacob to support a wife?"

"I don't know, but I don't think William will welcome him back to his practice."

Chapter 5

Halfway through the first week of September, Alex decided a visit to Forest Spring was long overdue.

"If the mountain doesn't come to Mohammed, Mohammed must come to the mountain." She wrapped her new shawl around her shoulders.

"I don't think Jenny will take kindly to being likened to a mountain," Matthew said, before going back to his work.

"Who would?" Alex dropped a kiss on his head and held out her hand to Adam. "Want to come?"

"It's a long walk for a wee lad," Matthew warned.

Alex bent down to scrape at something sticky that decorated Adam's worn smock. "I can carry him part of the way."

"I can walk." Adam lifted his bare leg in the general direction of his father. "Look, Da, I have strong legs."

"Aye, you do, laddie, very strong." Matthew smiled at his son. "Take Angus with you," he added, looking at Alex. She made a face but didn't even try to argue; a male escort was a prerequisite.

With Angus a silent shadow in her wake, Alex strolled along hand in hand with her youngest son, listening to his very long account of how Daniel had helped him set Mrs Pollyanna's leg.

"...I held her, and she squawked something terrible, she did."

Alex smiled down at him. "How did she break her leg to begin with?"

Adam shrugged. He had found her lying on her back in the hencoop, and gone rushing for help.

"She's getting on a bit, honey. Soon she'll be dead."

Adam looked up at her from wide, dark hazel eyes. "Not yet."

"No, of course not," Alex murmured.

Their youngest son collected hurt animals, and over the last year, the stable had seen a badly injured sparrow that had died despite Matthew's best efforts, a frog with no legs that Alex had secretly bashed to death to put it out of its misery, a baby raccoon that expired in less than an hour, and the newborn piglet that Adam had dragged half alive from below its farrowing mother. The piglet thrived, and Alex had recently confided to Matthew that she was going to have major problems slicing ham from a pig that had once been called Arthur.

They had detoured off the path to pick chanterelles when Alex spotted the gleaming yellow hats in a mossy hollow. She smoothed down Adam's curling hair, allowing her fingers to linger on his nape. Her youngest son was a restful person to be with, had been from the moment he entered the world. Placid and calm as a baby, he was now a placid and calm three-year-old who gracefully allowed himself to be pampered by the rest of his very large family.

From one son her thoughts leapt to another: her Jacob. Where was he now, her boy, and was he alright? Her belly turned at the thought of weeks at sea, and especially in boats that in her considered opinion should be restricted to small lakes. Alex was swamped by a sudden wave of loss. What if Jacob never came back? Maybe he would disappear into a life very far from here, and all that she'd ever get from him would be the odd letter, like once a year or so. It made her heart shrivel. She wanted him here, close. She wanted to thread her fingers through his thick blond hair, and see him rear back in irritation at this far too motherly gesture.

"Mama?" Adam tugged at her hand. He pointed at the approaching horse, a wide grin on his face.

Alex smiled. To Adam, his big brother Ian was very close to God, coming second only to Da in his inner ranking.

Ian held in his horse and grinned back, lowering Malcolm to the ground to allow him to throw himself at his granny.

"Off to visit us, are you?" Ian asked.

44

"Not you as such," Alex told him, hugging Malcolm back. "I see you all the time, don't I? I was planning on having a cosy chat with Jenny."

An unreadable expression flashed across Ian's face and then the smile was back, hazel eyes regarding her warily. "A chat?"

She knew him too well to be fooled by his bland smile. For an instant, she met his eyes, could read in their depths just how much he was hurting. His lashes swept down and, from the set of his mouth, Alex knew there'd be no point in trying to talk to him – at least not now.

"You know," Alex said instead, "about how best to turn a heel, or if it makes sense to use butternuts to dye homespun." And somewhere along the way, she intended to interrogate Jenny as to the true state of the Ian-Jenny marriage, although it didn't exactly take a genius to conclude things were far from peachy.

"In that case, maybe I should take both lads back with me," Ian said. Adam nodded eagerly, clearly not all that keen on visiting Forest Spring if Ian wasn't there.

"You do that." Alex swept the surrounding woods and looked back at him with a frown. "Is she alone?"

"Nay, Patrick's there, repairing a fence." Ian's brows pulled together for an instant. "And you? Should you be walking alone?"

In reply, Alex pointed to where Angus was standing to the side, almost invisible in his immobility.

"Ah." Ian gave Angus a nod. The tall young man mumbled a greeting, but remained where he was, cradling the loaded musket.

"It's like having your own private ghost," Alex said in an undertone. "And I'm not quite sure how much good he would be should it come to the crunch."

"Wee Angus is a good shot," Ian replied, just as low. "He'll see you safe."

"Yeah, because otherwise Matthew will use his guts for garters." She gave Ian a little wave and set off at a brisk pace, Angus trotting after.

By the time Alex reached the turnoff to Forest Spring,

45

she had almost forgotten that she had Angus with her. Walking several yards behind her, he moved like a wind through the shrubs that bordered the bridle path. Alex concentrated on her surroundings rather than on her elusive bodyguard, noting that yet another part of the forest had been cleared and fenced, in preparation for more cows.

Just as Alex emerged from the path, she saw Patrick appear in the dairy doorway and hurry off in the direction of the fields. Alex made a face at his disappearing back. She was going to be very glad when Patrick's term of bondage was up next year, hoping he'd leave as soon as possible. Capable and quiet, but with dark eyes that saw and noted everything, he gave her the creeps. Also, unlike Angus, it was evident Patrick resented his servant status, and at times she'd catch him looking at her elder sons – in particular Ian – with a cold gleam to his eyes and a sneer on his lips.

Forest Spring was built on a much smaller scale than Graham's Garden. The main house was a weathered cabin, the heavy logs having aged into a silvered brown. There was a small stable and a separate dairy situated beside the spring that gave the small homestead its name. A cat was lying on the door stoop, a couple of hens were scratching at the ground, and Jenny was nowhere to be seen.

Alex found her in the dairy, her back to the door as she packed the diced cheese curd into the wooden pans. When Alex called her name, Jenny jumped, wheeling round so fast she almost dropped the pan she was holding. Hmm... Alex pursed her mouth at Jenny's bright red face.

"Mother Alex!" Jenny's shoulders slumped. "What a surprise! I didn't hear you, and to suddenly have someone calling my name like that, it unnerved me. For a moment there, you even sounded like my mother."

Alex seriously doubted that. Elizabeth Leslie had spoken with a nasal tone to her voice, far from any noise Alex ever produced. Still, she made a vague confirming sound, and followed Jenny into the main house. Something wasn't right.

Alex studied her daughter-in-law while she bustled about the kitchen. Jenny's generally impeccable exterior looked unravelled, and whenever Alex met her eyes, the younger woman ducked her head to hide cheeks that went an uncharacteristic shade of pink.

Had it been one of her own children, or even Naomi, Alex would simply have asked and waited until she got an answer, but her and Jenny's relationship had never reached that element of familiarity, to a large extent due to Jenny's mother, who even after death cast a substantial shadow over her most beloved daughter. Alex accepted the offered mug of barley water, smiling when she recognised her own recipe with plenty of ginger and cinnamon.

"I miss you," she said, seeing a pleased smile appear on Jenny's face.

"You do?" Jenny sat down opposite to her.

"Yes, you never come over anymore, do you?"

Jenny looked away and muttered something about being very busy with the last of the summer milk.

Alex drank some more barley water. "Your mother wouldn't approve." She was taken aback by the dark flush that flew up Jenny's face. A warning bell rang in Alex's head.

"Approve?" Jenny asked in a flat voice.

"Of you spending so much time alone." Alex noted how the tensed back relaxed somewhat, but decided not to push things – at least, not for now. She sighed. Both Jenny and Ian were hurting, and she had no idea how to help. "You don't spend time with us, and you don't ride over to see your brother and father. All the time you spend up here, with the occasional visit from Agnes or Naomi."

Jenny's light blue eyes narrowed. "I don't want to see my father!"

"No, I suppose that might be difficult."

"Eight months dead she was when he informed me he was marrying again." Two bright red spots appeared on Jenny's cheeks. "The woman he'd been married to for more than thirty years, and she's barely cold in her grave before he goes a-courting again!"

"Maybe he was lonely," Alex tried, although she totally agreed with Jenny.

"Lonely? Then he could have wed a widow, someone closer to his age, not that...that..."

"Girl?" Alex offered.

Jenny bit her lip and nodded.

"It isn't her fault. I dare say your father, for all his stellar qualities, did not come top of her wish list – he's older than her father!"

"Stellar qualities?" Jenny stared at Alex before breaking out in harsh laughter. "There are babies all over Leslie's Crossing," Jenny said once she'd stopped laughing, her voice darkening. "Nathan and Ailish seem intent on populating the world by themselves, and then there's Constance, and I...I..." She looked away.

"Jenny..." Alex clasped her hand. "The babies will come. You'll see, they'll come." Jenny hung her head, refusing to meet Alex's eyes. "But don't lose your husband on the way. Don't let this become a wall between you." To Alex's surprise, Jenny slid to her knees, buried her head in Alex's skirts, and cried.

When Alex left an hour or so later, she was very pleased with herself. They'd had a long heart to heart about the importance of nurturing a relationship, and a red-nosed Jenny had promised that she'd follow Alex's advice and use the trip to Providence to try and find her way back to Ian.

"Don't forget to touch him – often," Alex had said, having to smile at Jenny's scandalised look. "Not like that, silly. Like this..." She'd exemplified by brushing her hand gently down Jenny's arm.

Alex smiled pleasantly at Angus when he popped up from behind the woodshed. He gave her a shy smile in return before falling in behind her. Alex swung her basket and hummed to herself. A good day's work, all in all, and on top of that her basket was full of mushrooms. She decided to fry them with finely chopped onion and parsley, and then she and Matthew could have them for supper – only he and she, in the privacy of their bedroom. And while she was at it, she was going to talk to him about Patrick – she hadn't liked the way he had looked at Jenny when they came out of Jenny's kitchen, a lascivious glint in his eyes.

★

Jenny waved Alex off, ignored Patrick's heated gaze and stepped back inside, leaning heavily against the door. She wasn't sure how all this had started. There'd been the time when she had run into Patrick in the forest, and he had handed her a flower. There'd been the time when he held her hand to help her across the stream, and all that had been innocent enough, at least on her part. And then, several months ago, he had cornered her in the stable and kissed her. Jenny had been so angry, raising her hand to slap him away, but all he had done was grab her hand and kiss her again, forcing himself into her mouth and leaving both of them panting – him with arousal, her with what she assumed to be rage. But she hadn't told Ian, and next morning, Patrick had smirked and grazed the back of his hand against her bosom.

He hounded her; he kissed her again, holding her still against the stable wall; he fondled her breasts leaving her in a state of severe disarray.

"I'll tell my husband!" she'd hissed back in June, backing away from him while she adjusted her bodice.

"Do that," he'd sneered. "Do that, and I'll tell him you've been kissing me back for weeks."

"No, I haven't," she'd protested, her cheeks mottling with shame – because she hadn't stopped him either, had she? She was filled with conflicting emotions. One part of her was insulted, another part was mortified, but there was a third part as well: the very big part that liked the way Patrick held her, how his lips felt. That made her even more ashamed, and suddenly the time frame in which she could have told Ian was gone, and she had no idea what to do.

Patrick was like a predator. Confidently, he circled his wounded prey, the circles narrowing until that day in July when he found her in the dairy shed, pressed her down on the workbench, and took her. Not a sound had she uttered, and when he was done, he'd re-laced his breeches, smoothed down her skirts, and walked off. She'd heard him whistling when he resumed his wood chopping, and between her legs, his come had oozed. Jenny had remained where she was for a long time, her eyes firmly shut.

After that, she was trapped. Should she attempt to say no, he threatened her with telling Ian, and no matter how much effort she put in staying away from him, he always found her. He had the upper hand, and he enjoyed it, caressing his crotch as he used his head to indicate that he wanted her to go to the stable, or behind the privy, or into the woods, and Jenny would do as he wished. Even worse, Jenny looked forward to these quick copulations, finding a release in them she no longer found with Ian – not now that their lovemaking had become nothing but a chore.

She cleared away the mugs, brushed the table clean of crumbs, and sat down to think. This had to stop, and it had to stop now. Three days in a row, she had thrown up behind the privy, and her courses were four weeks late for the first time in five years. She leaned her forehead into her hands to stop her head from spinning with shame and hope and revulsion, and took several deep breaths. Oh God, what was she to do?

Chapter 6

Peter handed Constance Leslie down from her dappled mare and turned to beam at Alex, pointing at his new son, fast asleep in the arms of his nurse.

"Two sons!" Peter looked proud enough to burst.

"Three if we're going to be correct," Alex reminded him, receiving a grateful smile from Peter's eldest son, Nathan Leslie, who was busy unhorsing his sizeable family. Ailish snickered and winked at Alex before sliding with considerable grace into the receiving arms of her husband, despite her pregnant state.

"You know what I mean," Peter said with an edge. "Two boys in two years. Is she not a marvel?"

Constance smiled weakly, her overlarge eyes flashing in the direction of Nathan. No love lost there, Alex concluded.

After spending an adequate amount of time admiring Peter's baby son, Alex went over to greet Thomas and Mary Leslie, at present busy talking with their daughter, Naomi. Where Peter was all bluster and show, his elder brother Thomas was a nondescript, quiet man. As always, Thomas was in his customary grey, with grey eyes and sparse grey hair that hung lank down to his shoulders, and beside him stood his plump little wife, as colourless as her husband. Compared to them, Naomi sparkled with colour and energy, her skin rosy, and what little could be seen of her hair gleaming in the September sun.

"Do you think she might be a changeling?" Mark asked Alex.

"Mark!" Alex hissed.

"One can always hope," her son muttered, before hurrying over to greet his parents-in-law. Alex tilted her head. Naomi was in no way a beauty, but somehow her parents' best features had combined into a pleasant whole, and thankfully the girl seemed to have inherited her brain from her father rather than her mother. Shame on you, she chided herself, Mary is a nice woman. Yeah, with the intellectual agility of a ten-year-old.

Matthew appeared from one of the storage sheds, cradling a cask of beer.

"Just what one needs on day such as this." Peter flapped his hat to create some air.

Matthew nodded and winked at Alex, no doubt to remind her that this was her idea, not his. She stuck her tongue out in response, before suggesting in a loud voice that they should all take their seats at the trestle tables set up below the trees.

Alex had on purpose placed Jenny at the very far end of the table, with Peter exactly opposite, his new wife beside him. But, with the sensitivity of a bull in a china shop, Peter insisted that his daughter come and sit closer so that she could properly admire the new addition to the Leslie family: little James.

"James?" Jenny gave him a cool look.

Peter looked up from where he was studying the vegetable pie that Alex had set in front of him. "James," he said, through his half-full mouth. "Mmm," he added, directing himself to Alex, "quite tasty."

"James is dead." Jenny's voice was loud enough to stop all activity at the table.

"Jenny," Ian said, placing a hand on her shoulder, but she shook it off.

"He died with your wife, my mother, in April of 1676, and at the time of his death, he was eight years old."

"I know how old he was," Peter snapped back.

"And still you give his name to that?" Jenny made a face and stood up. "And if you have a girl, will you name her Jenny? Or why not Elizabeth, in honour of the wife who gave you ten live children?"

Peter had gone an interesting shade of dirty pink, glaring at his daughter. "I'll name my children as I see fit."

52

He looked her up and down and expanded his chest, raising his receding chin in a gesture of defiance. "I can't help it that my wife is fertile, daughter. And mayhap you should wonder at your own barrenness and pray that the good Lord forgive you whatever transgression it is that's making you incapable of bearing children."

"Peter!" Alex exclaimed at the same time as Jenny raised a pitcher of ale and upended it over her father before stalking off.

"That was very cruel," Ian said to Peter before hurrying after his wife.

"It wasn't my fault," Alex said defensively to Matthew much later. She sank down to sit in one of their few armchairs and frowned. "He shouldn't have said that, and when that little tight-arsed wife of his proceeded to tell us how it was a known fact that barrenness was a divine punishment, well…"

Matthew added another log to the fire and sat back down. "It didn't help when you told her that someone with as little sense as she did best in keeping her mouth shut."

Peter had been out of his seat like an aggravated stoat, demanding an apology, and Alex had exploded, telling him not be such an old fart, and so the party had come to an end before it had even begun, with an apologetic Thomas trailing his brother.

"True, nonetheless," Mrs Parson said. "And it was a mightily heartless thing for a father to say to his lass."

"Aye, that it was," Matthew agreed.

Alex pursed her lips. The expression on Jenny's face had been not only of hurt and anger, but also of something else but, try as she might, Alex couldn't quite figure out what.

"But Mr Leslie's right," Betty said from behind them. "My mother always says how a woman unable to conceive must look deep within and pray for forgiveness." She flushed under their combined eyes.

"Easy to say if you conceive with the ease of a rabbit," Alex snorted.

Betty's face turned crimson.

"I didn't mean your mother," Alex said hastily. "You know I'm very fond of Esther. I was thinking more along the lines of sweet Constance."

"Sweet?" Betty looked confused. "I don't find her sweet." She pressed her lips together, her eyes brimming. "She asked me if I was the little fool who had opened my legs on the basis of a worthless promise."

"If you plan on weeping every time someone tells you the truth, you'll spend most of your life in tears," Mrs Parson said to her. "It was a daft thing to do, no?"

Betty shook her head. "No, it wasn't."

"Ah, lass." Mrs Parson sighed, not unkindly. "And what if you'd been with child? How would you have cared for it, with the father on the high seas?"

"I can sew, or go into service," Betty replied, without much conviction.

"That won't be necessary, lassie. You bide with us, aye?" Matthew patted the stool beside his chair. "You're family now."

With a shy smile, Betty went and sat beside him.

Alex smothered a smile at the tenderness in Matthew's voice. Children and puppies, kittens and babies in general, brought out a very soft side in him, a side generally reserved for her only. She slid her eyes sideways to study him in the firelight, and it struck her, as it sometimes did, that both of them were growing older. There were permanent creases on his forehead, a deep groove from nose to the corner of his mouth, and several small wrinkles around his eyes.

As if in response to her cataloguing, he straightened up and smiled into the fire. Just like that, he reverted to being as he'd been when she first met him, on a heat infested day in August when a bolt of thunder rent the veil of time apart and sent her hurtling through it. Her man: tall and strong, with magical hazel eyes and a long, generous mouth. Alex raised the back of her hand to his cheek, and he leaned into her touch with an almost inaudible sigh.

★

"It would help if you moved out of the way," Alex said a couple of days later, prodding at the huge dog that lay across the threshold. Narcissus yawned and settled his head on his paws, the deep brown eyes never leaving Hannah who was playing with a soft doll made from leftover yarn and bits and pieces.

Naomi grinned at Alex and went back to her kneading. "He's very protective of her, aren't you, little Narcissus?"

The dog wagged his tail in response to his name.

"Little? He's the size of a calf!" Alex bent down to scratch his yellow head. "But he's probably the best nursemaid I've ever seen. So," Alex said, sitting down to watch Naomi work, "have you spoken to your parents?"

Naomi snorted loudly. "You know I have." She used the back of her forearm to wipe a strand of hair out of the way, dusted some flour over the dough, covered it, and set it to the side. "Constance has quite the tongue on her. As long as Uncle Peter isn't around, of course – then she is silent and meek."

"Aye." Mrs Parson nodded. "She's wily, that one."

Agnes looked up from where she was slicing beets and frowned. "She should be silent in his presence. Mr Leslie is so much wiser than her, and he's her husband." She nodded vigorously, dislodging a strand of pale blond hair from under her cap.

Naomi rolled her eyes at her. "Wiser? If he were wiser, he wouldn't have married a girl that young. Look at the discord it's causing in his family." Naomi gnawed at her lip. "Poor Jenny, first she loses her mother, and now she's lost her father."

"Not a major loss, if you ask me," Alex muttered. "At least, not in his present besotted state. But, to be fair, one must remember it can't exactly be a bed of roses for Constance either."

Agnes choked and raised grey eyes her way. "Bed of roses? Marriage is a duty."

"If that's all it is, let me tell you there would have been no more than one, perhaps two Graham children," Alex retorted, grinning at the expression of mild shock that flew over Agnes' face. Seven years living with them, and Agnes still had days when she regarded Alex as a potentially demented woman.

"Anyway," Naomi went on, "Uncle Peter has stated that he expects a full apology from you before even considering to resume his friendship with you."

"From me? For what?" Alex said.

Naomi and Mrs Parson just looked at her.

"You told the wife she was simple, and then you told the husband he was even simpler, a pathetic old goat ruled by his cock," Mrs Parson said.

"Oh, that." Alex shrugged. "Well, that's true." She leaned over and nabbed a carrot from the basket at Agnes' feet and, with a small wave, stepped outside.

"I reckon that means she won't apologise," Mrs Parson stated, her voice carrying through the open door.

"Did you ever consider that a possibility?" Naomi said.

"Poor Mr Graham," Agnes put in, "to be saddled with such a headstrong wife."

Mrs Parson laughed. "Poor Mr Graham? I don't think he sees it quite that way, aye?"

He'd better not, Alex chuckled, and set off in search of her unfortunate husband.

"I think Agnes feels sorry for you," Alex said, leaning back against the sun-warmed wall of the woodshed.

"She does?" Matthew threw her a look. "Aye well, that's nice of her. I have a hard life, do I not?"

"You do? How?" She moved that bit closer. Matthew grunted as he brought the axe down, splicing the wood in two.

"You, of course. What was it Peter Leslie said? Oh aye: that a wife as opinionated as you needed regular beating, and that in his experience it helped, mellowing Elizabeth as the years went by."

"You think he did? Beat her?" Peter sank even lower in Alex's estimation.

Matthew wiped at his forehead and picked up the next

piece of wood. "Aye, I do. But as far as I can make out, it didn't mellow her much, did it?"

"Not much."

A couple of chops, a few more pieces of wood, and then he was done, sinking the axe into the chopping block. It quivered, and Alex's eyes flew automatically to his thigh, since some years back decorated with a scar the size of a kitchen knife. He noticed and gave a little shake of the head. "I know how to wield an axe. I didn't do myself the damage."

No, that had been courtesy of Walter Burley, an attempt on Matthew's life that was foiled at the last moment by their Indian friend – was he a friend? – Qaachow.

"Do you think he's still alive?" Alex asked.

"Who? Walter? You know he is – however unfortunate."

"Not him. Qaachow." Alex willed away the disturbing images of the Burley brothers that flew through her mind.

"I have no idea. The Bacon Rebellion and its subsequent aftermath crushed most of the local Indians, did it not? They even razed the Susquehannock forts, and them good allies all along."

Alex gave herself a little hug. It had been a fearful time, with Matthew called to serve at times in the militia, but mostly left at home to defend his own as best he could. Ian, Matthew and Mark had spent months on permanent sentry duty as the situation deteriorated all through 1675 to explode in 1676.

The Indians had retaliated as best they could, leaving a bloodied path when they moved south to avenge the Susquehannock chiefs killed in an attempted parley. But for all that they trampled crops both at the Chisholms' and at Leslie's Crossing; for all that they stole livestock from all their neighbours, Graham's Garden was never touched, safe behind an invisible wall of gratitude because Alex had once saved Qaachow's wife and son.

"I hope he is," Alex said. "He and Thistledown; alive and very far away. And I hope they stay there." Yes, please stay away, please don't come back.

"It isn't that easy. He might find his welcome cold among other Indian tribes – he might even be dead, killed in an Indian skirmish."

Alex hitched her shoulders, ashamed of the relief that flowed through her at the thought of Qaachow dead. "Maybe you're right, but I think he's still alive. Somehow, I know he is."

"If so, one day he'll come for Samuel," Matthew said in a low voice.

Alex gave him a black look. "Don't remind me, and it wasn't me that promised him our son for a year." She was being unfair, she knew that. Matthew had not been in a position to refuse, but there were days when she was very angry with him for agreeing to Qaachow's proposal that Samuel be raised into manhood with his son – as an Indian.

"Nay, and it wasn't me that suckled Qaachow's son at my breast, thereby making him and our Samuel foster brothers – at least in Qaachow's eyes."

"He would've died otherwise. What was I to do?"

"You did as you should." He reached forward to brush an escaped lock of hair off her face. "And as to Samuel, it probably won't happen. Qaachow might simply forget, or mayhap he'll never come back."

"Yeah," Alex said. Qaachow didn't strike her as a man that forgot.

Chapter 7

Jacob shouted with joy and ran from one side of the boat to the other, eagerly pointing at the dolphins that seemed to be racing the *Regina Anne*.

"Look!" he said to Captain Miles. "Look how fleet they are!"

"Aye, lad, I've seen dolphins before. And as I recall, you should be below deck, working with Iggy."

Jacob made a face. To spend hour after hour in the galley had not been what he'd had in mind when he snuck aboard the *Regina Anne*, but after his initial surprise, Captain Miles had decided that, if the lad was on board, he was going to earn his keep and more, so Jacob swabbed decks and peeled turnips, polished the captain's boots, kept the captain's cabin neat, and in general was at the captain's beck and call.

"I want to learn to sail," Jacob grumbled, earning himself a neat clip on the head.

"You do as I say," Captain Miles said.

"Put him on the night watch," Smith suggested. "They're good men, all of them, and you can count on Johnny to keep him in line."

Jacob nodded eagerly. Aye, he'd do the night watch, and of course he'd still mind the goats and help Iggy in the galley, and—

"We'll see," Captain Miles said. "You'll not be quite as light on your feet a week from now."

The first few nights were mainly exciting. So much to learn and understand, and Jacob tagged after Johnny and repeated words and terms, tugged at ropes, retied knots, hoisted sails, took in sails, and scrambled up the rigging to free a corner that had caught. He kept his eyes firmly on the flapping white above him, because the single time he looked down he nearly fell, uncomfortably aware of how high up he was, and how difficult it was to make out the deck in the dark of the September night. He collapsed into his hammock just before dawn. For five hours, he slept like the dead, and then he was shaken awake and told to get himself down to the galley to help with the food.

By the end of the week, Jacob was cross-eyed with lack of sleep, but he wasn't about to complain; not now that Johnny had clapped him on the shoulder and told him he had the makings of a fine sailor. Instead, he became adept at crawling away to hide during the afternoons, snatching the odd hour of sleep in the straw behind the goat pen, or in the narrow space beyond the forecastle.

He was ridiculously happy. He was on his way to see the world, and it didn't matter that he hadn't washed since he came on board, nor changed his clothes, that his hands were full of blisters, and that his shin was one black bruise from where he had fallen the other night. Very rarely did he think about home, and when he did it was mainly Mama he thought about, effectively blocking out Da. Occasionally, he woke to a hard cock, and he would rub himself to release, his eyes closed as he visualised Betty. His wife, he reminded himself with a small grin, and then the smile was wiped away as he wondered if she was alright.

"You think he'll let her wait for you?" Johnny stared at him and burst out laughing.

"But we've bedded and married by consent."

Johnny just shook his head. "If she ends up with child, mayhap. But, if not..." Johnny spat over the side. "No, lad, you must forget her. As you tell it, her father's a fine man. He won't wish to wed his lass to a sailor, will he?" His words dropped like stones through Jacob.

"I don't aim to be a sailor forever. Once I've seen a wee bit of the world, I'll return to her."

"And how will you earn your living? Will your father give you land to farm?"

Jacob admitted that no, that was probably not the case. "I can scribe. I can draw up documents and deeds."

"Hmph," Johnny snorted.

"Or I could become a healer – mayhap even a physician."
Jacob sighed. How was he to do that? He frowned down at
the black waters below them. "Betty will wait. She knows
I'll come back for her."

Johnny shrugged and changed the subject by pointing
towards the faraway shore.

Jacob could not turn his head fast enough. So many people!
And what a city! He beamed at his surroundings, hurrying
after Captain Miles who was making his way with dogged
determination through the crowds. Jacob's eyes widened
at the sight of the wenches: pretty lasses that hung out of
windows or loitered in doorways, their bodies exposed far
beyond the limits of modesty.

"Whores," Captain Miles told him, "and you'll stay well
away from them."

Jacob nodded, but his hand closed around his little
pouch. He had been very surprised when Captain Miles had
given him three half-crowns, four shillings and three groats,
gruffly telling him he had earned it. Never had he had this
much money before, and he had an urgent need to spend
it all – at once – and a visit to one of the taverns down by
the docks did not seem a bad idea, not at all. And then he
was going to buy something for Betty, he decided; perhaps
a ring.

The city was a warren of ongoing construction. Jacob
had to weave in and out of scaffolding, step over piles of
timber, and generally avoid being run over by the builders
who were a ubiquitous presence all over the place. New
multi-storeyed brick buildings tottered to impressive
heights above him, storeys were added to already existing
houses, and the narrow streets bristled with energy when
the citizens of London went about their daily business in
their half rebuilt city. Yet again, he marvelled at all the
women; now substantially more sedate and prim than the
ones down in the port area, but loud and commanding,
their garments in vibrant colours, and their necks and wrists

adorned by gold and jewels. He shook himself and caught up with Captain Miles who had stopped at the corner to wait for him, an irritated crease between his brows.

"Have you been here often?" Jacob asked.

Captain Miles grunted and nodded. "The port, aye. The city, no, not for many years. I don't hold with the English or that sad excuse of a Scotsman who sits the throne." He spat into the gutter and wrinkled his nose. "Filthy place, full of all sorts… You must go canny here lad, you hear?" He leaned towards Jacob and, after a furtive look at the people passing them, muttered that, as he heard it, times were hard on the papists – very hard. "It's yon Titus Oates, him and that popish plot of his. Pah!"

"Popish plot?" Jacob scanned their surroundings, hoping that out of nowhere would appear a band of papists, swords aloft.

"According to Oates, they aimed to kill the king. And to hear Oates, even the queen was embroiled in the plot – to poison him, like."

"His wife?" Jacob gasped.

Captain Miles gave him an exasperated look. "Lies – or fancies. Aye, the queen is unfortunately a papist but, as I hear it, fully devoted to her husband." He pulled a face. "Unfortunate, that there is no royal issue. The Londoners are not much pleased with having a papist heir." This Jacob already knew, having heard Mr Hancock expound more than once on the fact that the Duke of York was a Catholic. He hadn't found it interesting then, he didn't find it interesting now. Instead, he followed the captain through a series of winding alleys, coming to a halt by a huge stone set in the midst of a busy street.

"The London Stone," Captain Miles said. "Older than the city itself."

"I thought you said you didn't know the city," Jacob said.

"I didn't say that: I said I didn't visit it much, not now. It used to be I'd go into the city, but after the big fire I've never been."

"Why not?"

"None of your concern, laddie," Captain Miles said, but told him all the same about his business dealings with the Widow Farley, and how it had all ended the day her establishments burnt to the ground.

"I was here at the time. It wasn't pretty, not at all." Captain Miles went on to describe those September days thirteen years in the past, when all of London had stood ablaze, huge plumes of dark, acrid smoke colouring the sky. He told Jacob how he'd watched it all from the safety of his ship, moored off the wharves that were engulfed in flames. Iron melted, stone burst with the heat, the lead roofs of the churches became molten drops of fiery heat that flew through the night to land sizzling in the river. "So many people lost it all," he summed up, "and no one knows how many lost their lives."

"Not that many, Johnny said."

Captain Miles snorted. "When iron and lead melt 'tis very hot. Do you think there would be much left of a person burnt to death in that?" Nay, probably not, Jacob reflected, thinking that it must hurt frightfully to burn to death.

"I have an uncle here," Jacob said, following the captain into an inn.

"An uncle?" Captain Miles sat down at a table, motioning for Jacob to do the same. He called for beer and food before returning his attention to Jacob.

Jacob nodded. "Luke Graham."

"Ah, the evil brother."

"Aye." Jacob's attention was distracted by the serving wench who smiled broadly at him as she set down plates and a brimming jug of beer. He took a huge bite of pie, and just as quickly spat it out, grabbing for his mug.

"Hot?" Captain Miles teased.

"He works for the king," Jacob said once he'd finished drinking.

"He's been doing that since well before the king was king," Captain Miles said. "Have you ever met him?"

"Aye, but I was but a wee bairn at the time." Jacob

63

took a new bite and chewed for some time. Luke Graham was a name rarely mentioned in his home, and only by eavesdropping and laying an intricate puzzle had Jacob managed to form some kind of picture of his uncle.

Mark had told him that Da had cut Luke's nose off, and how in revenge Luke had Da abducted and sold into indenture. Then there was Ian who had at one time been raised by Luke, despite really being Da's son by his first wife, Margaret. They had lied, Mama had said. Margaret had sworn on everything holy that Ian was Luke's son, insisting Luke was the father for all that Ian was born while she was still married to Da. Jacob had spent a lot of time getting his head around this. For Margaret to make such a claim, she had to be bedding with both Da and Luke.

Then it all got even more confusing, because Margaret and Luke had a son of their own – wee, red-haired Charlie – and Ian was returned to Da, discarded in a way Jacob found callous. Even more disturbing was the fact that Margaret and Luke had been lovers before Da married Margaret, and Jacob didn't understand that. Nor had anyone ever given him a good explanation for why Da had sliced Luke's nose off in the first place – it seemed a cruel thing to do.

"There's no love lost between your da and your uncle," Captain Miles said. "And, as I recall, for good reason. Your uncle has ever been a viper at your da's breast, lad, and you best remember that."

Jacob shrugged. It wasn't as if he was bound to ever meet Luke Graham, was it?

"Nay, that you're not. You're coming with me to Edinburgh, and there I will turn you over into the loving hands of your other uncle, Simon Melville." The captain looked Jacob up and down. "You'll get a welcome to remember, lad." He laughed and mimed an aching backside.

Jacob nodded morosely. He already knew that.

"So where does the king live?" Jacob asked, once they were back outside.

"The king?" Captain Miles shook his head. "The king doesn't live here. He's no friend of the city of London, and the city of London is no friend of his. You know about the Commonwealth, don't you?" He lowered his voice, looking guardedly at the men that thronged by them.

"Aye, and Da says how London stood on the side of Parliament and free men."

"Against the king." Captain Miles pointed in the general direction of the west. "The king lives yonder, in the palace of Whitehall; an hour or so by foot." He had lost his audience: Jacob was staring at a young girl sitting in an upstairs window and smiling down at him.

They parted company on Cheapside, the captain to conduct his business negotiations, and Jacob, according to the captain, to return to the ship.

"Straight back, or you'll be swabbing decks all the way from here to Edinburgh."

Jacob rolled his eyes. "I'll be doing that anyway."

"Aye." Captain Miles grinned and clapped him on the shoulder. "We sail with the tide," he added as he turned away. "I have most pressing matters to attend to in Edinburgh."

Jacob took his time getting back to the wharves. He strolled up and down the narrow streets, spent two shillings on a small silver ring for Betty, bought himself a sticky bun, and eyed every lass he saw with interest. His Betty would be like a dull pigeon among a flock of glamorous peacocks had he brought her here, he reflected, feeling somewhat disloyal. Always in muted colours, always with high-cut bodices, she'd stick out like a sore thumb among these enticing creatures.

Low necklines, frothy lace and gleaming silks and velvets… He gaped at the creative hairdos, intricate compositions of braids and curls that succeeded in displaying very much hair to the world, despite the immaculate caps or hats that perched atop. And their faces…cheeks that glowed a delicious pink, mouths that looked suspiciously red, and darkened lashes that lowered themselves at his overt staring.

He was in a state of half arousal when he turned into the alley leading down to the water, and there, leaning against a wall and highlighted by a lantern above her, stood a wench that smiled at him. Jacob was not an entire innocent, and he knew this was a whore, but she was pretty for all that. His cock was nosing at the cloth of his breeches, and he was young and had money in his pouch. Captain Miles would never know, nor would Betty, so he followed when she led him up the creaky stairs. He gasped when her hand closed on his member, and for a moment he was sure he loved her, this woman who spread her legs for him and helped him come inside of her.

Half an hour later, it was dark outside, and the evening fog had transformed itself into a drizzle that seeped through Jacob's coat in a matter of minutes. Not that he cared, humming to himself as he relieved himself into the river. He shook his cock and adjusted his breeches, ensuring the little pouch still hung where it should, very close to his privates. He didn't hear the murmured conversation behind him, nor see how the girl he had just paid nodded her head in his direction, laughing under her breath. And he definitely didn't hear the footfalls until it was too late and a club came down upon his head, bringing him to his knees. Two things happened that saved his life: one, he toppled over the edge and fell into the swirling waters of the Thames; two, he wasn't entirely unconscious and managed to keep himself afloat until he bumped into a wooden jetty.

Chapter 8

"Have you seen Daniel?" Alex frowned at Ruth, who was busy folding her brother's clothes. "And really, Ruth, he should be doing that himself. You're not his servant."

Ruth shrugged. "I don't mind. Tomorrow he'll be gone." Her back curved, and Alex came over to sit beside her.

"He'll be back."

"In a year and that's a very long time." Ruth's arms wound themselves round her waist in a self-hug.

"But he was gone all last year as well."

"Nay, he wasn't. He came home for Hogmanay, and he was here for the spring planting." Ruth wiped at her eyes. "This time he goes away, and when he comes back he will have changed. Just like Jacob."

"Jacob? How do you mean?"

"The year he was gone from harvest to harvest on account of him being ill over Hogmanay – he had changed."

Alex smiled slightly at the memory. The thirteen-year-old came back a tall fourteen-year-old, the boy permanently supplanted by the young man. She looked down at Ruth and stroked the dark red head. "It was still Jacob, wasn't it?"

"Aye, but not quite. He sat with the men, talked with the men, not with us."

"But he still played with you, didn't he? And he chased you all over the farm the night you and Daniel stuffed his pillow with crickets."

Ruth grinned. "Aye, that was fun. But it was still me and Daniel, and soon it won't be, because he'll be gone." She sounded forlorn.

"That's the way it is, honey." Alex kissed her daughter on her brow.

"I'll miss him; so very much will I miss him."

"You still have Sarah, and—"

"Sarah?" Ruth gave an irritated shake of her head. "That's not the same. You can't talk to her, and all we do is quarrel and fight."

"And whose fault is that, hey?" With that parting shot and a little tug at Ruth's braid, Alex left the room.

Alex continued her desultory search for her son, but neither David nor Samuel had seen him.

"Agnes, have you seen Daniel?"

Agnes looked up from the butter churn. "I saw Angus and he was waiting for him," she said, going back to her long, steady strokes.

"Angus?" Alex was surprised. Daniel and Angus had never been close. Agnes didn't reply and Alex took off in the direction of the river. Daniel was a water child, and she suspected he was going to miss the river much more than he was going to miss anything else.

If it hadn't been for the deer, Alex might not have seen them, but the sudden movement startled her, making her head snap up, and that's when she saw Angus and Daniel on the other side of the clearing. Daniel was stiff as a board, his back pressed against a tree, and before him stood Angus, his hands on Daniel's shoulders, his pelvis pressed against Daniel in a way that made Alex's hackles rise.

The pale blond head bent itself towards Daniel who twisted his face violently to the side. Alex was inundated by an urgent desire to do Angus some grave, bodily harm. Instead, she ducked behind a bush and called loudly for Daniel. When she straightened up, Daniel was alone, slumped against the tree.

"Daniel?" Alex kneeled down beside him. He seemed to be crying, and this stumped Alex, because maybe Angus and Daniel were closer than she'd understood, and... Oh my God, maybe Daniel was homosexual, but would a thirteen-year-old know that? And if he was, what kind of an unfulfilled life would he be doomed to live?

She cupped his face and forced him to look her in the eyes. "What were you doing? You and Angus?"

Daniel stared at her with very blue eyes. "I didn't know what to do. He was weeping and telling me how it would all be worthless with me gone, and…" He wiped at his arms. "He touched me, he pressed himself against me, and then he kissed me." He scrubbed at his lips with the back of his hand. "I didn't want him to," he groaned, his eyes wide. "Why, Mama? Why did he do that?"

Alex thought long and hard. She was going to nail Angus' skinny arse, but at the same time she couldn't help feeling sorry for this troubled young man.

"He hasn't had an easy life," Alex said, sitting down. "His mother died when he was very young; then came the soldiers and arrested his father for being a Covenanter, and you know how they were all sold off into indenture to clear the fines."

Daniel nodded. "Like Da."

"No, your da was never arrested or fined. But he probably would have been had we stayed – which was why we chose to come here. Anyway, Angus' father died on the way over, and Agnes and he were separated once they landed here. He was only twelve…" Alex sat back against the tree and tilted her head in Daniel's direction. "I think he's very lonely and, sometimes when you're lonely, things happen in your head and you do things you're not supposed to do." She took her son's hand, running her fingers over his smooth skin. "He won't do it again, but I don't want you telling anyone about this."

Daniel obediently agreed. "Is he a sodomite, do you think?"

"Daniel Graham! Where have you learnt a word like that?"

"It's in the Bible, how the men of Sodom wished to have carnal knowledge of the angels God sent, and Lot begged them not to." He peeked at her from under dark lashes. "I never understood why he offered them his daughters instead."

"No, that does seem a very uncaring thing to do. Is it a bad thing to be a sodomite?" Alex asked, contriving to sound as innocent as possible.

Daniel looked away. "It's an abomination. It's stated clearly in Leviticus that man should not lie with mankind."

"Oh." As far as Alex recalled, Leviticus was one very long, tedious description of sacrifice after sacrifice after sacrifice. It was obvious she'd never gotten to the juicy parts. She pretended to think for some time. "No, I don't think Angus is a sodomite. I think he's a very unhappy man." And if he as much as laid a finger on one of her boys again, she was going to tear his balls off, but that was something she kept to herself.

For the first time ever in their long marriage, Alex chose not to tell Matthew about something. She needed to think, and decided she would talk to him upon his return from Providence instead. Ultimately, of course, she had to tell him, and her guts twisted when she considered what the consequences might be for Angus – and for Agnes.

"What is it?" Matthew asked her when she served him breakfast. Outside in the yard, Mark had saddled up the horses, and Angus and his sister were busy distributing the packing on the three mules.

"Nothing."

He made a disbelieving sound, wrapped his arms around her, and pulled her down to sit on his lap. "Is it Daniel?"

She shrugged and nodded, trying to look very dejected. From the way he narrowed his eyes at her, he wasn't entirely taken in.

"You'll tell me when I get back," he said as he stood up, and to her huge irritation, Alex could feel her cheeks heat with telltale blood. Lucky she'd never aspired to being an undercover agent, because she'd have failed miserably, most of her thoughts standing plain on her face for the world to see – okay, maybe not the world, but definitely her man.

He grinned and set a finger to her cheek. "When I come back, aye?"

Alex stood for a long time waving after her son and husband, scowled in the direction of where Angus had dropped out of sight, and went off in search of Mrs Parson.

"Hmm," Mrs Parson said once Alex had finished telling her. "You should have told Matthew. It would be best if wee Angus leaves."

"That's precisely why I couldn't tell him. We should at least try and find out what happened to him and see if we can help him."

"Some men are born that way," Mrs Parson informed her, making Alex blink.

"How would you know?"

"You don't get to my age without seeing a thing or two," Mrs Parson said drily. "Angus is a man; a young man, and mayhap a damaged man, but all the same a man, nigh on nineteen. And Daniel is a half-grown lad. Nothing can excuse what you saw."

Alex swallowed. Mrs Parson was right and, upon his return, Matthew would be very angry with her for not having told him.

"Maybe I should talk to Angus."

Mrs Parson raised her brows. "That isn't for you to do. 'Tis the master that must handle such."

Over the coming days, Alex did some discreet sleuthing. An odd question here, another one there, and given that Agnes was a sweet but rather dense girl, she didn't find this newborn interest in her brother strange, but replied offhandedly. Yes, he was much shyer around people now than she remembered him being as a child, and, no, she didn't think it strange that he didn't have a lass to go out with – he was still but a lad. Alex rolled her eyes at this but made a hemming noise, feeling very devious. Was he sorry that Daniel had left? Ah, aye, that he was; wee Angus had a fondness for Daniel. Agnes went on to comment how fond he was of the wee lads. She didn't notice the shudder that passed through Alex.

"It's going to be quite cold tonight," Alex said to Agnes late one afternoon. Agnes didn't reply at first, but concentrated on the load of dripping steaming linen she was transferring from the cauldron to the rinsing trough.

The laundry shed was full of steam, Alex's hair curling into heavy ringlets with the damp. Betty helped pour cold water over the hot sheets before she and Alex began the tedious process of first scrubbing and then rinsing the lye out, after which the sheets were wrung and placed in one of the wicker baskets for Ruth and Sarah to carry outside and hang.

"I won't mind," Agnes said, sighing as she filled the cauldron with yet another load. "It will be a right relief to have some cold air after a day in here." She wiped her sweaty face with her apron and scowled at the barrel in which the remaining unwashed clothes were soaking.

"I was thinking of Angus," Alex said. "It might make sense for him to sleep with Patrick in the room off the stables rather than up in the loft."

"Angus?" Agnes frowned. "He won't sleep behind a door."

Betty gave Agnes a curious look. "He won't?" she said, scrubbing at a grey stain on one of the sheets.

Agnes shook her head and used a wooden ladle to stir the lye into the boiling water. "Not since he was brought here. The master doesn't mind."

"Why not?" Betty asked.

Agnes stopped stirring and looked at Betty. "I don't know; mayhap it's a sense of freedom he misses?"

That made some sense, Alex conceded. Being only twelve when he arrived in Providence, Angus had been bonded for fourteen years to pay for his and his dead father's passage. He still had seven years left on his contract.

"He was very wee," Agnes said, her face softening.

Not so wee anymore, Alex sighed. Now he was a lanky man with guarded light eyes and an aversion to any type of contact beyond the absolutely necessary. He even avoided his sister, and at first Agnes had come to Alex to ask for advice, but now she no longer did, having seemingly given up. Always alone, Angus was, never interacting – except for the few times he played with her boys. Alex tightened her hold on the sheet she was presently rinsing, and decided then and there that until Matthew got back, her boys wouldn't be having any alone time with Angus – however prejudiced that sounded.

"Two more loads and then we're done," Alex said, forcing her thoughts away from Angus. "And I don't know about you, but I'm going to treat myself to a long, very hot bath in the tub afterwards."

Betty looked at the well-scrubbed pine tub. "Must we?"

"Not this time." Alex grinned. "This time I was suggesting it as a reward."

Her constant vigilance of Angus was disrupted by the Indian. One early morning, Alex snuck out of the house, making for the privy. When she came back, an Indian was standing in her yard, blocking her path. Alex came to a halt, feeling vulnerable in only her shift and shawl. The Indian was dressed like a white man, in ragged breeches and a white shirt that was in severe need of a wash. A coat several sizes too big completed the ensemble, decorated by the odd feather and what looked like braids sown onto the shoulders. Were braids, Alex amended: several long, dark braids of human hair.

"What do you want?" she called, hoping either Mark, who was in the stables, or Mrs Parson would hear her.

The man didn't reply. Instead, he extended a wrapped package to her. Alex backed away; the man came after.

"For you," he said.

"No thanks." One of the dogs began to bark. The Indian threw a look over his shoulder, and when the large yellow dog came loping towards him, he moved swiftly. The package was shoved into her hands, and he set off at a run in the direction of the woods. In a matter of seconds, he was swallowed up into the forest. The dog made as if to follow, but Alex called Dandelion back.

"Mama?" Mark came running from the stables, tagged by Patrick. "Are you alright?"

She nodded, but had to bite down on her lower lip to stop it from wobbling. The man had come and gone unhindered. Had he wanted to, she'd have been dead, her braid added to his gory collection.

"What's that?" Mark indicated the package.

"I don't know." She told him of their visitor, and her son's face set in an impressive scowl.

"Here? In our yard?" He shook his head. "Worthless dogs."

"Not all of them," Alex said, patting Dandelion. "Besides, he can't have been here long, and I guess he knows how to move so as to avoid setting them off."

By now Mrs Parson had joined them, a rather impressive appearance in starched nightdress, bed jacket, overlarge cap and a shawl.

"So what did he give you?" she asked.

"I'm not sure I want to know. Somehow I don't think it's a delayed birthday gift." Alex unwound the dirty cloth to find a small wooden box, around which was wrapped a paper.

In the box was a heart, pierced by a miniature knife. Alex threw it away from her.

"It's a pig's heart," Mark said after inspecting the organ. Alex nodded. She'd seen that too.

She held out the sheet of paper to him. "Read." It cost her just to say that one word.

"*Someday I aim to have the pleasure of delivering your husband's heart in a similar way*," Mark read out loud. "Bastard," he hissed, crumpling the paper into a ball.

The letter was unsigned. In Alex's head rang Philip Burley's laughter, and to her shame she began to cry, blubbering like a child in her son's arms.

Chapter 9

On the morrow of their departure for Providence, Jenny had woken to Ian's kisses. From kissing, he decided they might as well progress to other things, and Jenny was still half asleep but her body was most willing.

Afterwards, she made a contented sound and shoved at him. "We have to make ready. Your father will be by shortly."

"He can wait," Ian said, but rolled off her anyway. "Are you sure you should be going?" he asked as he pulled on his breeches. He dragged his hands through his dark hair in lieu of a comb, tying it back with a scrap of ribbon.

"We have been over this," she replied, rifling through her few petticoats in search of her flannel one.

"But the wean…" He covered her flat stomach with his hands.

"The babe will be fine, and we've agreed that I ride with you, just in case." She shooed him out to start loading her cheeses into the pannier baskets while she made breakfast.

"Patrick will be coming by later on account of the cows," Ian said, swallowing down the eggs she served him. Jenny arranged her face into a mask of blank indifference before she turned to nod at him. Patrick…the name made her breath hitch with anxiety.

"…and Mama will send Agnes or Naomi up for the milk on a regular basis," Ian went on, oblivious to her agitation. He stood up, grabbed another piece of bread, and told her to hurry; he would be waiting for her by the horses.

Jenny took several deep breaths to calm her thundering heart, and leaned her head against the smooth timber of the wall. Despite her best intentions, Patrick was still very much a part of her life. A quick look, that smile that made the right corner of his mouth turn upwards, and she'd come running, all of her burning for his touch. Tumbles in the hay, hurried meetings in the forest, his cock inside of her as she leaned over the kitchen table, eyes glued to the yard outside in case Ian should suddenly appear from the stables. Jenny swallowed and clenched her hands. Patrick had to go. Somehow, she had to find the fortitude to wipe him out of her life. She straightened up, grabbed her woollen cloak, and hastened outside to her husband.

It was very restful to sit in front of Ian on the horse. But when he slipped his hand in under her cloak and splayed his fingers across her midriff, part of her wanted to shy away, because God, what had she done? It might not be his child, and how would he ever forgive her? And then the other, saner part kicked in, and she pressed herself against his touch. No one would ever know, she assured herself, and at least in colouring Patrick and Ian were not dissimilar, except for the eyes.

Jenny was lulled half to sleep by the time they stopped for a quick break, and it was only as she returned from a visit behind a thicket that she noticed Daniel was looking apprehensive. She paused on her way to find the food and patted him on the cheek.

"It'll be alright. I'm sure you'll love Boston."

Daniel made a non-committal sound.

"And you'll like Harriet," Jenny went on, smiling at the thought of her energetic cousin.

"I hope she'll like me," Daniel said in a small voice.

"Of course she will." Jenny handed him a huge slice of cake.

Matthew was still trying to work out what it was that Alex had held back from him. His instincts – and the way Alex had blushed – were telling him it had something to do with Daniel. He was considering how to raise the issue with his son when Ian sat down beside him with a stone bottle of beer in his hand.

"She's breeding," he said in an exultant tone. "But she doesn't want me to tell you yet." He handed Matthew the bottle.

76

"Then why did you?" Matthew smiled.

Ian shrugged and took a huge bite out of his cold egg. "I just had to," he said through his food. "It makes it more real, like. A spring babe, and I'm hoping for a lad." For an instant, his face softened with yearning, and then he thrust the rest of the egg into his mouth and stood up to go and find something more to eat.

"So who will you miss the most, then?" Matthew asked Daniel once they were back on their horses. Daniel gave him a look that indicated just how stupid a question that was.

"Ruth," he replied, tugging a bit too hard at the leading rein of the mule.

"Not your wee brothers?" Matthew teased.

"You mean the scamps who filled my shoes with thistles as a going away gift?" Daniel laughed. "No, not them. Maybe Adam; he's a sweet laddie."

Matthew nodded, smiling fondly at the thought of his youngest lad.

"Sarah?"

Daniel gave him a black look. "Sarah is a right tease, she is. And I don't like it when she says I'll grow up dull and boring on account of becoming a minister."

"She wouldn't mind being a minister herself."

Daniel turned very surprised eyes in his direction. "Sarah? But she can't! She's a lass."

"She knows that, but she's a good Bible reader that lass is, and she has a bright head on her shoulders, and a tongue that can charm the squirrels down the trees…"

"…and scare them back up again," Daniel muttered, sounding irritated by this description of his youngest sister.

"Aye, that too." Matthew laughed. He peeked at his son. "And Angus, will you miss him?"

The reaction was so immediate Matthew knew he'd hit home, and over the coming minutes he wheedled the whole story out of Daniel, silently cursing Alex for not having told him before.

"He kissed you?" he asked in a disgusted tone.

Daniel nodded unhappily. "And he—"

"What?" Matthew sank his eyes into Daniel's.

"He put his hand on my cock and rubbed at it, like," Daniel said, blood surging through his downy cheeks. "And my cock…"

"Merciful Christ!" Had he had Alex in front of him, Matthew would have been sorely tempted to belt her for not telling him. And as for Angus… He wanted to wheel Moses round and set off back home immediately, because he had other sons – small, vulnerable lads that wouldn't understand until it was too late. What was the woman thinking of, leaving a man like that close to their lads?

When they'd made camp for the night, Matthew found the opportunity to tell Ian what Daniel had told him.

"Angus?" Ian sounded incredulous. "He wouldn't hurt a fly, Da." He scratched Narcissus behind his ear, making the large dog sigh with pleasure.

"You think?" Matthew stirred forcefully at the fire. "Is it not to hurt someone to make unwelcome advances? And he's a man – he must have urges to quench like all men do."

"But not like that. And as you tell it, Daniel himself says how he was weeping with it."

Matthew remained unconvinced. In his head, he saw Angus one summer day by the river with David, and his stomach heaved when the previously so innocent little scene acquired connotations he hadn't seen at the time. Both had been naked, swimming in the water, and at one point Angus had taken David on his lap, held him close, and an instant later thrown the laddie squealing through the air. And he hadn't thought more of it, but had strolled down to the water's edge and watched them play.

"Sleep," he said to Ian. "I'll sit here a while, aye? I'll wake you some hours from now."

Ian nodded and moved over to where Jenny was already sleeping, draped in quilts and blankets.

Matthew sat and stared into the fire, his hands tight around a piece of wood. He increased the pressure until the branch splintered in his hold. Very rarely did he feel the urge to hurt someone, but right now he did: Angus, for being a sodomite; Alex, for not telling him.

Matthew hugged his son one last time and shoved him gently in the direction of the gangway. "Go. Make me proud, lad."

Once Daniel was safely aboard the sloop, Matthew smiled, receiving a wavering smile in return. The lad hadn't said much for the last half-hour or so, and Matthew suspected it was due to not wanting to weep – not here, in front of all the people that were always present in the port.

The sloop was unmoored, it glided off, and Matthew strolled along the waterfront, waving at his son for as long as he could see him. He turned away with a small sigh. It was difficult letting the bairns go, he thought morosely, before squaring his shoulders and setting off to visit William Hancock.

The shove sent him sprawling. It was only by sheer luck that he didn't bash his head into the adjacent tree.

"How unfortunate," a voice said from behind him. "Here, Mr Graham, allow me to help you back up." Strong hands closed on Matthew's arms, closed with far more force than necessary, and Matthew was lifted back on his feet.

"Take your hands off me," Matthew snarled, wresting himself free from Philip Burley's hold.

"Really, Mr Graham! And here I was but offering you assistance." Philip Burley took a step back from Matthew's unsheathed dirk, hands held open and empty in front of him.

"You pushed me to begin with." Matthew wiped at his mouth. Three pairs of disturbingly similar light eyes stared at him, eyes that regarded him with the intent interest of wolves circling an injured prey.

"We did? And how do you know? Eyes in the back of your head?" Walter Burley smirked and, beside him, Stephen Burley laughed.

"What do you want?" Matthew straightened out of his defensive crouch. At well over six feet, he was taller than any of the brothers, a slight advantage he needed to flaunt. Besides, there were too many people about for the

Burleys to try anything, he noted with relief, nodding at an acquaintance.

"Want? Why, Mr Graham, we're just passing the time of the day – with a man we will never ever forget, will we?" Philip said, and his brothers laughed again.

"Not likely." Stephen's voice sounded strange, a wheezing reedy sound, until Matthew recalled he'd taken an arrow through his throat.

"You see, Mr Graham, we don't take kindly to people killing our brother and scarring us for life." Philip nodded at Stephen. A badly healed sword-cut bisected Stephen's destroyed face, giving the impression the nose was on the verge of falling off.

"That's what you get. Four against one, trying to murder me, so what did you expect? That I not fight back?" Matthew forced himself not to wipe his damp hand against his breeches, nor avoid those ice-cold eyes.

Philip took a step forward. "Next time, we won't just try. We'll tear the heart out of your living body and send it to your wife – as a keepsake." It sounded like a certainty, and Matthew's right knee buckled, causing the leg to fold before he got it back under control.

Philip snickered softly and stood out of Matthew's way. Beside him, Stephen Burley fingered his puckering scar and looked at Matthew with open dislike.

Matthew hawked, spat, and, with a huge effort, turned his back on all three. He walked away as fast as he could without appearing craven. As he left the port behind, the narrow streets grew increasingly empty. Matthew could hear his pulse thudding through his head, an irritating whooshing that made it difficult to concentrate on whatever sounds he heard behind him. Footsteps echoed on the cobbles to his left. Matthew wheeled, hand on his dirk. Ian came to a halt, skidding on the wet stones.

"Are you alright?" he asked.

"Aye," Matthew said, but was very relieved to see his tall, strong son. He was still weak at the knees; there was sweat congealing on his back, and he stopped, inhaling repeatedly in an effort to bring his thumping pulse back under control. They frightened the daylights out of him, those three brothers with their inhumanly pale eyes. One on one, they didn't worry him – he was quite confident he could defend himself against any of them – but together there was something of a pack of rabid dogs to them, an insane light in their eyes that had his whole body going into flight mode.

"I saw the Burley brothers," Ian said, "and I felt it best to ensure you were hale. Vermin!"

Matthew nodded. Definitely vermin, but dangerous vermin. "I don't think they plan on staying, they're not welcome here." The Burleys had collected quite a number of enemies among the worthies of Providence, in particular after Stephen Burley had knifed Minister Walker's nephew a year or so ago.

"Nay, I dare say not. I'll drop by Mr Farrell; have him set the constables on them," Ian said.

"Aye, do that." Matthew resolutely shoved any further thoughts about the Burleys to the back of his head, adjusted his hat, and smiled wryly. "Don't wait up for me. I fear the discussion with William will take a long time."

Esther Hancock let him in and, with a tentative smile, ushered him in the direction of William's study. He noted with interest how her hand came down to rest on her belly, had his suspicions confirmed when she blushed at his questioning glance.

"Are you well?" He liked Esther, and to his eye she looked peaked, dark smudges under her eyes. She just smiled and opened the door for him.

The interview with William did not go well, at least not at first, but once Esther interrupted their loud quarrel by inviting them to supper, they settled down to attempting to find a solution rather than apportioning blame.

"How is Betty?" Esther asked once supper had been cleared away.

"Well enough. She's an easy lass to like."

Esther nodded, and, for an instant, her face fell apart into an expression of utter misery before she collected herself. The mother was pining for her daughter – far more than the daughter was pining for the mother. Mayhap to be expected; in particular given Esther's pregnant state. Esther ducked her head, thereby avoiding Matthew's eyes, and scraped at a non-existent stain on the tabletop.

"Is she...?" she asked.

Matthew shook his head. "Nay, she isn't with child."

"Thank the Lord for small mercies." William stood and disappeared into his office, returning with a small flask of brandy.

"It will be relatively simple," William explained, topping up two glasses. "The vows can be annulled, and if we ensure Betty is married at some distance from here, no one need ever know."

"She doesn't want to annul the marriage." Matthew twirled his glass. He raised his eyes to meet William's irritated glare. "And if she doesn't want to then I won't see it done. My lad will stand by her and, until he's back, I'll care for her as my own."

"And how long do you propose she wait?" William sat back and regarded Matthew in silence. "When does she give Jacob up as lost?"

Matthew's throat constricted at the thought. "He isn't lost," he said, setting the glass back untouched on the table. "It's an unkindness to insinuate he might be."

William made a small sound. "It's not my intent to hurt you, Brother Matthew. I know the pain of losing a son... five we've lost." His eyes flew to his wife for an instant before returning to Matthew. "My intention is rather to protect my daughter. Is she to live forever in hope? See the years go by, let her life slip through her fingers as she waits for one who may be dead – who may have found himself a new life far from here?"

"If he does, he'll write. My lad wouldn't want his mother to spend her remaining years wondering where he may have ended up."

"If he can," William said, "but sometimes life happens."

"William!" Esther hissed. Matthew closed his eyes for instant, seconds in which his brain was taken over by graphic images of what fates might befall his son.

Well over an hour later, Matthew shouldered his way into Mrs Malone's. As always, the inn was full of male patrons, some like him there for the beer, others for the lasses. From the kitchen came enticing smells of baked onions and sausages, the whores smelled abundantly of perfume, and the men reeked of lust and grime. Matthew made his way over the floor, ducking here and there to avoid the lanterns that suffused the room in a hazy golden light – most becoming to the whores, some of whom were getting on a bit. One of the wenches came dancing towards him, her cleavage so generous he could see most of her heavy breasts. She simpered at him, but Matthew waved her away and ordered a beer.

Matthew sat down in a dark corner to nurse his drink and his foul mood. These last few days hadn't been good days, what with Alex holding back on him, wee Daniel setting sail, the damned Burleys, and then this long conversation with Hancock. In the end, they'd decided that, for now, nothing would be done, but that should Betty reach eighteen with Jacob still not back, well then…

Matthew drained his beer and beckoned for another one. And another, and another. He sat sunk into black gloom and regarded the bustle around him; the lasses that flirted and laughed; the men that panted with expectation.

Mrs Malone herself appeared for an instant, a statuesque woman with the most magnificent red hair Matthew had ever seen, even if Alex had drily informed him that it was dyed – anyone could see that. The madam let her eye rove her small kingdom to ensure her girls were working diligently, and after satisfying herself that all the private rooms were in use, she nodded at her barman and disappeared up the stairs – in all probability to count up her profits.

There was something of a commotion by the door, and Matthew looked up blearily to where a group of men were exclaiming in anger and disgust, glaring at a black stranger.

Black? Matthew knuckled his eyes. Aye, black, or at least a deep brown. One man, whom Matthew recognised as Mr Farrell, was waving his arms around in agitation, pointing at the dark man and repeatedly slurring an angry "slave". And then Mr Farrell wasn't standing up anymore, but was flying in a neat arc through the air to crash against the counter.

Women shrieked; men screamed and raged. Matthew ducked instinctively when a bottle came flying through the air towards him. The barman was attempting to regain control when Mrs Malone reappeared with a musket. The roar was deafening, and for a split second everyone in the establishment stood frozen to the spot. That was all Mrs Malone needed. Using her musket as a club, she made her way through the crowd until she reached the door where she pointed at the black man and told him to get out – now.

Matthew was impressed. In dishabille, with her hair hanging undone down her back and her heaving bosom very much on display, Mrs Malone looked verily like an Amazon, and the way she wielded her musket only served to further strengthen that opinion. She stood panting by the counter, resting back on her arms in a way that had the gawking men drooling over all that exposed flesh.

"How is he?" she asked, indicating Mr Farrell who lay groaning on the floor.

"The effrontery," Mr Farrell managed, sitting up with his hairpiece in his hand. "A black man to bear hand on such as me. I'll see him punished, I will." He got to his feet, one arm hanging awkwardly by his side. "What say you? An escaped slave is on the loose, and you've all seen how wildly he attacked me." An assenting rumble rose around him.

"I say we go a-hunting!" one man called out, and several men hooted their agreement.

Mrs Malone frowned and murmured something to the barman.

"Before you do," she interrupted, "let me offer you something to drink – on the house."

Not only an Amazon, but an Athena as well, Matthew concluded, throwing the madam an admiring look.

Chapter 10

Matthew woke very late next morning with uncomfortably indistinct memories of the remainder of last night. A very pretty lass…Henriette? Caroline? Matthew groaned and hid his face in his pillow. What had he done? His head throbbed, but a careful inspection assured him all of him was whole. He sniffed at his torn shirt and grimaced. He smelled like a bawdy house! Oh God; Alex would flay him alive.

The door opened, and he flinched at the sharp shaft of light.

"Awake?" Ian's dry voice sounded amused.

"Uhhhh," Matthew replied, hoping Ian would understand. A hand appeared with a cup of cider and Matthew gulped it down.

"It seems I got you out at the last moment," Ian went on with an element of reproof. "That wee lass had a good grip on you."

"I was drunk," Matthew informed him haughtily. He closed his eyes. "I'm still drunk."

"I don't think Mama would care why."

"Nay." A quick shudder at the thought of Alex's reaction flew through Matthew.

He was still very sore on the inside of his skull when he stepped out into the street some hours later. The voice that called his name cut through his sensitive brain tissue and made him wince, but he turned in the direction of the speaker, if nothing else to stop whoever it was from calling his name again.

"Kate!" Matthew shone up with genuine pleasure – it had been some time since he saw her last, one or two years back. "I hear you've managed to evade the hunt," Matthew teased, looking her up and down. Widowhood became her, he reflected, and especially now that she had left the sober colours of her widow garb behind and moved on to this far more attractive golden red. It brought out the colour of her hair and lightened her eyes, and, all in all, she looked most pleasing.

Kate Jones rolled her eyes and tucked her hand into the crook of his arm with far more familiarity than he was comfortable with. He shook his head and increased the space between them, making her smile.

"You fear word of our cuddling might reach Alex?"

"Aye," he replied, miming a cut throat. Alex might have forgiven, but she had definitely not forgotten, that he'd bedded Kate all those years ago, when he was a slave and Kate the single thing he had to hold onto.

Kate laughed and dropped her hand to walk beside him, no more.

"You look well," Matthew said, having concluded a detailed but surreptitious inspection. Well, he assumed being rid of a husband like Dominic Jones had to be a relief.

"I am well." Kate brushed at her velvet skirts.

"And the bairns? Are they well?"

"Bairns?" Kate laughed out loud. "The youngest is seven, Matthew, and the eldest is seventeen." A shadow flew over her face.

"Is seventeen?" Matthew asked perceptively.

Kate sighed. "John died of the measles two years back, so now it is only Henry left of the twins."

"I'm so sorry," Matthew said.

Kate looked away, her chin quivering. She cleared her throat and turned to face him. "And you? I hear that one of your sons has taken to the seas."

Matthew kicked at the ground and muttered something about gossiping women.

"Esther is my friend. She's quite upset by the whole situation, and what with her breeding again..." Kate made a face. "She misses her daughter. But then all mothers miss their children once they're gone."

Matthew inclined his head in silent agreement. "And

yet all children must ultimately leave the parent nest." He looked thoughtfully at Kate. "Don't you miss it? Someone to help you place the bairns and order your affairs?"

"I can take care of my affairs on my own, and as to the children, I haven't begun looking for suitable partners – they're still too young."

"Henry is seventeen," Matthew reminded her. "And the next lad is what? Fourteen?"

"He'll not wed yet. I'm of a mind to send Henry to Boston for some years." Her eyes slid over to meet Matthew's, and a slow smile spread over her face. "How old is your eldest girl? Twelve?"

"In a few months." Matthew smiled back.

"Mayhap that would be a suitable match for my Henry."

"Alex won't want her to wed too young," Matthew prevaricated. Alex wouldn't want Ruth anywhere close to Henry Jones. Nor did he, not really, but he liked the mother well enough, and the lad stood to inherit a sizeable property.

"We can wait, and we don't have to decide anything as yet. But it's an interesting thought, isn't it?" Kate smiled again, leaned forward to peck him on his cheek, and told him she was late for her appointment with Mrs Malone.

"Mrs Malone?" Matthew must have sounded very surprised because Kate burst out in laughter.

"I'm not applying for a position, but Mrs Malone happens to be the best dressmaker in town. Quite a lucrative sideline, I gather." With that, she was gone, nodding in passing to Ian who bowed before taking the few steps necessary to bring him abreast with Matthew.

"Gone," he said.

"Gone?" Matthew asked.

"The Burleys. Young Farrell told me they'd been seen riding south towards St Mary's City late last afternoon."

"Ah." That was good news, even if Matthew feared it was but a matter of time before he ran into them again. Those three demented brothers were nothing if not persistent, and what had begun as a hunger for revenge on account of their miscreant of a brother's death had swelled into an obsession, further fuelled by all the times when the Grahams – be it him or his wife – had bested them.

They walked along in relative silence for a while, Matthew nodding to the odd acquaintance, Ian commenting on the new houses that had sprung up since last he was here.

Providence – or Anne Arundel's Town, as the minority Anglicans insisted on calling it – was growing at an impressive pace, and, for all that it remained more of a village than a town, it had something of a bustle to it, a quality it shared with most ports, Matthew reckoned. The area round the docks was a beehive of activity, one warehouse after the other lined the waterfront, and on the opposite side were the slave pens, at present very empty. There was even talk of erecting a windmill down by the wharves, but so far nothing had come of that; as Matthew heard it, because Mr Farrell was reluctant to part with the land in question.

At present, the little town was thronged with people, most of them farmers like himself, come to attend the Michaelmas market. Matthew came with hams and sausages, smoked fish and pelts, further supplemented by Jenny's cheese and Alex's stone jars of honey. From what Matthew could see, Jenny was holding her own in their stall, giving them but a hasty wave before going back to her business endeavours.

Ian suggested they repair to an inn for some beer, but Matthew shook his head: no beer, not yet.

Ian laughed. "Why were you there? And why go to Mrs Malone's in the first place, when you know Mama doesn't like it that you do?" Precisely because she didn't like it, Matthew thought, recognising how childish that was. He was still angry with her over Angus, and after that dismal discussion with William, he had needed some cheering up.

"The beer is good," he said.

"Aye, that it is," Ian said. "But the lasses are good as well. I had to pay that wee redhead off last night before she would let go of your balls."

"Thank you," Matthew muttered. "I didn't want to."

"Oh, aye? It didn't seem so."

Any further discussion about this uncomfortable subject was cut short when they entered the main square. A triumphant Mr Farrell was watching while the stranger from last night was stripped and put in chains, despite his loud protests that he was a free man, as free as any of them, and all this was a mistake.

"Hey, man, what d'you think you're doing? Just let go of me, okay?" His dark skin glistened with sweat, he struggled like a fiend, but the odds were overwhelmingly against him, and in less than ten minutes, he was being dragged away, as naked as the day he was born.

"No!" he shrieked. "What the fuck is this? No!"

Matthew shifted restlessly from foot to foot. This was wrong, somehow, and he was on the point of interrupting when Ian placed a hand on his arm.

"No, Da, it won't help him, and it may harm you."

"He says he's free, and now look at him, chained like a beast."

"Do you know for sure that he isn't lying?"

"Nay." It was just something about how the man carried himself, how confidently he had stepped into Mrs Malone's last night, and how he spoke – definitely how he spoke.

Ian hitched his shoulder. "You don't know, Da. And it's rare for a black man to be free."

William Hancock appeared beside them, nodding at this last statement. "If he is free, he's a fool to come here without documents to prove his freedom. The man couldn't properly explain where he came from or what he was doing here." William frowned and shook his head. "He kept on repeating something about a crossroads and a thunderstorm, and when Mr Farrell called him a lying Negro, he got most upset and loudly demanded he be called an…em…Afro-American – yes, that's it, an Afro-American."

Matthew had stopped listening beyond the word crossroads.

"Where?" He asked in a breathless voice that had both Ian and William looking at him with concern. "Where was this crossroads?"

"Down south," William said.

Matthew felt the strength drain away from his legs so fast that, if it hadn't been for Ian's support, he would have fallen to the ground. A crossroads, here! He'd hoped all such time nodes were left forever behind in the old country, ensuring Alex was safe with him.

He stared in the direction they'd dragged the poor bastard. The stranger came from another time, a time when black people were as free as white men were. He was as vulnerable as a newborn babe in the here and now. Without a backward look, Matthew hastened over to talk to Mr Farrell.

"No," Mr Farrell cradled his broken arm to his chest. "He isn't for sale, Brother Matthew." He looked over to where his latest human asset was being chained to a cart and smiled nastily.

"Everything is for sale, Mr Farrell, as long as the price is right."

"Not this one. This one will work his life out for me." With that, he bowed and turned away.

"Explain," Ian said, having followed Matthew across the square.

Matthew blew out a long gust of air and looked at his eldest son. "It isn't really my story to tell."

"I won't spread it, but you have to explain why you attempt to buy a slave when you know Mama doesn't hold with slavery."

"She wouldn't mind if I bought this one." Matthew grabbed Ian by the arm and led him off towards the bay. For a long time, he walked in silence, having no idea how to begin – or even if he should begin.

"Well?" Ian said. They were well out of town by now, surrounded by nothing but reeds and water.

Matthew looked about for somewhere to sit and perched on a rock. "You know how we've always told you that me and your mama met each other on a moor?"

Ian sat down beside him. "A right huge thunderstorm, and Mama's father went missing and you thought him dead."

"Quite," Matthew said.

"But he wasn't, and I still don't fully comprehend how he came to be in yon thorny thicket back home."

"Nay, that was a surprise." Matthew frowned down at the tear in his shirt, fingering the ragged edges. "As you said, it was a thunderstorm, and one of those bolts of lightning threw Alex to land at my feet." He smiled at the memory. "She was a strange lass, dressed in long blue breeches she called 'djeens'. And her hair was short." He indicated with his hand how her hair had been no longer than to her ears, seeing Ian's brows rise in surprise.

"Had she been ill?"

Matthew laughed hollowly. "Ill? No, not as such." He took a deep breath. "She was thrown through time."

Ian looked at him for a long time and then began to laugh. "You're making this up," he said once he had calmed down.

"I wish I was, but no, I'm not. Alexandra Lind was born in 1976, and a few weeks short of her twenty-sixth birthday, time unravelled beneath her feet and sent her spinning to land in 1658."

It was almost amusing: his son blinked owlishly, mouth gaping wide.

"Is she…?" Ian licked his lips. "Is she…?" He stood up, all of him twitching.

"A witch?" Matthew filled in. "Do you think she is?"

Ian sat back down. "Nay. If she is, she's not a very good one."

Matthew smiled in agreement. He wasn't about to tell Ian about Mercedes, because there he had no doubts: Alex's mother had been a witch, her paintings throbbing with magic, horrible little squares of greens and blues that sucked you in and spat you out in another time.

"And Magnus?" Ian asked.

"Magnus…" Matthew hedged. Dear Lord! The man had tumbled out of the year 2016 to arrive here in 1672. "He was ill, and he wanted to see his daughter before he died."

Ian bit his lip. "How?" he said hoarsely. "How did he do

that?" He had paled to the point of acquiring a bluish tinge to the skin around his mouth.

"A painting," Matthew said. "A wee, accursed painting, that was how." Matthew saw Ian's hand form itself into a protective sign against evil and smiled sardonically.

"Aye," Matthew agreed, "it's enough to make your head ache – even without Mrs Malone's excellent beer.

"Crossroads," Matthew continued. "That first time, Alex was standing on a crossroads when she was caught in a thunderstorm – a huge thunderstorm by all accounts." He smiled briefly at his son. "That's why Alex is so terrified of lightning – and crossroads. Twice, time has opened at her feet at the crossroads on the way to Cumnock; twice, I've managed to keep her here with me." He swallowed, recalling just how close a call it had been.

Matthew cleared his throat. "Yon crossroads is very exact, and Magnus told us how such crossroads can at times mark points where the weave of time is weaker than it should be."

"So it rends more easily," Ian said, his face reverting to a more normal colour. He turned to stare at his father. "And that black man: he has fallen through as well!"

"I don't know for sure, but, aye, that would explain some." Matthew painted a brief description of a future society in which all men were equal, no matter race or creed, and Ian listened with an incredulous expression on his face.

"No king?" he said.

"Not here," Matthew said, and both of them grinned.

"And the paintings?" Ian asked.

"I don't know, lad," Matthew lied. "Magnus reckoned they were depictions of the fall through time, painted by someone who'd had the misfortune of falling repeatedly from one age to the other; someone who desperately tried to paint their way home. Magic, son, black magic." He swallowed, feeling a twinge of pity for Mercedes, a woman he had never met nor ever wished to meet, but who had by all accounts led a miserable life, thrown hither and thither through time. In his head, he heard a sultry laugh, a soft woman's voice telling him it hadn't been all bad. After all, she'd had all those years with Magnus, and… Matthew recited the first few lines of the Lord's Prayer, relieved when the voice faded away.

"Repeatedly?" Ian croaked.

Matthew nodded. "An accursed existence, don't you think?"

"Very." Ian shuddered.

"You can't help him," Ian stated after a couple of heartbeats of silence.

"Nay," Matthew agreed. "Poor man."

"Farrell will make him pay."

"Aye, that he will." Matthew frowned down at his clenched hand. To be free, and have it all taken from you, to be degraded to an animal. To father bairns – and Farrell would make sure the well-built stranger fathered several – and see them sold away from you and not be able to do anything about it. But, most of all, to live that day when you bowed to the ground and admitted that, yes, you were a slave, a beast of burden… Like he himself had done, eighteen years in the past on a plantation called Suffolk Rose, crawling at the feet of that accursed Dominic Jones, may he rot in hell.

Matthew shook himself free of these unwelcome memories, and turned his mind to other concerns. "I'll be riding back after dinner. I don't want to be gone for longer than I have to. Will you and Jenny manage on your own?"

"Aye, we will. I met one of the Ingram men in town so we can ride together." For an instant, Ian rested his hand on Matthew's shoulder. "Don't be too harsh on her. She did what she thought best."

"She was wrong. She should have told me about Angus pawing at Daniel – it isn't her right to withhold such from me."

Chapter 11

One of the more irritating things about life in the seventeenth century was that nothing was ever on time – departures and arrivals were at best approximations, dependent on the vagaries of the weather. To ride back and forth to Providence could take anything between five days and eight, and adding a further four or five for the business Matthew had to conduct meant that at earliest he would be back nine days after setting out. So it was with surprise – and some apprehension – that Alex watched Matthew ride into their yard on the afternoon of the seventh day, on a winded Moses with Narcissus an exhausted shadow at their heels.

He only had to look at her and she knew. A lump settled heavily in her stomach, and she turned her head to look at Angus, who was trailing the rest of the household towards the master. Matthew intercepted her look, and his eyes went very green, never leaving hers. Shit, he was mightily pissed.

She hugged herself and went forward to greet him with his children, but hung back. He didn't stretch out his arm to envelop her in an embrace as he would normally do, but allowed the children to monopolise him instead, laughing down at them, tweaking cheeks and ruffling hair. From the pocket of his coat, he brought out ribbons for the girls, boiled sweets for the boys, and a wooden rattle for little Hannah.

"And Mama?" Adam asked, tugging at his coat tail. "Didn't you bring something nice back for Mama?"

Matthew threw Alex a cool look. "There are plenty of things for Mama, but they come with the mules."

Right; stuff like bolts of fabric, needles and thread, a new kettle to replace the old one, but nothing specifically for her – not this time. She tucked her hands in under her arms and retreated a few paces. She wanted to tell him about the Indian and the horrible gift, needed to feel his beating heart under her cheek, but as he made no move to come to her, she stood to the side, feeling abandoned.

He had ridden like the wind in his haste to get back home. Home to ensure nothing had happened to his sons while he was gone, but also to reassure himself Alex was still here, with him, and not yanked back through time. The whole incident with the black man had left him edgy and nervous, all too aware of the times he'd nearly lost her.

But on the long ride back, it had been his anger that had swelled and grown, so that when he rode into the yard and saw her standing to the side, he felt at first a weakening relief that she was still here, then a flaming rage that she should have taken it upon herself to decide what he should know or not.

He looked over to where Angus was leading Moses off towards the stable, and his right fist closed. By tomorrow, Angus would be gone, he decided, feeling very small and mean-minded. But what was he to do? Keep him on and risk that one day he would not attempt to woo, but force himself on one of his sons? Angus' narrow shoulder blades shifted under his stare, and Matthew dragged his eyes away from him to smile down at Samuel, who had taken his hand in an effort to catch his attention.

"Mama saw an Indian," he said.

"You did?" His eyes flashed over to Alex, who was standing some feet away, her arms crossed in a forlorn gesture over her chest. For some reason she paled, tightening her hold on herself. "Well, did you?"

"Yes."

"A brave? An Iroquois?"

"I have no idea; he wasn't wearing Indian garb." She gnawed at her lip, seemed on the verge of saying something, but shook her head instead. "I can tell you later."

All through supper, Matthew exchanged but a minimum of words with Alex, submerging himself in his bairns while she busied herself with serving up meat soup, slicing bread, and insisting that all eat at least one carrot stick. When Matthew told the household that he wished to speak to his wife alone, the kitchen emptied so quickly it was almost risible, with Agnes mumbling she would handle the dishes later before darting after Naomi and Betty.

Matthew sat back in his chair and extended his legs towards the hearth. The lesser man in him was enjoying her evident discomfort. "Why?"

Alex hitched her shoulders. "I'm not sure. Maybe because I was afraid you'd overreact and—"

"Overreact?" He looked at her with dislike. "How can I overreact? That man, crawling over our son!"

"It wasn't quite like that, and it's not as if he's undamaged himself, is it?"

"I don't care if he's been buggered every night by the men he shared a hut with."

"He was?" Alex gasped.

Matthew closed his eyes at her innocence. "I have no idea, but men will be men. Angus is a pretty lad, near on girlish. So I guessed. He wouldn't have survived three years on a tobacco farm without some protection, and he paid for it the only way he could, by offering up his arse."

"Jesus," Alex muttered.

"As I said, I don't care. He touched my lad in an untoward way, and had you told me, I'd have had him off our land that same day – as you well know."

Alex nodded: that was why she hadn't told him, because however mad she was at Angus, she was also sorry for him – and for Agnes. But she'd been vigilant, she assured him, ensuring Angus was never alone with her sons.

Not good enough, he told her, not at all good enough. "Never again. You will never take it upon yourself to choose what I should hear or not when it comes to our bairns."

"But—" Alex protested.

Matthew brought his hand down so hard on the table it made her jump. "Never," he said, his eyes inches from hers.

"Never," she promised, and in her eyes he saw just how humiliated she felt. At the moment, he didn't much care.

"Good," he said as he got to his feet. "And now I must speak to Angus."

Angus was mute. He sat slumped on a stool, his mouth slack as Matthew told him in a matter-of-fact voice that he wished him gone next morning. His contract had been revised, Matthew explained, and he was free to go. There would even be a pouch with a few shillings and a change of clothes for him, but he was not welcome to stay.

"Why?" Angus asked. Matthew stood looking down at him for a long time, pity warring with disgust.

"I won't have you making catamites of my lads," he said and turned on his heel.

"What have you done to your shirt?" Alex asked later that evening, in an attempt to regain some kind of normality between them.

Matthew looked down at his tear. "Oh, that. I caught it on something."

"Caught it on something," she mimicked and held out her hand. "Give it here. I'll have to mend that before I wash it." Matthew drew the shirt over his head and lobbed it at her before going over to the little writing desk.

Alex was faintly disappointed. The whole idea had been for him to come over and hug her, complaining about being cold. Fine, mister, if that's the way you want it then that's the way you'll have it, and until you ask, I won't tell you about the damned Indian either. She stabbed the needle through the cloth, not really caring that the resulting mending was nowhere close to her normal standards.

"I've been in discussions regarding marriage for Ruth," Matthew said suddenly.

"Ruth? But she's a child!"

Matthew gave her an irritated look. "For now, aye. And nothing is set on paper. It's just a preliminary discussion."

"With who?"

Matthew continued with his writing, the only sound in the room being the scraping of the quill against the thick paper.

97

"Who?"

"Henry Jones," Matthew replied, swivelling on his stool to face her.

"Jones!" Alex let his shirt fall to her lap. "No way. I'm not going to share grandchildren with that bastard – or his wife."

"That's not for you to decide," Matthew snapped.

Alex studied him for a long time. "I see, this is my punishment, is it? For not telling you about Angus." She crumpled the shirt together and threw it in his face. "Over my dead body, Matthew, you hear?" And then she was out of her chair so fast the candle flame guttered and died. Without a further word, she left the room.

Matthew shrugged, tossed the shirt to land in Alex's basket, relit the candle, and went back to his letter. She'd be back soon enough, even if he heard the door slam as she left the house. He finished his letter and sat for some time before the fire, nursing a pewter mug of whisky. Still no Alex, and with a little sigh he banked the fire and retired upstairs.

He was used to this, Matthew reminded himself as he lay in bed. Alex always did this when she wanted to punish him. Out she'd go to wander in the dark, and he'd be left lying awake and restless in bed, not knowing for sure where she was or if she was hurt. Mostly he'd go after her, but tonight he had no intention of leaving his warm bed to go traipsing around in the dark. The silly woman could sleep in the hay for all he cared. Two nights sleeping on the ground had him exhausted, so he rolled over, pummelled his pillow into a more comfortable shape, and closed his eyes to sleep.

He woke much later, and something was wrong. Alex still wasn't back, and Matthew's nostrils were invaded by the smell of smoke. Fire! He was out of his bed so fast he stubbed his toe against the floor, and then he was outside in only his shirt, staring in the direction of his stables. He heard Alex scream, there was a loud clatter and a thud, and he ran in the direction of her voice.

From his cabin came Mark, as undressed as he was, and Agnes came running with Betty at her heels. When

Matthew threw the doors open, he was met by a wall of heat. The hayloft was on fire, the horses were shrieking in fear, and on the floor was Alex, lying by the fallen ladder. For an eternal second, he feared she might be dead, his eyes stuck on the blood that was trickling down her face. But then she moaned, pointing upwards to where the loft was burning, and he was suffused with relief that she was alive, no matter that her sleeves were singed and that there seemed to be something wrong with her foot.

Around them, pandemonium reigned. Thick acrid smoke billowed from the loft. Agnes rushed by with her arms full of implements, dropped them just outside the door, and rushed back inside, all the while praying in a high, carrying voice. Mark struggled with the oxen. Betty had managed to lead out one of the horses and was rushing back in for the next one. Matthew swept his wife into his arms and carried her outside, ignoring her unintelligible gibbering.

"Here," he said to Mrs Parson, who had made it from the house by now. "See to her. I must help with the beasts."

Mrs Parson creaked down on her knees and wrapped her arms around a crying Alex, nodding at Matthew to go and do what he must.

"The pigs!" Mark wheezed through coughs. "I can't get the pigs out."

Matthew rushed over to the pigs' enclosure. The sow had backed into a corner, screeching in terror at the fire that dripped from the hayloft floor above her home. Matthew threw himself at the stable wall behind her, he kicked and tore, and Patrick was on the outside, grabbing at the planks and tearing them apart until there was a hole large enough for the pigs to escape through.

Behind him, Matthew heard the hayloft give. Just before crawling through the aperture, he turned, transfixed by the conflagration. A blackened, elongated shape plummeted from one of the roof beams to land in the roaring fire.

"Oh God!" he said, his voice cracking. "Dear Lord, no!" With a roaring sound, the last of the hayloft collapsed, and Matthew threw himself outside.

The entire household was standing before the burning stable when Agnes realised one of them was missing.

"Angus?" She turned this way and that, looking for the lanky shape of her brother. "Angus?" There was a wobble to her voice. "Angus!" she shrieked, and threw herself towards the building.

Patrick grabbed at her waist and pulled her back, making low shushing sounds into her hair.

"Oh Lord," Agnes whimpered when the roof fell down in an explosion of sparks. "Where is he? Where is my brother?"

Alex woke next morning with one arm neatly bandaged, her forehead stitched, and her husband fast asleep beside her, still in a shirt that smelled of smoke. She used her aching fingers to prod him, and with a start he woke.

"What happened to you?" she croaked, taking in his torn nails and damaged hands. His hair was singed on the left side, and there was a huge bruise on his face.

"The pig kicked me." He fingered the purple discoloration.

Alex laughed, even if it hurt like hell. Shit! Well, that's what you get when you fall from the hayloft. She closed her eyes at the remembered horror. "She's not the most polite of creatures. Did you get them all out?"

Matthew nodded. "But the hay is gone, and I don't like feeding them on grain throughout the winter. I'll have to go to the Leslie place and barter for some feed." A lot of the oats were gone as well, he told her, and most of the tack and the saddles. Matthew muttered that it would be a costly effort to replace all that. At least the plough was undamaged, and Agnes and Betty had managed to save most of the expensive iron equipment from the blaze.

"That's good." Alex fiddled with the tassels of the new quilt. "But Angus..." she whispered. If only she'd been a few minutes earlier, she might have stopped him. If, if, if. If she'd seen the light in the hayloft sooner; if she'd not slipped in the mud while crossing the yard; if she'd been faster up the ladder – oh God!

"We found him, what was left of him that is — a few charred bones, no more."

"Ah." She blinked: the swinging body, the stool kicked aside, knocking the lantern off its perch to land in the stacked hay. A matter of seconds, and it was all on fire.

Matthew smoothed her hair off her face. "Why didn't you tell me?"

"Tell you what?"

"About yon Indian. You should have told me the whole story."

"At the time, you didn't seem all that interested, did you?" She turned her face away.

"I was—"

"...pissed off, I know. As does every single person in our household."

"I had the right of it," he said, sounding indignant.

"Fine." She waved him silent. She had no energy to quarrel with him. "Those Burleys, they're sick obsessive bastards," she muttered instead.

"Aye, I can't say I was much thrilled to stand eye to eye with all three of them."

"What? You've seen them? When?" She took his hand. His heart...that damned Philip Burley threatened to send her Matthew's skewered heart, and...Alex coughed.

Matthew raised their interlocked hands to his chest, pressing them close enough to his skin that she could feel the reassuring thump of his heartbeat.

"In Providence," he said, going on to recount his recent encounter with the brothers. "I swear, those brothers..." He broke off, and tugged at one of her curls. "Do you want me to braid it for you?"

She nodded and sat up, biting back on a surge of pain when she put too much weight on her burnt hand. Matthew clambered up to sit behind her, brushed her hair until it lay thick and untangled, and braided it together into a plait.

"You scared me," he said to her nape. "I saw you bleeding by the ladder, and feared that the last words you'd ever hear from me were words of anger. And it broke my heart to think that perhaps you'd die and not know how much I love you."

Alex leaned back against him, pillowing her head on his chest. "I always know that, just as you know how much I love you." He wrapped his arms carefully around her, but it still hurt. "That doesn't mean that I'll let you marry Ruth to Henry Jones," Alex went on, yawning hugely. "Just so you know."

Matthew squeezed, making her yelp. "We'll discuss that later," he said, indicating this subject was not done and dealt with.

"Later," Alex agreed, and her voice was as steely as his. She craned her head back to look at the small patch of sky visible through the window. "Poor Angus."

"Aye, poor lad. But it was a wicked thing to do, to set the stable on fire. I didn't think it of him."

Alex shook her head. "He didn't do it on purpose. He just didn't want to die in the dark."

"Merciful Lord," Matthew groaned. "What have I done?"

"You didn't know he'd do that."

"I forgot. I was too angry and afraid to remember that greatest of all virtues is compassion."

Alex raised a bandaged hand to his cheek and gave him a clumsy pat. "It wasn't your fault."

"Aye, it was. I could have waited to talk to him in daylight; not left him alone to mull it over in the dark."

She didn't reply, raising her good hand to wipe at her eyes. A lost boy, she thought, a damaged young man with no one to turn to.

"You make a very bad patient." Mrs Parson scowled at Alex. "I tell you, no? You must stay off that foot for a week or so, and you mustn't use your hands, and what do I find? Mrs Graham hobbling around in her kitchen!"

"What am I supposed to do? Just lie here like a stranded whale?" Three days in bed had her crawling out of her skin.

"Aye, why not? You could use the time to meditate on your sins. Lack of patience for one—"

"But I have work to do! The boys need new breeches before the winter, and I haven't even finished their stockings yet and—"

"Shush! Betty is doing a fine job with the knitting, and Naomi has already made new breeches for David and Samuel. And Adam can stay in smocks a wee while longer, no?"

"No choice, apparently." The moment she was up and about, she'd make sure Adam got his first pair of breeches. She glanced at the chest where the new bolts of serge, broadcloth, linen and cotton lay stacked. The dark blue would make Agnes a nice bodice... She turned to face Mrs Parson. "How's Agnes?"

"Not well," Mrs Parson replied with a slight shrug. "Matthew and I have decided not to tell her the full sorry tale. It wouldn't help, we think."

"No, probably not." Alex studied her hands, overcome by an image of Angus on his stool, the noose already round his neck.

From outside came the sound of hammering and sawing, and, to her surprise, she could hear Peter Leslie's voice among the others.

"Peter?"

"Helping Matthew with the stables," Mrs Parson said, "and Peter Leslie is a right good carpenter, he is."

"So is Matthew," Alex said proudly. She extended her hand to caress the carved roses decorating the closest bedpost, thinking her husband was more of an artist than a journeyman. She swept her eyes over the small room: the bed, the chest that contained their few linens and stockings, the stool, the dressing table in maple wood – all of it created by Matthew.

"Right besotted you are," Mrs Parson snorted. "Unseemly, almost. Here." She handed Alex a thick, folded square of paper. "This might keep you still for some time, no?"

Alex hefted the letter in her hand. She recognised Simon Melville's scrawled handwriting, and for an instant she held the letter to her nose, hoping to catch a faint smell of home, of peat fires and wet bogs, of gorse and heather.

Rather clumsily, she opened the letter, giving Mrs Parson a distracted little wave when she left the room.

Some time later, she folded together Simon's long letter, and, with a little sigh, settled herself deeper in bed. From what Matthew's brother-in-law described, the Lowlands were infested with strife, the few outspoken Covenanters that remained chased like deer through woods and moors. Much better here; for all that there were Indians and Burleys – no, don't think about them – it had been the right decision to come here and carve a new life out of nothing. She drew a long, shaky M with her finger on his pillow. Coming here was why he was still alive – had they stayed in Scotland, he would have been rotting on a gibbet since years ago, and all for the sake of his religious convictions.

"Unbelievable," she muttered to the pillow. "Absolutely unbelievable what people do to each other in the name of their God." The pillow seemed to agree, voicing no opinions to the contrary. Alex yawned and closed her eyes.

Chapter 12

Jacob woke to a clawing headache and the sensation that his tongue had outgrown his mouth, hanging like a strip of dried leather between his cracked lips. He was shivering, he had no idea where he was, but after ascertaining that he could still move both arms and legs, he sat up and took stock of his surroundings. He didn't know how long he'd been lying where he was, but seemed to recall waking a couple of times before, and it had been dark and cold. But now it was well past noon, a weak October sun shining down through thin veils of cloud. He got to his feet, and a careful inspection of his head assured him it wasn't broken, however much it hurt.

The jetty was a platform on stilts. He blinked down at where the water should have been. The tide was out...the tide was out! In panic, he tried to get his bearings before dropping off the jetty to squelch up the stinking sluggish stream – more of a ditch – that disgorged into the river proper. He sniffed at his clothes and grimaced. Mama would have stripped him had he come home like this, and then she would've burnt his clothes and probably scrubbed him with lye all over. He was overwhelmed with sudden longing for her, for the way she would have hugged him, laughing and crying at the same time.

Jacob turned right onto Thames Street and hurried as best as he could in the general direction of the Tower. The *Regina Anne* lay at anchor just beyond the fortress, and as Jacob ran, he prayed that she still be there, because what was he otherwise to do? Captain Miles wouldn't leave him, he comforted himself; not here, not without knowing what had happened to him. He sidestepped stinking piles of ordure, ignored the mouth-watering smell from a bakery, and ran.

The tide was out, the tide was out, drummed his brain, and when he finally reached the wharves, the tide was beginning to flow back in, but the *Regina Anne* was gone. He had no idea what to do. His legs folded under him, and he sat down with a heavy thud, staring at the spot where the ship should have been. For an instant, he thought he might cry, but instead he sank his nails hard into his palms and counted slowly to a hundred.

"Left behind?" A soft cackle accompanied this statement, and a very old man creaked into view.

Jacob nodded morosely. "I was knocked on my head last night, and by the time I got my wits back, it would seem the ship had left without me." His head hurt something frightful, not at all helped by his recent run.

"You're no sailor," the old man scoffed.

"I might still be," Jacob bit back, insulted by the derision in the old man's voice.

"No, not you." The old man sniffed at Jacob, and his whole face squished itself together. "You stink."

"You don't exactly smell like a posy yourself." The old man smelled of fish and tar, and a lot of other things.

"But not of shit." The old man grinned. "Have you been swimming in the river?"

"Not out of choice, aye?"

"No one does," the old man nodded, "not in the Thames at any rate. Full of offal and bodies and whatnot." He pointed his cane at what looked like a bloated cow – was a bloated cow. "Have you been to the Customs House?"

Jacob gave him an irritated look. Did he look like a merchant with wares to declare and tolls to pay?

"To see if there's a message for you," the old man said. "Any real sailor would know to go there first. Over there."

With a curt nod, Jacob moved off. Sweetest Lord, but he did stink! The stench wafted off him in little puffs, making people detour round him.

There was a message. A terse note explaining that Captain Miles couldn't wait – he was entrusted with a most urgent delivery, a matter of life and death – but that he hoped Jacob was alive and capable of coping on his own. With the note was a sizeable purse, enough to tide him over for some months at least.

"They spent all night looking for you," the harbour master said. "The captain was beside himself, near on weeping." He tut-tutted at Jacob for being such an inconsiderate lout, but when Jacob asked for some paper, he produced the three required sheets and even allowed Jacob the use of his little carrel. One letter to Captain Miles, sent by overland mail to Edinburgh, one rather long letter to Mama, and a third fervent letter to Betty, in which he included the little ring.

"These might just make it," the harbour master told him. "The *Clarissa* is set to sail for Virginia tomorrow. Last ship out this year."

"Tomorrow?" Jacob went over to study the ship in question. Home… But no, he wasn't done with seeing the world yet, and he had money in his purse and a whole city to explore. He paid for the postage, wrung a promise from the master to get them aboard the *Clarissa,* and left before his nerve failed him. Jacob rushed into the warren of streets, leaving the heaving river behind.

He found a water conduit and sluiced himself from top to toe, teeth chattering when the cold water seeped through his clothes, but at least the pervading stink of shit was gone. An older woman looked at him and clucked in sympathy, and, to his surprise, extended a piece of linen to him, suggesting he dry off as well as he could.

Feeling much better, if very hungry, Jacob spent some time moving from patch to patch of sunshine, slowly regaining some warmth. He burnt his fingers on the hot pasties he bought off a street vendor, and now both clean and fed, he set out to properly explore, making for the huge bridge he had so far only seen from the water.

It was a longer walk than he'd expected, through alleys and narrow streets that teemed with people, with offal, with hand-drawn carts, with dogs, cats, the odd pig and rats. Well-dressed men hurried by, often accompanied by a burly servant or two; chairmen hollered for people to get out of the way as they lugged sedan chairs through the streets.

Jacob's senses were assaulted by noise, by smells – most of them unsavoury. His head swivelled to follow a pretty lass on her way, his eyes sliding elsewhere when confronted by yet another set of urchins, so dirty he could see the vermin crawling through their hair and rags. He'd never seen people this thin before, aghast at having to step over beggars that sat slumped on the streets, emaciated hands held out to him. Bairns as young as Adam ran wild through the crowds, fought for scraps of bread, for the odd bit of kindling. Men cursed, bairns wailed, women laughed, and everything stank – of shit, of rotting foodstuffs, of accumulated grime. It was with some relief he arrived at his destination, halting for a moment to gape at the structure that spanned the river.

This was more than a bridge: it was a floating town, with houses banding the narrow thoroughfare that connected London proper with the southern shore of the Thames. Pedestrians jostled with ox-drawn carts and riders on horses; people went in and out of the myriad of shops that lined both sides of the bridge; and women hung out of windows to yell and converse with each other. At one point, all traffic ground to a halt as the drawbridge roughly at the bridge's centre was raised to let through a ship. Jacob studied this display of advanced engineering, but was more interested in the nearby food stalls.

He spent more than an hour walking London Bridge back and forth, sticking his head into small shops, gawking at peddlers and jugglers. Never had he imagined that so many people could live on such a constricted space, and on both sides of the wee open place where he was presently standing rose huge buildings, with the bridge proper tunnelling itself through them. Seven, no, eight storeys... He shook his head in amazement. Who could ever have imagined something like this, and why had Mama never mentioned it? The Tower she'd talked about; he even recalled her mentioning the huge kirk they had seen grow out of the ground of Ludgate Hill yesterday – that would have been the old one, the one that according to Captain Miles burnt so ferociously the stones in its walls flew like projectiles – but never had she mentioned this marvel, this city within the city itself.

Jacob's stomach rumbled, and after yet another hot savoury, he meandered his way up through the city, stopping to buy himself stockings and a new shirt. He studied his battered shoes: the swim in the river had not done them any good, but for now they would have to do, as would his coat. Instead, he began looking about for an inn, and when he finally found one, close to Blackfriars, he didn't even haggle about the rate. He just paid up the sixpence and stumbled up the stairs to sleep.

By next morning, a vague plan had formed in Jacob's head. If he was marooned in London over the winter, he might as well do something useful with his time. So, first on his list was to find a physician and attempt to find employment. Second on his list was something he was far more ambivalent about, not at all sure Da would approve. Jacob smothered a laugh. Da would flay him to the bone anyway when he got back, so how could one more transgression matter one way or the other? He sipped thoughtfully at his mulled beer, turning his idea over in his head.

Around noon, Jacob sank down into a dispirited heap and kicked at the ground. Three times he'd been laughed out of the room; twice he had been told that being a physician required years of schooling, something he didn't have, did he? They laughed at his accent, snickered when he attempted to tell them he had studied on his own, and all five of them had gone decidedly greenish when he mentioned Culpeper.

"Nicholas Culpeper was no physician," the latest of his potential employers had sneered. "He was a dabbler in plants, a mere apothecary."

What most rankled was the way they regarded him as being somehow backwards on account of coming from the colonies – that and the impertinent questions about his faith given his accent. Scotsmen – in particular Presbyterian Scotsmen – were not held in high regard.

"You can't sit here!" A broom came down inches from his leg, and he scrambled to his feet. The woman in front of him glared at him. "I won't have loiterers outside my shop," she went on, thrusting the broom at him. "And, in particular, not large louts such as you. You scare away my custom."

Jacob looked up and down the deserted little alley. "Aye, I can see that."

The woman sighed, the aggression running off her as quickly as it had surfaced. "It's not easy," she said, thrusting her chin forward.

"What isn't easy?" Jacob kept a cautious distance.

"Being alone." The woman gripped her broom and shook it at him. "Now, be gone, you!"

"I'm alone too," Jacob tried. "I know no one here."

"Then why are you here?"

"I was attacked and left behind by my ship." To his embarrassment, his voice wobbled, making the woman's face soften.

"How old are you?"

"Sixteen," he replied, straightening to his full height. "In December."

An hour later, Jacob had made his first friend in London, listening with interest as Mistress Wythe told him her story. The youngest daughter of five to a well-off London merchant, she had been wed at sixteen to a haberdasher, and when he had died three years ago, she had found herself the inheritor of a small but profitable business.

"I should have listened to my father. He had chosen a new husband for me, but I was reluctant to wed yet another man more than twenty years my senior." Instead, she'd embarked on a hectic social life, setting in motion a hunt for her wealthy person that ended the day one of the suitors bribed his way into her bedroom and took her to bed, despite her protests. "So I was wed again, and my husband sold it all and set me up with this as my jointure, and now he lives a life of gambling and whoring on the south bank, and I, well, I sit alone."

110

"And sew." Jacob looked at the embroidered chemises and shirts that hung in the little shop.

"And sew. It feeds me at least – and him, when he chooses to come home."

Hesitantly, Jacob shared his plans with her.

"A physician?" Mistress Wythe laughed. "What would a lad like you know about such?"

"Nothing – but I'd like to learn."

"Would you now?" She shook her head. "They're right, the masters you've spoken to. A physician is an educated man. No, you should talk to an apothecary instead." She drummed her fingers against the tabletop. "My cousin Alice is married to one of the officers in the Society of Apothecaries. I'll talk to her tomorrow."

"You will? For me?" He beamed at her.

Mistress Wythe flushed. "I can't offer you to stay. It would not be seemly."

Jacob just nodded, gratified that she should so clearly consider him a man.

The next afternoon, Jacob found himself inspected by a man who reached him to the shoulder. His hands were turned back and forth, accompanied by small grunts of satisfaction at his obvious strength and size. He was barraged with questions. Feverfew? Foxglove? Garlic? St John's wort? Milk thistle? He was given dried samples to identify, was told to describe the principal healing qualities of a number of plants. Quite often, Jacob had to admit he didn't know, but on several of the plants his replies were evidently satisfying, because the little man – Mr Castain – nodded in approval.

"Will you mind living out in the country?" Mr Castain asked.

"How out in the country?" Jacob hadn't travelled across the world to end up living in something like Graham's Garden.

"Chelsea," Mr Castain said. "A village an hour or so by foot from here."

"If you walk very fast," Mistress Wythe muttered. "And

111

how would you know? You always go by barge, don't you?"

"I can't very well be walking." Mr Castain sniffed. "It's far quicker to go by boat."

"Boat?" Jacob asked.

"You'll have to walk," Mistress Wythe said, "unless you're rich enough to pay for the fare, that is."

"It's not devoid of entertainments," Mr Castain put in. "There are a couple of inns, and a lot of coming and going from all the stately homes and mansions."

"And what would I do?" Jacob asked.

"Do? You'll work with me and my assistants in the best herbal garden in the world, the Apothecaries' Garden."

"John," Mistress Wythe sighed, "at best it's a garden in the making."

"No, it isn't. We've been at it for six years by now."

"But still…" Mistress Wythe said. "It's mostly a lot of turned earth."

Mr Castain gave her a chilly look, puffed out his chest, and told her he'd prefer it if she kept her disparaging comments to herself. Mistress Wythe muttered an excuse, and Mr Castain turned to Jacob. "I'll teach you two hours a day, give you food and board and a shilling a week."

Jacob did some quick calculations. "Two shillings, and I have need of a new pair of shoes and breeches."

"Done," Mr Castain said with such alacrity that Jacob understood he had sold himself too cheap. But he liked this little man, and from the way he handled the plants, this was a man who knew what he was talking about. Even more, he liked the way this John Castain smelled, of mint and lemon balm and all those other herbs that reminded him far too much of Mama. Besides, Jacob Graham needed a profession, and this could be a starting point. So, half an hour later, he bade his newfound friend farewell and hastened after his new employer, making for the river and the barge that would convey them to the as yet unknown village of Chelsea.

Chapter 13

"Some more?" Alex set a full plate in front of Peter Leslie.

Matthew looked up from his own food, and winked at Alex. If ever a man was to be seduced by good food it was Peter Leslie, who at present lived in a household dominated by tasteless stews. Constance had few – if any – cooking skills, and Ailish was at best a disinterested cook, who ensured all were fed and that was that.

Peter closed his eyes, drew in the smell of pork boiled in ale and topped with a golden piecrust, and exhaled happily. Matthew eyed his wife with amusement. Alex had no intention of ever apologising for what she'd said, but had no compunction whatsoever about winning their neighbour's heart – nay, stomach – back by serving Peter one succulent dinner after the other now that he was here on a daily basis to help with the stable.

"Not much left to do," Peter stated once they were back outside, sounding rather regretful. "Your man is quite handy," he added, indicating Patrick who was balancing barefoot on the roof.

"Aye." Matthew frowned. They would be short-handed over the spring planting without Angus. And Patrick's contract expired after the harvest next year, and while he had no wish to replace him with a new bond servant, he knew that he would, because other labour was hard to find unless one went for slaves. Slaves: the thought brought him up short. He hadn't told Alex about the black man down in Providence.

"Where?" Alex's voice came out as a croak.

"I don't know, but William said how it was down on the eastern side."

113

"Yet another part of the world I won't be seeing."

"Nay, that you won't." Matthew lifted a leg, let it fall back with a splash into the hot water, and sank even lower in the tub. "He said 'okay', and then there was something about how he moved. You could see this was no slave."

"And now he is." Alex sighed, reclining against her end.

"Aye, that he is." Branded on the spot, and his loud, despairing yells had made the men around him laugh.

"There's nothing we can do, is there?" Alex asked in a small voice.

Matthew shook his head: nothing at all. He took hold of her hand and pulled her towards him through the bathwater. Firmly, he banished any thoughts of the unknown man from his head and concentrated on his wife, how warm and slippery she lay against his chest, how her hair tickled his nose.

"Mmm," Alex said very much later. They had taken their lovemaking out of the tub to the wide bench that ran the length of the shed. Her legs were splayed wide under him and his cock remained buried deep inside of her, shrinking back in size. She hitched a shoulder and patted him on the bum. "You're squashing me."

Matthew grumbled, but shifted to lie half on her, half off her, and propped himself up on his elbow to look at her.

"Esther Hancock is with child." He nodded at the pitying expression on Alex's face. They were of an age, Esther and his Alex, and yet another pregnancy must be more of a burden than a joy.

"That's her seventeenth pregnancy!"

"It is? There are only seven bairns to show for it: six lasses and wee William." He cupped her breast and squeezed. "Not like you, my fruitful wife, ten pregnancies and nine live bairns…"

"…and there will be no more," she told him.

"Nay, no more." He bent his head to kiss her, his mouth lingering a long time. He released her mouth and smiled at how dark her eyes were. He kissed her brow, her nose, the hollow at the base of her throat, her navel…

Matthew slid down her body and alternated between nibbling at the insides of her thighs, and kissing the soft folds of pinkish flesh that always reminded him of a flower, a blushing rose hiding its core from the world. Alex undulated below him, hands resting lightly on his head.

"Your turn," he said, guiding her down his body.

"Aye…" he added dreamily a bit later, helping her straddle him. How well they matched each other: all of him inside of her, his hands on her hips to hold her there, impaled on him. He tensed his thighs, rose upwards, and she sighed. He did it again, and her breath rasped in and out. He cupped her breasts, holding her upright when he knew that what she wanted to do was to fold forward, fall over him, kiss him. He clenched his buttocks and she gasped, pressing down on him. A surge of bright red heat exploded through his loins, up his cock, and for a brief second he was sure he would die.

"No more babies," she murmured from where she had collapsed on top of him. "But definitely much more sex."

He laughed, hugging her close. Oh, aye, much more sex.

Betty froze by the privy when the door to the laundry shed opened. Now? In the middle of the night? A cloud of steam escaped from the hot space inside, Matthew appeared in only his shirt, hair still damp, holding a lantern. Alex fell out after him, laughing at something he had just said. Betty had never seen an adult woman look quite so…so… dishevelled? Her shift was undone, leaving one shoulder bare, and the dark hair was a nest of messy curls. Their hands met and braided. Instinctively, he adjusted his stride to hers and they swayed in perfect synchronisation in the direction of the house. Betty was overwhelmed by a wave of jealousy. That should be her, with Jacob, not his old parents! On quick and silent feet, she scampered after them, slid in through the kitchen door, and tiptoed into the room she shared with Agnes.

★

Betty was tired of Agnes' constant panegyric over her poor, dead brother. From what Betty had managed to find out, it would seem Angus had been a conflicted soul, and then there were all those times when she'd seen Alex more or less supervise Angus the moment he interacted with the younger boys. Betty pulled her brows together into a thoughtful frown. She'd heard of men that abused other men; the Bible was rather explicit when it came to the sins of Sodom, but men lusting after boys? Small boys like David and Samuel? She studied Agnes from the corner of her eye.

"What happened to Angus once you got here?" she asked, interrupting Agnes halfway through yet another description of Angus as a wee lad, already so well versed in his Bible.

Agnes fell silent, her fingers tightening on the feathers of the dead hen in her lap. "He was sold off," she said in a curt tone. "He spent several years on a tobacco farm down south, and then the master bought his contract and brought him here – where he died in that unfortunate fire."

Betty gnawed at her lip. She had overheard Alex describe to Thomas Leslie how she'd seen Angus hang himself from one of the roof beams, but, after careful consideration, she concluded this wasn't something she should tell Agnes. Instead, she went in search of her favourite among Jacob's brothers, Ian.

Ian enjoyed his conversations with Betty, flattered by being singled out as her confidant. To be quite honest, he also enjoyed basking in her admiring looks, but this he preferred not to dwell too much upon. The lass was easy on the eye and sharp of wit, so mostly their conversations were light-hearted things, with him laughing much more with Betty than he had ever done with Jenny.

The thought of his wife made him sigh, and for some moments he stopped listening to Betty, immersed in yet another attempt to comprehend what was gnawing at Jenny.

"...so did he?"

"Hmm?" With an effort, he returned his attention to Betty.

"Angus. Did he…err…?" The lass blushed.

Ian wasn't sure whether to tell her the truth. Betty Hancock – no, Graham, at least for now – was a bright enough lass, but young, just sixteen. She had hoisted herself up to sit on one of the workbenches, and was swinging her feet back and forth. When she leaned forward to listen to what he was saying, she reminded Ian very much of a squirrel, her reddish brown eyes intent on him. The bridge of her nose was covered with a myriad of small freckles, as was the skin along her sedate neckline. But it was to her tightly braided hair – visible here and there, despite the cap – that his eyes leapt repeatedly. He wondered what she might look like with that head of copper curls undone and floating free round her shoulders. If his inspection disconcerted her, she didn't show it, shoving her hands in under her thighs.

"Aye," he finally said, "Angus made untoward approaches to one of my brothers."

Betty gasped. "But they're babies, they're as small as Willie is."

"Not the wee lads; it was Daniel." Very briefly, he told her what Matthew had told him.

"How could he?" she said, wrinkling her nose.

Ian shrugged. "I reckon he couldn't help himself, lass." He gave her a teasing glance. "Just as you couldn't, that last night with Jacob."

That was the wrong thing to say because, just as quickly as she'd come, she was gone, her back very straight as she stalked off in the direction of the woods.

For some reason, Ian's comment had Betty feeling hot and bothered – angry even. She preferred not to talk to Ian about Jacob. She wanted to talk about…Ian, a small voice whispered in her head, or Betty, or maybe Ian and Betty, but she definitely didn't want to talk about Jacob. Dear Lord, what was the matter with her? She scrubbed at her face and smoothed at her apron in an effort to regain some

117

composure, but it didn't much help. A brisk walk was what she needed, so she increased her pace, making for the forest.

Some way in, Betty stumbled, slipped on the mossy ground, and tumbled down a small incline to land in an undignified heap. She straightened out her limbs and sat back against the stone behind her. This was a nice, secluded place, and the late October sun was warm on her face and body. She dug into her bodice, pulled out a folded and refolded letter from her mother, and read it once again, hearing between the short lines how much her mother missed her.

Betty folded the letter before returning it to its keeping place, close to her heart. She longed for home and her mother – even her father – more than she longed for Jacob. She scratched at a small scab on her arm and sighed. She had no idea what she wanted anymore, but two years seemed an interminable amount of time. She looked down at her hands: long, thin fingers, each of them crowned with an oval, well-tended fingernail. Very bare hands – nothing to indicate she was a married woman. Betty laughed at herself. She wasn't sure she was.

The warmth in her protected hollow made her drowsy, and she yawned, pillowing her head on her arms. A little nap…she yawned again, thinking of Jacob, or was it Ian? At some point, she must have fallen asleep, because she woke to the sound of agitated voices very close by, and shrank back against the boulder, fearing that they might be Indians. Betty peeked out from behind the thorny thicket, and, to her surprise, it was Patrick and Jenny. They were arguing, with Patrick holding Jenny's arm in a way that seemed to hurt her, and she kicking at him.

Betty's eyes widened when Patrick yanked Jenny close and kissed her. She squeaked a 'no', but neither of them heard, and Betty was no longer quite sure what she was seeing. Jenny was still struggling, but her hands were locked round Patrick's neck as if she was holding him close, and her body leaned into him, rather than away from him. Moments later, they were on the ground, Jenny's legs bared most indecently when Patrick pushed her skirts out of the way. Jenny moaned loudly.

Betty tried to rush to Jenny's help, but the thorns tore at her skirts, thereby hampering her progress as she tried to force the thicket. By then, it was too late: she could see that in the way Patrick's bared buttocks clenched and unclenched, and in how passively Jenny lay beneath him, her arms tight around him. Tight around him? The angry shout died in Betty's mouth, and halfway through the brambles, she ducked down to hide until Patrick was gone.

"Jenny?" Betty shook her. "Are you alright?"

"Alright?" Jenny raised a face covered in tears and snot to glare at her. "How can I be alright?"

Betty's face heated at her own idiotic remark. "I saw—"

"Saw? What did you see?" Jenny sounded angry rather than distraught.

"How he...how he made free of you." Betty avoided looking into Jenny's pale blue eyes. "We must tell Ian and Father Matthew, and they'll know what to do."

Jenny's hand came down like a clamp on Betty's arm. "You'll tell no one!"

"No one?" Betty was very confused.

Jenny stuffed the handkerchief she had used to wipe her face back into her sleeve, brushed down her skirts, and raised her arms to order her hair, hands like lark wings as she rebraided the dark hair that floated free around her face.

"Don't you see?" Jenny said with her back to Betty. "They'll blame me."

"But—"

Jenny interrupted her with a harsh sound. "It's always the woman's fault." She turned to face Betty and placed a hand on her stomach. "I'm with child. I don't want there to be any doubts cast as to this child's paternity."

Betty nodded that she understood, even if she didn't. The child was already there, so how could what she had just witnessed have any bearing. Unless... Fragmented images thronged her brain, of Jenny's hand in Patrick's hair, of how Jenny's bare calf had come up to rest on Patrick's leg, of

119

Jenny's arm round Patrick's waist, holding him close rather than trying to dislodge him. No, she was misinterpreting things. After all, hadn't Jenny attempted to tear herself free? She'd even kicked Patrick.

Jenny grabbed hold of Betty's hands. "Will you promise never to tell unless I ask you otherwise?"

Rather unenthusiastically, Betty promised. "But what will you do?"

"Do?" Jenny laughed hoarsely. "I'll pretend it never happened, and that is what I want you to do as well."

Jenny took her time walking back to Forest Spring, her brain in overdrive. If the little goose told, Patrick would be forever banished from her life, either thrown out or, even worse, dead, and that was something she couldn't bear even to think about. She must be a depraved woman, because she wanted Patrick to do what he did to her. She liked it when he was hard and careless, his hands forcing her to do just as he wanted. Not at all the considerate lover her husband was, and yet...

Jenny came to a halt, and took a couple of deep breaths. She had to put an end to all this. If she didn't, she might find her whole life bursting apart. She placed a protective hand over her womb. After five years of trying, there was a child growing in her, and the sensation was one of utter joy — except for when she was afflicted by the horrible insight that she had no idea who the father was.

When Ian returned late, she was waiting for him, newly bathed and in her best embroidered shift; nothing else.

"Malcolm?" he asked when she wound her arms round his neck.

"Asleep, and tomorrow is Sunday."

"So it is," he nodded, and the shift was already on the floor. He carried her over to their bed and made love to her until the candles guttered one by one.

In the dark, Jenny lay awake beside his sleeping shape and held on very hard to his hand. She loved this man, the way his hazel eyes shifted with his moods, the way his hands were warm and soft on her skin – of course she loved him. So, why was it Patrick she saw while they were making love? Why was it Patrick she wanted to hold her, take her?

She rolled over to face Ian and traced his sleeping profile. "I'm so sorry," she whispered. "Oh God, Ian, I am that sorry." And she knew that she wouldn't put a stop to it – at least not yet.

Chapter 14

"She is too!" Naomi nudged Betty. "See?"

The two girls giggled, watching Agnes balancing across the frozen yard towards the stables with a pie in her hands.

"She's what? Ah," Alex said when she saw Patrick pop his head out of the stable door before opening it wide to allow Agnes and pie entry. "I don't think he is." She went back to her cinnamon rolls.

"No," Betty said with surprising sharpness. "But he knows she's in love with him."

That wouldn't exactly take a genius, Alex thought with an exasperated smile.

"I don't like him," Betty added unnecessarily, given her tone. "Agnes can do much better than that conceited man."

Mrs Parson looked up from where she was steeping willow tea for Matthew, who was in bed with a fever, and nodded in agreement. "He thinks much of himself, young Patrick does. But then I suppose he would, no? He's a comely lad."

"Who is?" Ruth came into the kitchen with Hannah in her arms.

"You're supposed to be in bed, young lady," Alex said.

"I was in bed, and then who crawled all the way up the stairs on her own?" Ruth kissed her niece tenderly on the top of her dark head and set her down. She coughed, a heavy dark sound, and sat down close to Mrs Parson to rest her head against her. "My chest hurts, and Sarah just coughs and coughs."

"I'll be up with a cordial presently, but now be off with you, back to bed, lassie." Mrs Parson smiled fondly at Ruth, who nodded and padded off. "At least the lads are up and about again."

"More than up and about – try tearing the whole place down!" Alex was tired: two weeks of colds and fevers, interrupted sleep, and sheets that had to be changed in the middle of the night were taking their toll. She moved over to Betty and gave her a quick hug. "I don't know how I'd have managed without your help," she said, receiving a shy smile in return.

"I couldn't help." Naomi sounded defensive.

"Nay, of course not," Mrs Parson said. "You had one sick man, no? Enough to run any woman off her feet."

"Alex?" came a demanding, very hoarse call from above, and all four fell over in helpless laughter.

Alex came back down to find that the buns were done and that Mrs Parson had made them both a cup of herbal tea. For once, the kitchen was empty, the large table containing nothing but a bowl of late apples and two fat tallow candles. On one of the long benches, one of the household cats was sleeping, and Mrs Parson was sitting in Matthew's armchair, feet propped up on a stool.

Alex liked her kitchen. It was airy and clean, agreeably warm, and very neat. There was a workbench under one of the windows on which stood a clay pot that housed Alex's precious aloe vera plant, as well as a large, battered pewter basin. A narrow door led to the pantry, and beside it were a set of shelves that contained what little crockery they had. The walls had been recently whitewashed; pots and saucepans hung on nails within easy reach of the hearth and the small baking oven, and firewood was stacked in one corner.

Alex sank down to sit. "I don't know how you do it." She bit into a freshly baked cinnamon roll.

"Do what?" Mrs Parson moved the chair so that the afternoon sun hit her squarely in the face, and sat back with a contented sound. The new kitchen was a light place, with two windows replacing the former single one, even if Matthew had grumbled loudly at the cost.

"You've never been sick. Not one single day in all the years I've known you."

"That would be a bad habit to break now, no?" Mrs Parson cradled the earthenware mug in her hands and blew.

"Yeah, so please don't."

"Oh, I don't plan to. I'm aiming to live to a hundred or so. After all, how would you cope without me?"

"Not at all." Alex clasped the old woman's liver-spotted hand. "You know that, don't you?"

"Tsss! It's my knitted goods you're after, Alex Graham – that and my meat pie recipe." But she sounded quite touched, an uncharacteristic wet glimmer to her bright black eyes.

"I love this time of the year," Alex said to Ian a couple of days later, efficiently gutting one trout after the other. She drew in a long, invigorating breath of crisp November air. It was a beautiful, still day, the kind that brought roses to your cheeks the moment you stuck your face outside, with the fallen leaves crunching with frost under your booted feet.

She rubbed her frozen fingers together and stamped her feet. "Not perhaps if you stand still too long," she hinted, making him laugh.

"Is it a wee walk you want, Mama?" Together, they strung the fish up and carried them over to the smoking shed.

"A long walk, but Matthew doesn't want me walking about too much on my own, and he's stuck in bed for another day or two."

They walked in silence for a while, Alex setting a brisk pace that Ian easily followed.

"Thank you," she said. "I don't know how we'd have coped without your help these last few weeks."

Ian grunted in reply, saying that he liked being here, surrounded by his whole extended family, and Malcolm pined for his uncles if he didn't see them daily.

"All the same, Jenny can't be too thrilled, can she, to be spending so much time alone." It worried her, how Jenny isolated herself, rarely accompanying Ian and Malcolm. Ian hunched under her inquisitive look, but chose not to reply.

"Do you think of him often?" Ian asked instead, making

a hasty grab at her skirts to stop her from overbalancing on a fallen log.

"Who? Jacob?" All the time, more or less, spending an idiotic amount of time scanning the lane for the implausible arrival of an anachronistic postman, complete with a letter from her son assuring her he was alive and well.

"Nay, Isaac."

"Oh." She glanced at her twenty-five-year-old stepson. She was still in two minds about him knowing the truth about her, and disliked his repeated attempts to discuss all aspects of her future life – and especially her son living in the twenty-first century. "Of course I do, but not exactly on a daily basis," she said, feeling rather ashamed. She increased her pace up a short incline and waited for him at the top, breathless with exertion. "Does that make me an awful mother?"

"Not to me, but perhaps to him."

"There wasn't much I could do about it, was there?"

Ian gave her a long look. "Would you like to go back?"

"No."

"Why not?"

"That's a rather stupid question, isn't it? I have my family here, not there."

"And if you could take us with you?"

Alex fell silent, mulling this over. "No, I somehow think you'd all be quite unhappy there." Rednecks, the lot of them, and where here Matthew and his sons were looked upon with respect, there they'd be considered uneducated. "It's very different: people live in cities, and the jobs they do keep them mostly indoors. And for your father, it would be difficult to adapt to an age so devoid of God."

"Devoid of God? How can any time be devoid of God?"

"Oh, believe you me it can." She gave a short laugh. "If the Second Coming happens in my time, no one would really care, and poor Jesus would have his work cut out for him to even achieve being heard."

"So you're glad that you happened upon this time?"

"Glad? Well, now I am. But if it hadn't happened then

I would probably have been pretty okay with the life I was leading there, in the future. Of course, that would have meant I would never have met Matthew Graham, and that would have been a terrible loss." She snaked her arms hard round herself. Quite unbearable, actually.

"Besotted," Ian said, rolling his eyes.

She laughed and swiped at his arm.

It was probably because they had the advantage of higher ground that they saw the Indian before he saw them. Still in the same gruesome coat as last time she'd seen him, but Alex could swear there were more braids decorating the dark broadcloth, one of them an eye-catching red colour that for a moment had Alex choking on her heart: that could have been Ruth's hair.

Beside her, Ian had gone still, sinking down on his haunches with an admonishing finger to his lips. Alex nodded, lowering herself to a crouch, eyes never leaving the silent shape that was gazing so intently at her deserted yard. Not entirely deserted, because suddenly Narcissus loped into view, his heavy snout raised to the wind. The dog barked and took a couple of steps in their direction. Below them, the Indian raised his bow, notched an arrow, and aimed at the dog.

Alex just couldn't stand it. "Hey!" she called out, barging down the slope.

The Indian wheeled, still with his bow raised. Belatedly, it struck Alex that this was a very stupid thing to do, to rush a man with a lethal weapon. She faltered. The Indian pulled back the bowstring.

"Mama!" Ian's arms wrapped themselves around her thighs, tackling her to the ground. The arrow whined through the air, striking a nearby tree at head level. Narcissus was barking his head off, and from all over came canine reinforcements, adding their voices to the cacophony of sounds. Ian whistled, and here came the dogs, making a beeline for the intruder.

The Indian set off for the river. Ian roared and charged after, dirk held high. With him went the Graham pack, now running in sinister silence. Alex rose to her feet. A couple of hundred yards to her right, the Indian had reached the shore, but Narcissus was snapping at his heels. When the dog sank his teeth into the man's thigh, the Indian screamed. Ian yelled, rushing for the Indian. Some of the younger dogs were leaping about like demented rabbits, but, step by step, the Indian dragged himself towards the water, with Narcissus like a huge yellow leech on his leg. With a splash, the man went under, and Narcissus released his hold.

For a moment, Alex thought the Indian might be dead before the dark head resurfaced halfway across the river. Without a backward look, the man swam to the other shore, limped his way to the bordering woods, and disappeared.

"Are you alright, then?" Ian was breathing heavily by the time he got back to Alex.

"Yes, I scraped my knee, that's all." She patted Narcissus on the back. "He'll sleep in the yard for now."

"Aye, they all will." Ian slid his dirk back into its sheath and took her hand.

The Indian had come with a purpose they discovered some time later, finding yet another little package where he had been standing.

"Burn it." Alex nudged it with her toe.

"Shouldn't we open it?" Ian said.

"Whatever for? We know what's in it. Yet another calling card from the damned Burley brothers. Sick bastards."

She told Matthew of the whole incident while she served him hot broth for supper. For all that he was hot with fever, he tried to get up, insisting he was well enough to leave his bed and take over the defences of their home.

"Forget it," she told him, pressing him down on the pillows.

"I must," he said, trying to stare her down.

"Ian and Mark will handle it, and then there's Narcissus. Somehow, I don't think our Indian friend is all that eager to meet him again."

Matthew's lips stretched into a faint smile. "He bit him?"

"Like a clamp. Must hurt like hell."

"Aye, if we're lucky, the wound will fester. Nasty things, dog bites."

For several days, Betty had stayed close to the house, unnerved by the notion of finding herself face to face with an Indian man who collected braids. But when she saw Ian enter the resurrected stables, she decided it would be safe enough for her to brave the yard as well. Moments later, she slid into the dusky light of the stables and seeing as Ian was nowhere in sight, busied herself with Moses.

She had finished with the mane before Ian came back, pushing a creaking wheelbarrow.

He set down his load and nodded a greeting to her. "You like horses?" he said.

Betty went on with her currying, standing on tiptoe to properly reach across Moses' wide back.

"They smell nice, and they're warm and they don't talk."

Sarah and Ruth recently out of sick bed made for enervating companions, Naomi was sick, and as to Agnes... After several weeks of Angus anecdotes, it was Patrick this, Patrick that, and had Betty noticed how beautiful his eyes were, and did Betty think he preferred grey or green, and should she perhaps leave her hair unbound now and then? She sighed. It lay like an uncomfortable rock in her belly, the scene she had witnessed in the woods, and she was still not sure it was the right thing to do, not to tell. Would Ian not want to know?

Betty crouched and combed her way through the white feathers that adorned Moses' fetlocks, and tried to make him lift his hoof. Moses stood like a rock, sinking his head into his manger. Betty tried again and sat back with an irritated sound.

"You can't do it by force," Ian said mildly from above. He entered the stall and ran a firm hand down the leg, squeezed, and waited until Moses lifted his hoof.

"See?" Ian smiled at her. His eyes were far too close, and so like Jacob's – except that he had a ring of small yellow spots all around his pupils, and Betty couldn't recall if Jacob

128

had those. She drowned in these hazel pools, widening her own eyes in response.

Ian stood up abruptly, slapped Moses on the rump, and backed out. "Tell me if you need help."

"I did it!" Betty crowed. She gave Moses a carrot and exited his stall, looking for Ian. He was down by the pigs, and Betty danced towards him.

"Oh, aye?" Ian wiped his forehead with his sleeve and grinned at her. "There are four more horses – and the mules."

She stuck her tongue out and came over to hang over the railing to look at the huge sow. "She could do with a wash; she looks very dirty."

"I wouldn't try," Ian said. "She's not in the best of moods at the moment."

"Who would be?" Betty extended a piece of bread to the pig. "Look at that belly!"

"Aye." Ian sighed. "Breeding females are difficult." A shadow flitted over his face as he sank his pitchfork into a heap of soiled straw and lifted it into his barrow. Betty waited for him to say something more, but after some minutes she trailed back to the horses.

Ian worked himself into a sweat, all the while thinking about Jenny. Something wasn't right, but he couldn't put his finger on it. At times, she was like fire in their bed, and he allowed himself to be devoured by this wild, unknown woman who was insatiable and demanding. Other times, she was a stiff board, insisting that they blow out the candle first.

During the days, she was incessantly occupied with her work, as was he, but now, with the shortening days, the evenings were long, and there should have been opportunity to talk, to somehow bridge the distance that had grown between them during these last few years. Instead, she escaped into more chores, insisting the table had to be scrubbed with salt, or how could she have forgotten to mend Malcolm's breeches.

She never touched him out of bed, gliding away like a

fleeing doe when he tried to hug her or simply take her hand. He didn't understand. He tried to show her how overjoyed he was with the coming child, but when his hands spanned her expanding waist, she shrivelled under his touch, her face acquiring a distant look. He had to talk to someone about all this before he burst, but not with Betty, not with a pretty lass that followed him around with her adoring beautiful eyes wherever he went.

"Maybe she's afraid," Alex said, having listened to a very hesitant Ian.

"Afraid?" Ian slurped the hot soup.

"That things might go wrong; that something might happen to her – or the baby."

Ian shook his head. "She's fit as a fiddle, and Malcolm was an easy delivery."

"How would you know?" Alex said with some acerbity. "And, even if it was, maybe it scared her. Some women just hate it." She came to stand behind him, and stroked his hair. Hair so like his father's used to be, a deep vivid brown that even in winter retained a tone of chestnut to it. Her fingers unravelled tangles, dragged their way through wavy soft curls that had gone a long time unbrushed. Alex produced a comb from her apron pocket and began to tug her way through his hair. Ian sat immobile under her ministrations and to her surprise, Alex realised he was crying.

"Ian?" She hugged him, kissing his cheek.

"Don't mind me," he said in a gravelly voice. "It's just…"

"Just what?" Tenderly, she smoothed a lock of hair in behind his ear.

"She doesn't touch me like this," he admitted in a pained whisper. "Not anymore."

"Oh, Ian." Alex kissed him again. "She will. Just bear with her for some time, okay?" And if she didn't shape up then Jenny was going to find out just how protective Alex Graham was of her children – all her children.

"A lioness," Matthew agreed with a weak smile when she told him this. His hair had also been brushed into some kind of order, his face washed, his sore nose anointed with grease that smelled of peppermint, and he was sitting up in bed, nursing a steaming cup of something he insisted tasted like horse piss.

"Much more dangerous than a bloody lion." Alex sat down beside him and adjusted his clean shirt. "Better today?"

"Aye." He tentatively pulled in air through his nose, sounding as if he were gargling. Alex smiled and indicated the mug.

"That's why you have to drink that. All of it."

He made a face but drank all the same.

"He's right," Alex said, snuggling up to him.

"Hmm?" Matthew yawned and put his arm around her shoulders.

"Something's bothering Jenny, and I don't believe it's the baby or her strained relationship with her father."

Matthew yawned again. "Breeding women are a strange kind, aye? It will sort itself once the wean is born."

Chapter 15

It was touch and go who was the most surprised: the Burley brothers or Matthew. There was no doubt whatsoever as to who was the most frightened, with Matthew sinking back with a little hiss into the trees, musket in hand.

"Why if it isn't Mr Graham himself," Philip Burley said. "Just the man we wanted to see."

"You're trespassing," Matthew told them, putting some more yards between them. A few paces behind the brothers limped a fourth man, and when Matthew saw the grisly coat, he concluded this was the accursed Indian scout.

"We are? Oh dear, oh dear." Philip caressed his musket, looking at Matthew. "We heard the hunting is exceptionally good here."

"And so we came," Stephen filled in.

"No dog?" Philip asked, taking a step towards him.

Matthew wheeled and ran.

He was fast, and had the added advantage of knowing his land where they did not, leaping over trunks and crevices with the grace of a buck. A musket ball whistled past him, and he increased his speed, hoping Ian or Mark would have heard the shot. He slipped on a patch of ice, lost his footing, and rolled to the bottom of a long incline, scrambling to regain his feet.

He was up, veering to the left, but Walter was far too close. Matthew bounded up the next hillside, crashed through a thicket of blackberry brambles, and heard Walter curse. From his right came Philip, musket held aloft as a club. Over the relatively flat expanse of ground, the younger man gained on him, and it was but a matter of yards before that musket would strike him over the head, or between his shoulders.

Philip cheered, increased his speed, and the stock of his gun came down, whooshing through the air. It caught

132

Matthew squarely over his left arm, a blow strong enough to send him staggering. For an instant, he was down, knee on the ground, and here came Philip, musket raised for yet another blow. Matthew swung his own weapon, striking Philip over his legs. A misdirected swipe, not at all enough to do Philip any serious damage, but at least Matthew was back on his feet while Burley was down. Matthew tightened his hold on his musket, preparing to deliver one final blow. A shot: it nicked his arm. Stephen screamed as he came running with Walter at his heels. Matthew fled.

His breath was catching in his chest. His teeth ached with the effort of pounding up and down the undulating, wooded hills. From behind came the sounds of determined pursuit, and Matthew knew that, unless he made it back home, he would soon be dead – a protracted and painful death, no doubt. His ankle was beginning to throb, his boots dragged at his tired legs and there was blood trickling down his arm. He heard Walter jeeringly call his name. Out of the corner of his eye, he saw him closing in. Another shot, this one uncomfortably close to his head, and Matthew ducked and wove amongst saplings and boulders.

Matthew's mind cranked into ice-cold logic, and he led them deeper into the woods, where their speed and youth would be less of an advantage. He skirted the abandoned Indian village, dropped heavily down the steep side of sheer rock that bordered it, and ran flat out for the distant opening in the trees, for the safety of his fields. Matthew could hear his own ragged breathing, his heart was beating like a drum in the constricted space of his chest, and he sensed them closing in on him like wolves round a wounded deer. He opened his mouth and screamed.

Ian frowned. Was that Da? He couldn't recognise the voice, distorted with fear, but moved towards it nonetheless. The kitchen door slammed open, and there was Mama running like the wind towards the sound, kitchen knife in one hand, skirts in the other. In only her stockings, she burst across the frozen yard, and Ian fell into step with her, pitchfork still in hand. From the river came Mark, lithe and swift with his flintlock already at his shoulders, and now Ian could hear the thrashing sound of someone running for his life through the underbrush.

"Matthew!" Mama gasped. "My Matthew."

A crash, someone keened – a triumphant sound – and Da burst into the open, legs stumbling as he rushed towards them. Indians? The shrubs parted, and out came the Burleys. Here? How came they to be here? Ian tried to scream a warning. Fifty yards in front of him, the Burleys had almost caught up with Da; so intent on bringing him down, they hadn't noticed the three of them.

Mama shrieked. It near on made Ian jump, and it definitely had an effect on the Burleys. Heads snapped up, and Walter threw his musket into a firing position. Da collapsed on his knees, crawling as fast as he could towards them. Ian increased his speed, brandishing the pitchfork like a three-pronged lance before him. His vision narrowed into a chute with Walter his target. He heard Mama exclaim, felt the rush of air as a musket ball whizzed by him. Thirty yards...twenty-five. He tightened his grip on the worn wood of the pitchfork handle. Twenty yards...fifteen, and the Burley brothers turned and ran. Mark fired and Philip yelped, clapping his hand to his head. Ian hollered, all of him filled with a need to chase them down and beat them into lifeless pulp. Mark grabbed at his arm and brought him to a standstill.

"Nay," Mark panted, "we can't risk that they turn on us."

Ian wrested himself free, scowling at his brother. So close!

"They all had muskets," Mark said, "and I don't think a pitchfork is the best of weapons when you go hunting wolves."

Ian glowered, but nodded, wishing that he'd had the smooth stock of his flintlock in his hands instead.

Matthew couldn't find the energy required to rise. Instead, he sat down, extending his shaking legs before him.

"What are they doing here?" Alex asked in a voice that was markedly unsteady.

Matthew found that a most idiotic question, so he just

shook his head and concentrated on calming his heartbeat. He couldn't collect when last he had run for so long and so fast. Distractedly, he noticed his breeches had tears and burrs in them after his panicked rush through the woods.

"Are you okay?" Her hands inspected him, travelling down his damp back, his sleeves.

He nodded and gulped for more air. "I lost the bird," he said.

Alex stared at him. "You lost the bird," she echoed.

He grunted. A big fat turkey, but he had thrown it away in his haste to flee.

"Small price to pay," Alex said, and now she was weeping, falling to her knees to envelop as much of him as she could in her arms.

For three days, they rode in search of them, him and his sons, and for all that they picked up the trail for a while, it was as if the Burleys had gone up in smoke.

Matthew was in a foul mood when he entered the kitchen, hanging up his wet cloak with an irritated gesture before sitting down at the head of the table, waiting for his food.

"South-west," he said through the piece of bread he had stuffed into his mouth, "they've gone south." He sighed. He didn't like it that the Burley brothers knew where he lived, where his family was. How easy it would be to sneak down at night and set the farm alight and then…

Several times over the last few months had come news of isolated homesteads burnt to the ground, people and beasts seemingly swallowed by the forest. The Burleys, he'd wager, back to their original slave-trading business but now dealing in whites rather than Indians.

"No!" Alex said when he shared this with her. "Who would want to buy them?"

"Indians, I presume, and some whites as well."

"But they're free men!"

"And you think anyone will care?" he asked her with a crooked smile. "The bairns will forget soon enough, the women will be made to forget, and the men die quickly."

★

Slowly, they relaxed back into normality, into winter days spent catching up on all the undone chores of summer and autumn. But it was there: all the time, the Burley threat hung over them, tainting their lives, seeping in to undermine the safety of their home.

"Should you really…?" Alex said, breaking off when he scowled at her. She frowned back, took a determined breath and continued. "Is it really wise to walk about alone?"

Matthew pulled on his gloves and stamped his feet into his boots before replying. "I won't be a prisoner to fear. Besides, we know they're gone."

"For now," Alex replied.

"They won't be back." Matthew heard himself how utterly ludicrous that sounded. Before she could say anything, he stepped outside, whistled for one of the dogs, and hurried off into the forest.

He came back late in the afternoon, light of heart and mind. He had reclaimed his land over the day, walking very much on purpose to where he had run into the brothers. From there, he had tracked his own frantic progress through the woods, allowing himself to relive the fear he had felt.

For a moment, he stood scanning his empty winter fields, mentally seeing his sons and his wife converge on him as they had done that day, all of them determined to keep him safe, and something warm and soft settled in his chest. He looked over to where Alex appeared from the smoking shed, her basket filled with what he supposed to be trout, given the tails he saw sticking up, and strode to meet her.

"Hi," she said.

"Hi, yourself." He took the basket from her.

"Good walk?"

He nodded and gave her a short description of what he'd done. "I even found the turkey," he finished, setting down the basket to root around in his leather game bag.

"Matthew! It's been dead well over a fortnight!"

"Aye, nothing but bones and feathers left." Matthew produced a hare instead, laughing at her relieved face.

Chapter 16

"This has to stop," Jenny said as she always did afterwards, never meaning it. She got up from her knees and turned to face Patrick. "I can't do this anymore. It's wrong, and should Ian ever find out..."

Patrick tightened his belt into place before raising his eyes to her. She flushed at the look he gave her, all too aware of how she must look, her bodice gaping open over breasts he had recently fondled, her skirts still rumpled, straining over her large belly. His child, she moaned inside, this was Patrick's child. At times, all she wanted to do was to run away with him, sacrificing everything she had just to be with him, a bond servant with nothing to his name.

Patrick pouted. "I like my little wanton," he said, sticking his hand up under her skirts. "So does my cock. Where would we go, he and I, for sport?"

"I'm not wanton!" Oh yes, she was, a little voice told her, because all this man had to do was jerk his head and she came running, so eager to please, so eager for him to use her as he just had.

"No?" Patrick laughed. "And what would your husband call you if he found out? He'd call you even worse."

She slapped him. "Get out, and never come back. If you do, I'll—"

"What?" Patrick was very close, his hand rubbing at his reddened cheek. "What?" he repeated, winding his hand into her hair. She gasped when he forced her towards him.

"Nothing," she said, all of her melting with want.

"Jenny?"

The voice from outside had Jenny's heart skipping a beat or two. Sweet Jesus in his meadows! Alex Graham was coming this way, and suddenly they were scrambling away,

Patrick to throw himself out of sight behind the hay, Jenny to duck into the furthest stall and adjust her clothing.

"Mother Alex?" she replied in what she considered a very calm voice. "I'm here, down at the end." She smoothed down her hair, clapped her cap into place, did laces with trembling fingers, and arranged her shawl.

Alex stood by the door and peered in the direction of Jenny's voice. Her daughter-in-law rose into sight from behind one of the cows and came towards her, brushing at her apron as she went.

"Isn't Patrick here?" Alex asked as she entered the byre.

"Here, mistress," Patrick replied from behind her, appearing with an armful of hay.

Alex looked from her daughter-in-law to her bond servant. She could taste the tension in the air. Besides, she could smell it as well.

"Matthew has need of you," she said to Patrick. "The three furthest wheat fields are to be tilled today."

Patrick bobbed his head head, mumbled a farewell to Jenny and hurried off to where he had left the mule.

Alex turned the full force of her eyes on Jenny. Under her inspection, Jenny shrank back for an instant before straightening up to walk outside. Hmm. Was that hay in her hair?

"Finally spring," Jenny said, extending her arms towards the March sun.

"Don't remind me; first major laundry run tomorrow." Alex smiled though, as pleased as Jenny was with the fact that winter was over. And today she was going to make nettle soup for supper, thrilled to bits at eating something fresh and green again, however unenthusiastic the majority of her family was.

"Betty will be accompanying us down to Providence," Alex said once they were settled by the kitchen table. "She misses her family, poor thing, and for a girl used to living in a town, this must be the back of beyond."

Jenny nodded and lowered herself to sit. With a little face, she stood back up again, smoothing skirts into place before sitting down.

"Your back?" Alex asked sympathetically.

"My everything." Jenny grimaced, making Alex laugh.

"Only two more months." Alex reached forward to pat Jenny's hand.

"How is Naomi?" Jenny asked.

Alex broke out into a wide grin. "Horribly recovered, and the baby thrives." A boy: her first biological grandson, with eyes she was convinced were going to be as blue as her own, even if Matthew kept on reminding her that most babies were born with blue eyes.

She studied Jenny for some minutes, drew in a huge breath, and locked eyes with her. "What's going on?"

"Going on?" Jenny sounded confused, but Alex saw just how tightly she pressed her legs together, hands twisting into her skirts. "How going on?"

In reply, Alex sniffed and Jenny went an almost painful red. "With you and Patrick."

"Nothing." Jenny laughed. "How can you possibly think there is?"

Alex set her mouth and met Jenny's wide, innocent stare. "I love Ian very much. I'll not see him hurt. Not by you, not by anyone."

Jenny swallowed audibly.

"So whatever it is you and Patrick are up to—"

"I just said: we are up to nothing!" Jenny interrupted in an angry voice.

"Don't give me that!" Alex snapped, leaning forward. Jenny retreated, her back hitting the wall behind her. "As I was saying, whatever it is you are up to, end it. Now." With that, Alex stood up and grabbed at her basket. "I actually came by for a cheese."

Jenny was on her feet immediately and led the way to the dairy.

On the way back home, Alex mulled things over. There was no doubt in her mind that she had more or less caught Jenny and Patrick *in flagrante*, and then there were the other times. The time Patrick had ducked out of the dairy just as Alex arrived, the two or three times she could swear she'd seen Jenny in the woods far too close to Graham's Garden, the evening when Patrick appeared from among the trees and several minutes later there came Jenny, from a slightly different direction, but still... What was the stupid girl thinking of, and what was she, Alex, going to do? Well, at least she knew she had to do one thing: speak to Matthew.

"She knows!" Jenny was panting from her hurried run through the forest, cutting across to where she knew Patrick would be working. "Oh sweetest merciful Jesus, she just looked at me, and I could see she knows!" She was dancing on her toes with panic.

"How can she know?" Patrick said. "No one has ever seen us, have they?"

Jenny had never told him about Betty, but decided this wasn't the time to update him, so she just shook her head. Besides, Betty wouldn't tell now if she hadn't told before, would she?

"We have to end it." Jenny looked Patrick in the eye. "I – we – can't risk being accused of adultery!" She shuddered: adultery could carry the punishment of death, for both.

"They can never prove anything without our confession."

"Oh God," Jenny groaned, twisting her hands together. "What have I done?" She glared at him. "It's your fault. You forced yourself upon me, and I, weak woman that I am, couldn't stop you."

"You didn't want me to stop. If you did, you could have told your husband."

"Ian!" Jenny's throat closed up at the thought of how he would react. He'd look at her with those beautiful eyes, and she'd see the love in them extinguished to be replaced by ice. She didn't want that. Now that it was nearly too late, she was filled with the certainty that she wanted nothing but to be a good wife to him, from now until the day she died. No more Patrick, ever, she swore, and her heart cracked at the thought. Dear Lord, she loved them both.

Jenny grasped at the smooth trunk of a maple sapling. The sky was whirling above her, the treetops chased each other round and round, and with a little 'oh' she collapsed to sit in the grass. Patrick crouched down beside her, his hand running up and down her back.

"We end it now," he told her, helping her to her feet. "And whatever they ask us, we just repeat that, no, we've never done anything untoward. Agnes will help, I think."

"Agnes?" Jenny didn't understand.

Patrick chuckled. "Agnes is in love with me, and I've pretended not being entirely adverse to her little advances." He shoved at her. "Go, hurry back home." Jenny nodded and turned to rush off. He caught up with her ten yards into the forest, drew her close, and kissed her roughly.

"Take care of my child," he said, and in his eyes flared a tenderness she had but rarely seen. His thumb came up to caress the wet skin under her eyes, and he kissed her again, a soft, warm touch of his mouth on hers, before returning to the field.

Once home, Alex set off in search of Matthew, finding him in the stables. He gave her a long look, brows in a forbidding line.

"Where have you been?"

"Forest Spring, for a cheese."

"I don't want you walking alone through the woods! How many times must I—"

Alex waved him silent. "We can talk about that later, okay?" Quickly, she shared her suspicions with him.

"Jenny? With Patrick?" Matthew was dumbfounded.

"I'm not sure, but there's something there...and today..." She cleared her throat. "I could smell it."

"But you've never seen them."

"No, not as such. I hope I'm wrong, that I'm just overreacting." Alex found a carrot in one of her pockets and broke it into pieces to feed it bit by bit to Moses.

Matthew wrinkled his brow and went back to his currying.

"I can't tell Ian," Alex said, "but I must, right?"

"Unless you're sure, you can't tell him."

141

Alex felt her shoulders collapse with relief. "No, I can't, can I?" She sidled over in the narrow stall to end up behind Matthew, her arms round his waist, her cheek leaning against his back. "What do we do?"

"Nothing, but I'll have myself a wee talk with Patrick."

She rubbed her cheek against his back. She could hear in his voice how affected he was, no doubt drawing horrible parallels between what might be happening to Ian and what had happened to him, when Ian's mother – Matthew's first wife – took Matthew's brother to bed.

"I'm so sorry," Alex said quietly. "I don't want you to relive all that."

"Mostly I don't, but this…" He shook his head. "I'll not see my son as badly treated. I'll—"

"Shush, we don't know, okay?" She tugged at him, making him turn in her arms before cupping his cheek. "We'll deal with it together if we have to, and let's just hope it'll never come to that."

"He denies it," Matthew said later that evening, "but then he would." He kept his voice low, a cautious eye in the direction of Betty and his daughters, who were involved in a game of draughts.

Mrs Parson muttered that otherwise he would be a fool, and whatever else Patrick might be, a fool he was not. Alex agreed, but was at the same time relieved. If both insisted on denying, maybe all of this could blow over. She was just about to say that when there was a loud shriek from the gaming table. The board flew into the air, scattering pieces all over the place.

"I didn't cheat!" Sarah glared at Ruth. "I was winning, and then you say I was cheating."

"Now we'll never know," Alex said. "What with you throwing it all up into the air, who's to know if you were cheating – or winning?"

Sarah transferred her bright blue stare to Alex. "She always wins – always. And now I was winning, and she said I was cheating."

"She was," Betty agreed.

"What? Winning or cheating?" Matthew asked with a small smile.

"Pfft," Betty snorted, "you can't really cheat at draughts, can you?"

"Sarah can," Ruth put in. "She can never beat me honestly."

"I can so!" Sarah kicked in the general direction of her sister. "I beat you at chess last week."

"That was a lucky game!" Ruth flashed back. "You'll never win again. I dare you, Sarah Graham, I dare you to a new game."

"Oh dear, sore point that," Alex murmured.

Betty came over to join them by the hearth, still smiling. "At least they'll spend the rest of the evening in silence," she said, indicating where two heads were now bent over the chessboard.

"You think?" Matthew said.

The game ended with a triumphant Ruth knocking Sarah's king over.

"I'm supposed to do that!" Sarah protested. "It's me that pushes the king over when I give up."

"Lassie, you've been staring at the board for the best part of half an hour without finding any way out of Ruth's wee trap." Matthew beckoned his youngest daughter over, and settled her on his lap. "How would you like coming with us down to Providence when we go in April?" Ruth's eyes flew to his, green with jealousy. "You too," he hastened to add, and found himself fending off two highly excited daughters, who nearly tumbled him to the floor in their attempts to ensure he knew just how much they loved him.

"Is there a church in Providence?" Sarah asked once they had calmed down.

"A meetinghouse, you know there is," Matthew replied, "and we'll go to service there."

"Not one of our meetinghouses," Sarah said, shaking her head. "Is there perhaps a convent?"

"A convent?" Betty made big eyes at her. "Why would there be a convent in Providence?"

"There should be," Sarah grumbled, "for us lasses that wish to become a nun."

"A nun?" Alex was working very hard to avoid laughing out loud. "Why would you want to be a nun?"

Sarah mumbled something about not being allowed to be a minister, so then she could at least become a nun.

"Nay, that you cannot," Matthew said. "Nuns are papists, and that you're not."

Sarah pouted. "Then I'll be a lady pirate."

"More in keeping with your character," Mrs Parson commented.

"Let's just hope you're not prone to seasickness." Alex lowered her sewing to her lap, and let her eyes stray out of the window to the dark March sky. Was Jacob seasick? She sighed, and sent off a silent prayer that wherever he may be, he be alright.

Chapter 17

London in late March was a fine place to be, Jacob reflected as he strolled down Bread Street in the direction of Mistress Wythe's shop. Helen, he corrected himself; she was Helen to him now. He gripped his posy of daffodils tighter, and polished off the top of his shoe against his stocking. He inspected his hands, frowning down at his fingers. No matter how hard he scrubbed, his fingertips were a permanent greenish brown, courtesy of days spent digging and planting in the garden that was his workplace four days out of six, the other two spent in the master's shop.

Master Castain kept him hard at work, from early in the morning to well into the twilight of the spring evenings, and then there were lessons to study, huge tomes of plant lore to memorise, and long calculations to be made of how to mix up different tonics. At times, Jacob's brain felt about to burst, but he'd never been so certain of something as he was of this. He was meant to do this.

Occasionally, the master threatened to use the switch on him, like the time when he'd forgotten to cover the rosemary plants before the frost came. Mostly, he was a good and generous teacher, and, with each day, Jacob's admiration for him grew, because what this little man didn't know about herbs was probably not worth knowing.

Mistress Wythe – Helen – opened the door to him with a pleased expression on her face. Recently widowed again after her husband had the misfortune of falling off one of the river boats at full tide, she had decided she wasn't going to marry again – at all.

"Why should I? I'm better off on my own, controlling my own purse strings."

"But don't you want bairns?"

Helen shrugged, telling him that she'd had eight years with two men, and not once had she quickened. Hmm, Jacob had sharp eyes, and he'd noted already on one of his first visits that Helen had a sizeable supply of tansy and rue in her kitchen. Not his concern. Mayhap with this second scoundrel, she hadn't desired a wean.

Helen arranged the daffodils in a chipped stone bottle and set them on the table before offering Jacob something to drink.

"And Peggy?" he said, referring to Helen's maid.

"I gave her the afternoon off. Her mother is ill."

"Again?" Jacob asked, thinking that Peggy's mother had to be as old as Methuselah, given that Peggy herself was a grandmother several times over.

"Yes." Helen sipped at her cider. She frowned at a dash of flour on her bodice, wet her finger, and rubbed it off.

"It doesn't become you," he said, waving his hand at her dark clothes. "I liked you better in that green you had before."

"Jacob Graham," she huffed. "I'm a grieving widow!" She grinned broadly, making him laugh.

In Mistress Wythe's – Helen's – company, Jacob felt strangely adult. It might have had something to do with the way she looked at him when she didn't think he noticed, or how her cheeks coloured when he paid her a compliment. She was very bonny, for all that she had once attacked him with a broom. He smiled at the memory of that incident, and went on to wonder how long her hair would be if it was unbound from that heavy bun that hung a dark honey at the back of her head, very little of it covered by the elegant lace cap she wore. Very long, he thought, well down to her arse. And her arse... He assumed it was a nice arse, but he didn't really know, but he knew for a fact that her breasts were high and round. They peeked most invitingly at him from above her bodice, even if the linen of her chemise covered most of them.

Since Jacob's unfortunate experience down at Trig Lane, he'd kept well away from the whores, and Master Castain's colourful depiction of the pox had but strengthened his resolve to go nowhere near any of the stews. His weeks were spent in an almost entirely male environment – with the exception of Mrs Castain and nine-year-old Miss Castain – and the few hours of leisure he had, he spent wandering the surroundings of Whitehall Palace in pursuit of his other little plan, so far disappointingly fruitless. He took another gulp of the beer Helen had served him. He enjoyed his visits here, to sit and talk for some few hours with a woman who appreciated his company, to pay court to her, if somewhat clumsily, and to now and then feel his face heat from the way she looked at him.

"Have you tried the school?" Helen asked after he bemoaned his lack of progress in his other matter. She was the only person to whom Jacob had confided his intentions.

"What school?"

Helen blew out loudly through her nose and shook her head at him.

"Westminster: that's where all court lads go." She was very taken with this tale of sundered families, brothers who had torn each other apart on account of their love for the same woman, and now one of their sons hoped to mend the rift. Jacob had given up on trying to clarify that Da had stopped loving Margaret years ago, allowing her to embroider his story however it pleased her.

He looked at her from under his heavy fringe. She was sitting very close, close enough that, when he extended his legs, his calf brushed against her skirts. She moved even closer, a hand resting on his arm as she stretched across the table for the pitcher of cider. For an instant, the soft swells of her breasts pressed against his forearm. Jacob swallowed, crossing his legs in a futile effort to keep his member from stirring.

"Pie?" She smiled at him.

"Aye, please," he croaked.

Helen stood, fetched a piece of pie and sat down, watching him as he ate.

"Crumbs," she said, using her apron to wipe at his

mouth. So close. Jacob shifted on his stool, not quite sure if he minded or liked it. "There." She smiled and, just like that, kissed him.

Jacob sat very still, holding his breath. She shouldn't be doing this, he shouldn't be doing this, but he leaned forward and kissed her back.

"Wait, wait," she gasped, "not like that. I don't want to drown or choke." He felt himself flush and pulled back. Her hands cupped his cheeks and she kissed him again. Her mouth opened, and he opened his and... Jacob stood up abruptly.

"I—"

"Shh," she replied, standing up as well. "I know. And her name is Betty, and you love her very much."

He nodded, because he wasn't sure he could speak, and he swallowed in an effort to clear his throat of this unfamiliar tightness. Then her hand was on his breeches and to his great shame, that was it.

Helen laughed in a nice way. "You're young; young men are like that at times. Over-ardent." She bolted her door, shuttered the window, and took his hand. He didn't attempt to protest – he didn't want to.

She did have hair down to her arse, and a very nice arse it was, but it was the breasts he liked the best, heavy and warm in his big hands. Not at all like Betty's small, pointed breasts, he thought, feeling a flash of shame at his disloyalty. Betty was a lass, Helen was a woman, and now he was on his way to being a man – a real man. His cock stood upright in anticipation, and Helen chuckled.

"See? A young man...always so easy to rouse." But she opened herself to him and helped him inside, smiling when he whispered that he thought he might love her too, aye?

"Westminster School? What would you be wanting there?" The man on the horse looked Jacob up and down with evident disdain.

"I just wanted to see it," Jacob mumbled, "on account of my grandfather having been a pupil there."

The man raised one eloquent, incredulous brow. "Over there," the man waved with his riding crop. "Behind the Abbey."

Jacob bowed and walked off unhurriedly in the indicated direction. Only a daftie would rush to see the school his grandda had attended.

The place was teeming with lads. The eldest were of an age with Daniel, and the youngest somewhere around seven or eight. Some of them looked forlorn, standing to one side and trying to be as inconspicuous as possible, while others demanded attention in the way they moved and spoke, their manner indicating these were lads that knew their worth – and it was high.

Jacob grimaced when one big lout boxed a laddie over the ear, screaming at him to get his arse off the ground and into class before he had to report him again. The laddie fled, crying, and his tormentor laughed, nudging a tall lad beside him in the ribs. The nudged lad shoved back, in the process dislodging his hat, and at the sight of that fiery red hair, Jacob was convinced he had finally found his cousin.

Over the coming weeks, Jacob spent a substantial amount of his leisure time in the environs of the Westminster School. He charted the red-haired boy's days, from the morning when he rode in with a manservant beside him, to the late afternoon when he set off back home. He discovered where the boy lived – a house less than a quarter of a mile from Whitehall proper that had him gawking at the iron railings, the elegant brickwork and the impeccable knot garden. But from one day to the other, the time he could invest in this little pastime shrank dramatically, because his workload doubled, with Master Castain saying that the whole garden had to be completed by the end of August.

"All?" Jacob shook his head in disbelief. "But we haven't even opened the new beds yet!" He gave his master a despairing look. "No matter how hard I work, that can't be done, not unless you bring in some more lads to help with the digging."

Ned, the head gardener, muttered an agreement: impossible, absolutely impossible – even with more lads.

"Hmm," Master Castain said. "Well, your period of service has just been extended – until the garden is finished."

"That will take another year," Jacob moaned.

"Oh, stop whingeing, boy! Start using your spade instead. You have all the seedlings to plant, and the hyacinths have to be dug up and moved to wither in the shade, and I want you to replant the artemisia, cut the lavender all the way down, and then there's the monk's hood, and where have you settled the hyssop, and—"

Jacob held up a hand. "I know what I have to do, aye? Just leave me the time to do it." He stomped off in his heavy pattens.

Later that day, Master Castain came to find him, looking pleased. Somewhat rushed, he told Jacob that he'd had a meeting with his fellow guildsmen, and even if it was all most unorthodox, they'd finally agreed.

"Agreed to what?"

"It's not as you came untutored to begin with," Master Castain went on, further confusing Jacob, "so here." He held out a formal-looking document.

Jacob read it through – twice – and looked at him. "Truly?" he said.

"Truly," Master Castain said, "but it will be fifteen hard months, young Graham, and you'll be subjected to a formal and most extensive examination at the end of it."

Jacob swept his thumb over the deed. He'd be worked to the bone, he reckoned, but at the end of it he would be able to call himself an apothecary – a most junior apothecary, to be sure, but still.

"Starting September, you'll work in my shop over on Watling Street," Master Castain continued, "and I expect you out here two days a week to work in the garden. Of course, your evenings will be taken up with study, so there will be very little time for any other pursuits." He gave Jacob a prim look, making Jacob squirm. His master had on several

150

occasions asked pointed questions as to his relationship with Helen, while now and then reminding Jacob in a casual tone that marriage vows were there to be kept.

"One day a month off," Master Castain went on, "and every other Friday evening."

"Starting when?" Jacob asked, feeling trapped.

"Today is Thursday, so let's say Monday and you can have three days off." He extended his quill to Jacob, who took it and signed his name.

With so little time at his disposal, Jacob decided to act, spending most of his precious free Friday loitering outside Whitehall. Just as the red-haired lad showed up, Jacob threw himself before the horse, screaming like a gutted pig. Quite a competent rider, he concluded between his shouts of pretend pain. The lad dismounted and kneeled beside him.

"Are you alright?"

"Aaaagh," Jacob said, attempting a weak wave of his hand. "I don't think so." He allowed the manservant to help him to sit up, and clenched his arms hard around his waist. "I think the horse trod on me."

"No, he didn't," the lad told him, green eyes flashing into his.

"Nay? Well, that's good." Jacob grinned, before allowing that expression to convert itself into a grimace of pain.

"What happened?" the lad asked.

"I don't know. It all began to spin, and my head throbbed something terrible. It still does." Jacob eyed the lad curiously: eyes very like his own – except that these were mostly green – magnificent red hair, and a nose that somehow reminded him of Ian. "Jacob Graham, at your service."

"Graham? You said Graham?" The lad began to laugh. "But that can't be! I'm Charles Graham."

Now it was Jacob's turn to look confused, which he seemed to manage quite well. "Charles Graham? Wee Charlie?"

The lad sat back on his heels and regarded him cautiously. "You know me?"

151

"I've never seen you in my life, but I suspect we may be cousins."

Charles stood up. "My cousins live in the colonies somewhere."

"In Maryland, and your da's Luke Graham, and my da is Matthew Graham. And you have a wee brother called James and a sister called Marie, and then there is a fourth one as well, right?"

"James is dead," Charles informed him in a stilted voice. "And my sisters live out in the country."

"I'm sorry to hear that." Jacob got to his feet. Charles regarded him in silence, chewing his lip in a way that made him look very much like Ruth.

"You must meet Father," he finally said and turned on his heel, motioning for Jacob to follow.

If Luke Graham was surprised by finding himself face to face with a nephew he had last seen as a lad of four, he didn't show it. Instead, he sat back and allowed his eyes to travel up and down Jacob's worn clothes.

"Hard life?" he asked, crossing legs sheathed in dark silk stockings and blue velvet breeches.

"It would make no sense to dress up when one works in a physics garden," Jacob replied, forcing himself not to stare at the opulence that surrounded him. His uncle must be a wealthy man, he reflected, feeling a stab of anger at the fact that his own parents should live without any of the comforts this man had: books, an exquisite wooden cabinet with intarsia, upholstered chairs, cut-glass goblets... It almost made him uncomfortable. As did his uncle's silver nose, glinting dully in the sunlight from the windows.

"A herbal garden?" Luke sounded amused.

"Aye." Jacob straightened up. "I'm under apprenticeship to be an apothecary."

"Oh, aye? And is that what your father has chosen for you?"

Jacob squirmed. "Nay, Da wanted me to be a lawyer's clerk. But I didn't like it much, and I wished to see the world, like, so I took ship—"

"Ah." Luke steepled his fingers. "And so you ended up here, on my doorstep."

Jacob grinned at him. "Strange, no?"

Luke stood up and came over, bringing his eyes very close to Jacob's. They were of a height, Jacob noted with pride. If anything, he overtopped his tall, elegant uncle by a scant inch or so.

"Strange? Yes, it would seem so. In particular, when you don't believe in coincidences," Luke said.

"Not a coincidence," Jacob said, wanting very much to touch that silver nose. Was it cold or was it warm? "Nay, it seemed the polite thing to do, to visit with you now that I'm in London."

Luke stared at him a moment longer and then he laughed. "Polite? Well, I assume it is." He shook his head in reluctant admiration. "Cheeky lad."

"Aye." Jacob mock sighed. "'Tis one of my graver faults."

Luke laughed again, clapped his hands together, and invited his long-lost nephew to join him at the table.

Chapter 18

"Seriously, Matthew, what were you thinking? Both girls to go with us? My hair will be as white as Mrs Parson's by the time we come back." Alex drew her cloak closer around herself and sat down beside him. He fed some more wood into the fire and extended his hands towards it.

"Are they asleep then?"

"Finally." Alex glanced over to where the three lasses lay curled up close together. "Betty's very jittery. I suppose she's worried about her welcome."

"Aye." He nodded at the two Chisholm brothers who came over to join them. In general, their Catholic neighbours kept mostly to themselves – except for serving together in the militia, or bartering beasts and produce – but travelling together made sense, especially now with recent sightings of wolf and, far more worryingly, Indian braves.

"Will they be alright?" Alex asked in a low voice.

"Ian and Jenny are at Graham's Garden," Matthew said, "and with Mark and Patrick that makes three men."

"Whoopee, three men to defend four women and six children."

"They don't kill, Alex, they come to steal, to find food. And that goes for both the wolves and the Indians." Not for the Burleys, he thought, but since that December day he'd seen nothing of them, and neither had the Chisholms nor the Leslies.

"I don't like it, that Ian and Jenny live on their own like they do," Alex said, "especially not after what happened some months back. And they did kill."

Sadly, she was right. The homesteads to the north-west of them had been attacked in January, and two of the settlers had been killed, leaving widows with half-grown bairns to fend for themselves.

"Aye, they did, which is why Ian and I have cleared that space beyond the barn. We'll build a new cabin for them there."

"That won't thrill Jenny much. She likes being mistress of her own place."

"It isn't her decision. Ian doesn't want them all alone, not now, with all that restlessness." Matthew poked at the fire, sending a shower of sparks into the air. "And it will put a stop to anything that may be going on."

Alex rested against his shoulder. "What would you do, should there be something between Jenny and Patrick?"

"What would I do? It's more what Ian would do." He dug into the fire again, an angry movement that dislodged a piece of burning wood.

"But we don't know – not for sure – even if at times… I don't know. It's as if the air between them crackles with tension, even if they're on opposite sides of the yard."

Matthew muttered something long and foul under his breath. He had eyes of his own, and, just like Alex, he sensed it, that burning heat between his daughter-in-law and his bond servant. Had he been able to do without him, he'd have dismissed Patrick outright, but during the spring planting he needed him, and, besides, how was he to explain to Ian if he ousted the man now, with the busiest time of the year looming? But, come May, he'd gladly see the young man off his property and urge him never to return – no matter that Patrick's contract did not expire until September.

"We don't know," Alex repeated in a dejected voice.

"Nay, we don't," he sighed.

An uneventful two days later – except for the constant chattering of his daughters – Matthew bade the Chisholms farewell and turned towards Providence. Their neighbours, being papists, were bound for St Mary's City, preferring to conduct their business there.

He held in his horse for an instant, allowing his lasses to take in the wee town spread out before them. Four – no, five – streets arranged in a rough fan-shape with the central docks and the adjoining marketplace as their starting point, the most imposing of them leading up to the meetinghouse. Here and there, narrow alleys connected the streets, houses stood cheek to jowl, some of them narrow and tall with at most one room per floor, others somewhat more well-proportioned with leafy backyards. The original western palisade was looking dilapidated; the northern had all but disappeared, absorbed into a crooked alley that was bordered by stables and houses. To the east, Matthew could make out the half-finished shape of the new Anglican church, twice as big as its predecessor, no doubt to house its growing congregation. As of last October, Reverend Norton was a member of the town council, and for all that he was Anglican and therefore near on half-papist, Matthew liked Norton, an energetic and cheerful man who didn't hesitate to roll up his shirtsleeves and pitch in when needed.

"It's..." Ruth stuttered from where she sat behind him.

"Big," Sarah filled in, leaning so much to the side that Matthew feared she might slide off the mount she was sharing with Alex.

"Not that big," Betty laughed.

"Big enough," Matthew said, "and you'll not be going anywhere on your own, y'hear?"

Both lasses promised that they wouldn't.

"Do you think there will be letters waiting for us?" Alex asked as they made their way down the long slope.

"No, it's still too early in the year." He squinted at the grey horizon. "Although if I'm not much mistaken, there's a ship on its way in. Probably a sloop from Massachusetts or Virginia."

"Where? Where?" The girls craned their necks eagerly.

"I was hoping for a ship from England," Alex sighed.

"Aye, I know." He leaned over to clasp her hand. "He'll do fine. Our Jacob will be fine, aye?"

She nodded, giving him a brilliant smile. Tears hung like dewdrops in her lashes.

With the sloop came Mrs Walker, and it was somewhat of a relief to Matthew to be able to give his wife reassurances as to the well-being of one of their lads.

"So he's alright?" Alex gave Mrs Walker a watery smile and clutched Daniel's letter to her chest.

"Very," Mrs Walker said, "he's settling in well. Harriet is taking good care of him, and he has several friends – good boys all of them." Mrs Walker launched herself into a description of the wholesome life Daniel was leading, with much opportunity to advance his spiritual progress, regular church visits, occasional evenings spent with his friends, but with most of his time and effort being spent on school. Matthew nodded approvingly at this.

"He's considered a serious and disciplined student by his tutors," Mrs Walker finished with a smile. "I'm sure he'll make an excellent minister."

Matthew snuck Alex a look, noting that, if anything, she seemed sad. "What is it?" he asked once Mrs Walker had bustled away.

"It gets at me: my son, and he's leading a life I know nothing about, with people I don't know, and when he graduates, it might be you'll be there, but in all probability not me."

"Of course you'll come as well." Matthew kissed her tenderly on the nose. He was still glowing with pride after having read the short letter from Daniel's teacher, praising his son for his diligence. "He seems happy," he said after having read Daniel's own letter, a cramped two-page effort, obviously written under duress.

"Very, seeing as he barely can find it in his busy schedule to write us."

"That's as it should be. He's making his own way in the world now."

"But he's so far away," she groaned, "and I miss him."

"So do I, lass." Matthew drew her close. "So do I."

After installing themselves in the inn, they accompanied Betty to the Hancock home. The lass was nervous – as was her father. A somewhat stilted greeting, a clumsy hug on both sides, and then they were all ushered inside, with William leading the way to the parlour.

"He has some effrontery," William said, handing over

a letter to Alex. "He absconds from my service, secretly weds my daughter, and then sends his letters care of myself." An unwilling smile tugged at the corner of his mouth. "That Jacob is quite the scamp." He produced yet another letter and handed it to his daughter. "For you."

Betty curtsied and turned the letter this way and that. "May I remove myself to read this in private?"

William nodded that she could, and she whirled out of the room.

Alex opened the letter and read it with Matthew hanging over her shoulder, his eyes flitting over the scrawled words.

"When did these arrive?" Matthew asked, frowning at the date.

William flushed. "November? Yes, I think it was late November – came with the last ship."

"You've had the letter in your keeping since then without passing it on?" Matthew didn't even attempt to disguise the anger that coloured his voice. "That was an uncharitable thing to do – have you any notion of how worried Alex has been?"

"I was irate," William said.

"But not with my wife, I hope."

"With all of you. The son's behaviour is a reflection on his parents." William sounded very defensive, ignoring Esther's protesting gasp. Matthew watched him in silence for some minutes before holding out his arm to Alex.

"We'll come by for our daughter-in-law when we ride back on the Monday." With that, he propelled Alex before him out of the room, calling for his lasses.

"He's right, I suppose," Alex said later that evening. Their daughters were fast asleep on their pallet beds, exhausted after a full day spent gawking at the assembled populace of Providence.

"How so?" Matthew pressed his hand against the lower part of his back, grimacing at the way it all seemed to thud.

"Lie down." She set to with slow, strong movements that made him grit his teeth in pain. "Well, he is, isn't he?

158

If I hadn't talked so much about the world at large then maybe Jacob wouldn't have decided to take off." She sank her thumb into a painful spot, and he gasped.

"Uh," he said once she released the pressure. "Mayhap it was me, choosing to apprentice him here, so close to the sea and the ships. Had we kept him with us, at home, then…"

"And now he's in London," Alex said. "Cheeky bastard, isn't he? 'Hi Mama, I'm in London, everything's great' – well, more or less anyway. So, now I'm scared stiff as to what might have happened to him since he got there, and I don't understand why he stayed behind there. Captain Miles must have known he'd taken off without our permission, and if so he should've taken him to Edinburgh."

"Perhaps he didn't ask for leave." Matthew shifted under her hard hands.

"Lie still! London, shit, Matthew, that's a huge city…"

He nodded and closed his eyes.

"Maybe Simon can try to find him," Alex said.

Matthew grunted. One lad in a city the size of London – like looking for the proverbial needle.

Chapter 19

It had to be said: Philip Burley had a certain flair to him, in everything from how he carried himself to how he was dressed, impeccable linen contrasting nicely with the deep blue of his dashing coat. That didn't endear him one whit to Alex, and, in particular, not when he popped up most unexpectedly just as she was leaving the apothecary, her daughters trailing after her.

"Mrs Graham," Philip said, bowing. Alex controlled the urge to turn on her heel and run. Never, ever show him how much he scares you, she admonished herself, just stare him in the eyes. Except that she didn't want to, unnerved by the penetrating, assessing look in them – as if he was putting a value to her, estimating how much she might be worth should he sell her.

"Mr Burley, how unfortunate to find you still so very much alive."

He laughed, shaking his head so his signatory lock of black hair fell over his left eye.

"Why, Mrs Graham, one could think you don't like me much."

"Like you? I hate your guts, Philip Burley, and to my dying day, I'll regret not serving you toadstools the first time we met."

His eyes lightened into impenetrable ice. "Well, you didn't, did you? And so, here I am." He glanced over her shoulder, studying her girls with interest. "See?" he said, directing himself to the Philip lookalike that had appeared beside him. "Quite pretty, aren't they?"

Walter Burley grunted, his eyes stuck on Sarah.

"We're partial to fair girls," Philip said. "In particular to young, fair girls."

"You…" Alex swung at him, Philip ducked, and came up grinning, eyes like flint.

"Don't," he warned, and, at a snap of his fingers, yet another Burley brother materialised, this one so badly scarred Alex knew he had to be Stephen. She threw a look over her shoulder, relaxing somewhat at finding the street busy. Should they try anything, she'd scream – or stab them with her new knitting needles. Still, they were far too close, with Walter more or less drooling over Sarah. When he made as if to touch her daughter, Alex flew at him, slapping him hard over his wrist.

"Don't you lay a finger on her. Do that, and I'll—"

"…do what, Mrs Graham?" Philip purred.

"Kill him," she replied, staring into those eyes as firmly as she could. It only made him laugh.

A hand at her waist, and Alex's shoulders dropped an inch or two, safe now that her husband stood beside her.

Philip regarded Matthew, a jeering light in his eyes. "Not as afraid now as when we met last?" He chuckled at the responding wave of angry red that suffused Matthew's face. "You should be afraid, because someday we'll make you pay for Will."

"You can try," Matthew said.

"Oh, we can do more than try." Philip looked Alex up and down a couple of times. "You have a comely wife. What a pity she'll soon be a widow." He smirked. "And, once she is, then who is to stop us from taking what we want?" He nodded in the direction of Sarah.

Rage rose red before Alex's eyes. She didn't stop to think. She set down her basket, hitched up her skirts, and kicked Philip, swiping his legs from under him. Philip's smirk became a surprised squawk, converting into a grunt when he crashed to the ground. Walter rushed forward, shoving Alex so hard she fell. Matthew's fist drove into Walter's gut. Walter wheezed like a punctured accordion and doubled up. Stephen cursed and went for Matthew. By now, Philip had regained his feet, and in his hand was a knife.

Alex regained her feet. She raised her arms and crouched

to achieve balance, immensely grateful of the time she had spent on upholding her martial arts skills – even if one man and one woman against three determined Burleys didn't feel like good odds. Why was no one interceding? Why were the people of Providence content to watch, instead of putting a stop to this? And where were her girls? She wheeled, tried to smile reassuringly at her girls, standing very close together. Sarah squeaked, pointing, and Alex turned just in time to see Philip lunge at Matthew.

"Stop!" William Hancock shouldered through the crowd and came to stand beside Matthew, followed by the blacksmith and Reverend Norton, big men the both of them.

Philip fell back, flanked by Walter, who was holding a rock, and Stephen, who was growling like a dog, uneven teeth bared in a snarl. Philip returned his dagger to its scabbard and wiped his face with his hand. He was bleeding from his lip, and for what seemed like an eternity, he stood staring down at his bloodstained fingers before raising his eyes to Matthew. Seconds passed. It was as if everyone was holding their breath, but then someone laughed. Walter whirled and sent the rock flying. The crowd scattered.

Philip put a restraining hand on his brother's arm. "Not now." Just as suddenly as they had appeared, the Burley brothers melted away.

Alex tottered over to Matthew, her heart thundering with adrenalin. "I don't think I like them much," she said, noting that she couldn't unknot her hands from where they gripped Matthew's shirt.

He covered her hands with his, rested his forehead against hers. They stood like that for some minutes, oblivious to the people around them.

"They don't like us much either," Matthew voiced, one arm coming out to give first Ruth, then Sarah, a quick, comforting hug.

"No, that's kind of obvious." She took a deep breath, glanced at their curious audience, and stepped away from him, smoothing at her cap and apron before turning her attention to her basket and its spilled contents.

"Are you alright?" Matthew asked in a concerned voice, bending down to help her.

Alex nodded, even managing a smile. "No." She bit her lip. "They'll never give up, will they?"

"Maybe not, but they'll never do us any harm."

"Now, why do I find that difficult to believe?"

Matthew inhaled noisily, stared off in the direction the Burleys had disappeared, and turned to face her. He didn't say anything; he just held out his hand. Tight, tight, his fingers closed round hers.

"They'll not be back in a hurry," Minister Walker assured Alex some hours later. She was sitting on a stool in his little study, with Matthew hovering behind her. From the kitchen came the sound of her girls, who had been whisked away by Mrs Walker. In a paternal gesture, the minister patted Alex on the cheek and went back to frowning out the window. "Chased them for a mile and more – they're well on their way elsewhere by now."

Alex nodded, her fingers picking at her skirts, her bodice, the fringe of her shawl, back to her skirts. If only they'd been arrested; instead, they were still out there somewhere. She had to grit her teeth to stop herself from crying.

"Nothing happened, my dear," he said gently.

Alex gave him a false smile. "No, it didn't, did it?" With that, she stood, grabbed at her basket, and, in a controlled voice, informed Matthew that she had errands to do, and would he meet her later by the meetinghouse?

For the coming hour, Alex submerged herself in her purchases. Spices, sugar, salt and tea, wax candles, poppy seed and limes, bolts of linen and serge. Her mood lifted, the fluttering in her belly settled down, and she was humming to herself when her eyes alighted on Kate Jones, flirting mildly with Matthew.

She came to a halt, regarding them from the shadowy doorway of the haberdashery. Her man looked good, his best coat fitting snugly over broad, strong shoulders. Alex felt a surge of pride. He'd just turned fifty, but Matthew still carried himself like a young gallant, that tall lean body of his as fit now as it had been decades ago.

Kate tilted back her head, saying something that made Matthew laugh. Kate shifted closer, and her hand drifted to rest for a moment too long on Matthew's sleeve. Alex didn't like that. Even less did she like that he didn't immediately step out of range.

You're overreacting, she told herself sternly. So he slept with her all those years ago on Suffolk Rose – slept with her? He'd fucked her, not once but several times – but that was due to circumstances, to Matthew struggling to stay alive in an environment that had stripped him of all human worth and dignity, reducing him to a slave. Still, Kate Jones was far too attractive in her dark green velvet skirts and matching bodice for Alex to remain where she was any longer than necessary. She paid for her purchases and, with a quick nod at Mrs Wilson, darted outside.

"Alex! How nice to see you." Kate beamed, bejewelled fingers smoothing over the excellent cut of her skirts.

Bloody woman: she looked absolutely gorgeous, even if the skin on her face and neck was somewhat flaky. Alex flicked her skirts into place and adjusted her flower patterned shawl around her shoulders, wishing that she had something as becoming to wear as the outfit Kate was wearing. She felt dowdy in comparison, and it must have showed in her eyes, because suddenly Matthew was very close, his fingers brushing her arm.

"I was just saying to Matthew how I've presented the option of your daughter as a future wife to my Henry," Kate went on.

"Umm," Alex replied, shooting eyebolts at Matthew. She'd made her opinion on the matter clear enough, hadn't she? "Ruth is only twelve, and I find it somewhat premature to be thinking of her marriage."

"Time flies, and suddenly they're sixteen with a mind of their own – like your boy, Jacob."

Bitch. Alex fixed her with a cold stare. "Twelve is too

young to even be discussing this." Alex looked over to where her eldest daughter was bickering with her sister, this time over a piece of sticky gingerbread. "Esther isn't looking well," Alex continued, firmly changing the subject. "The baby is due when? In two months?"

Kate shook her head. "A matter of weeks, no more; halfway through May, I think. But it's been a difficult pregnancy, and I think she would have preferred it not to happen. But William so wants another son, little Willie is somewhat frail."

"It might be a daughter," Alex said – or kill the mother.

"Let's hope for a boy," Kate said, "a healthy, strong son."

They spent a couple of minutes on more small talk before Kate hurried off, saying she had a cargo of sugar to inspect.

"I thought I'd made it very clear that Ruth isn't marrying Henry Jones," Alex said to Matthew once Kate was out of earshot.

"And I told you we haven't finished discussing it." Matthew nodded in the direction of the barber's. "He's a good-looking lad."

Alex turned to look at the eldest Jones boy. Tall and big, with his mother's honey-coloured hair, he was talking to Mr Farrell's son. Yes, he was handsome, and his clothes were of excellent cut, his boots polished to a shine, and, as she watched, he threw his head back and laughed loudly, revealing a lot of teeth.

"Do you really want to risk holding a grandchild that stares up at you with Dominic Jones' piggy eyes? Because, let me tell you, I definitely don't!"

"It's a good match," Matthew said mulishly.

"A match that won't happen, okay?" Alex gripped the handle of her heavy basket and hurried away from him before she do something really stupid like slap him for being an inconsiderate idiot. How could he think she'd want their daughter to marry the son of his former lover?

★

Matthew watched her out of sight and hitched his shoulders. Ultimately, he'd do as he pleased in this matter, and Ruth would do well out of a marriage with Henry Jones – very well. He approached the two young men and shared some words with them, all the while sizing young Jones up. Very much like his mother, he noted with relief; nothing of his father in his eyes or face, except for a certain tightness of the mouth.

Young Farrell was saying something with marked agitation, and Matthew forced himself back to the conversation, shaking his head in amazement as he listened to the tale that was spilling out of the younger man's mouth. With a mumbled excuse, he hastened off to find his wife.

"...and so the new slave ran away," Matthew said, "taking with him a further ten or twelve of the Farrell slaves."

"How did he manage that?" Alex asked.

"They just walked off the plantation back in February, him still in chains. They forced the local smith to strike the irons off them and disappeared into the woods." He threw her a worried look. "They caught them three days ago, after nigh on two months of freedom. Half-starved they were, and some of them most grateful to be captured."

"What will happen to them?"

"They've brought him into town. He's going to be punished publicly tomorrow."

"And the others?"

Matthew didn't answer. He hadn't enjoyed listening to young Farrell's detailed description of the floggings.

"You won't be going," was all he said.

Alex found the place they were holding him after hours of walking her way here and there through Providence. She should have thought of this immediately. Of course Farrell's slave would be held in Farrell's house, not in the makeshift holding cells belonging to the town buildings. She'd never been anywhere close to the impressive Farrell home before, had only exchanged nods with Mrs Farrell on her previous visits to town, and as she stood looking into the cobbled yard, she had no idea how to reach the poor man. All she knew was that she had to try and set him free, whatever the risk to herself.

She shivered and moved closer to the fencing. She knew where he was, because she could hear him, continuous sounds of something that sounded like despair and fear. She eyed the heavy doors to the storage shed and gnawed her lip. Somehow, she suspected waltzing across the yard with a chirpy 'hello' wasn't going to work very well.

She strolled by the house, turned up the small dirt track that led up to the meetinghouse, and stood looking for some time at the narrow overgrown passage that bordered the back of the Farrell complex. After ascertaining no one was about, she ducked into it and made her way towards the buildings, cursing at the amount of offal and garbage that lay in heaps along the way.

"Hello?" Alex heaved herself up as high as she could get, her feet scrabbling for purchase on the planks. The muted sounds from inside stopped briefly before resuming. Alex dropped down, hunted about, and found a discarded stool that she dragged back to stand on. Her nose cleared the lower sill of the small light gap, and she looked down at a man who was staring back at her with a mad glint in his eyes. He was in leg irons, the chain wound round a pole.

"Are you okay?" Alex said.

"Okay?" The man laughed weakly. "She asks if I'm okay..." His head snapped up. "Okay?"

Alex nodded. "Yeah, one of those expressions as yet not invented."

"No way!" The man struggled to sit. He squinted at her. "Lucky you, you're white."

"Yes, I suppose that helps. What have they done to you?" Her eyes rushed over a body that looked very much the worse for wear.

"Done?" He coughed and dragged at his feet. "First, they stripped me, then they branded me on my butt, and then they dragged me out to work in the fields." He held up large hands in her direction. "I'm a musician," he said with irony. "I play the piano – Beethoven sonatas mostly. I never will again, will I?" Two fingers had been broken and inexpertly set. "Not that I'll ever see a piano again." He closed his eyes and emitted a low whimper. "I wanna go home. I hate this fucking place, and I'm still not sure what happened. All that thunder, and the ground kind of caved in, you know? So much light; bright, bright light."

Alex shivered, recalling with precision her own fall through time. Terrible, goddamn awful, and she'd been fortunate enough to end up at Matthew's feet, not like this poor guy, landing in a time and place in which he was automatically taken for a slave.

"You were on a crossroads, right?"

He nodded. "Just outside of Salisbury." He eyed her hopelessly. "There's no way back, is there?"

"Not as such."

He groaned and hid his face in his hands. "God, I hope they kill me tomorrow, because I sure don't want to live like this."

Alex wanted very much to touch him or take his hand, but there was no way she could reach him, just as there was nothing she could say. "What's your name?" she asked instead.

"My name?" He coughed again. "Apparently my name is Noah. I've been forcibly christened, even if I tried to tell them I was already baptised." He studied his hands in silence. "Leon, my name is Leon White. Ironic, huh?"

A rough hand yanked Alex off her perch, and she fell heavily to her knees.

"Mistress Graham?" Mr Farrell looked her up and down when she was marched into his yard.

"Master Farrell." She curtsied, glaring at the man who was holding her arm.

"She was conversing with the runaway slave," the man informed Mr Farrell.

"Now, why would you do that, Mistress Graham?" Mr Farrell nodded at the man, who unhanded her.

"Curiosity, I suppose," Alex replied, trying to look shamefaced. "My husband won't allow me to witness the punishment tomorrow, and I'd heard it was a huge man, black as the night with red eyes." She shrugged and tried out a discontented pout. "He looked rather ordinary to me."

Mr Farrell looked at her and burst out laughing. "Disappointed, my dear?" He shook his head and rearranged his features into a mask of severity. "I'll have your husband sent for, to accompany you home. I dare say he'll punish you as he sees fit."

"I have a good mind to belt you," Matthew hissed, a firm grip on her arm as he led her towards the inn. "The lasses have been so concerned for you, fearing all kinds of things, and then I'm summoned to collect you as if you were a recalcitrant child! What were you thinking of?"

"I was going to set him free, but that was kind of impossible to achieve, wasn't it?"

"I will belt you," he promised and tightened his hold.

"You try that, Matthew Graham, and let's see in what shape your balls emerge," she spat back.

He stopped and shook her.

"Ow!"

"You're my wife and you'll do as I say."

"You didn't tell me not to, did you?" she pointed out logically.

Matthew groaned, but released his hold. "I didn't think you'd attempt something that half-brained." He took her hand instead. "Mr Farrell has decided not to punish him here, on account of it being too much for female sensibilities. Instead, he'll take him down to the slave docks and there make an example of him."

"Will he die?" she quavered, imagining one torture worse than the other.

"Die?" Matthew looked away. "Oh no, Alex. Yon Noah has assured himself a long and painful life of servitude." Much, much worse than dying, his voice told her.

"Leon," Alex corrected, "his name is Leon."

Matthew sighed. "Leon then. But by the time he dies, he won't remember."

It was well after midnight when Alex gave up on sleep. Beside her, Matthew slept heavily, and on their pallets her girls were lost in dreamland, one sprawled on her back, the other curled into a ball. Alex rose and tiptoed through the room, collecting her clothes and shoes as she went. The door creaked. Alex held her breath and counted to fifty, but neither Matthew nor the girls as much as stirred. She opened the door wider and squeezed out onto the landing. Behind her, she heard Ruth cough.

Five minutes later, Alex hurried through the darkened streets of Providence, clutching the chisel and mallet she'd lifted from the inn's stables. Her stomach contracted into a hollow of fear, and every few paces she hesitated, thinking that maybe she should go back, because this little excursion could really backfire. But there was no choice, not if she wanted to be able to live with herself, and so she pushed on, nearly dying of fright when a male voice cut through the night. She shrank into a nearby bush. The voice was complemented by other voices, and a group of men walked by, leaving a stench of piss and beer and general grime in their wake.

There was no moon, so she walked almost blind down the little passage that led to where Leon was being kept. She bumped into the shed, shoulder first. A few paces to the right, and she could make out the light gap she'd been peering through previously, now a dark rectangle in the stout wooden walls of the shed.

"Leon?" she whispered, scratching at the wall. "Are you there?" No reply. Alex used the chisel to tap at the wall. "Leon?"

"Uhh?" A hoarse cough, followed by the sound of chains scraping against the ground.

Alex set the chisel to one of the planks, brought down the mallet, and winced at the loud splintering noise. There were no warning shouts, no barking dogs, and so she did it again, pleasantly surprised by how rotten the lower end of the planks were. In a matter of minutes, she'd created a hole, and after one last look round, she slithered through it.

Leon was a dark shape a foot or so away from her.

"Hi," she said, and the big man laughed, a rather wheezy sound.

"Hi," he replied, "how's things?"

"Stressful," she said, using her hands to inspect the chain that fettered him. The sound the chisel made on the iron links was like that of a loud gong.

"Shit," she said when a dog began barking.

"Let me." Leon took over mallet and chisel. He must have skinned himself at some point because she heard him suck in breath, but he drove the mallet down furiously several times. The dog was at the shed doors, barking excitedly. From somewhere in the yard came a curse; booted feet rang over the cobbles.

"Hurry!" Alex hissed.

"I'm trying," Leon hissed back, and finally the chain gave.

The hole seemed smaller this time. Alex's skirts got stuck, she couldn't move forward or backwards, and now she could hear someone unlocking the door to the shed. Oh God, oh God. Any moment now and they'd be inside the shed, and how was she to explain this? She bit back a surprised gasp when hands grabbed at her shoulders. With a tearing sound, she was pulled outside. Matthew? Yes, Matthew, in shirt and breeches only.

Leon came crawling after, but whatever advantage he had was shrinking fast, because there were angry shouts in the shed, and here came the dog, poking his head through the hole. Matthew kicked the animal, hard. The dog howled and retreated.

"Go, run, man!" Matthew shoved Leon in the direction of the nearby alley. "Up," he said to Alex, motioning towards the roof.

"Here?" To Alex, that seemed a very bad idea. They'd be like cornered rats.

"There's no time!" He helped her up, heaved himself after, and they lay as flat as they could.

In a matter of minutes, the area round the shed was full of men and dogs. Lanterns threw weak beacons of light on trampled grass. Mr Farrell himself made an appearance in nightshirt and coat, and, after having inspected the hole, he shrilly told his men to find the accursed slave, find him and bring him back – alive. Dogs bayed, the men set off at a steady trot, and it didn't require all that much intelligence to conclude that the odds for Leon getting away were ridiculously low.

Matthew had them remain on the roof until the sounds had faded in the distance. Once they were back on the ground, he crawled into the shed, returning seconds later with the chisel and mallet.

"Can't leave them here, can we?" he said, leading them off in the direction of the inn. He didn't take her hand, he didn't talk to her, and in the returning light, Alex could see just how angry he was in the set of his shoulders.

They were passing the graveyard when Matthew came to an abrupt halt.

"What?" Alex whispered.

Matthew pointed down the road before throwing the chisel and mallet over the low graveyard wall. Towards them came a triumphant procession, headed by Farrell's eldest son. Four men were dragging a gagged and tied Leon behind them, and Alex bit back on a sob at the sight of him. Bring him back alive, Mr Farrell had said, and alive Leon most definitely was, no matter that he looked as if he'd been savaged by the dogs.

"Mr Graham!" Young Farrell stopped, eyes flying over Matthew and Alex. For a long time, his gaze lingered on the tear in Alex's skirts, on her hands that she suddenly realised looked rather the worse for wear after worrying at the wall planks. She retreated to stand behind Matthew, clasping her hands behind her back.

"Edward." Matthew bowed slightly.

"Out and about this early?" Edward Farrell asked, eyes drifting yet again to Alex, who gave him a weak smile.

"As you see," Matthew said with a shrug.

"Ah, and may I enquire why?"

"Is it of your concern?"

"It may be. This slave…" He broke off to point at Leon. "…attempted to escape a few hours back, and how he succeeded in breaking his chains is a right mystery." Edward pursed his mouth. "We suspect an accomplice."

"Not me," Matthew said.

"No, no, of course not! But mayhap your wife? She did show inordinate interest in the man earlier, did she not?"

"Not my wife either," Matthew said, sounding very affronted.

"So why is it she is looking so…well, pardon me… dishevelled?"

"She sleepwalks." Matthew sighed. "A right nuisance it is, aye?"

"Sleepwalks?" Edward gave Alex a curious look. "But she is fully dressed."

"Aye, this time. At times, she wanders round in shift and nowt else."

"Ah," Edward said, an interested gleam in his eyes, as if he was imagining what she might look like in her chemise and nothing more. The young man bowed and stepped aside to give them precedence down the street. Matthew bowed back, offered his arm to Alex, and off they went. When they passed Leon, Alex threw the unfortunate man a sidelong look. Two dark eyes met hers, and the anguish in them tore her heart to shreds.

"Sleepwalking?" she said as they approached the inn. He had dropped her hand the moment they had left the Farrell party behind.

"I had to think of something." He wheeled, bringing eyes an unusually light green very close to hers. "You are a fool. How could you do such?"

"I had to."

"And have you helped him, do you think?"

Alex looked away. If possible, she'd made things worse for the poor man.

173

"Well? Have you?"

"If he had gotten away…"

"Gotten away? Where to? The man is, however unjustly, a branded slave! Someone would always find him."

"I…" She wet her lips. "…I just had to try, I guess."

"Fool," he repeated, "and what if I hadn't woken, what then? What if they'd apprehended you there in the shed?"

Alex hitched her shoulders; she hadn't really considered that part. "I guess Mr Farrell would have yelled a bit."

"Yelled a bit?" Matthew's voice soared into a falsetto. "Dearest Lord, spare me! They'd have hanged you, Alex; for theft."

"Oh," she said, her hand fluttering against her neck.

"Aye, oh, indeed." Matthew spat to the side and entered the inn, clearly not caring if she followed or not.

Chapter 20

Alex snuck into the room well after him, and it sufficed with one look for Matthew to conclude she'd been weeping – for the unfortunate Leon, he assumed.

Daylight was seeping through the shutters, patterning the interior of the room in elongated streaks of light, but Matthew was so drained after the recent events that he just had to stretch out on the bed. He covered his face with his arm, peeking at his wife as she hesitantly moved in his direction. Thank you, Merciful Father, he prayed, thank you for Ruth's cough that woke me, because if not…

"I'm sorry," she mumbled, sitting down on the bed.

He clasped her hand hard in his. "Think, Alex, beforehand, aye? You're no mindless lassie to act so rashly."

She inhaled, a long ragged breath, and nodded.

"Come here," he said, patting at his chest. "Come here, my heart." Her lower lip wobbled, the corners pulled down as they always did when she was about to cry. He shushed her, pillowing her head against him. Some time later, she slept, a warm breathing weight on his chest. Matthew stared at the ceiling. He'd never be able to sleep, not when his brain was an explosion of jumbled images from the passed night.

"Da?" Sarah shook him hard, and Matthew reluctantly opened an eye to find his youngest daughter's face scant inches from his.

"What?" He yawned, sitting up.

"I'm hungry."

"So am I," Ruth said, popping up beside her sister. Matthew had to smile. Where Sarah's hair stood like a messy haystack round her face, Ruth had already braided hers and placed a cap on top.

An hour or so later, the lasses had been safely deposited with Mrs Walker. Matthew had business to conduct with one of the timber merchants, and he'd decided that he wanted Alex with him, to keep an eye on her. Yesterday had been overly exciting, what with the Burleys and yon Leon, and Matthew intended to ensure today contained no such spicy ingredients.

"A word, Brother Matthew?"

Matthew sighed when he recognised the voice, but stopped all the same, sending an admonishing look at his wife.

"Mr Farrell," he said, inclining his head in a polite greeting. Beside him, Alex curtsied.

Mr Farrell nodded curtly. "And how is your wife today?"

"As you can see, she is well."

"Hmm." Mr Farrell twirled his cane, his normally rather fleshy mouth set into a displeased gash. "I find it too coincidental," he blurted.

"What?"

"Don't give me that, Brother Matthew. You know full well what I'm referring to. First, your wife is found talking to my slave. Come night, said slave escapes. Mighty strange that: a man chained to a pole contrives not only to strike the chains off, but also succeeds in creating a hole through a stout plank wall – with no tools but his hands."

"Aye." Matthew nodded. "That is right strange, that is."

"He had an accomplice," Mr Farrell said. "How else explain it."

"An accomplice? Another slave, you think?"

"No, Brother Matthew, I think not. I think your wife."

"My wife?" Matthew pulled his brows together into a ferocious scowl. "What makes you say such?"

Mr Farrell took a step or two back. "I hold you in the highest regard, Brother Matthew, and never would I utter such an accusation lightly. But, as I said, I don't believe in coincidences. On the same night my rebellious slave escapes, your wife is apparently sleepwalking through our settlement, and in the process she not only tore her clothes, but somehow mangled her hands."

"I do that a lot when I sleepwalk," Alex put in, "tear my clothes, I mean. I fall over."

Matthew glared her silent. "I can assure you, my wife it was not, and I'd gladly take on anyone who says differently."

"We'll see." Mr Farrell adjusted his hat. "I dare say he'll tell us the truth – ultimately. There is only so much pain a man can bear."

"The word of a slave counts for nothing," Matthew said, but his heart was thronging his throat, and out of the corner of his eye, he could see Alex had gone very still.

"Interesting all the same." Mr Farrell looked Matthew straight in the eye. "I expect you to be present at his punishment so you can hear first-hand what he has to say."

"His punishment?" Alex said. "How can you even think of punishing him? He looked close to death this morning!"

"That slave has to be taught a lesson," Mr Farrell said, "and, once I'm done with him, he'll be as docile as a lapdog."

"He's not a dog, he's a man," Alex flared.

"He's a slave, Mrs Graham, a disobedient, difficult slave." Mr Farrell gave her a crooked little smile. "And why should you care? Unless, of course, it was you that helped him."

Alex went a bright pink. "I most certainly didn't!" She sounded insulted rather than guilty. "That doesn't mean I can't feel sorry for him."

"Most inappropriate," Mr Farrell said severely before turning away.

"Shit," Alex muttered to his retreating back. She cleared her throat. "Maybe we should leave, now."

"How would that help?" Matthew said. "No, we have to brazen it out, no matter what yon poor bastard says."

Matthew was so sickened by the brutality he was forced to witness later that afternoon that it was only through staring intently at his shoe buckles that he succeeded in retaining his composure. Mr Farrell was true to his word, stripping his absconding slave of every shred of human dignity before he was done, at which point the tall man was reduced to a whimpering, crawling creature that abjectly begged his master for forgiveness. But no matter how the man was tortured, no matter how deeply the leaded tips of the flogging whip sank into his flesh, he refused to name his accomplice, screaming that he didn't know, Jesus, he didn't know, but he thought it might be a man.

Afterwards, Mr Farrell approached Matthew and apologised for his accusations. Matthew bowed and assured him it was already forgotten, and as they were strolling back towards Mrs Malone, he asked if Mr Farrell had considered selling the slave, troublemaker that he was. In reply, the trader laughed, saying that, now that the man was well and truly broken, he had no intention of selling him – ever.

Alex wasn't in the mood for church next day. Matthew's terse description of what had befallen Leon had left a sour taste in her mouth, and the thought of running into Farrell at church made her want to throw up. Worst of all, there was absolutely nothing she could do to help the poor man – nothing at all.

All through the sermon, she sat lost in a silent monologue with God, entreating him to pull out a spectacular lightning bolt or two and propel Leon back to whatever time it was he came from; alternatively, fry Mr Farrell to a crisp. Every now and then, she dropped out of her internal musings to ensure her girls were behaving as they should, which was quite unnecessary given the fact that Matthew's presence was enough to guarantee they sat like angels throughout the long service.

"I don't want to be a nun," Sarah said afterwards. "And I'm that sorry for Daniel. Is this what he's going to do? Talk people to death?"

"Shh!" Alex suppressed a laugh. "That wasn't the best sermon, and I'm sure Daniel will find a way to liven things up a bit. He could start by keeping it substantially shorter and sweeter."

Sarah looked doubtful, saying that in her opinion Daniel had a tendency to ramble.

Ruth poked her with a sharp elbow. "No, he doesn't.

It is just that you never listen, so he has to repeat it, several times."

"Will you be sorry to be going back tomorrow?" Alex asked her daughters as they strolled back towards the inn. She was walking arm in arm with Matthew, while their daughters skipped around them.

"No," said Sarah.

"Aye," said Ruth.

"Yes? Why?" Alex asked.

In response, Ruth indicated a group of girls her own age that were walking a few yards before them. "It is nice with all the people."

Sarah made a dismissive sound. "I miss home, and I miss our brothers and the woods and our river."

"So do I, but I wouldn't mind going to school." Ruth sounded very yearning.

"Lasses your age don't go to school," Matthew said, making Alex roll her eyes. So bloody unfair, that their brightest child, their Ruth, was by gender excluded from any kind of higher education.

"Not even in Boston?" Ruth asked.

"No, not even there. The skills a lass needs she has to learn at home."

"Huh," Alex began, but broke off, staring down the street. It couldn't be, could it? She blinked, looked again. It was, oh my God, it was! With a whoop, she tore herself free from Matthew, and off she went, running at full pelt. From behind her, she heard Matthew's loud exclamation, and to her great irritation it only took him a couple of seconds to sweep by her, a sound of pure joy hanging in the air behind him.

"I can't believe it!" Alex hugged Simon, Joan and little Lucy – not so little anymore – and then did it all again. "Oh, my God, what are you doing here?"

"I would expect that to be obvious," Simon Melville said, "we want a slice of currant cake and some of that new-fangled tea that you're so fond of." He was visibly shaken, wiping at his eyes between hugging his brother-in-law and Alex. "It's good to see you, Matthew," he said hoarsely, and

Matthew looked back at him with eyes as wet, and nodded that, aye, it was.

Alex wasn't quite sure whether to cry or smile when they hugged each other again, these two men that were almost like brothers, for all that one was short and shaped like a bulging barrel while the other – her hunk – was an impressive six foot two with not an ounce of excess fat on him.

"You look just the same," Alex said, although that wasn't strictly true, at least not in Joan's case. Matthew's sister had always been very thin and very tall, hovering around six feet, but the last decade or so had permanently rounded Joan's shoulders, and there was a gauntness to her face that made Alex worry she might keel over at any moment. But Joan's eyes, grey and luminous, were just the same, fringed with the thick dark lashes she shared with her brother.

Simon did look very much himself, emanating that general likeness to a fat, strutting pigeon, even if his girth had expanded dramatically, reminding Alex of a mother of twins in the last month of gestation. But his eyes were still an inquisitive, mischievous blue, his hair still fluttered in reddish strands around his head, and he still heaved himself up and down on the balls of his feet while he talked.

"And she's stunning," Alex said, indicating Matthew's niece. Lucy Melville was indeed so beautiful that men were already taking note of this new arrival, quick looks being thrown her way and then thrown again when they took in the general roundness of her, eyes just like her mother's, and hair somewhere in between her father's reddish colour and Sarah's blond, hair that hung, surprisingly, uncovered and unbound down her back.

"And deaf," Joan reminded Alex.

"Not that much of an impediment, it would seem." Alex inclined her head in the direction of where the girls were walking in front of them.

"She lip-reads," Joan said, "and she always carries paper and a stub of coal with her. And she talks with her hands, but you won't understand that, I fear."

"So why are you here?" Matthew said. "You've never indicated any wish to leave Scotland."

An unreadable look flashed between Simon and Joan.

"Nor did you," Simon retorted. "As I recall, it took a lot of convincing to make you see you had to go, for the sake of yourself and your bairns."

"Are you saying you had to leave?" Matthew said.

Simon came to a stop and turned to face Matthew. "I'm fifty-one. All my life I've spent building a practice in Scotland. Do you think I'd be here unless forced to?" He stuck a finger down his collar and grimaced. "And it's a frightfully hot place – hot and damp, like."

"Hot?" Alex said. "This isn't hot; this is comfortably warm. It's better up where we live, up in the higher country."

"So why?" Matthew repeated.

Simon squirmed. "I had to." From the set of his mouth, it was clear that for now that was all he was going to say.

Repeatedly, Alex clasped Joan's hand, smoothed her hand over Lucy's head, ignoring the irritated ducking movement this generated. To Alex, all of this was a dream come true, except that of course it wasn't, because something must have gone very wrong for them to set out so late in their lives to build a new existence for themselves. Also, there was a reticence between Joan and Simon, and with all her antennae waving madly, Alex caught far too many looks between them, heard too many undertones in the comments they made to each other. Behind her sister-in-law's back, she caught Matthew's eyes, and from his infinitesimal nod, she understood that he noticed it too: the silent but constant reproach oozing from every pore in Joan's body.

Alex took Joan for a walk, leaving the girls in the care of their fathers. After a guided tour through the town, they strolled off along the water, opposite to where the ship from which the Melvilles had disembarked earlier that morning lay at anchor, small boats plying back and forth.

"How fortuitous," Alex said, "that you should arrive today, on our last day here."

"Do you have to leave tomorrow?" Joan asked.

"We're riding with a party. It's best not to ride alone." Especially not now, when the risk of running into the Burleys was significant. But she didn't say that. Instead, she stroked Joan over her thin arm. "It's so good to see you, and once you've settled in, maybe you can come up and visit us for some weeks."

"Settled in? Here? In this small place so far from home?" Joan kicked at a stone and burst into tears.

"Oh, Joan." Alex hugged her sister-in-law. "It'll be alright. It does have its advantages, you know. Like much less rain and fog in winter, and none of that constant grime hanging in the air like it does in Edinburgh."

"I like Edinburgh," Joan snivelled. "I didn't want to leave."

"No, in general, you don't want to leave your home, do you?" Alex pulled them down to sit on a rock facing the water. "So, why did you?"

Joan burst into a new bout of tears.

"It would have been better if he had visited the whores," she said, once she'd gotten herself back under control. "I could have understood that, aye?" She blushed and looked away. "I can't...not since several years, on account of always being in pain." Joan placed her hand on her abdomen – ever since Lucy's birth, she had been plagued by constant pain in her nether parts. Joan straightened up and looked at Alex. "So I wouldn't have liked it had he gone with the whores, but he's a man, and men have needs. Instead, the wee daftie had to fall in love, and not only fall in love, but with the wife of one of the aldermen."

"Ah." Alex nodded, although in reality she had no idea beyond seeing an enraged husband appear at the bedside and threaten Simon's life.

Joan gave her an irritated look. "Ah? So you know then? What it's like to have your husband write love notes to another woman? To hear your neighbours whisper behind your back, tittering to themselves while you know nothing, nothing at all, because you'd swear on the life of your child that your husband wouldn't do something like that?"

"No," Alex said, "I guess, I don't."

Joan exhaled loudly. "He never did anything, he says. He just loved her from afar…" She wasn't sure she believed him, she went on, but he insisted that was how it was: a passionate verbal relationship no more. When the alderman found out, intercepting one of the love letters, he'd hauled his wife in front of the courts for adultery, demanding that the marriage be dissolved, and who would step in to defend the wife if not the honourable Simon Melville.

"He didn't! He was compromised, wasn't he?"

"Aye, one could say that," Joan said, "but, strictly by law, no adultery could be proven, and so the alderman was obliged to settle generously with his wife or keep her." Joan picked at her skirts. "He kept her."

Oh dear, Alex thought. The poor wife would probably pay until the end of her days.

"I was made a fool in everyone's eyes," Joan continued. "They looked at me and nodded that they could understand why Mr Melville strayed. And I have problems forgiving him for that – I have problems forgiving him at all." She sighed. "He made Simon pay, the alderman did. In a matter of weeks, his custom dried up, and on top of that he hounded us – Simon mostly. But, one day, a gang of apprentices set upon Lucy, chasing her all the way back from the butcher's shop."

"No!"

"And then, one March evening, Simon came home and told me we were leaving on the morrow, that he had passages booked, and had no intention of staying one more day in this accursed, damp-ridden gutter of a city. So that selfsame night we packed and, come daylight, we were in Leith, boarding the ship."

"Wow, very abrupt."

"I told you, we had to. It was unbearable, it was!"

Alex eyed her sister-in-law. Dear Joan wasn't telling her the whole truth – she saw that in how Joan avoided her eyes and, much more tellingly, in how she'd clasped her hands together.

"I am so angry," Joan said after a minute or two. "It is a Christian thing, to forgive, and I try. But some days..."

"So, why did you come with him?"

"And what else was I to do? He's my husband. Besides, I love the silly, puff-breasted man." Joan picked up a clod of earth and crumbled it through her fingers. "I think I do at least," she qualified, staring off towards the east.

"...it's so sad." Alex finished recounting her conversation with Joan.

"Aye," Matthew said, "but I'd warrant Joan is but telling you selected pieces of the whole sorry tale. Simon is far too competent a lawyer not to weather such a storm. No, there's something else at the root of this sudden decision to leave."

"Yeah, I think so too." Alex went back to her packing, wondering how all this stuff would fit in the pannier baskets.

"Simon and I spoke to William and he's willing to attempt a partnership," Matthew said, "and I've found them lodgings with Mrs Redit. I reckon it may do Joan some good, to have a female companion to show her about."

Alex threw him a look. Mrs Redit was a widow, and a bloody old one at that, but seeing as she had lived here since Providence was three houses and a hen coop, she knew everyone in town, and was probably a good introduction.

"I hope they'll come up to us soon," she said.

"They're welcome whenever they wish," Matthew said, "but it's better if they're a wee bit settled first."

Probably. But that might take a very long time, given Joan's open dislike for her new home.

Chapter 21

"Did you have a good time?" Alex asked Betty, holding in her mare.

"Yes." Betty's brows creased together. "Mayhap I should have stayed. Mother did seem rather poorly."

"So, why didn't you?"

Betty mumbled something about wanting to go home, kicked her horse into a trot, and bounced off to join Matthew and Sarah further up the line.

Alex gave her a long look, wondering what it was that was exerting such a pull on the girl. Not the younger boys, not Ruth or Sara, maybe Naomi, definitely not Agnes... hmm. That didn't leave all that many, did it? Ruling out herself and Matthew, it was either Mark or Ian, and, as far as she could recall, Betty had spent very little time with Mark. She turned this interesting little conundrum round for some time, but was distracted by Ruth's excited cries that she'd seen a moose, a huge moose.

Late in the afternoon, three days after setting out, they were home. The moment Alex set foot on the ground, her three young sons swarmed over her, and she had to kiss and cuddle and hug, exclaim at how big they'd grown while she was away, and was that a baby raven Adam was cradling? He beamed that it was, and Alex was dragged away to inspect the cage that Mark had helped him build, and did she know just how many worms this little bird could eat?

Very carefully, he ran a finger over the soft fuzz on the baby bird's back. "I'm going to teach him to talk. Mark says you can."

Matthew came over to study the bird and ruffled his son's hair. "I had a wee corbie when I was a lad, bigger than this when I found it, with a broken wing."

"And did it talk?" Adam asked.

"Nay." Matthew laughed. "But it was a wise bird for all that." He inspected the worms and shook his head. "Meat is better. See if you can trap a few mice, and give it to him in pieces."

"In pieces?" Adam looked quite distraught. "Must I slice them up?"

Matthew ruffled his hair. "'Tis a hard job being a parent, laddie."

Samuel came next, showing her a huge bump on his brow. David had learnt to whistle – rather tunelessly. Naomi proudly held out little Tom for inspection, Hannah clutched at Alex's skirts, Agnes popped out from the dairy to welcome them home, and even Mrs Parson bustled outside for a quick hug.

Two people kept their distance. Jenny smiled vaguely in Alex's direction before disappearing in the direction of the dairy, and Ian gave her the briefest of hugs before turning his attention to the stabling of the horses. There was a tightness to his mouth that increased when she came after him, a quick negating movement of his head making it clear she was intruding. Alex sighed: there wasn't much she could do unless he let her in, and so she left him alone – at least for now.

Once all her people had been adequately greeted, Alex took a little turn around her home, a slow walk to ensure it was all still there. For the first time ever, being home was not the same as feeling safe, and every now and then she stopped, staring at the encroaching forest. What she had always perceived as a natural barrier protecting the frail little clearing that was her home was now a threatening darkness that could hide dozens of lurking Burleys, and at one point she stooped, picked up a rock and lobbed it at a shadow, exhaling when the only resulting reaction was the angry chatter of a bird.

"Mama?" Mark's voice made her jump. Her son strode towards her, his dark hair lifting in the breeze. "What's the matter?"

Alex eyed him from under her lashes. Normally, she would have chosen Ian as her confidant, but seeing as he seemed reluctant to spend one-on-one time with her, she slid a hand in under Mark's arm and told him about their latest meeting with the Burleys. Mark listened in silence, his brows pulled together.

Alex made a sweeping gesture with her free hand. "We don't know. They can be anywhere out there, and we won't know until it's too late."

"The dogs—" Mark began.

"The dogs? And what good are they against armed men?" Alex shook her head. "We're like sitting ducks, all of us."

Mark frowned. "That's not true. We can fight back, defend our own." He set his jaw and gestured to where his daughter was playing in the grass. "The man who tries to harm me and mine, I'll kill." He looked quite determined – and very young.

Alex patted him on the arm and said nothing more.

The sun was setting as she made her way up from the river. The yard was full of children and dogs, Ian was working on his cabin, and from the main house came the comforting scents of soup and bread. Alex counted the dogs: six all in all, and four of them bloody big. By the barn stood her man, laughing at something David was saying, and when she stepped into a patch of evening sun, he saw her and came to meet her. He looked indestructible, his elongated shadow thrown before him, his head and shoulders silhouetted against the golden light.

They strolled towards the house, hand in hand. Just before they reached the door, he drew her to a halt.

"It'll be alright," he said, looking her in the eyes. The conviction in his voice was such that the fist-sized knot in her belly softened. His hand cupped her face, the rough texture of his calloused palm stroking her cheek. She leaned into his reassuring touch.

"I hope so."

"It will be fine, lass." Matthew's eyes glimmered in the

setting sun, a beautiful golden green that had her thinking of sun-drenched meadows.

"Of course it will," she said, relegating the Burley bogeymen to a locked drawer in her mental filing cabinet.

"It's nice to be home," Matthew chuckled once he and Alex closed the door to their bedroom behind them for the night.

"Do they always talk so much?" Alex mock groaned.

"Like their mama." Matthew ducked to evade the pillow she threw at him. "It's no better, is it?" he asked in an entirely different tone, helping her undo the lacings down her back.

Alex sighed and shook out her clothes before hanging them neatly on their respective pegs. She threw a considering look at the burst seam on her stays and made a mental decision to cut back on puddings for some weeks.

"No," she said, "Ian tries and Jenny flees."

Matthew batted away her hands and undid her hair. He picked up the brush and set to work, a deep furrow of concentration between his brows.

"It may be the bairn."

"Perhaps." Jenny was huge, and the baby was due any time within the coming two or three weeks, but in Alex's experience those last few weeks were weeks when she'd needed Matthew very close, all the time. She said as much.

"Ah." Matthew smiled. "But you weren't the norm." He swept aside her hair and kissed her just behind the ear. "Pink, you were; pink and rounded with my bairn, and always eager for me."

"Still am." She grinned. "Lucky you."

He helped her to her feet and turned her to face him. "Very." He stooped slightly to place a soft kiss on her mouth. More butterfly kisses on her cheek, her mouth, and Alex slid her arms round his waist and leaned back, head thrown back to give him access to her neck. He backed towards the bed; she followed. His fingers on her lacings, and the worn linen of her shift slid down her arms, her back. She released him to shrug the garment to the floor.

Matthew slid his warm hands down her flanks. "Dance for me."

"Like this?" Alex felt rather self-conscious, dressed in only her hair.

"Aye," he said, eyes burning into hers.

So she did, humming to herself as she did some rather explicit dance moves.

"Like Scheherazade," she said with a smile, shaking her head so that her hair fell like a veil before her face. She fluttered her eyelashes, rose on her toes, and twirled, her hands cupping her breasts.

"She didn't dance, as you tell it. She mostly talked – a typical woman." He grabbed at her, pulling her close. They swayed together, a coordinated series of movements in which eyes locked into eyes, hips ground against hips. He released her, she danced away, he caught her extended hand, and she did a slow spin, ending up trapped in his arms, her back to his chest. She rested her head against his shoulder while pressing her bottom against his growing erection.

"You want it this way?" he said, nipping at her earlobe. His hands flowed over her belly, settled on her hips and yanked her against him.

"Whatever way you want it."

"Aye," he breathed in her ear. "Whatever I want, my wife gives me."

Moments later, she was on her knees in the bed, her cheek pressed to the pillows, her hips held still by his grip.

"I love you," he said, entering her. "So very much do I love you," he went on, thrusting into her again. "So much, so much, so much…" He picked up pace, she clutched at the sheets, meeting his thrusts as well as she could.

They lay close together afterwards, Matthew's body like an outer peel round hers. He found her hand and braided his fingers with hers.

"He's hurting," he said, sounding sad.

"Who?"

"Ian."

"Yes," Alex said. "And so is she."

189

★

Betty woke, blinked, and was ridiculously happy to be here, no matter that she had to share a bed with Agnes, no matter that already at this early hour the house was loud with noise, several young voices talking and laughing in the kitchen. She dressed, stuck her feet into clogs, and near on danced across the yard to the stables and the waiting cows. And Ian.

"I heard you had a letter from Jacob." Ian tugged at Betty's thick braid in passing. She didn't reply, lugging a stool and an empty pail to the next cow in line. She liked milking, and, according to Matthew, she was right good at it for someone who'd never tried it until the advanced age of sixteen. Betty leaned her forehead against the warm flank of the cow, used the cloth that hung at her apron to wipe the teats clean, and took them in a firm grip, using her whole hand to tease the milk from the udder.

"So what did he write?" Ian asked from where he was sitting three cows down.

"That he was in London and aimed to stay there awhile. He hoped to see if he could find a physician to apprentice himself to."

"Fool. A physician is an educated man, a university man. Nothing else?" he asked after a while.

"He sent me a ring."

"A ring? Let me see!" Ian's head appeared for an instant above the cows.

Betty held up an empty finger.

"Ah, it didn't fit."

"Yes, it did. It's just that I'm not sure I want to wear it." She met Ian's eyes.

"Oh." Ian ducked out of sight. "Why not?"

Betty carried the full pail out into the passage, and massaged her hands for an instant before finding another bucket and moving towards the last cow.

"I don't know. Maybe it's because I don't feel married." The silence was very heavy for some time. "He..." Betty swallowed. "Somehow he convinced me to do something I'm not sure I really wanted, and then he just left."

Ian's head reappeared, his eyes unfathomable in the weak light of the stable. "He shouldn't have done it, lass. No one will think the worse of you if you decide to break the contracts."

The moment she did, her father would be there with another suitor, and that was something Betty definitely didn't want. And yet...she gnawed her lip. Among her few private belongings lay a half-written letter to Jacob, and as she sat with her cheek against the comforting warmth of the cow, she made up her mind. She would write to Jacob and tell him she no longer wanted this.

Once she was done with the milking, she followed Ian out, carrying the heavy pails over to the dairy shed. She watched him move, the way his muscles shifted under his worn shirt, and she wanted so very much to lay a hand on him, blushing at these sinful thoughts. Very rarely did she confront the dawning realisation that she, Betty Hancock – or was it Graham? – had fallen in love with a married man, a man nine years her senior and Jacob's brother to boot. When she did, she did what she did now. She closed her eyes, and for some seconds allowed herself to be swept away to a world where such a love might be possible.

"Malcolm might just as well be their son." Jenny shrugged off Ian's arm. "He eats with their three youngest, he sleeps with them, he takes the holy weekly bath with them... I hate living here. Why can't we just go back to Forest Spring?" She was about to fragment under this unbearable pressure. Her eyes strayed after Patrick whenever she saw him, all of her wanting him to turn towards her, command her to come to him.

"You know why," Ian said. "You heard about the Chisholms."

Jenny swore under her breath. "Indians! Why don't we just kill them all?"

"What a terrible thing to say." Alex entered the kitchen, carrying a basket of eggs.

"But the way they've behaved lately doesn't greatly endear them to us, does it?" Ian said.

"No." Alex sighed. "How is poor Andrew Chisholm?"

"He won't walk again and his poor wife…" Ian shook his head.

"She shouldn't have bit him." Alex sat down beside them.

"It served," Ian pointed out. "It stopped them from further hurting her husband."

"Thank heavens three of them were killed – three less to worry about," Jenny said.

"And now they're most aggravated, and we don't know where they'll show up next, which is why we're staying here." From the look on Ian's face, Jenny knew it was futile to argue. She heaved herself onto her feet and left the room without a word.

Once in the yard, Jenny made for the gap between the privy and the barn, throwing an angry look at the half-built cabin that was soon to be her home. She puffed as she crawled under the slats that fenced the paddock, clumsily got to her feet, and made for the woods beyond.

The child kicked inside of her, and Jenny had to stop for a moment to regain her breath, clasping her hands protectively around the baby.

All around her, the woods stood in bright greens. Orioles and cardinals whistled from the thickets, blackbirds chirped and squabbled higher up the trees, and the ground was dotted with the white of trilliums and the heavy heads of early lupines. Not that she cared: Jenny barged through the undergrowth, aiming for the river. She stood staring down at the swollen flowing waters. Maybe she should just walk into it and let the current take her. It would be quick, and she'd heard drowning was a painless way to die. No, she didn't want to die; not yet, not now. She hurled a stone into the river, sat down on the log Matthew had placed there as a bench of sorts, hid her face in her hands, and cried.

Betty was picking flowers, meandering through the woods closest to the farm. She broke off a twig of new birch leaves and added it to her sizeable bouquet, wondering whether to give it to Alex or Mrs Parson. To her surprise, she could hear the river and realised she'd walked in a circle, lost in her daydreams.

Jenny was sitting by the water, and Betty hung back. Since that episode in October, Jenny had avoided her just as much as she'd avoided Jenny, and, even if she could see Jenny was crying, Betty suspected her presence was not what Jenny needed or wanted.

She was considering what to do when Patrick appeared on the path above them, leading one of the mules. He came to an abrupt stop at the sight of Jenny, left the mule, and went over to where Jenny was sitting. He didn't touch her; he didn't seem to talk to her either. He just sat down beside her and rested his hand close to hers. Two little fingers brushed against each other and hooked together. Very, very slowly, Jenny leaned her head against his shoulder, and, just as slowly, his arm came up to hold her close, his other hand sliding up to rest on her belly.

Betty sank down into a crouch. Poor, poor Ian.

Chapter 22

"What should I do?" Betty asked Mrs Parson, once she'd finished telling her what she had witnessed back in October as well as the recent tender scene down by the river.

Mrs Parson arranged her flowers in silence, deep in thought. "What do you think you should do?"

"Tell Ian?"

Mrs Parson shook her head. "That's not for you to do, lass." She exhaled loudly. "You must tell Matthew, aye?"

Betty looked at her, aghast. "I can't talk to him about... Couldn't you?"

Mrs Parson sat back down in her chair. "Nay, that I can't. It's not I that have seen anything, is it? But if you can't tell Matthew, then you must tell Alex."

"Bloody hell," was what Alex said, feeling how her knees weakened so abruptly she had to sit down. "And you're sure you saw them having sex back in October?"

"Sex?" Betty looked confused.

"Fornication," Alex elucidated.

All of her twisting, Betty repeated her earlier description, and Alex had to agree it left very little room for an alternative interpretation.

"At the time, I thought he might have forced her, and she begged me not to tell on account of the shame always being the woman's." Betty pulled at her lower lip in a gesture that made her look remarkably like her father. "Now I'm not that sure – although at first she seemed terribly aggrieved with him, kicking and hitting at him." She moved restlessly in her seat. "Was I wrong not to tell?"

"Hmm?" Alex looked at her blankly. "Oh! No, no, of course you weren't. She asked you to keep it quiet." It would have been much easier if Betty had held to that promise, Alex reflected, because now there was no way back – glossing it over and pretending nothing had ever happened was out. She'd have to tell Matthew and then… She quailed.

Matthew's reaction was one of absolute stillness. In the shaft of sunlight falling in through the wide open barn doors, his eyes went a deep gold, his pupils shrinking down to pinpricks. It made him look rather sinister; the impression further helped along by the way his hand gripped the hammer.

"So now we know." He sat down with a thud.

"Unfortunately." Alex sat down beside him and scrubbed her cheek against his shoulder. "Oh God, what do we do?"

He stared down at the floor. "I have no choice," he said in a voice that was on the point of breaking. "I can't let this lie. I must tell him."

"Or not – after all, it might work itself out. If we send Patrick away and—"

"I have to," he cut her off. "I can't keep something like this from him. It would be wrong." He bowed his head further and mumbled something.

"What?" Alex asked.

"I was just quoting the Holy Writ: *Father, if thou be willing remove this cup from me…* But he won't, will he?" Matthew stood up, and from the slump of his shoulders to the way he held his hands, Alex could see how heavy this burden was.

"Do you want me to come with you?"

Matthew extended his hand to her. "I don't think I can do it without you."

It felt like a wake, this slow trudge up to where Ian was hewing logs into shape for his cabin. He saw them coming, and his right arm dropped, the axe falling out of his hand. He looked from one to the other in a way that reminded Alex so much of how he'd been as a boy, a child torn in two because no one could tell him for sure who his father was. She smiled wryly. To her, it had always been obvious that Ian was Matthew's, not Luke's – every single line of the tall body facing them screamed it out loud: that he was Matthew Graham's son. His son in more ways than one, Alex shivered, because now they were to tell him that his wife had betrayed him, just as his mother had betrayed his father.

"Jenny," Ian whispered. "Something has happened to Jenny and the babe."

Alex's heart went out to him – to them both – as Matthew went over to his immobilised son and wrapped his arms around him.

"Not as such," Matthew said, and Ian slumped. Matthew led him over to sit, keeping an arm around him. It was terrible. Even for her, standing to the side, it was almost unbearable to hear Matthew tell his son that his son's wife was being unfaithful, and it was made even worse by the brittle look in Ian's eyes, a pleading expression that begged them to laugh and tell him this was all in jest.

It didn't register at first. Ian heard what Da was saying, but somehow he couldn't string the words together into sentences that made sense. And then his brain connected the random words into a meaningful whole, and for a moment the world tilted.

"Betty?" Ian kicked at the ground. "She saw?"

His parents nodded, and he kicked again. Was that why the lass looked at him the way she did? Was she sorry for him, when he'd thought her in love with him? When Mama told him about that day in early March up at Forest Spring, he flew to his feet.

"You knew already then, and you didn't tell me?"

"Not for sure. How could we tell you something like this without knowing for sure?" Mama placed a hand on his sleeve. "But now we do know, and we have no choice but to tell you."

"Thank you," he said, twisting out of her hold.

He sat down beside Da again, and felt a strong arm come round to hold him close. It didn't help, because all of him was disintegrating, small parts of him floating off into the air and disappearing like melting snowflakes. How could she do this to him? Whore! His hands knotted themselves, all of him was shaking, and had he had her in front of him he would have… His hands itched. He was within his rights to punish her, to whip her until she bled, and throw her out to face the world, and, God, he wanted to, very much did he want to. Patrick he was going to hurt, that much he knew, but he didn't really care about him – it was her betrayal that had him swimming in a sea of burning rage. He lowered his head and concentrated on breathing. One breath, two breaths, three breaths…

"The babe might still be mine," he said after a long, strained silence.

"Aye, but we'll never know for sure," Da said.

Ian shrugged and looked away. "Apt, isn't it?" He attempted a laugh but failed miserably. "Here I spend most of my childhood not knowing who my father is – and Mam couldn't tell me either – and now I am to welcome yet another ambiguous child into the world."

"You're my son," Da said, gripping his shoulder.

Ian shook himself free. "You don't know that; not for sure."

Da opened his mouth to protest but Ian waved his hand at him. "You're my da. I made that choice very long ago. But we will never know." He got to his feet again, picked up his axe, and returned to the log he had been working on when he saw them. "I want to think," he said, sinking the axe hard into the wood. "Alone."

He sent wood chips flying; he chopped and chopped, venting anger and humiliation on the length of timber at his feet. He choked on his rage, a hard knot working itself up and down his gullet. God, how gullible she must have found him! He drove the axe head into the wood, and worked until his shirt stuck to his back.

It helped to gouge his way through the log. With each stroke, the red anger inside of him receded, the heat that threatened to boil over cooled, until he was left with a controlled, icy rage that lay like a lid across the angry whipping thing in his guts. The babe, he reminded himself as he envisioned various scenarios, he must think of the wean. And so Ian made up his mind to not do anything at all – for now.

"She'll be birthing soon," he told Da with a callous shrug, "and then I'll see."

It cost him to keep his voice this low and matter-of-fact, and it cost him even more to nod in the direction of Patrick and find a smile for Jenny, but he did, even if he set Malcolm beside him as a bulwark between Jenny and himself. Nor did he attempt to touch her, or converse with her beyond the small talk over the kitchen table. Once he'd finished his food, he told the table at large he'd be working late in the carpentry shed, ruffled Malcolm's hair, and escaped outside.

"Another evening like that and I'll burst," Alex said to Matthew later. She tucked the quilts around Adam's small body and smiled down at her three sons, lying so close together in their bed. At Ian's insistence, Malcolm was sleeping downstairs with his parents, and Alex guessed he would be wedged between his mother and father, however little bed space that left for Ian and Jenny.

"If he wants it this way then that's the way it'll be," Matthew replied, trailing her into the girls' room.

Ruth as always slept on her back, one hand thrown high above her head, the other resting on her chest, while Sarah was her normal whirlwind self, the bedclothes tangled round her legs. Matthew freed quilts and sheets, ensuring Ruth got her fair share back, while Alex smoothed down hair and kissed brows.

"What will Peter say?" he asked once they were in their bedroom.

"Nothing compared to what Elizabeth would have said," Alex said. "Her favourite daughter to so shame the family."

"Mmm." Matthew worked the willow twig over his teeth, splashed some water in his face and retired to sit on the bed.

"They'd have flayed her." Alex sniffed at her latest concoction. "You like it?" She held out the stone jar to him.

Matthew smacked his lips together. "It makes me think of a nice piece of pork." Right; not quite the effect she wanted to achieve. Alex shoved the jar to the side and decided to go easier on the thyme next time round.

"Ian might," Matthew said. He stretched out on the bed, gesturing for her to join him.

"Might what?" Alex slid down to lie beside him.

"Whip her. He'd be within his rights."

"Bloody barbaric... Hey, you've stolen my pillow." She made a grab for it.

"I like this pillow." He sank his head into it.

"So do I," she said, but gave up at the sight of his smirk. She'd get it back tomorrow anyway.

"So how would you see Ian deal with his adulterous wife?" Matthew asked, spooning himself tight around her.

"I don't know...divorce her, I suppose." Alex felt a twinge of pity for Jenny, soon to be cast out on her own.

"And the bairns?"

"The children stay with him; at least, Malcolm does." She turned to face him. "It is a grievous thing to take a baby from its mother."

"Aye, but it's his right."

"And what rights does she have?" Alex asked, even if she already knew the answer.

"None." Matthew rolled over onto his back. "An adulterous wife has no rights, no rights at all."

It gave Ian very little satisfaction to exact his revenge on Patrick. He looked down at the gasping man and was disgusted: with Jenny, with Patrick, but just as much with himself for having set upon an unsuspecting man. Patrick groaned and righted himself to a sitting position.

"What was that for?" Patrick slurred.

"You know why. You have been making free with my wife." Patrick began shaking his head. Ian loomed over him, hands fisted. "Don't lie to me."

199

Patrick licked his lips, looked away. "I never meant it to happen," he croaked, his shaking hands held up in a conciliatory gesture.

"Since when?"

"Last summer." A taunting look appeared in Patrick's eyes, and Ian's next blows had blood spurting from Patrick's nose, his mouth.

"Get out," Ian said. "Get yourself off our land while you can, aye?"

Patrick fled.

He didn't like it how disapproving Mama looked when he recounted what he'd done to Patrick.

"What would you do then?" Ian challenged. "In your time?"

"Well, I wouldn't have kicked the crap out of him – or her in my case. Divorce her, that's what you'd have done in my time – and found out if the child was yours, which isn't an option at present." She came over to join him by the workbench. "The first question you have to ask yourself is if you love her. Love her enough to try again."

Ian cleared his throat. "I've tried. All through these last months, I've tried, but she...and now it's too late. I can't forgive her for this." He threw the piece of wood he was presently working on into a corner.

There was another complication as well, a complication in the form of wild reddish-brown hair and eyes to match, but he pushed that thought away from him. He had never acted upon it.

"If it had been the once, or at least no more than a couple of times, then maybe I could. But from what Patrick confessed, it has been going on for nigh on a year. A year of putting horns on me and laughing at me behind my back."

"I don't think Jenny's been laughing at you. She cares too much for you."

"Not enough to remain faithful. Not enough to ensure the wean she's carrying is mine." A bitter taste flooded his mouth. "No, I don't love her enough to try again. I don't love her at all, not after what she's done to me."

"And the baby?"

"The wean is mine." Ian went over to stand in the doorway.

"You don't know that," Mama said from behind him.

"It's mine. I won't let it go." His eyes rested for a moment on Naomi, who walked by outside with Tom tucked neatly into a shawl and Betty laughing by her side. As if on cue, the lass turned her head in his direction, and for an instant those red-brown eyes met his, sending a flash of heat through him.

"Just as long as you hold to that." Mama ducked under his arm and turned to face him. "A child deserves to know where it belongs – but I don't need to tell you that, do I?"

"Nay, that you don't." He stretched out his hand and tweaked at a curl that had escaped from her thick bun.

"Mama," he whispered in a broken voice. "My mama."

"Always," she said, standing on her toes to kiss his brow.

Chapter 23

"Where's Patrick?" Jenny asked in a casual tone. "I haven't seen him of late."

"Gone." Alex gave Jenny an appraising look. The baby was due any day now, the whole belly having sunk down to hover just above her pubic bone.

"Gone?" Jenny's fingers whitened with pressure when she clenched them round the handle to the baby basket she was presently lining. "Why?"

"I have no idea," Alex lied and went back to her cooking.

Jenny made a strange sound, like a muffled honk, and with a muttered excuse fled the room. Alex was overwhelmed by a wave of compassion for her. How alone she must feel, even more now that Ian so clearly avoided her, exchanging a minimum of words with her, no more.

"Oh God, what a mess," Alex said to Mrs Parson once the kitchen was empty of anyone but them.

"Aye, you can say that again." Mrs Parson nodded, frowning down at her knitting. She used her fingers to ensure she hadn't dropped any stitches before going on.

"You do have spectacles," Alex informed her.

"Spectacles? They're for old people, no?" Mrs Parson snorted.

Alex grinned. The old woman was pushing seventy, but apart from a general stiffening of her joints, she was almost disgustingly healthy.

"Will he keep her?" she asked Alex.

Alex shook her head. No, Ian had made up his mind, and with every day she could see him hardening his heart towards Jenny, his eyes regarding her with an impassiveness that Alex found quite disturbing. At least Jenny wouldn't be destitute, some of her jointure being settled on her in case of divorce. Luckily, as she suspected Jenny would not receive much of a welcome should she choose to go back to Leslie's Crossing. Little Constance would have a field day.

"Enough," Matthew said, drawing the oxen to a halt. "Tired?" He smiled down at his son.

David straightened up from the crouch in which he'd been working for the last few hours and nodded. "So much stone," he moaned, looking down at his reddened hands.

"And just as much there." Matthew nodded at the next patch of half-cleared land. "But this we can plant this afternoon and then do that tomorrow, aye?"

David nodded again, boyish shoulders sloping downwards.

Matthew sighed inside. The laddie was too young to have to work this hard, but there was no choice, not now that Patrick was gone. A few weeks, no more, and then the new fields would all be cleared and planted, and he could release his son to go back to playing.

They were coming up the river path, the oxen ambling along, when a sudden movement caught Matthew's eyes. David squawked and took hold of Matthew's hand. On the other side of the river stood a group of Indians, and a tremor coursed through Matthew. These were not Susquehannock. These were Iroquois, and just the name had the hair along his spine rising. One of the men took a step forward and raised a hand, and after a couple of heartbeats, Matthew smiled in relieved recognition.

"Run, lad," he said to David. "Run and tell your mama we have guests for dinner."

"Guests?" David breathed.

"Aye, lad, guests."

For a moment, Matthew thought Alex was about to hug Qaachow, but at the last moment she remembered herself, giving their Indian friend a nod instead.

"Qaachow," she said, "it's been years."

The former Susquehannock tribal leader bowed back. He was much greyer than last time they'd seen him, his body far too lean, with a disfiguring scar on his right arm.

"What happened?" Alex asked.

"Snake bite," he said in English that sounded rusty, not at all as fluent as it once had been. Mayhap he had little opportunity to practise it where he lived now. Qaachow extracted a small pouch and handed it to Alex. "From Thistledown."

Alex shook out several seeds into her hand.

"Squash," Qaachow said, "and beans."

"Thank you." Alex curtsied, making Matthew grin at the sheer incongruity of the gesture. His guest seemed to agree, smiling as he bent his naked torso in a slight bow in her direction before turning back to him.

"How is your son?" Matthew asked.

Qaachow smiled, his eyes travelling over the younger Graham boys. "He's well." He beckoned to Samuel, who at first hung back but, after a glance from Matthew, obediently stepped forward.

"This is for you." Qaachow held out a small pouch decorated with quillwork and beads. "It contains your Indian name and spirit. A gift from your foster brother and me, your foster father."

Samuel received it carefully. Matthew smiled crookedly. The lad knew that he had an Indian foster brother, having heard often enough how Mama had saved the little Indian baby from starvation, but not until this moment had Samuel realised that, as a consequence, he had an Indian foster father. Matthew swallowed down on the lump that was clogging his throat. His wee laddie, and from the way Qaachow was eyeing him, it was clear the Indian leader hadn't forgotten Matthew's promise all those years ago.

"My name?" Samuel said. "My name is Samuel."

Qaachow smiled down at him. "Your Indian brother and you are like bear cubs, twins to the same mother. So he is Little Bear and you are White Bear."

"White Bear," Samuel repeated and hung the amulet pouch around his neck.

★

204

Alex watched all this from a distance, clenching her hands in her skirts to stop herself from doing something dangerous – and rude – such as rushing over to tear the amulet pouch off her son and throw it in the river. She made an effort, pasted a bland smile on her face, and invited their guests to dinner.

As always, Qaachow refused to step inside, but he studied the new house with interest, complimenting Matthew on its general size. Mark and Ian set up trestles outside, and Alex served the Indians and her men bread and meat and beer, before retreating to leave them space to talk.

In the kitchen, Betty and Naomi were staring through the window, with Agnes hanging over their shoulders.

"Has he come to take the lad with him?" Mrs Parson piped up from her corner.

"The lad?" Alex's heart did some very strange arrhythmic things in her chest. "No, no, that's not yet. Not until Samuel is about twelve or so. By then, he'll probably have forgotten."

"You think?" Mrs Parson snorted. "I think not." She lowered her voice and told Alex that, in her opinion, it had been a rash and foolish thing Matthew had done, promising Qaachow to have the raising of Samuel for a year.

Alex just nodded. She looked over in the direction of Samuel, proudly showing off his new accessory to his brothers and nephew. White Bear, she thought, and in her mind she saw a polar bear raise itself on its hind legs and stare at her before it dropped back down on all fours and turned its back on her to walk away. She shuddered, and Mrs Parson put a hand on her arm.

"Nothing," Alex assured her with a weak smile. "Just a goose walking over my grave."

Mrs Parson gave her a very strange look. "You don't have a grave."

"No, not yet," Alex said.

"Adopted?" Matthew said. "So you're no longer Susquehannock?"

"The Susquehannock are a splintered remnant of a once

great tribe," Qaachow said, "and I have done what I must to ensure the survival of my people. So, now I'm an adopted son of the Mohawk, and my son speaks Mohawk, not Susquehannock, as do all our children. We're forgetting our language and our customs, for it is as Iroquois we now live and fight." It came out with a bitter edge to it, accompanied by a lingering look at Matthew's fields and home, land that had once belonged to Qaachow's tribe.

"And is that why you are here? To fight?" Matthew asked.

"We fight against the Piscataway. They have ever been a thorn in the side of the Susquehannock."

"And you attack the odd colonist," Matthew said.

"The odd one," Qaachow said, "but it wasn't us that harmed your old neighbour."

"Nay, but it may have been people of your tribe."

"It may have been." Qaachow gave Matthew a dark look. "And, on the other hand, it might not. A white man in buckskins and with feathers in his hair looks verily like an Indian in the dark."

"What is it you're saying?"

Qaachow hitched one shoulder. "A band of white wolves killing white men. They sell the children and women into slavery, they steal the horses and the cows, and all is blamed on us." And not only that, he said, at times they raided Indian villages as well, taking the young women with them and leaving the men dead or dying behind.

Matthew made a disgusted face. Yes, he could well believe it could happen – he knew it happened, courtesy of men such as the Burleys.

"Brothers?" he asked.

"Brothers: three of them. One of them has a badly scarred face. We drove them off some weeks ago."

"Ah." Matthew's stomach shrank into a throbbing knot. They'd been here – again. More dogs, he decided, more muskets, and...

Qaachow placed a hand on his shoulder, dark eyes very close to his own. "We chased them all the way back across the great river, into what you call Virginia."

Matthew's shoulders softened with relief.

Qaachow seemed to consider this particular subject as dealt with, nodding in the direction of where Samuel was playing with his brothers and cousins. "He's a fine boy, tall and strong."

"Aye," Matthew agreed, not at all liking just how hungrily Qaachow regarded his son.

Qaachow stood up, and at his short command his men did as well, moving over to stand in a loose group some feet away from the table.

"I'll come for him," Qaachow said to Matthew. "He'll make a fine Indian."

"Not yet," Matthew said, hating it that there was a pleading note to his voice.

"No, not yet – but soon." With that, Qaachow was gone, him and his band of braves evaporating into the surrounding trees.

"Will I be an Indian then?" Samuel said in a small voice, rubbing his face against Matthew's chest. They were sitting on the bench under the white oak, finishing off what little remained of the food Alex had served their guests.

"Nay, you won't. You'll live with them for a while and learn their ways, and then you'll come back to us." Matthew stroked his boy over the knobbly back, pressing him close.

"Maybe I don't want to."

"I've given my word, lad. And you might find it quite an adventure." Matthew kissed the dark head and met Alex's eyes. What had at the time seemed nothing more than a gesture towards a man it behoved him to keep as his friend was now becoming a most uncomfortable commitment. He didn't want his son to be taken away and grow up among the heathen, but he had seen it in Qaachow's eyes: it was Samuel that ensured Graham's Garden wouldn't be touched by the Indians – or the Burleys – and Qaachow intended to claim his prize.

He could see it in her movements, in her eyes, how Alex

wanted to take him by the hand and lead him away for a talk. He knew exactly what it was she wanted to discuss – Samuel – and also what she needed him to say. Lies, he sighed, she needed lies; worthless reassurances that of course Qaachow would not claim on his promise – reassurances he didn't know how to give her, not now.

She waited until they were alone, cleared her throat, and looked at him beseechingly, eyes the colour of cornflowers at dawn. She opened her mouth; he held his breath. Just at that moment, Agnes burst from the house, asking the mistress to hurry because Jenny's waters had broken.

"Ian?" Betty shoved the door open. "Ian? Mama Alex says that you must come. Jenny has begun her labour."

Ian didn't reply and went on with what he was doing.

"Ian?"

"She can do it without me." Ian kept his back turned. He had no intention of sitting in the kitchen waiting, while his false wife birthed a child that might or might not be his.

"Oh," Betty said, edging closer. "Don't you want to be there?"

"No." He set down a pail of slops for the sow and scratched her behind the ears. The pen was full of half-grown piglets, and Betty bent to fondle soft ears, scratch at bristling backs before straightening up.

"But maybe…"

"Didn't you hear?" he exploded. "I don't want to be there. I don't care!"

"That's not true," she replied, coming even closer. "If you didn't, you wouldn't be this upset."

He laughed hollowly and rested back against one of the walls, crossing his arms. "Mayhap I'm upset because she's cuckolded me."

Betty blushed at his matter-of-fact statement, but came to stand beside him. "I'm sorry," she said clumsily.

"Sorry?" He turned to face her. "Is that why you tag after me like a wee dog, because you pity me?" He winced inside at the hurt expression that flew up her face. "Well, is it?" he challenged, overwhelmed by a need to know.

"No," she breathed, her eyes luminous. "No, I don't think this is pity." With that, she stood on her toes and pressed her lips against his. A soft kiss, warm and tentative, promising and daring, her tongue flitting out to run over his lips. For an instant, her tongue met his, and then she wheeled and ran.

Ian sank into a crouch and groaned. The wee lass loved him, and, God help him, he thought he might love her. A hypocrite, he thought with dark amusement, that was what he was. So quick to condemn Jenny for loving elsewhere, and all the while this russet lass had been worming herself bit by bit into his heart.

"A perfect girl." Alex handed the child to Ian. He nodded, settling the weight of the child in his arms.

"Elizabeth," Jenny said weakly from the bed. "I want to call her Elizabeth."

Ian shook his head. "Nay, this is Margaret." He handed the girl back to Alex and left the room.

"He knows, doesn't he?" Jenny said. "All of you know."

"More or less," Alex said.

"Stupid girl," Jenny hissed. "Why didn't she keep her mouth shut?"

"Why didn't you keep your legs shut?" Mrs Parson said.

"He made me, he forced me – ask Betty."

"And that is why you didn't tell?" Mrs Parson's voice dripped with incredulity. She moved over to study the child. "So, it was just that once, was it?"

Jenny attempted a feeble nod but averted her eyes.

"And you can swear on your immortal soul that this wee lass is Ian's daughter?" Mrs Parson peered down into the little face, ran a honeyed finger inside its mouth to verify the palate was whole.

"Yes," Jenny whispered.

"You lie," Mrs Parson said, "and your lover admitted it all before he left."

"What will happen to me?" Jenny asked Alex in

a surprisingly level voice, staring at the door that was still reverberating after Mrs Parson had slammed it shut.

"I'm not sure. I suppose you must ask Ian that."

Jenny held her little girl close, one finger tracing the small rosebud mouth, the finely formed eyebrows, the nose.

"I truly don't know. I have no idea who fathered her." She raised her face to look Alex straight in the eyes. "But at least I know she's mine."

"Not that it will help her much," Alex sighed, sitting down to a late meal in the kitchen. Matthew set down a plate of fried eggs before her, got her some bread and a large slice of cheese.

"No," he said. "What a terrible way to be welcomed into the world: no congratulations, no rejoicing, only this compact, heavy silence."

Alex swallowed the last of her eggs and nodded. "Where's Ian?"

"Out." Matthew waved at the blue May night. "With a stone bottle of beer and my flask full of whisky."

"Ah. Should we go after him?"

"Nay." Matthew placed an arm around his wife and drew her close. "What a long day."

Too right. Her head wheeled with Qaachow, Jenny, the new baby and Ian – her beloved son who was hurting so badly and whom she couldn't help – not at all.

Chapter 24

Jacob was very pleased with himself. Helen had appreciated his little gift, and after a couple of agreeable hours spent in her company, he was hurrying in the direction of Whitehall, tugging at his coat as he went.

Since that first interview with his uncle, he'd been invited back a couple of times, and he was looking forward to an afternoon with a man he found as fascinating now as the first time he saw him. Everything about Uncle Luke breathed success: his clothes, his furnishings, the quality of his horses, his unobtrusive servants… Nothing about Uncle Luke breathed happiness, rather the reverse, and to Jacob this was something of a conundrum.

"He lacks a woman," Helen told him when he tried to explain this to her. "I'd wager he still grieves for his wife, his one single love." She sighed happily at the sheer romance of it all, making Jacob silently wonder if she was feeble in the head. There was no lack of women in his uncle's life; that much Jacob had quickly understood from the odd comment made by Luke, mainly along the lines that, should Jacob feel the urge, it was best he came to his uncle, who would see him introduced to some of the more reputable establishments in London.

If Jacob was fascinated by Luke, that was nothing compared to how entranced Luke was by this nephew of his. Cheeky, bright and full of bubbling energy, Jacob reminded him very little of an older brother he snidely remembered as somewhat dull and dreary. He supposed the lad must take after his mother, except that, at times, Jacob tilted his head just like Matthew did, or pinched the bridge of his nose while frowning down at the chessboard in a way that made

Luke experience a most unwelcome sensation of loss for a brother he'd expended so much energy in hating.

Sometimes he'd watch the two lads, his Charles and Jacob, and the similarities between them were such that they could have been brothers, so clearly stemming from the same root. Mostly though, it was Jacob's sheer boldness that captivated him, from the fact that he had set off to see the world with nothing but a shilling or two in his pouch, to how he had managed to carve himself a place here in London, mainly due to his engaging manner and quick head.

Some discreet enquiries had brought back the information that Master Castain was much taken with the lad, lauding him for his tenacity and diligence. Strangely enough, that made Luke proud – odd seeing as Jacob wasn't his. He did some further sleuthing, and discovered that the lad had found a welcoming bed as well, and Luke chuckled, quite convinced dear brother Matthew wouldn't approve, in particular as the lad was married.

"It holds," Jacob said, "marriage by consent, and it was consummated. She's my wife." They were strolling up Lombard Street, Luke having business to conduct at the Royal Exchange.

"You're too young for that." Luke laughed. "Far too young to tie yourself to someone for life." He took a hasty step to the side to avoid being spattered by mud as a cart trundled by, having to grab Jacob by the arm to pull him out of the thoroughfare.

"Oh, aye? But you were even younger when you bedded Margaret that first time."

"That was different. I had known her since we were bairns. And we didn't wed at the time."

"But you wanted to," Jacob said. "Mama always says how much misery could have been avoided had old Malcolm made you wed her instead of throwing you out."

Luke gave him a surprised look. That was mightily generous of Alex, all things considered.

"She wasn't rich enough," Luke said, feeling a wave of ancient, bile-green rage rise through him. But the old fool had paid. He smiled coldly: one well-placed push and Da had gone into the ice-cold water of the overflowing millpond, and Luke had watched as he drowned.

"So what does she look like, this Betty of yours?" he said to change the subject. He grimaced as he stepped around a stinking pile of ordure, nimbly leapt aside when a sedan chair came rushing by.

Jacob shrugged. "Brown eyes, brown hair, and freckled, all over like." He smiled. "She doesn't like her hair – I think it's nice, soft and curly, all fuzzy."

"Ah." Luke nodded, thinking the lass sounded rather plain. "And if you come back and she's wed elsewhere?"

Jacob came to an abrupt halt, causing a man to barge into him. There were several minutes of raised voices as Jacob went down on his knees to retrieve the man's spilled wares.

"Wed elsewhere?" Jacob looked at his muddied breeches. "She can't – she's wed to me."

"And her father can tear up the contracts as easily as that." Luke snapped his fingers. "Would you mind?"

Jacob's brow furrowed into a concentrated frown. "I would be devastated," he said, making Luke laugh out loud.

"Nay, you wouldn't, Jacob Graham, and you're an awful liar, you are." He clapped his nephew on the back. "If you truly loved her as much as you say, you wouldn't be spending the odd night in Mistress Wythe's bed, would you?" They had by now reached Cheapside, as always thronged with people, and he took hold of Jacob's arm and guided him to the right, towards his destination.

"Oh, so you were celibate, were you? All those years when you were away from Margaret?" Jacob threw back.

"No, but mostly I paid for it, and rarely I cared. But you care for…Helen, is it not? You buy her trinkets, bring her the odd flower." Luke smiled at the way Jacob's face had turned a bright pink. "I'm not judging you. I am but pointing out that maybe it was all a bit too rash."

"I've given Betty my word," Jacob said stonily.

"Aye, but what if she doesn't want it?"

Jacob looked away. He seemed on the verge of replying, but whatever he'd intended to say was drowned in a shriek. Luke frowned when he saw the horse and the man it was dragging behind him. Cheapside was lined with spectators, loud, angry people screaming at the wretch that had no possibility of avoiding the rotting foodstuffs that were thrown at him, fastened as he was to a primitive wooden frame.

"Another one?" Jacob sounded dismayed and moved closer to Luke.

"It would seem so." Yet another papist accused of one more grievous sin after the other, foremost amongst them a lurking intent to kill the king – or a magistrate, a reverend, a good honest Anglican merchant. Luke would wager a sizeable purse that the broken man presently being transported to his execution was as innocent as all the other papists that had been killed in recent years, but that mattered not one whit, not when the people were baying for blood.

"What kind of king condones such?" Jacob said. "Look at him, tortured and beaten until he admitted to whatever was said of him."

"Hush, lad!" Luke threw a nervous look at the men closest to them. "And it's not the king," he added in a low voice. "His Majesty had yon troublemonger Oates jailed nigh on two years ago on account of his perjury." Luke moved his nephew along by the simple expedient of placing his hand on Jacob's back and pushing.

"The people wanted him freed," Luke said, once they were out of the press of people. "It's parliament, not the king, that condones what is being done to the papists."

"So why doesn't the king stop it?"

"He can't," Luke said shortly. From the way Jacob looked at him, Luke could see his nephew found this unbelievable. Luke gave him an irritated look, considering whether to launch himself in defence of his royal master. No use, he concluded: the finer aspects of politics would be lost on someone as young as Jacob.

★

214

Charles and Jacob quickly became close, and Jacob looked forward to Charlie's frequent visits to his workplace, enjoying having someone to talk to while he created bed after bed of sweet-smelling herbs and plants. Mostly, Charlie would beg Jacob for details about his huge family, listening with particular interest when Jacob talked about Ian.

"I never knew him," Charlie said, "and Father has never spoken much of him. But Mam did – until the day she died, she would talk about him, her Ian."

"Do you miss her?" Jacob asked, throwing his cousin a look.

Charlie lobbed a clod of earth in the direction of the water gate. "I do, and so does Father. At times—" Charlie broke off.

"At times what?"

"At times I wake up at night, and I can hear him talking to her."

"She's a ghost?" Jacob asked, much impressed.

"Of course she isn't! Father talks to the portrait he has of her."

"Ah," Jacob nodded, thinking this was rather strange behaviour. If someone was dead, they were dead. "Mayhap it's time he finds a new wife."

"A new wife means half-brothers and sisters, and I have no desire to see myself or my sisters displaced in Father's affection." Charlie threw yet another clod of earth, this time hitting the two-headed rhinoceros that decorated the water gate.

Jacob laughed. "Why would you be? I don't think Mama loves me less because of my younger siblings."

"But that's what happened to Ian," Charles blurted before going a bright red – rather unbecoming, given the colour of his hair.

"It did?" Jacob had never heard the full story.

Charles squirmed, admitting that he didn't know; he'd pieced this together on his own, snatched comments from the servants, the very long ramblings of his mother the few times she had drunk excessively...

"I was born and Father no longer wanted him," Charles summarised succinctly.

"Oh." Jacob shook his head. "But he shouldn't have been with your father to begin with. He's Da's son." This was all very bewildering.

"Umm," Charles replied.

"And you're definitely Luke's son," Jacob went on with a grin. "But if you prefer, we can set him up with a widow instead. An old widow."

"Set him up?" Charles squeaked. "With an old lady?"

Jacob hitched his shoulders. "He's no spring chicken, is he?"

"We don't serve working women," Master Castain told Jacob one evening. "It will bring us into disrepute."

"Working women?" Jacob pretended confusion. "So no seamstresses, no serving girls, no cooks, no—"

"You know what I mean," Master Castain interrupted him.

"She was in search of something to help with her cough," Jacob reprimanded. "Nothing else."

"Her cough? Consumption, I'd warrant."

"Aye." The city was full of people who were constantly coughing, and the lass from earlier in the day had held her handkerchief to her mouth throughout their short conversation, the thin cloth stained with blood.

"So what did you give her?" Master Castain asked.

"Dried elderberries and raspberry leaves to be boiled slowly with linseed, sugar and lemons," Jacob replied, without raising his head from the notes he was making.

"Linseed?" Master Castain thought about that for some time, nodding in approbation.

"It releases an oil – most soothing."

"Another of your mother's cures?" Master Castain smiled.

Jacob shrugged. "Aye."

They had a major argument a week later, with Jacob glaring at his master across the workbench in the back area.

"She's a bairn! Look at her! She's too young to carry

a child!" Jacob threw a glance out into the shop proper where a pale lass was gripping her older sister's hand. "And with her stepfather, no less," Jacob went on with disgust.

"That is what she says, but we don't know the truth of it. And what is to say she hasn't invited the man into her bed? Girl children can be full of wiles." Master Castain studied the two young women, clearly not quite as taken in by the abject expression on the youngest girl's face as Jacob was.

"Please, we have to help them. She's desperate, and what help you don't give them they'll look for elsewhere. And we both know how often that goes wrong..."

Master Castain looked at his wife, who was sitting in the furthest corner of the room, her small desk piled high with ledgers. "What do you think, my dear?"

"It may be too late as it is," she said, "and the girl may bleed to death if the dose isn't accurate. Pennyroyal is a dangerous herb. Besides, if he's bedding her, he'll have her back in his bed shortly, and so what good will it do?"

"We must stop him!" Jacob exclaimed.

Mrs Castain laughed shortly. "Stop Richard Collin? That I think you'll find beyond yourself, Jacob. No, husband, I suggest you tell them pennyroyal may help, but that unfortunately you have none to offer."

When next he met Luke, Jacob was bubbling with indignation. A young comely lass in the hands of a ruthless stepfather – it was right terrible, wasn't it?

"Richard Collin?" Luke twirled the cup round in his hands. "I'm prone to agree with Mrs Castain. He's not a man you want to antagonise."

"And so we sit and watch as he abuses a lass not yet fifteen," Jacob spat.

Luke sighed. "She's his ward, Jacob. And should she end up pregnant, he'll wed her."

"And how does that help? The poor lass hates him."

"How do you know? How?" Luke repeated, when Jacob at first chose not to reply.

"How? She was weeping, begging me to help."

"Ah. So what did you do?"

"I..." Jacob attempted to look away from the bright green eyes facing him. "I prepared something for her, and it was easy enough to find his house." But not the lass. To his chagrin, he'd had to leave his package in the hands of a maid.

"Yes, it would be, I imagine."

Jacob made a face. A goldsmith, Richard Collin was very successful, having made a series of marriages that had, one by one, brought him his former competitors' businesses as well.

"Four widows," Luke said with an element of admiration. "The last one brought him that new house just off Maiden's Lane." He eyed Jacob, shaking his head from side to side. "His stepdaughter comes well dowered, and Richard Collin isn't about to let such a plump bird escape his hand." He extended his legs in front of him and crossed them at the ankle, studying his pink silk stockings. "Stay away from young Mistress Collin."

"Her name is Charlotte Foster," Jacob said.

Luke's warning didn't help, nor did Master Castain's. Jacob gravitated far too often in the direction of Maiden's Lane, on the off chance of at least getting a glimpse of fair-haired Charlotte Foster. And he did, often enough, seeing her dart across the muddy road on her pattens with the grace of a deer in flight, her head sedately covered as she hurried down Gutter Lane on her way to the newly rebuilt St Mary-le-Bow.

Jacob became an avid churchgoer. As the weeks progressed, he moved closer and closer to the hunched figure in her pew, his heart thudding loudly in his chest. The day she patted the pew and shifted to allow him to sit beside her, his stomach did an uncomfortable somersault. The afternoon she raised her blue eyes to his and smiled, he was lost. Jacob Graham had fallen in love, and he had no idea whatsoever what to do with the sensations that rushed through him whenever he saw her.

"I told you," Luke barked. "I told you to stay away from her, and instead you've been sniffing around her like a dog after a bitch in heat." He sat down beside Jacob's bed.

"I love her," Jacob mumbled through his broken mouth, trying to open his swollen eye wide enough to see his uncle. Richard Collin's two apprentices had been quick and efficient, cornering him as he came out of the church after yet another rendezvous with Charlotte.

"Love! Pff! And you a married man as well." Luke lowered his face to stare Jacob firmly in his eyes. "Either you promise to do as I tell you, or I'll put you aboard the first ship out of here."

Jacob swallowed heavily. He couldn't leave, not now that he had a lass to save from an ogre of a stepfather. He looked out at the July evening and nodded. But beneath the bedclothes, his fingers were firmly crossed.

"She lies," Luke told Master Castain. "Richard Collin isn't taking her to bed. She's too young for a start; he has always preferred his women somewhat more mature."

Master Castain nodded. "Let's hope Jacob stays away from her for now, because next time they will be less gentle with him."

"Gentle? The lad's got one black eye, a split lip, and bruises all over his arms and chest!"

Master Castain's brow wrinkled. "As I said, next time it will be worse."

Chapter 25

"Leave?" Jenny had to bite her lip to stop it from trembling. "How leave?" Over the last months, she'd succeeded in convincing herself that Ian would forgive her, even if nothing in his behaviour towards her indicated that was the case – rather the reverse.

He avoided any contact with her beyond the necessary, sat for hours studying the baby's face, and, on occasion, Jenny could feel his eyes bore holes into the back of her head. The cabin stood finished since some weeks back, and Ian had moved in but made it clear she wasn't welcome to live there with him and their son.

"We ride down to Providence tomorrow," Ian said, "and you won't be coming back."

Jenny's heart seemed to stop for a second. She bowed her head to brush her lips against the wispy softness of her daughter's head.

"Not come back?" She cleared her throat and blinked in an effort to stop herself from crying.

"I'm divorcing you, on account of adultery. I assume you won't contest it, will you?"

"They will put me in the pillory," she whispered. "I'll be shamed before all."

Ian gave her a look that made her twist. "However much you deserve it, I'll try to ensure it doesn't come to that," he said, and left her to pack.

It was late in the afternoon before Jenny fully comprehended what this leaving meant. She stood aghast and listened when Ian explained that Maggie would be staying behind with Naomi, and that Malcolm wasn't coming with them either.

"My bairns stay with me."

"Your children?" She found her voice and her anger. "Well, there's no doubt Malcolm is yours, but Maggie isn't, you hear? She's mine, only mine!"

Ian's face hardened into a mask of dislike. "My birthmother once told Da that the babe she held in her arms wasn't his, so he let her go and take the wean with her. I won't repeat his mistake. The lass is born under my name, and will be raised by me and mine, not you."

"I'll contest it!" she screeched. "God damn you, Ian Graham, I'll deny it – all of it!"

"You do that, and I'll bring forth enough evidence to place you in the pillory for a week."

Jenny made a run for the baby basket, but Ian was quicker and stronger, easily blocking her way.

He picked Maggie up and held her to his chest. "She won't miss you," he said in a cold voice. "She's but two months old."

She jerked at his words before slumping in defeat. "And Malcolm? What will you tell him?"

"The truth: how you bedded with another man and shamed us all."

"You'll paint me a whore to our son?" Jenny groaned.

"Nay, you've done that yourself." Ian met her eyes, and Jenny wept inside as she realised that any love he'd ever had for her had been swept away by the damage she'd done him. This was a vulnerable man, a man whose manhood had been stripped away from him, and in his eyes the hurt stood naked.

"I'm so sorry," she whispered far too late. "I truly never meant for you to be hurt."

"But I was," he replied just as softly. He held out his daughter to her. "You may kiss her goodbye."

"Now?" she quavered. "Why now? Why not on the morrow?"

"Now. We leave at daybreak."

"I wish I could ride with you." Matthew clasped Ian's hand. "But I can't leave Mark to cope on his own with only Daniel at his side – not now, with all the harvest work."

221

Ian waved away his continued apologies. "I know why, Da, and Mama is coming."

As was Betty, already mounted, her brow set in a permanent expression of worry since the messenger had arrived some days back to let her know her mother was doing poorly.

Matthew gnawed his lip, eyes flying over the loaded pistols that Betty and Alex carried. A very long ride, and he would never have allowed it if he hadn't known for sure the Burleys were still in Virginia – this courtesy of Thomas Leslie, who had recently returned after visiting one of his daughters there.

He went over to his wife, waited while she finished talking to Daniel, and helped her up on her horse, allowing his hand to remain on her thigh. Her eyes remained stuck on their son, now standing beside Mark. Already as tall as Mark, but nowhere near Mark's width of shoulders, Daniel had returned home a few weeks ago, and after several days of constant comparisons between this life and his new exciting life in Boston, he'd settled down to pull his share of the workload.

Matthew regarded Daniel with pride. The lad was halfway to being a man, a bright young lad who spoke with enthusiasm about his studies and his teachers. But he was still young enough to have blushed a bright red at his mother's effusive welcome, an embarrassed "Mama" escaping his lips while Alex hugged and kissed, wept, hugged some more, and finally released him to be greeted by the rest of his family.

"He's so...I don't know, so adult somehow," Alex said, smiling at Daniel.

"Adult? That's not what you said yesterday." Matthew grinned.

"Okay, so he's a very young adult with streaks of infantile behaviour," Alex amended with a laugh. "I think there's still a frog or two left in the girls' room."

"Aye, well, I'll set him to chasing them out." Matthew took her hand. "You don't have to go. I know it tears at you to ride off when Daniel's here."

"No choice, is there? One of us has to be there for him, don't you think?" She looked over to where Ian had sat up on his horse.

"Take care, aye?"

"Of who? Of me or of him?"

"Of both," he smiled, "but mostly of you."

At the top of the lane, she turned and waved, eyes flashing in the sun.

Jenny threw a hateful look in the direction of Betty and manoeuvred her mule so that she was as far away from them all as possible. All of her was aching, all of her was swollen, and she'd cried so much during the night she'd thought there were no tears left – until she'd said goodbye to Malcolm.

One fat tear slid down her cheek. Her son had not said a word, standing as close as he could to Ian. But when she'd hugged him, he'd thrown his arms round her neck, and she could feel it, in every inch of him, how hard he was struggling not to cry. Her son, her daughter – lost to her and all because of… She muffled a sob and averted her face from Alex's concerned eyes. No more weeping, she told herself; it doesn't serve anyway.

It was hard to keep that promise during the ride down to Providence, and it was even harder not to succumb to tears the day Ian and she stood before the ministers.

"Adultery?" Minister Walker wrinkled his nose and looked Jenny up and down. "And you don't deny this accusation, daughter?"

Jenny shook her head, keeping her eyes on her clasped hands. If only someone would hold her, not leave her standing this alone in front of the elders of the congregation.

"And you want a divorce," Minister Walker went on, directing himself to Ian.

"Aye."

The men before them huddled together in deep discussion, several disapproving looks thrown in the direction of Jenny who shrank further into herself, sinking her nails into the skin of her wrist to stop herself from crying.

"And the post-nuptials are in order?" a minister Jenny didn't recognise asked. In reply, Ian handed over the contracts, drawn up by Simon.

"Well," Minister Walker cleared his throat, "that was most generous of you, young Ian."

Ian hitched his shoulders in a gesture that showed just how unimportant he found this aspect of the whole affair, and Minister Walker nodded compassionately.

"She must be punished," the new minister said. "Such behaviour cannot be condoned."

Jenny's knees dipped, but she remained silent, concentrating on her breathing.

"I don't want to," Ian said.

The minister smiled benignly at him. "No, of course you don't. This is, after all, your former wife. But this is a matter for us to decide, not you."

"I don't want to," Ian repeated. "Isn't it enough that I have to live through this pain? Must I also be humiliated in public?"

"You? But it isn't you, it's her," the minister said. "A few hours in the pillory to make an example of her to all women here."

A murmur of agreement rose from his colleagues.

"Aye, and all will ask themselves why." Ian shook his head stubbornly. "No, I ask you not to do this to me."

They had walked into the meetinghouse a married couple, and they walked out divorced, with Ian carrying the deeds. The midday heat struck them like a wet blanket, and they hurried for the shade afforded by the meetinghouse building.

"Will you be alright?" Ian asked.

"Do you care?" she snapped back, unable to help herself. She raised a hand to her tender chest and liked it that he noticed, a faint blush colouring his cheeks. Let him realise what he was doing, stealing her daughter from her!

"Not as such." He shifted from foot to foot, looking uncomfortable. Finally, he gave her a stilted bow and made as if to leave.

"Ian?" He turned back towards her, and she tried to

224

smile, although to her consternation her eyes were filling with tears. "Thank you for not allowing them to put me in the pillory."

"I promised you, didn't I?"

She scuffed her shoe back and forth over the cobbles. "Take care of my children."

"I will."

There was nothing left to say. For some minutes more, they stared at each other before he shrugged and turned away. "And I do care," he added as he was leaving.

"I know you do," she whispered to his retreating back, "and that makes it all such a waste." Oh God, what had she done? She stood very still until he had disappeared from sight. Never until this moment had she been utterly alone, entirely without protection. Jenny sighed, bent down to pick up her few belongings, and, with a constricted throat, took the first steps of her new life.

"So, are you settling in?" Alex asked Joan after having made appropriately impressed sounds as she was guided round the new Melville residence. The small house was surprisingly light, with two small glass-paned windows to the front, and light filtering in from the open kitchen door that gave onto a small yard where a couple of hens were clucking.

"Well enough, even if it's quite a small place."

"A small place," Alex echoed with a laugh. "Shame on you, to disparage our thriving town."

"Not much bigger than Cumnock."

"Oh yes, it is, if you include the docks."

"Ah," Joan said. "I don't go there much."

"No, I don't think you should, nor should Simon."

"He does as it pleases him," Joan said in a cool tone. "As I hear it, Mrs Malone's attracts its fair share of the male citizenry."

"And Lucy?" Alex asked to get off this uncomfortable subject.

Joan's eyes drifted over to her daughter, who was sitting in the small backyard. "Men look at her; all the time they look at her. And she, God help her, she looks back."

"She has to. It isn't as if she can eavesdrop or something, is it?"

Joan shook her head. "You know what I mean. Some lasses just have that...that...knowingness about them. No, the sooner she's wed the better – in particular given her deafness."

"But not at fifteen!"

"Nay, of course not, but once she's betrothed, it will be easier." Joan fiddled with her cup and smiled down at the table. "There's a lad much taken with her, a right bonny lad of good family."

"Oh," Alex muttered, not that interested. She glanced at Lucy, who was sitting on the small bench under the single tree, her head bent over some mending.

"Henry Jones," Joan continued. "Have you perhaps heard of him?"

"Henry Jones?" Alex strangled a surprised guffaw. "Kate Jones' eldest?"

Joan leaned forward eagerly. "Aye, that's him. Rich as I hear it – very rich."

"Let's just say I have no fond recollections of his father, Dominic Jones."

Joan looked nonplussed and Alex sighed.

"Jones was the overseer who so mistreated Matthew, all those years ago in Virginia." Alex nodded at the shocked look that flew up Joan's face.

"Hmm." Joan gnawed at her lip. "The lad seems polite enough. And you can't hold him responsible for the ill deeds of his father."

"No, that would be unfair, however biblically correct."

Joan flashed her an irritated look but didn't say anything, shifting the conversation to other matters.

"I'm not sure." Betty studied Simon Melville cautiously.

"You're not sure that you want to remain married, or you're not sure that you want to end the marriage?"

"Isn't that the same thing?"

Simon tilted his head to one side, and Betty had to quell an urge to laugh. Mama Alex was right: he did look like a large bird.

"Aye, probably, but it's a question of progression. First, you begin to consider whether you wish to remain married; then you move on to thinking about ending it." He picked up a leather-bound tome from his cluttered desk and used it as a clumsy fan. "Hot, no?"

"It's even worse come August."

"Worse?" Simon looked down at himself. "I'm melting away in this heat!"

"Not a bad thing perhaps," Betty said before she could help herself.

He raised his brows. "You've been talking to my wife," he said, wagging a finger at her. He leaned forward on his elbows. "Why?" he asked, throwing her entirely. He rolled his eyes at her. "Why do you want to end the marriage?"

"I..." Betty hesitated, uncomfortable under his penetrating eyes. "I'm not sure my marriage is valid," she ended lamely.

"Aye, it is, as long as you want it to be. You know that, Betty Hancock." He smiled broadly at her. "And so does your father, which is why you come to me to voice these belated concerns of yours, because should he hear them, he'd insist you come back to live with him while he makes arrangements for a new, rather hasty marriage."

Betty gave him a pleading look. "I don't want that."

"Nay, of course you don't, because you already know the man you want to marry." He grinned and winked.

"Yes, but I'm not sure he wants to wed me..."

"No, not at the moment," Simon agreed. "He's but recently divorced."

Betty's face, her neck, went uncomfortably warm. How could he possibly know that?

He tapped his nose. "In my business, lassie, it comes in handy to read faces. And it's not as if there's an interminable supply of young men up in the woods, is it?"

"Oh." She didn't know what to say.

"You don't need to worry. I won't be telling." He sat back. "I'll draw up agreements for you to end your marriage, but you must tell Jacob yourself."

"I've already written a letter, and I'll include an annulment if you prepare it for me and ask that he send his reply to you." The letter had been burning a hole in her petticoat pocket for well over two months, but until the receipt of Jacob's latest letter, there'd been no address to which to send it.

"And to Ian you will say that you've decided to end this farce of a marriage, but that you're holding back on telling anyone on account of your father," Simon said.

"Yes," she said, "if he should ask, that is…"

"I dare say he will. Men are most flattered by lasses that fall in love with them, and you're quite a comely lass, wee Betty."

"Oh." Once again, she had no notion what to say, so she curtsied and fled the room.

For all that this was a trip Alex would have preferred not to have made, she enjoyed the brief visit to Providence – even if the summer heat made it all rather sweltering. As an additional plus, there'd been a letter from Jacob waiting, and she'd spent a couple of happy hours penning him a reply.

On one of her walks through the settlement, she bumped into Mr Farrell, who complained loudly about the heat, the disappointing development of the price on tobacco, and the ever-increasing taxes. Alex hemmed and hawed, listening with pretend interest. There was really only one thing she wanted to discuss with Mr Farrell, and when he at last fell silent, she drew in a deep breath and asked about Leon.

"Leon?" Mr Farrell's face was an absolute blank.

"Noah," Alex corrected herself. "You know, the slave that tried to run away."

"Tried to run away? He had run away, but was caught." Mr Farrell gave her a stern look. "You should not concern yourself with such. Slaves are wild and dangerous creatures."

"He's a man, Mr Farrell – and last I saw him, he looked close to death."

"He did?" Mr Farrell hitched his shoulders. "He was in a bad way for some weeks, but by now he is fully recovered, and docile as a lamb." He grinned. "I'll have no more trouble from him, Mrs Graham. Noah knows his place now, and I'll get many years of hard work out of him yet." He leaned towards Alex. "I've told him, you see, that next time he does something foolish, I'll have him sold down to the West Indies. Tobacco is a harsh crop, Mrs Graham, but sugar cane is much, much worse." With that, he was off, bidding Alex a good day as he hurried towards the meetinghouse.

Alex felt sick to the stomach, but had no idea what to do. When she discussed this with Ian, he sighed and told her there was nothing they could do. As he heard it, Noah was living out his life down in the south of the colony, on one of Mr Farrell's plantations.

"Besides, Da wouldn't want you to meddle," Ian said. "Last time you did, it cost the poor man hours of suffering."

Alex squirmed, but had to concede he was right. Her misdirected efforts had, if anything, made Leon's life even more of a living hell than it already was.

"Still," she said.

"Aye, poor bastard. But maybe he's reconciled himself to his new life."

"You think? Would you, if it were you who'd been unjustly enslaved?"

"Not at first, but with time..." Ian sighed. "He's been flogged a number of times. There comes a point where it is either give up and adapt or die, and most of us prefer to live – however reduced our lives." He patted her hand. "Hopefully, he will forget. Forget who he was, what he could have been. That will make it easier for him, I think."

Alex spent the rest of the morning moping, but after an afternoon spent safely out of the sun with Joan, she was in a much better mood, and it was with relish she set off for the short walk to the inn, accompanied by Ian and Simon, who was regaling her with one story after the other from his practice in Edinburgh. Mostly, he recounted amusing anecdotes, making them laugh, but she kept on hearing it:

the sad tones of homesickness and yearning. She was on the verge of asking him what had really happened to make him come this far, when from the further side of the square came a babble of angry voices.

Seconds later, a lone man burst into view, running as fast as he could to get away from the mob on his heels. He was barefoot and half-dressed, his long shirt covering him down to his knees. Long, dark hair streamed behind him, and in his right hand he carried a musket.

"That's the Indian!" Alex said, eyes riveted to the signature coat the man was wearing, the heavy braids bouncing up and down as he ran.

"You know him?" Simon said.

"We've seen him before," Ian said, "and we have no cause to like him."

"You can say that again." Alex frowned. If their Indian companion was here, did that mean the Burleys were here as well?

By now, the pursuing men had disappeared up the street the Indian had taken, and in their wake came a number of people headed by Mrs Malone, who looked quite ferocious in hunting green and a musket. The long, red hair had escaped whatever restraints had been in place to begin with, and Alex was rather taken aback by the expanse of cleavage the madam was exposing to the world.

"Castrate him!" the madam yelled. "That's what men like him deserve!" She halted and pressed a hand to her side.

"A stitch?" Alex asked.

"Aaah, I haven't moved this fast in years." Mrs Malone dabbed at her sweaty face with her sleeve and scowled in the direction the Indian had gone. "Miscreants, you and your scar-faced companion. But, this time, you'll not get away with it, you hear?"

Between breaths, she told them of how the Indian and his companion had mistreated one of her girls, leaving her half-dead and without hair. "That Stephen Burley is a sick bastard," she said, spitting to the side. "Took a knife to her, he did."

"Stephen Burley?" Alex inched that much closer to Ian.

"In the flesh. That face is difficult to disguise."

"Oh, and his brothers?"

Mrs Malone hitched a shoulder, causing the neckline of her dress to slide down her arm. "I haven't seen them. He came with the Indian."

"They're not welcome here," Mr Farrell put in, giving Alex a brief nod. "Brigands, the lot of them. Whenever they're in town, slaves disappear from the pens, so I make them thieves as well. Hang them, I say, hang them as high as we can!"

"Hear, hear," said the butcher.

The butcher's wife appeared from a nearby house and handed Mrs Malone a shawl. "Will she be alright?" she asked.

"My lass?" Mrs Malone's mouth shaped itself into an elongated spout. "I hope so. Hair grows back, and the gashes will heal eventually."

Loud whoops carried from the direction of the palisade.

"Caught him," Mr Farrell said.

"And Stephen?" Alex asked.

"They're looking for him down by the docks." Mr Farrell waved a hand in the general direction of the port. "Unless he can fly, we'll get him as well."

The Indian was dragged back to the square, and a rope was produced, while loud voices chanted that the man should hang, and hang now. Alex backed away. She had no intention of witnessing this, and seeing as both Ian and Simon had joined the loud group of men, she decided to walk the last two hundred yards or so to the inn on her own. The evening was still light, the street looked empty, and when the Indian screamed, twice, Alex hurried off.

It took her only a few minutes to regret setting out alone. At every shadow, at every sound, she jumped. Idiot, she chided herself, you're overreacting. Stephen Burley is miles from here – anyone with any sense of self-preservation would be. She vacillated for a couple of seconds, considering whether to return to the square or continue. A series of catcalls and jeers interspersed with the screams of someone in pain made up her mind, and she continued towards the inn. The last part of her walk was through a narrow alley, bordered by buildings of assorted heights. She squinted into its dusky interior. Nothing. At the other end, she could make out the entrance to the inn. Alex picked up her skirts and ran.

Halfway across, she stumbled, slipped in something soft and fell. She landed heavily, her palms stinging from the grit and gravel.

"Shit." Alex got to her knees. There was a thud, a hand closed on her arm and pulled her upright.

"Mrs Graham." Philip Burley bowed, courteous as ever. But his fingers were sinking into her arm, and he was standing far too close, pinning her against the wall.

"Mr Burley. I heard you were in Virginia."

"I was – last week. But now, as you see, I'm here." He looked her up and down, shifted that much closer. "You humiliated me last time we met," he said in an even voice.

"Tough, that's what you get when you become obsessive pains in the butt. It's you harassing us, not the other way around. It's you that threaten and intimidate. It's you that—"

"I loved my brother," Philip interrupted, "and your husband killed him!"

"How you gripe! Isn't it time you got over it? He was killed fair and square – no, wait, he was killed despite you being four against one." She yanked at her arm. Quite useless. If anything, he tightened his hold. "Let me go!"

"Why should I?" His eyes swam very close to hers; his breath tickled her cheek. "You taunt me, woman. Every time we meet, you rile me." He squashed her against the wall and trailed a finger down her neck. A shiver ran through her, even more so when his finger continued along her neckline.

"Don't..." she spluttered.

Philip laughed. "Or else?" He continued with his groping, Alex slapped at him, heaving in an effort to dislodge him. "I should reconsider," he murmured, his lips at her ear. "Why kill Matthew Graham? Why not steal his wife instead? More enjoyable for me, more devastating for

232

him." He chuckled, the sound converted to a low yelp when Alex bit him in the shoulder. "Slut!"

"Get off!" She raked him over the face.

He gripped her by the shoulders and slammed her into the wall. It left her dazed, and he pressed his advantage, one strong leg forced between her thighs, his hips pressing against her. Two icy eyes bored into her. "You're coming with me, and, come morning, you'll be much more biddable."

"In your dreams!" Alex filled her lungs and screamed. Philip tried to cover her mouth. Alex bit his finger. He cursed. Alex screamed again.

"Mama?" Ian's voice rang down the alley.

"Here," she yelled, "I'm h—" Philip slapped her into shocked silence.

Ian charged, pistol in one hand, Simon hollering like an aggravated bull at his heels.

Philip pulled Alex to stand in front of him. "She goes with me. Alive if you leave, dead if you don't."

Ian came to an abrupt halt. Philip relaxed the throttling grip on her throat. Alex stomped down on his foot, grabbed hold of his forearm with both hands, took a step to the side to achieve some momentum, and crashed her hip into him, bending forward to send him flying over her head. He landed with a thud and lay still.

"We got him!" Alex said, looking down at Philip.

"I think not." The disembodied voice floated down from one of the sheds. Walter aimed his musket at Ian. "Don't move," he warned. "Nor you," he added, nodding at Simon. "Not unless you want to scrape off young Graham's brain from the planking behind him."

Ian trained his pistol on Philip, and from the way his arm was twitching, he was sorely tempted to pull the trigger, no matter Walter's threat.

"No," Alex whispered.

"Best not," Walter agreed. "Help him," he said over his shoulder, and Stephen jumped down, landing a yard from Alex. He stank, of rotten vegetables and fish, of mud and shit. He must have hidden in the offal heaps behind the docks, and during his headlong flight he'd hurt himself, because he was limping, favouring his left foot as he moved.

"Philip?" Stephen shook his brother. There was a muted groan in response, and slowly Philip Burley heaved himself up on his knees, one arm dangling uselessly by his side.

"My arm," he said.

"Nope, your shoulder," Alex said. Too bad he hadn't landed on his head and broken his neck. This looked like a dislocation, no more.

"You—" Philip broke off to gasp.

"Not now!" Walter said. "We must be off, brother."

"Ian! Do something! We can't let them get away!" Alex made as if to grab Philip, but at Stephen's snarl, she fell back.

"If he as much as twitches, I'll shoot him." Walter watched his brothers out of sight, and dropped down to land like a graceful cat in front of Alex.

"The debt increases every time we meet," he said, walking backwards away from them. His musket was still trained on Ian. "We will collect, Mrs Graham – we always do."

"Wherever they are, they're not here," Mr Farrell said much later. "We've searched the whole town, the port, and even the closest plantations, but they've gone up in smoke."

"Great." Alex hugged herself. The earlier euphoria at having given Philip a lesson had evaporated, leaving behind a debilitating and overwhelming fear.

"They're probably haring back to Virginia," Mr Farrell said. "And unless they boarded a ship, they're on foot. We found their horses."

That was a relief – a very minor one, but still. She wrapped Mr Farrell's cloak even tighter around her, trying to stop the shivers that were flying up her legs, her back.

"Oh God," she said in an undertone to Ian. "Now they'll be even angrier."

"Aye, but at least they won't be up to much for the coming days." Ian gave her arm a pat.

"Whoopee." Alex found that no comfort whatsoever.

Chapter 26

Alex was in a hurry to get home. They left at dawn the day after the Burley incident, taking the long turn round town so as to avoid the spectacle of the hanging Indian that still decorated one of the plane trees in the square. All that day, they pushed on, and next day Alex had them in their saddles by daybreak, hoping to cover the remaining miles in one long day. The heat was oppressive, and as the day progressed, the clear skies disappeared behind dark, brooding clouds.

"Thunderstorm," Ian said, pointing to the east. "We'd best find cover while we can."

"We ride on," Alex insisted, "we're only hours from home." One night sleeping in the open had been bad enough, with Alex spending most of it wide awake, clutching Ian's loaded musket. Every time she glanced at the surrounding forest, she expected to see Philip leering at her, or Walter aiming his musket, or... She swallowed and urged her horse on.

They'd only covered a couple of miles when Ian refused to go any further. The clouds had sunk low enough to seem to skim the treetops, and to Alex's irritation, Ian dismounted and started setting up camp.

"We would have been home by now," Alex grumbled some time later. She speared a piece of cheese with her knife and glared at her son. She hated the thought of being outside in the coming storm.

"Mayhap – or maybe it would have caught us unawares. Fickle things, storms."

"Fickle things, storms," Alex mimicked in an undertone. What would he know? When a magnificent fork of lightning cleaved the sky in two, Alex squeaked, shifting to sit as close as possible to Ian.

"It's just lightning," he said.

Easy for him to say; he hadn't had quite the same close encounter with the potential consequences of lightning as she had, and this had all the makings of spectacular fireworks. She caught an amused look between Betty and Ian, and grabbed hold of Narcissus instead.

The dog was as spooked as she was when the sky exploded. She buried her face against his side, and tried to block out the sounds and the lights, but it didn't much help. Light zigzagged through the air only feet away, the ground shivered with the impact, and Alex squished her eyes shut and prayed.

Alex wanted Matthew. The air crackled with electricity, the sky was torn apart by dazzling light, and she needed his arms around her, his reassurance that all would be well, that he'd keep her safe. But no Matthew; only a panting, frightened dog that leaned its considerable bulk against her and whined.

The next bolt of lightning struck a nearby tree, and the night was suffused with the scent of scorched wood. The ground shook. Alex whimpered and hugged Narcissus. One of the horses shrieked, the mare beside it joined in, and just like that they took off, hobbles snapped like cotton thread.

More thunder, yet another bolt, and then came the rain, a torrent of water that drenched them in seconds – not that Alex cared, because now the air was light and fresh, and the thunder was moving westwards.

An hour or so later, they huddled together round the small fire Ian had succeeded in lighting.

"How are we to get this home without the mules?" Alex kicked in the direction of the pannier baskets. Stupid animals. With the exception of Narcissus, they'd all taken off, leaving them stranded.

"Tomorrow," Ian yawned, "we'll think of something tomorrow, aye?"

Betty was sitting very close to him and, even in the dark, Alex could see they were holding hands. At present, she was too drained to do more than register this interesting little fact, just as she was too tired to worry about the Burleys. With a little grunt, she settled herself to sleep.

Alex woke to a dawn that glittered with returning light. She rolled over on her side and regarded the immobile heap beside her. A wild fuzz of brown hair appeared, and Alex closed her eyes and pretended to sleep, peeking from under her eyelashes to watch Betty disentangle herself from Ian and stand up. Betty smiled down at Ian with a smile of such sweetness it made Alex's stomach contract, and then she ducked in among the trees.

Alex was busy tying her apron into place when Ian rolled onto his front and got to his feet.

"Good night?" She winked, grinning at the red that flew up his face.

"Aye," Ian mumbled, and all through breakfast, he and Betty maintained a distance. Still, Alex intercepted a number of radiant smiles and covert looks. Betty was glowing from within, and as to Ian… She sneaked him a look. Hazel eyes so like his father's rested on Betty, eyes that lightened into gold when he smiled at her. She pursed her lips. This whole matter required careful handling, but she decided to leave this for later. Right now, her more immediate concern was to get home before Matthew went frantic with worry.

Matthew was restless. Every day he wandered up and down the lane, hoping to see them come riding back even if he knew they wouldn't, not yet. He disliked being separated from Alex, and even more when it was him left at home while she was riding unprotected through the woods.

He submerged himself in the harvest, working well into the evenings, and still he found the time to take that last hopeful walk up the lane – just in case. Around him, the family drooped. Naomi was struggling to feed two weans, and as such was excused from any other labour except cooking, which left Matthew, Mark, Daniel and Agnes to carry the brunt of the work. Matthew urged them on, worried that the dry weather might break, and as the week progressed, he could feel the heat begin to build, the heavy smell of dry dust permeating the air.

The Indians worried him as well. Twice, he'd seen bands of braves cut across his land, and he hadn't recognised any of them. Even more worrying, they had been dressed for war, their normally long hair reduced to waving crests. And so, on top of their daily work in the fields, he and his eldest sons shared sentinel duty at night, leaving them cross-eyed with exhaustion. The few hours Matthew slept, he tossed from side to side, his mind invaded by a never-ending list of tasks.

Matthew woke in the middle of the night, and his tongue was glued to the roof of his mouth, his head aching fit to burst. A thunderstorm...he frowned, resting his hand for an instant on Alex's pillow. Was she out in this? He was filled with an urge to ride out and find her, but waved the thought away as ridiculous – he had no idea where she might be.

All through the storm he lay awake – it would have been impossible to do otherwise, what with the sheer force and beauty of it. With the rain came a steady drumming on his roof, and he was almost asleep when he heard the sound of horses. Now? He stumbled out of bed and grabbed at his musket.

"It's our beasts." Mark yawned and nodded at the closest horse. "Tore itself, I reckon."

The hobbles were in tatters, but otherwise the three horses and the mules seemed undamaged, if somewhat overexcited.

"I'll ride to meet them," Matthew said.

"Now?" Mark asked. "It's not yet dawn."

"Now," Matthew told him, throwing the saddle onto Moses. "How else are they to get home?"

"Walk?" Mark suggested in a dry tone.

"And the panniers? Are they to carry them home on their backs?" He took the mules on a leading rein and urged Moses into a trot.

He found them no more than six miles from home. Alex leapt to her feet at the sight of him and hurried towards him.

It made him smile to see her thus, running barefoot in her haste to reach him and throw her arms around his neck. His son hung back, saying something in an intense voice to Betty before coming over to take the mules.

Matthew looked from Betty to Ian, from Ian to Betty. Under his inspection, Betty coloured while Ian paled, splotches of red decorating his cheeks and throat. Matthew chewed his lip and slid a look at his wife for confirmation. Her brows rose, her mouth quirked into a little smile. Matthew sighed. He should put a stop to this, send the lass back to her father immediately.

"Not now," Alex murmured.

A mere half-hour later, Betty and Ian were gone, double-mounted on Moses and with the mules in tow. Matthew loaded his musket, offered Alex his hand, and set off for home. On the long walk back, Alex told him about her latest encounter with the Burleys. Matthew's windpipe felt as if coated with ice as did his lungs, making it difficult to inhale. Vivid images of his Alex, nude and helpless under Philip, crowded his brain.

"Too bad they got away, huh?" she sighed.

"Aye," he said, and the freezing fear was replaced by a red-hot rage. He should have been there to protect her, to finish them off with his bare hands.

"Was he badly hurt?" he asked, hoping that Philip Burley, accursed bastard that he was, would live out his life severely maimed.

Alex hitched her shoulders. "It probably hurt like hell, but, no, unfortunately not."

They were both hot and tired when they reached the turn-off, sometime after noon. David came rushing to meet them, tailed by Samuel and Malcolm, and making up the rear came Adam, with Hugin perched atop of his head.

"The day the bird shits in his hair is the day that bird becomes history," Alex muttered to Matthew, making him laugh. "Bath?" she suggested, once they'd greeted their children. "I could do with one."

239

"Aye, why not?"

By the shore, she shed her clothes, one garment after the other dropping into a pile. He followed suit, dove in first and amused himself by splashing her with water when she complained the river was bloody cold.

"What's this with Ian and Betty?" he asked as he lathered her hair.

"Well, it's something, for sure." She tilted her head back and grinned up at him. "They slept very close together – but at least they were fully clothed."

"As if that is a hindrance should you want to." He waded towards the shore.

"You talk to him and I talk to her – or we talk to both of them together." She threw herself backwards into the water to wash out the last of the soap in her hair, did a slow backwards somersault, and swam to the shore where he stood waiting with towels. "I actually think they're well suited."

"She's his brother's wife," Matthew said.

"Not much of a marriage – we both know that. As you said, whatever Jacob was thinking with at the time, it was definitely not his brain." She opened her stone jar of homemade lavender lotion and applied it all over.

"And what do you think Ian is thinking with?" He took over, motioning for her to turn this way and that. He slowed his hands up her back, dug his fingers into her stiff neck and shoulders, making her groan with pleasure.

"I'm not sure," Alex said, "and I don't think he knows either."

Matthew spread skirts and linens and urged Alex down, thinking she looked lovely, her skin glistening with her oils, her glorious hair unbound. He tugged at her curls, decorating her pale skins with tendrils of hair that shifted all the way from darkest brown, through bronze and a vivid copper, to the odd strand of grey. She was uncharacteristically shy, his wife, lying unresponsive in his arms as he caressed her body. He traced the outline of her nipple and pinched it ever so lightly.

"What's the matter?" he asked, bending his head to nuzzle her throat.

"I…" She shook her head. "I'm just being silly."

"What?" He kissed her jawline, disappointed when she didn't squirm as she normally would.

"I keep on seeing him. You know: Philip."

It was the equivalent of being doused in a bucket of ice-cold water. Matthew rolled over on his back.

"Is that how you would have reacted?" she asked in a small voice.

"Reacted when?" he asked, even if he already knew what she meant.

"If Philip Burley…" She cleared her throat. "Well, if he'd…"

"…raped you."

She made an unhappy sound, hiding her face against his chest. Matthew sank his fingers into her hair, forcing her to lift her head to meet his eyes.

"If Philip Burley had tainted you with his body, I would have done my utmost to erase every single memory of that event from your mind."

"How?" she whispered, her tongue flitting out to wet her lips.

"Like this." He rolled her over so that her back pressed against the ground. Blue eyes stared up at him, her hands rested on his chest. He kissed her temple; he traced the contours of her beautiful ears, slightly pointed and tight against her skull. Normally, she giggled when he fondled her ears, but today she stretched towards him, offering herself. Her neck, the downy spot just below her hairline at her nape, the rounded shape of her shoulders, the sharp planes of her clavicles. He kissed his way across each and every one of these, and under his mouth and his touch, he felt her relax, those hesitant hands on his chest sliding round to caress his back instead.

He took his time over her breasts, suckling until her nipples stood dark and hard like ripe raspberries.

"Better?" he murmured, moving up her body.

She just nodded, opening her mouth to his. A long kiss, tender at first, but by the time he was done she was writhing

241

below him, her hands where they would normally be when he was loving her: in his hair. With his legs, he nudged her thighs apart, sliding one hand in under her waist to hold her perfectly still when he entered her. There! One thrust and he was so deep inside of her he heard her gasp.

His wife, his woman. Made for him, only for him, and God save the man who ever as much as laid a finger on her. Anger bubbled through him, mixing with his arousal. He dug his toes into the ground for better purchase and pounded into her, grinding his pelvis into hers. She moaned below him, legs coming up around his thighs, his hips. So close, so very, very close.

"Look at me," he panted. "Look me in the eyes when we come."

And she did, her eyes a wide open mirror to her soul and her heart.

After their long, uninterrupted session by the river, Matthew felt more relaxed than he had done in weeks. Over supper, he exchanged a number of looks with his wife, smiling inwardly when she winked, mouthing "I love you".

Once the meal was concluded, Matthew invited his eldest son and Betty to join them in the parlour, having to bite his lip not to grin at how flustered Ian seemed.

"I've already written to Jacob." Betty sat on the edge of her stool, keeping her eyes on anything but Ian.

"You have?" Ian gave her a surprised look.

Betty nodded. "I…well, I was never entirely sure."

"That's not what you said a year ago," Matthew reminded her.

"What could I say? I was frightened I might be with child, I had no idea what I wanted or not, and I was so upset with my father for…" Betty broke off.

"And now you're sure?" Alex said.

Betty raised her chin. "I know I don't want to remain married to Jacob."

"And does your father know this?" Matthew asked.

Betty's eyes flew so abruptly to him he had his answer.

"Ah," he said, "and why not?"

"Because," Betty whispered. And it all spilled out: how William kept on listing prospective bridegrooms, and how he kept on nagging at her to dissolve this 'ridiculous' marriage with Jacob Graham so that he could see her settled elsewhere.

"...preferably very far away from Providence. None of the men he speaks of live within the colony."

"You've shamed him," Matthew tried to explain.

"And for that I must pay the rest of my life?"

"I assume it's Simon you've spoken to regarding your marriage contracts, then," Alex said.

Betty inclined her head, and Matthew rolled his eyes. Wee Simon did best not to rile William Hancock.

"And now you think you love Ian," Alex stated.

The lass squirmed on her stool, her face so bright Matthew shared a quick smile with his wife. Ian wasn't smiling: he was staring at Betty like a thirsting man at a miraculous well in the desert.

"I don't think I do," Betty breathed. "I know I do." She fiddled with the edge of her apron, eyes lowered so that only a flash of bright brown was visible under her lashes.

"You're very young to be saying that," Matthew said gently. Betty hitched her shoulders. "And you? Do you love her?" Matthew continued, directing himself to his son who was looking at the lass in a way that made any answer redundant.

"I'm not sure," Ian said, "but I think I might."

Betty's eyes met Ian's. His mouth curved into a slight smile, and her face almost broke in two with the responding grin. Matthew sat back in his chair and regarded them.

"Have you bedded her?" he asked Ian.

"Nay, of course not!" Ian replied, glaring at him.

Matthew held up his hands in a conciliatory gesture. "I had to ask, aye? As I hear it, you were lying very close together this morning."

Once again, the blush spread like wildfire up Betty's face, this time reciprocated in Ian's cheeks.

"That was just for warmth," Ian said.

Matthew raised a brow, thinking that there was warmth and warmth. He threw a look at Alex; met blue, blue eyes.

"You'll do nothing improper." Matthew stood up to tower over them. "I won't have you bedding before you're properly wed – if you're properly wed." He looked down at Betty and smiled. "One of my sons has treated you badly, and I won't risk that you be so uncaringly used again. As I recall, you will be eighteen in October a year from now." Betty nodded. "Well then, if you're still sure you love Ian a year from now, I'll do my utmost to see you wed. But until then…" He wagged his finger at them. "You walk a very fine line, aye? Oh," he added as an afterthought, "and Jacob must be told, by both of you, that you have feelings for each other. My sons won't end up in enmity over a woman."

"So, I must get my younger brother's blessing?" Ian said acerbically.

"Aye, lad, you must. As I should have done before I wed Margaret." Matthew was very aware of Alex's eyes upon him.

"And would you not have married her had he said no?" Ian sounded breathless.

"I don't know, but I should have asked." Matthew let them go; watched them leave the room with well over a yard between them. By the time they reached the privacy of the stables, he suspected they would be scant inches, if that, apart.

Alex slid her arms round his waist. "Had you asked, he would have said no."

"Aye."

"And would you not have married her then?"

"I don't know." He glanced at her. "I was very much in love with her."

Alex averted her eyes and stepped away from him. It amused him – and flattered him – this lingering jealousy that she obviously felt for Margaret.

He took hold of her and gathered her close. "I love you."

"But once you loved her."

244

"Not as I love you," he said, kissing the top of her head. "I never knew her well enough to truly love her."

"Huh," she snorted, but he could hear she was pleased. She stood on her toes and kissed his cheek. "Bed? Before I fall asleep on my feet?"

He nodded, and together they closed down the house, bade Mrs Parson a good night, and, with a pitcher of hot water in his hand, Matthew followed Alex upstairs. She busied herself with soap and water while he undressed and retired to bed, too tired to bother with washing.

"I wonder how long Ian has felt that way about Betty," Alex said, making a very pleased sound as she slid into bed.

"Well, for longer than since yesterday," Matthew mumbled and rolled over on his side, yawning.

"And she about him?" She rolled over with him, rubbing her face against his back.

"I don't know, and I don't much care. Sleep, aye?"

"Probably for quite some time," Alex went on. "I'd guess since somewhere in winter."

"Oh, aye?" He twisted back to peer at her. "Why so?"

She sat up and grinned triumphantly at him. "First, Betty developed a fondness for the animals, always offering to curry and milk and whatnot, and, second, she stopped talking about Jacob." She nestled down beside him and patted him on his rump. "Now, will you please stop talking. I definitely need some beauty sleep, okay?"

"Me stop talking?" Matthew laughed softly. "It is you that can't keep your mouth shut."

His only reply was a soft snore.

Chapter 27

Five days later, Graham's Garden had unwelcome visitors. Out of nowhere, the Burley brothers rode into the yard, clearly unfazed by the barking dogs.

"Shit!" Alex croaked from where she was standing in the kitchen. The men outside meant business, muskets cocked. Alex was ridiculously grateful that Matthew was out on his furthest fields until she realised that might not be a good thing at all because, to her consternation, the men dismounted, using their muskets to herd the children to stand in the centre of the yard. One of the dogs snarled, but howled when the stock of a musket was brought down over its snout.

"I'll kill the younger ones first," Philip Burley called. "I'll keep on killing them until Matthew Graham comes out, unarmed." He aimed his musket at Hannah.

"What do I do?" Alex hissed to Mrs Parson. "There are six men out there!"

"Talk to them, delay them as much as you can." Mrs Parson shoved Ruth towards the back of the house. "Run and find your da, but make sure they don't see you." Ruth was a ghastly white, but nodded and slunk off to escape through one of the back windows. A shot rang out, someone screamed, and Alex flew to the door, throwing it wide.

"Don't!" she pleaded. "Please don't!"

"Your husband, Mrs Graham." Philip Burley eyed her with evident dislike and shifted his bandaged arm ostentatiously. Unfortunately, he didn't seem all that incapacitated.

"He isn't here," Alex hiccupped, counting the children. All of them still alive, even if Hannah was shrieking with fear, small hands clapped to her ears.

"Where, Mrs Graham?"

"He's over at the Chisholms'," Alex lied.

Philip shook his head slowly from side to side. "Do you take us for fools? Would he be visiting elsewhere when his fields stand ready for harvest?" He produced shot and powder, took his time reloading his musket, all the while sneering at Alex. He loaded, wadded, and raised the barrel at Hannah.

"No." Naomi was on her knees hugging her daughter. "Not my little girl."

"All of them." Walter grinned and cocked his head in the direction of his brother. "Waste to kill them."

Philip shrugged. "Matthew Graham, brother, that's why we're here. Once we have him, we'll see."

"They'd be worth a pretty penny, the children and the women," Walter said. Even from where she was standing, Alex heard Betty's gulp.

"We've never harmed you," Alex said, trying to keep her voice steady.

Philip raised a brow and looked at his arm.

"Different, that was self-defence," she said.

"Your man killed our youngest brother. He sliced his throat wide open." Philip's eyes travelled over the children, stopped for a moment on Sarah, who was holding Adam.

"Because you attacked him," Alex said. "You were going to kill him."

Walter Burley laughed. "We *are* going to kill him, Mrs Graham. Today."

"No," Alex whispered.

"Today," Philip repeated. "Find him."

"I can't," Alex said. "I don't know where he is."

"How unfortunate. For them." Stephen Burley jerked his head in the direction of the children. His eyes alighted for an instant on Samuel, dropping to the amulet pouch that hung round the boy's neck. "Come here." When Samuel hung back, Stephen grabbed him by the arm. A knife appeared in Stephen's hand, and Alex hurtled across the yard.

"No!" She was on Stephen and, moments later, she was flying, landing on her back. All air was knocked out of her, she registered that someone was hitting at her, opened her eyes to see Stephen's face only inches from her own, and then her head exploded with pain. Alex crawled on the ground, was vaguely aware of how Stephen Burley raised his foot to kick her. There was a jarring pain up her side. Another kick, and Alex tried to drag herself out of range, vaguely hearing Stephen laugh. She blinked up at him. He lifted his foot yet again. Philip appeared in her field of vision and, to her surprise, he was scowling at his brother.

"Leave her alone," Philip said. "You!" he snapped his fingers at Betty. "Where is he?"

Betty opened her eyes wide, let her mouth fall open, and managed to look quite imbecile.

"Oh, no," Philip snarled, striding towards her. "I know who you are, little Betty Hancock, so don't try that with me." Betty retreated, bumping into Mrs Parson, who appeared with a pitcher of beer.

"Mrs Parson! How can you!" Naomi gasped.

Yes, how could she? Through a rapidly swelling eye, Alex tried to glare at the old woman.

"Feeble-minded old woman," Betty scolded, eliciting a vague smile from Mrs Parson.

"They're guests, no? And right bonny to boot." Mrs Parson simpered at the closest Burley brother, who laughed. Mrs Parson's jet-black eyes flew to Alex, and there was nothing of hospitality or feeble-mindedness in them. She was trying to gain them some time, that's all.

Alex sat up, groaning with pain. Her face, her arm... She licked her mouth, tasting her own blood.

"Mama!" Adam slunk between the legs of one of the men, and crawled on all fours towards her. His small fingers deposited a knife in her hand. She tried to smile at him, shared a quick look with Mrs Parson, who was still serving the damn Burleys and their men beer, for all the world as if this was a friendly little visit. But with a mug of beer in your hand, it was difficult to keep your musket pointed quite as firmly at the children. A distraction, she needed a distraction.

"Call for Hugin," she whispered to Adam.

Obligingly, he whistled and the raven sailed towards them, circled a couple of times, and landed on Adam's head.

"He's tame?" one of the roughnecks asked.

"Aye," Adam said, "he says my name."

"He does?" The man sounded interested and took a step towards them. The muzzle of his musket wavered, pointing at the ground. Come closer, Alex urged silently, come just that little bit closer.

"He has quite the vocabulary," Alex croaked, gripping the handle of the knife in her hand. She even succeeded in smiling at the man. He obviously had no idea what vocabulary was, but he was curious about the bird.

"Spencer! Get back here!" Philip's voice was sharp, making Spencer jump. When he turned, Alex launched herself forward and buried the knife high in his leg. Jesus, he screamed! And bled, a fountain of blood standing from his groin. Philip rushed towards them, musket held high in a one-handed grip. Mrs Parson crashed the pitcher over the head of Stephen Burley. Naomi fled with the children, and Alex pushed Adam away from her, screaming at him to run.

With a thwack, the musket hit the ground beside her. Alex scrambled backwards, raised the little knife in a defiant gesture that had no effect whatsoever on Philip Burley. Oh God, here he came again, this time with the musket the right way round, and Betty was shrieking from somewhere to her right.

The last few microseconds of her life played out in slow motion: she could see her children, her home, every single strand of hair on Philip's head. His finger tightened on the trigger and Alex didn't even try to move – what was the point? Something yellow and huge landed on Philip's back, and the shot went wild. Philip staggered a few paces, regained his balance, and pulled his knife. Alex tried to grasp the fact that she wasn't dead. Not yet, anyway. The dog snarled, Philip howled, using his good arm to dislodge the dog from his back. A few moments later, poor Narcissus was dead, Philip's knife buried in his flank.

Just like that, time resumed its normal speed. Philip shoved the dog to the side and bent to retrieve his gun. Alex went for the musket; she had to stop him. Walter yelled in warning, and Alex grunted when her forehead banged into Philip's. She held on for grim life to the gun's barrel, and the air filled with war cries, with the hoarse roar of advancing enraged men.

From the river came Matthew, leaping towards the Burleys with death in his eyes. That in itself wouldn't have been enough, but beside him ran Qaachow, and behind them came Ian and Mark and a whole band of Indians.

Shots burst from all around. Philip cursed. With a decisive yank, he reclaimed his gun from Alex before hurrying over to where his brothers and their men were already scrambling up in their saddles.

Arrows whirred overhead, Matthew yelled – a loud carrying "*Alex*". One of the attackers fell off his horse to land in the dirt, screaming for help. The Burleys didn't look back. They spurred their horses away.

It was abruptly very quiet – or at least that was how it seemed to Alex. She opened her mouth to speak but closed it, because she had no idea what to say. The children... Adam fell into her arms, and Alex had to bite back on the surge of pain this caused her. But her son was whole and safe, and here came Samuel and David, rushing over the yard to her. Mark came with Daniel at his heels, Sarah came head to head with Ruth – all of them converging on Alex, who sat mute and stared at the man who was bleeding to death only yards from her feet.

Ian's hand on her shoulder, Mark's arm round her waist, and she was standing, facing Matthew. In his eyes, she saw the same fear that lay like a frosty layer round her heart. They would never give up. As long as the Burleys lived, they would try to avenge themselves on Matthew for the death of their youngest brother.

"He's dead." Mrs Parson nudged at Spencer with her toe. "May you rot in hell."

"And the other one?" Alex asked. It was difficult to talk through her swollen mouth.

"Oh, he's alive," Mark said, "for now."

It scared Alex to see the look in her son's eyes: all ice, no human warmth whatsoever. When she looked at Ian, it was the same, and Matthew's eyes were like emeralds.

"We turn him over to the law, right?" Alex said.

Matthew looked down at her with an unreadable expression on his face. "He goes with the Indians."

"But—" Alex fell silent at the implacable look in his eyes. "Too bad it wasn't one of the Burleys," she said, indicating the dead man.

"Aye," Matthew replied. "It's but a matter of time," he added ominously, and both his sons nodded.

Qaachow had by now joined them, and was eyeing Alex with respect. "Quite the warrior." He gave Alex a slight bow.

She shrugged. "They threatened my children," she said, experimentally opening and closing her mouth to ensure her jaw wasn't dislocated. Her face was blossoming with pain, she was bleeding from a gash down her cheek, and her side hurt like hell. To top it off, her right hand was covered in blood – not hers. Qaachow's eyes drifted over to Samuel, who was bleeding from a shallow cut down his neck.

"What happened to him?" he asked.

"Stephen grabbed him and I jumped Stephen." She was tired and scared, wanted nothing more than to hide herself away and cry. She hadn't intended to kill the unknown man, but there it was. He was dead as a doornail. She shied from looking in the direction of the body, but did so all the same, finding that it was already gone. But the blood still stained the ground, and Alex closed her eyes. Silently, she counted to fifty in her head, straightened up, and limped inside to see to the feeding of their Indian allies.

"They'll come back," Alex said to Matthew, once they were alone.

"Probably." He concentrated on what he was doing, large hands washing her face, her bruised side. He dipped linen cloths in the tea prepared by Mrs Parson and applied them to Alex's face, indicating she had to lie still. It was almost like having a facial, Alex reflected, lying back with a soft exhalation against the pillows. She groped for his hand and opened her fingers to braid them with his.

"I was so scared."

"So was I. And had Qaachow not been here…" He shook his head.

"How did he know?"

"He has sentries posted."

"Oh." Alex gnawed at her lip. "Sentries? All the time?"

"Aye." Matthew flopped down beside her. "To protect his foster son, and today Qaachow has placed me forever in his debt."

"I don't want him to take Samuel," Alex whispered.

Matthew raised their braided hands to his lips. "Nor do I, lass."

"Maybe—" Alex broke off.

"Maybe what?"

Alex shook her head. She had been about to say that maybe Qaachow would die before Samuel was twelve, but how could she even think that? They owed Qaachow their lives.

"We can send Samuel to school," she said instead. "Somewhere very far away."

"Aye, mayhap. But we don't need to worry yet, do we? He's only six."

Chapter 28

Matthew hurried over to help his sister off her horse, and it was like lifting a wee lass, all skin and bones. Joan disengaged herself with a little frown, making very clear that she'd have no patience with questions regarding her health.

"And you, Simon, have you become permanently attached to yon horse?" he teased, shading his face to peer up at his brother-in-law.

"I don't think I can get off," Simon said. "My legs are permanently splayed, and my privates will never recuperate."

"Aye well, if you choose to ride a carthorse…" Ian eyed the ugly horse Simon was perched on with some amusement. "Maybe it was the only one that could carry your weight?"

"You shouldn't make fun of your elders," Simon said haughtily and dismounted. "Nor should you judge on appearances alone. This is a true Rocinante, it is." He slapped the horse on its huge rump.

"Rocinante was a very thin nag," David piped up, looking this unknown uncle up and down. "That horse is fat – very fat."

"Aye, if it were a lady horse, one would think it big with foal." Sarah giggled.

"Is Uncle big with child then?" Adam asked.

"Laddie," Simon replied severely, patting his belly. "This is the accumulation of very many years of wisdom."

"And good food," Alex said, making Joan and Matthew laugh.

"And that." Simon's eyes leapt from one bairn to the other, looking somewhat taken aback. Well, Matthew reflected with some pride, it was a sizeable brood, and it was one thing to count names on paper, quite another to find oneself surrounded by nephews and nieces.

"Nine bairns and four grandchildren. You've been quite productive." Simon grinned at Alex. "I recall you saying that over your dead body would there be more than five."

"Things happened," Alex said.

"Oh, aye. Big things." Simon eyed Matthew's crotch insinuatingly.

"Simon," Joan admonished, but she was smiling all the same.

"Two menservants?" Alex asked Mark sotto voce.

"Aye, a reasonable precaution in these times. One man killed and two seriously wounded some days back. Indians against Indians, and they were caught between." Unspoken between them lay the ever-present threat of the Burleys. Mark reverted to studying Lucy. "I don't recall her as quite so eye-catching."

"No, she was an ugly baby. But, lo and behold, the duckling has become a swan."

That reminded her: she had as yet not told Matthew about Lucy's effect on Henry Jones. Alex looked at Ruth. Marriage to someone like Henry Jones would ensure material comfort well beyond what Ruth was accustomed to, so maybe she was stupid to refuse to countenance it on account of things that had happened so long ago. She studied her redheaded daughter and was washed by a wave of nausea at the thought of Dominic Jones' DNA mixing with theirs. No, definitely something that wasn't going to happen. With a quick smile at Mark, she hurried over to Joan, who was looking rather abandoned now that Matthew had dragged off Simon for a private tour.

"You still haven't told me," Matthew said to Simon. For the last half-hour, they'd spoken of the Burleys, with Simon interjecting the odd exclamation here and there.

"Told you what?" Simon clasped his hands behind his back.

"Why you're here."

"Aye, I have. I had to leave."

"Simon," Matthew sighed, "have we not always been honest with each other?"

"No," Simon bit back, "I recall a hasty ride back from Edinburgh to Cumnock, and not once did you see fit to tell me you'd hanged an English officer – not until after we were stopped and asked about your whereabouts."

Matthew gave him a long look. "Am I to take it this is something of a similar nature?"

"Somewhat."

"Ah." Matthew waited for some more, but for all that Simon looked most concerned, it was clear he had no intention of saying more. Instead, he turned the conversation back to the Burleys, suggesting that Matthew should initiate action to have the brothers outlawed.

"How will that help?"

"Outlawed and with a price on their heads?" Simon gave a little laugh. "If it were me, I'd keep well away from the colony."

"There's no one to uphold such, not here. In Providence, it might help, but out here…" Matthew spread his arms to indicate the wilderness that surrounded his home. His only protection here were his Indian allies, thereby increasing his debt of gratitude to Qaachow.

"Still, a first step."

"Hmm," Matthew said. Mayhap he was right.

He shared this with Alex when he ran into her by the smoking shed, and immediately regretted doing so. Of late, it took but the mention of the Burleys to make Alex acquire the waxy pallor of a tallow candle, and now she just nodded before changing the subject.

"Apparently Henry Jones' covetous eye has locked itself on pretty Miss Melville," she said.

"Aye? Well, she's a bonny lass." Matthew was only mildly interested.

"So you're not going to go all mad and insist Henry must marry Ruth?"

"It never got beyond a suggestion, and, in any case, you were dead set against it."

Alex flicked at some straw that had gotten stuck to his shirt. "I told you: just the thought of seeing anything of Dominic Jones in Ruth's future children...ugh!"

Matthew was on the verge of commenting that Henry mostly took after his mother, bonny woman that she was, but given that Alex was a trifle oversensitive when it came to Kate, chose not to.

It was almost like old times, back at Hillview, Matthew mused some days later. To have Simon and Joan here, to hear Alex laugh with his sister again, it warmed him all the way down to his toes. And for him to spend evening after evening with Simon, reliving his youth, discussing the matters of the world, it did him good, banishing the constant presence of the Burleys to the back of his mind. Still, he heeded Simon's advice and, together, they wrote a long description of the Burleys' colourful career.

Matthew signed the finished document with a flourish, blotted it, and sat back to read it yet again. The house was silent, all hands either in the fields or in the kitchen garden. He looked with irritation at his sprained foot – consequence of an unfortunate stumble yesterday – deciding that one day of rest was enough, and that tomorrow he'd start taking in the barley on the last two fields.

He stretched and hobbled out into the yard, sitting down in a shady spot halfway up the slope that led to the graveyard. They were almost done with the harvest, and this year it was good – it would go a good way to cover Daniel's fees for the coming school year, and mayhap there would be enough to set something aside for the wee ones. Adam...he smiled: if any child of his had the gift of healing in his hands, it was his youngest, and Matthew had already decided that Adam was destined to be a physician.

From physician, the leap to apothecary was rather short, and Matthew was invaded by images of his Jacob, in London and doing well for himself. His chest expanded with pride at the same time as his stomach twisted at the thought of Jacob spending time with Luke – and quite a lot of time, to judge from his latest letter. He was sorry to hear Luke had lost his second son, and slightly amused at Jacob's insistence his uncle needed a new wife – *preferably someone old who cannot have children by him but will love him dearly all the same.* He missed his son, especially now when his whole family was collected around him. He was overwhelmed by an urge to write Jacob a letter, and got to his feet in one fluid movement. He could still do that, he noticed with satisfaction, still get to his feet without using his hands – sprained foot notwithstanding.

"You don't have to accompany us tomorrow. The lad rides well protected with us, and I'll see him on the boat myself." Simon looked over to where Daniel was lounging on the swing, Ruth and Lucy hovering around him. "Good-looking lad, I dare say Lucy has quite a fondness for him."

"Cousins, and, besides, she's already spoken for." Matthew elbowed Simon hard, grinning at his brother-in-law's responding wince. "I'd be most obliged. I wouldn't mind saving myself the round trip down to Providence."

"Decided then." Simon hurried off to where Joan was calling for him.

Matthew went over to the swing and tapped Daniel on his shoulder. "Walk?"

They took a long walk, just the two of them, with Matthew listening to Daniel's enthusiastic descriptions of Boston and the life he led there. Once they reached the river, they sat down on the bank, Daniel commenting that it was never this hot in Massachusetts.

"No?" Matthew chuckled. He stretched out full length beside his son, pulled up a straw of grass and chewed at it, his eyes on the bronzed blue of the August sky. "Are you content?"

Daniel didn't reply at first. "I think so," he finally said. "I enjoy school, and the masters say I do well, and it will be exciting to enter university this autumn."

Matthew rolled over to prop himself up on an elbow. "Will you promise me one thing?"

"What?" Daniel asked, making Matthew smile. Jacob's

automatic reply would have been anything, but Daniel was far cannier than his brother – most of his brothers.

"If you at any time feel this vocation isn't for you, will you let me know? I don't want to force you into something that you have no love for, and the ministry requires full commitment."

Daniel pulled at the grass. "How will I know?"

Matthew sat up and put an arm around him. "All the way to the vows of ordination, you have time to think, lad. It's a hard road to the ministry, and that's very much on purpose, because once a minister always a minister. I won't think less of you if you come and tell me you can't take those vows. I will think less of you if you take them and don't uphold them."

Daniel leaned against him and nodded. "I'll think beforehand."

Chapter 29

"What's this?" Jacob had never seen anything like it before, and leaned closer. The blues and greens leaped out of the small gilt frame, whispering seductively that he should look, come closer and look. Jacob's stomach turned, and he straightened up, swallowing back on a rush of bile.

"What?" Luke looked up from his correspondence. "Oh, that." He waved his hand dismissively. "I generally don't have it out. It's a wee thing Margaret had after her mother."

"Her mother?"

Luke grunted. "Aye, she had a mother. All of us do." He set down his quill. "She died when Margaret was very young – well, we assume she did; here one day, gone the next – and that wee painting was all Margaret had to remember her by."

"Oh." Jacob peeked at the picture, closing his eyes at the resulting nausea.

"You don't like it?"

Jacob wasn't sure. "It makes me seasick, but the colours…"

Luke came over to stand beside him. "Seasick?" He shook his head. "Nay, not at all. But I don't much like it all the same, which is why I keep it in one of my drawers."

"Aye, do that," Jacob said, his eyes stuck in all that blue and green. But then he remembered why he'd come, and dug into his shirt. "Letters: one from Mama and one from Betty." This latter one he set to the side, not really knowing what he was hoping for: a heated declaration of love?

Mama's letter was a long, untidy scrawl, decorated with the odd ink splotch here and there, and he smiled at how she would surely curse every time that happened, blaming the quill, the ink, anything but her penmanship.

Betty living with them? Mr Hancock whipping her? Jacob swam in shame at what he'd done, his eyes leaping to the other news. The stable burnt to the ground, Angus dead, a new baby brother for Hannah, a wee sister for Malcolm, and then this very strange thing about Ian divorcing Jenny 'on account of her infidelity'. Poor Ian! And Jenny, what would happen to her? He folded it together and after a moment of hesitation, opened Betty's letter. He swallowed, took his time in smoothing out the pages, and began to read.

Luke saw him stiffen, and for a moment assumed the lad had found out he was now a father, but then Jacob began to breathe again, a look of absolute relief on his face. Luke smiled. The lass had changed her mind, and who was happier than young Master Graham, greensick with love for that Foster girl?

The letter included some kind of formal deed, and when Jacob held it out, Luke took it and read it. The marriage was not to be considered valid as it had never been consummated. Betty had signed it, and there was a space for Jacob to sign it as well.

"It wasn't consummated? You've told me you bedded her," Luke said.

"Difficult to prove it happened if both parties agree it didn't."

"And are you just going to relinquish this love of your life?" Luke teased. He looked closer at the document. "Well, well, and look who is her lawyer, if not that wee toad Simon Melville."

"Simon? Uncle Simon?" Jacob took back the document. "But he's in Edinburgh!"

"Not, I would say; rather in Maryland." He played with that for some time. Why would a well-established lawyer leave so late in life? He couldn't recall Simon as being overly religious, but Joan definitely was. Maybe she had somehow meddled with something she shouldn't. The timing suited, what with the crushing defeat to the Covenanters last June at Bothwell Brig, and the consecutive hunt for fugitives throughout the south-west of Scotland. Luke frowned: Joan had not been well since the birth of her deaf daughter, and last time he had glimpsed her in Edinburgh he had been shocked by how old she looked. Surely, she wouldn't do something reckless?

"There!" Jacob signed, wrote a brief covering letter, and sealed the document, addressing it as instructed to Simon.

"And why has she decided she no longer wants to be married?" Luke asked, watching all this with some amusement.

"She didn't really say. I…" Jacob sighed and looked at his uncle, his ears a bright red. "I don't think I forced her, not as such, but I don't think she really wanted to."

"Ah, a bit like Richard Collin is purportedly doing with his stepdaughter?"

Jacob flew out of his chair. "He forces her!"

"Hmm," Luke replied, steepling his fingers in his favourite thinking position. Charlotte Foster struck him as an unlikely victim, even more so knowing her eldest sister as well as he did. He hid a small smile at the thought of acrobatic little Frances, now since several years prim Mrs Holmes. Besides, if Richard Collin was bedding Charlotte regularly, it was surprising that she was as yet not with child – her two eldest sisters bred like rabbits. Luke turned this thought over a couple of times before directing the full force of his eyes on Jacob.

"What are you giving her?" he said.

Jacob attempted a look of incomprehension, making him look very much like dear, recently departed Rochester's pet monkey.

"Jacob," Luke warned.

"Queen Anne's Lace," Jacob said, "and rue and tansy to steep into tea."

Luke was tempted to slap him. Fool, to meddle in matters as sensitive as these!

"Does Master Castain know of this?"

Jacob shook his head. "No one knows. I barely dare see

261

her, and she goes accompanied to church these days." So he left her small packages, he told Luke, tucked away under her favourite pew.

"I told you to stay away from her! We both told you to." Luke frowned at the September rain pattering the window before facing his nephew. "What is it you don't understand? The lass is too valuable for Richard Collin to let her slip through his fingers."

"Then why hasn't he wed her?"

"Why? Because she's only fifteen, you oaf, and it is not quite a year since her mother died. And I very much doubt that he's bedding her."

"Are you calling Charlotte a liar?" Jacob's eyes tightened into narrow slits of green fire. "Well, are you?" he repeated, balancing on the balls of his feet.

Luke was tempted to laugh. This nephew of his was far more like him than he was his father, and the sheer audacity of continuing to see a lass he had been so explicitly warned away from, not only by Master Castain and himself, but also physically by Richard Collin and his apprentices, deserved some admiration. "I'm just making the point that none of us know. You have only her word, and I have only his."

"You spoke to Richard?"

The familiar use of the first name was revealing. Jacob was seeing Charlotte far more often than the glimpses in church he admitted to.

"Aye, I did. A casual comment, no more, as to the rumours that he was making free of his ward."

"And what did he say?" Jacob said.

The man had been most irate: curses had tumbled out of his mouth as he berated whoever it was that was spreading this calumny, grimly promising Luke that should he find him — or her — there would be very little skin left on their backs when he was done.

"He would say that."

"Yes, I suppose he would," Luke agreed, thereby mending his bridges with his nephew.

He poured them both some wine, sat down and crossed

his legs, regarding Jacob who was still sunk into thoughts of his own – more of dastardly Richard Collin than of fair Charlotte, to judge from his mien.

"It must itch," Luke said with a small smile.

"Itch?" Jacob looked confused.

"As I hear it, Mistress Wythe no longer has the pleasure of your company."

Jacob looked away. "I can't bed her and not love her, can I?"

"No?" Luke beckoned the lad over. "Let me show you that you most certainly can."

"Now?" Jacob looked at his everyday wear. Luke stifled a little laugh. Where they were going, it was the gold in your purse, not your exterior that counted.

"Now," Luke said, leading the way to the door.

"You have work to do!" Master Castain scolded.

"Aye," Jacob winced. "But will you please keep your voice down?" He groaned and held his aching head between his hands. "Never, never, never again," he said, and hurried outside to void his guts. He felt much better afterwards, and even better after Master Castain poured a bucket of ice-cold water over his head.

"Seeing as you've not been remiss before, you'll go unpunished this time," Master Castain said. "But next time I'll belt to you."

Jacob nodded carefully. Somehow, his brain had become dislodged during the night, skidding uncomfortably within his skull at any hasty movement. Jacob sat down and began the tedious process of mortaring the bundled herbs and spices into powder. A fragrant cup of herbal tea was placed before him.

"Ginger, cinnamon and mugwort," Master Castain said, "and I've asked the Mistress to make you some onion soup."

"Thank you," Jacob mumbled. "That's very kind of you, master."

Master Castain laughed and clasped his shoulder. "Believe it or not, but I have also been young – and very wild, according to my sainted mother."

Jacob eyed him balefully. Did he have to roar him in the ear?

In his befuddled state, he spent most of the morning without one single complete thought, but, by late afternoon, the small cogwheels inside his head began to interact again, swamping him with memories of the previous night and evening. He glossed over the end, a stinging feeling to his cheeks when he recalled himself, very drunk and very roused, swear his never-ending love to the pretty little whore, who had yawned in his face and told him to get on with it or she would have to charge him double.

To block out these embarrassing recollections, he mulled over his letters instead. More than one year away from home, and this was the first time he'd actually felt the sharp sting of homesickness. He longed for his family, all of them, but in particular for Mama and Da. Not at all for Betty, and he was washed again by that wave of relief that had broken over him yesterday when he'd read her letter. He squinted down at his measuring bowl, and attempted to bring to mind what she looked like, but all he could properly see was that wild hair that always fuzzed into a halo no matter how hard she braided it. He smiled fondly. How she had hated it and how he had loved it... Jacob yawned, pillowed his head on his arms and slept.

Jacob was flustered when Helen came into the shop the next day, standing unobtrusively in a corner until he found the time to serve her.

"Willow bark and peppermint," she ticked off, "sage and, if you have it, tansy."

"Tansy?"

She grinned at him. "For my face."

"I'm getting married come Michaelmas," Helen said in passing, curtseying to Mistress Castain.

"Oh, aye? And is he a nice man this time?"

Helen shrugged. "My father's choice, and a respectable enough merchant, even if he's rather old and has very little hair." She looked yearningly at Jacob's heavy mane, making

264

Jacob duck his head and hide behind the curtain of fair hair. "I was thinking," she murmured, "that maybe we could... one more time?"

Jacob studied her. She'd made an effort, the linen very white, and her hair recently washed. His cock swelled. One more time and never again, it begged. Look at her, and you like her soft, round breasts, don't you?

"Aye, that would be nice. One last time."

She smiled at him. "Tonight," she whispered and, with yet another curtsey to Mistress Castain, left the shop.

"I hear Widow Wythe will soon be a married woman," Master Castain said, coming over to stand beside Jacob.

"Aye, in less than a week."

Master Castain threw him an oblique look. "And so will young Miss Foster."

Jacob glared at him. "No, she won't. She doesn't want him."

"And how would you know that, Jacob Graham?" Master Castain could look quite threatening despite his short stature, and now he frowned at Jacob. "I've told you: Charlotte Foster is not for the likes of you. Twice, Richard Collin has had you beaten for sniffing too closely around his ward, and if you aren't careful, it will soon be thrice."

"I am careful," Jacob informed him. "Very careful. I don't see her at all." Which was not much of a lie: it had been but three times since July.

"Hmph," Master Castain snorted.

Jacob decided to change the subject. "Will you help me with my reading, master? I'm not entirely comfortable with the preparation of tonics against hair loss."

"They never work," John Castain snapped, but then smiled, shaking his sparsely covered head. "But it's hope we sell, and hope comes best in pleasing colours and agreeable tastes."

"Oh? Mama says beer is the thing. Beer and lentils."

"On your head?" Master Castain made a disgusted face.

Jacob laughed out loud. "Nay, you eat them. On account of the vitamins."

"Vitamins?" Master Castain said before waving his hand at Jacob. "No, son, I already know. It's something they have in Sweden." From the master's tone of voice, Jacob suspected he might be talking a wee bit too much about Mama.

"Well done!" Master Castain said halfway through October, clapping Jacob on the shoulder. "You did very well."

Jacob flushed with pleasure. For hours, he had been drilled by fellow apothecaries, in everything from the use of leeches, to tonics to strengthen the blood or reinvigorate a flagging manhood, and he hadn't stumbled even once. His head was full of recipes, of herbs and their uses, of how best to draw the essence of elderberries, and what remedy to recommend to someone suffering from excessive flatulence.

"I didn't list the properties of pomegranate as I should," he said, somewhat chagrined.

"No," Master Castain said, "there's still work to do."

Jacob nodded distractedly. Charlotte would be crossing London Bridge within the hour, and they had an assignation to meet outside the milliner's shop halfway across. It was the first time in weeks they had met, and Jacob's innards were filling with bubbles of expectation. He hurried after Master Castain, shivering in the easterly wind that promised at minimum rain and possibly sleet, and tugged his cloak tighter round him. The hood shadowed his entire face, leaving only his nose to brave the cold full-on.

"Home?" Master Castain said.

Jacob shook his head. This was his afternoon off and, after promising to be back before supper, he rushed off in the direction of the river.

She was waiting, her fur-lined hood pulled up, and only by the way she rocked from side to side did he recognise her. Charlotte moved to a rhythm uniquely her own, a soft swaying that men found most alluring. He stepped up to her, drew back his hood for an instant before letting it drop back down, and she did the same, her mouth curving into one of those smiles that had him promising her the moon should she want it.

266

They fell into step with each other, jostling their way through the crowds until they found a sheltered, quiet corner between two stretches of shops. Charlotte's maid followed them at a distance, turning her back to give them some privacy.

"Are you alright?" Jacob asked.

Charlotte muffled a small sound. Alright? How could it possibly be alright, did he think, when most nights she had to bolt her door to be left in peace?

"I wish—" he began, but broke off, shaking his head. It tore at him, to not be able to help her, save her from this cruel stepfather. He took her hand instead and caressed her palm with his thumb. They spoke briefly to each other, huddled against the icy wind. As they said their farewells, she allowed him to kiss her, whispered a new date, and rushed off.

Jacob remained where he was, stamping his feet in the cold. This was becoming quite unbearable, and in his head the most preposterous plans were being hatched, all of them ending with him and her forever. He laughed. He was seventeen soon, and too old to believe in fairy tales. If he stood on his toes, he could still see her, weaving her way in and out of the crowd, and suddenly her hood was thrown back and the light of a lantern spilled over her hair, making it gleam like gold. How apt: the daughter of a goldsmith, shimmering in golden hues. A wealthy lass, accustomed to a life of comfort. What could he possibly offer her?

He sighed and trudged back home.

Chapter 30

"I told you that wee kitten has lethal claws," Mark said.

"But still, to throw boiling sugar at someone and claim it was an accident!" Alex shook her head. "Ailish is going to be permanently disfigured, and from the way Nathan looked at Constance today, she should be fearing a trial – or a knife in the back. Are you okay?" she asked Mrs Parson, who was hanging on grimly to Mark.

"Aye," Mrs Parson replied through gritted teeth. "But maybe you could walk the horse instead?"

"Oh." Mark drew rein. "Better?"

"Ugh," Mrs Parson replied, and released her hold somewhat.

The rider had come at midday. One of the younger Leslie field hands had stormed into the yard on Peter's best horse and begged them to come quickly as the mistress was badly burnt. Alex had been shocked: the right side of Ailish's face, her ear, shoulder and neck, all a blistered mass made worse by her frantic attempt to get the sticky, burning sugar off her.

Constance had looked contrite, trying to blend into the wall, but at Ailish's anguished looks in her direction, Alex had evicted her and told her to make herself useful – if she could.

Once they were home, Alex went to find Matthew.

"Peter has a civil war on his hands," she said, "and I'm not sure he's fully aware of what the fallout might be, what with Nathan siding with poor Ailish, while that cow Constance flutters her eyes and says it was an accident."

Matthew grunted and went on with his leatherwork. "Constance Leslie is not a nice woman, but neither was she given the welcome she should have been accorded the day

Peter Leslie rode back to present his new wife."

Alex rolled her eyes at him. In her book, Constance was a conniving little bitch, and to fill a ladle with melted sugar and throw it at someone…

"She even had the effrontery to ask us to look at her hand as she had burnt herself."

"And did you?" Matthew asked.

"No, why should we? Oh, by the way, Jenny was there."

It had been a difficult meeting, with Jenny dropping a curtsey before shooing Ailish's brood from the room. Some stilted words in the kitchen with Jenny replying monosyllabically that yes, she was well, and no, she didn't intend to stay for more than some weeks – she was only here to sort out the details of her jointure.

"She wants to see the children." Alex looked over to where Betty was capably carrying Maggie in her shawl, while helping Malcolm balance on the paddock railings. Matthew came to stand behind Alex and slipped his hands around her waist.

"Canny lass," he said with a nod in the direction of Betty.

"Canny? How canny?" Alex smiled at Betty. Gone was the insecure girl of a year ago, and in her place was a high-spirited, confident young woman, eyes bright and hair even fuzzier than usual.

In response, Matthew pointed to where Ian was leaning against the stable door, his eyes glued to where his children were playing with his intended wife.

"I think she likes them for their own sake."

Matthew laughed into her hair. "But very much on account of their father."

Alex wandered over to the stables and gave Ian a short recap of the events at the Leslies' – including Jenny's presence there.

"Aye, I already know." Ian cast an eye at the lowering black clouds. "It'll snow soon."

"Ian!" Alex elbowed him. "We're not talking about the weather, are we?"

He looked down at her and stretched his lips into a faint smile. "Nay, we were talking about my erstwhile wife. About as interesting."

"Bullshit – and don't try that cool, impervious look on me. It makes you look quite inane. So, will you let her see the children?"

"I promised her, so aye, I will. But not here, not at home. I'll ride over to Leslie's Crossing with them in a day or so."

"Does he miss her, do you think?" Alex indicated Malcolm, who had joined his uncles for a wild game of football in the frozen yard.

"Aye." It came out very soft, a mere whisper. "Not as much now as in the beginning," Ian continued in a more normal tone of voice, "and, with time, even less. But for now, aye, the lad misses his mother."

"She never will." Alex nodded in the direction of Betty, who was walking towards them, singing something to the flailing bundle in her shawl.

"Nay. She has a new mother." Ian went over to reclaim his daughter.

"Not formally she doesn't," Alex muttered to his back.

Ailish remained in bed when Alex accompanied Ian to Leslie's Crossing some days later. The rawness had subsided, but already the puckering had begun, and where once there had been smooth skin, in the future there would be a huge and rather ugly scar.

"Thank God it didn't hit you closer to the eye," Alex said, breaking open the aloe vera leaves she'd brought with her to get at the gel.

Ailish didn't reply.

"I've made you some calendula tea to use as poultices," Alex said, "and then you must keep it as dry and clean as possible." She felt helpless. Burns such as these should be treated in a hospital by people with white coats and stethoscopes hanging round their necks, not by someone like her. She picked up Ailish's hand and held it for a while. The younger woman's silence was unnerving and, from what Nathan had said, this was the way she'd been for the last few days.

"I'll come and apply some more gel before I leave, okay?" Alex said, stroking back the thick hair.

Ailish remained mute, her eyes fixed on the rosary beads she was twisting through her fingers. It was with relief that Alex left the room, making a weak excuse along the lines of brewing more tea.

She found Nathan in the dark kitchen, all messy hair and tired eyes.

"How is she?" he asked, hoisting his youngest son to lie in the crook of his arm.

"It's not infected, but her face will be marked for life." Alex patted him on the shoulder. "I'm so sorry, but there's nothing to be done, I'm afraid."

"She's afraid I won't love her if she's disfigured," Nathan said with a perceptiveness that surprised Alex. To her, he had always been the spoilt eldest son, used to getting his own way in a household that consisted mostly of sisters.

"And won't you?" Alex found a mug, crumbled a generous amount of willow bark into it, and used a ladle to fill it with simmering water from the iron cauldron that hung over the hearth.

Nathan just shook his head. "Five children, Mistress Alex, as well as rearing my two by Celia as if they were her own. I never loved Celia – I've always loved Ailish – I always will."

"Then you'd better tell her that." Alex handed him the mug of willow bark tea and held out her arms for the baby. "Go on, she's awake. Make sure she drinks it all." She shoved Nathan out of the kitchen and went to find Peter.

"You're going to have to do something," Alex said to Peter, handing him his grizzling and damp grandson. "You can't expect Ailish to continue living with someone who intentionally hurt her."

"Constance says it was an accident."

"Accident, my arse! She filled the ladle and threw it at Ailish!"

271

Peter shrank together in his chair, his chin all but disappearing into his neck. His once so vigorous hair was now trimmed very short, and on the desk a hairpiece lay thrown on top of an unfinished letter.

"Nathan says she must be punished," he said.

"Yeah – harshly."

"Do you suppose Nathan will take it up with the ministers?"

"He should," Alex said, "but, for your sake, he won't."

Peter fidgeted with his cravat, his long fingers smoothing it down against his chest. He looked old and tired, and Alex felt sorry for him, even if this whole mess was his fault. She supposed there were days when he missed Elizabeth, even more when he regretted marrying Constance. From what little she'd overheard, there was no great fondness between man and wife, a minimum of words, no more. Not like with Elizabeth, Peter's companion and confidant in everything he did.

"I heard Walter Burley has been arrested," Peter said, thereby distracting Alex from his marital issues.

"What?" Alex stared at him. "Where?"

"In Jamestown," Thomas Leslie replied in his brother's stead, nodding in greeting at Alex as he entered the room. "For rape."

"Oh," Alex said.

"Fourteen, the girl is." Thomas produced his pipe and a pouch of tobacco. He frowned down at the pouch and, from the way his jaw was working, Alex assumed he was thinking about his own daughter, almost as young when she was brutally assaulted several years ago.

"If we're lucky, he hangs." Peter patted Alex's hand.

"If we're lucky?" Alex echoed.

Peter sat back. "It's her word against his. As I hear it, he's insisting she gladly went along with it. Besides, those brothers would have hanged years ago had it not been for their powerful friends in Virginia. That Philip has most of Jamestown eating out of his hand, one way or the other."

"Blackmail, probably," Alex said.

Peter nodded. "Maybe. But it's also a matter of lucrative business endeavours. The Burleys have enriched quite a few of their Virginian neighbours."

"Whatever the case, he won't be coming by here any time soon," Thomas said, "and that's really what's most important."

"For us, yes, but not for her, poor girl." Alex sighed.

"No, not for her," Thomas agreed.

It was only reluctantly that Alex agreed to stay for dinner, and if she found it difficult, Ian must have hated it, sitting very much to the side throughout the meal. Constance acted the lady of the house – to be fair she was, even if Nathan looked as if he'd gladly throw her out the door – serving them bread and beer to go with a watery cabbage soup. All through the meal Constance kept staring at them, dislike shining out of her eyes when she studied her husband and her stepson, but particularly whenever they rested on Jenny.

"Have you seen anything of – what was his name? Patrick?" Constance asked spitefully. A bright flush stained Jenny's face while Ian looked at Constance as if he was considering disembowelling her.

"Constance," Peter sighed from his end of the table, cutting his eyes in the direction of Ian.

"What? I am but asking – out of concern for my stepdaughter."

Alex raised her brows. "Of course, we all know how much you care for Jenny."

"Not as such, but her morals reflect on me, and I have repeatedly urged my husband to do his fatherly duty and whip her – drive the sins of the flesh out of her body once and for all."

Jenny made a strangled noise and pushed back from the table.

"Was it worth it?" Constance asked her, ignoring Peter's warning sounds. "Did he merit putting your soul at risk?"

Jenny was on her feet, making for the door.

"Or mayhap it was just a matter of needing a real man in your bed – Our Lord knows I can sympathise with that!" Constance called after her.

"That's enough!" Peter exploded, rising to his full height. "How dare you sit there, wife, and insult not only my daughter but my guests and myself?"

"Not my guests," Constance snapped back.

Peter lunged across the table, got her by the scruff of her neck, and dragged her screaming out of the room. All the way up the stairs, she kept on shrieking abuse at him, calling him a fool, a withered old man, a disgusting goat.

"If you don't unhand me, I'll—" she yelled.

The slap echoed down the stairs, and for some seconds there was silence before she started up again.

"We'd best go," Alex said.

"Aye." Ian was already at the door, holding Malcolm by the hand.

"I swear, Matthew, it was very embarrassing," Alex said, having recounted the events. "I never thought I'd say this, but if ever a woman deserves to be whipped, it is Constance Leslie." She frowned at the huge rent in one of David's shirts.

Mrs Parson murmured a fervent assent. "More than once, mayhap on a regular basis, no?"

"Hmm." Alex squinted as she threaded her needle. "I invited them over for Christmas Eve."

"Who?" Ian and Matthew looked at each other and then at her.

"Thomas and Mary, Nathan, Ailish, the children…oh, and Jenny." She concentrated on her sewing, her cheeks heating under their combined looks.

"Well, that will be nice and cosy, no?" Mrs Parson chuckled. "The ex-wife and the wife-to-be in the same room. You're a daftie, Alex Graham, you hear?"

"I couldn't exactly not invite her, not after witnessing Constance's humiliation of her. Besides, what is she to do? Help Peter whip his wife?"

Matthew came over to where she was sitting and crouched down to meet her eyes. For a very long time, they looked at each other, and then he raised a hand to stroke her cheek.

"It's never boring, life with you." He rose to clap his stunned son hard on the back. "We'll need a lot of beer. Will you ride with me to the Chisholms tomorrow and see if we can buy some casks?"

Jenny resented Betty for everything: for the way Malcolm smiled at her; for the way Maggie sat in her lap, the dark tousled head resting against Betty's chest; for the way she leaped to her feet to help Alex. Ingratiating little slut, it was all her fault! If only Betty had kept her mouth shut then it would've been Jenny who would have been complimented for the cheese, Jenny who would have sat beside Matthew as he carved the meat.

It took her some time to notice, but once she did she drowned in jealousy, hating every look that passed between Ian and Betty, every discreet little smile. The sheer effrontery of the girl: accuse Jenny of adultery and then make cow's eyes at Ian, despite being married to his younger brother. What would William Hancock make of all this, she wondered, and as to Jacob Graham… Jenny stood in a corner and hated Betty, planning just what she would do to bring this sweet little love affair to a harsh and brutal end when her arm was gripped by Matthew.

"You have a very transparent face."

Jenny gasped when he increased the pressure.

"Keep in mind that you brought it all on yourself, and should you do anything to hurt my son further, you'll never see the bairns again. That I promise you, aye?"

With that he was gone, calling in a loud voice for some more beer, and behind him Jenny wished that she was dead. She'd had it all, and she had thrown it away, and all for a touch that drove her wild, lips that inflamed her as none had done before. She dragged a shaking hand over her wet eyes and cleared her throat, wishing Patrick had been here to hold her instead of remaining in Providence.

"Why are you out here?" Ian kept his voice down, but made Betty jump all the same.

"I..." she wiped her face on her sleeve. "She doesn't like me." She patted the cow she'd been talking to and straightened up, stepping into the weak light cast by the lantern she'd hung from a nail.

Ian came to stand very close, his coat unbuttoned over his best shirt. He tweaked at her wild curls, left unbound for once, smiling at how the curl bounced back into shape the moment he released it. Sometimes, he forgot she was very young, a mere child in many aspects.

"Nay, of course she doesn't like you, but that need not concern you. I don't think Mama will be inviting her over again in a hurry."

Betty snorted with laughter, making Ian laugh as well. All evening, Mama had been like a trapped doe, hurrying back and forth across the parlour to avert any potential confrontation between Jenny and Ian, Jenny and Betty.

"It makes Malcolm uncomfortable to have us both there," Betty said, "so I thought I'd make it easier for him."

Ian ran a thumb down her nose. "That was nice of you."

Betty hitched her shoulders. "I like Malcolm."

It was cold in the stables. Her breath stood like a plume, and she stuck her hands deeper into her armpits, stamping her feet. He took off his coat and wrapped it around her.

"Now you'll get cold." She smiled, slipping her arms around his waist.

"Betty," he murmured, and he was shivering all over, but he didn't feel cold exactly. She smelled nice: of newly churned butter, of ginger and cinnamon, and something that was always there – an earthy warmth. All of her body he'd explored over the last few months, stolen hours spent tracing the line of her flank, the curve of her hip, the soft down on her belly all the way down to her pubic curls. But he hadn't taken her, because he'd promised Da he wouldn't, and promised himself the same. At times, it was driving him insane, like now in the dark and cold stable when all he wanted was to lay her down and love her properly. He laughed unsteadily. Here it was cold and dirty, and this was not the way it was going to be, not that first time.

Betty stood on her toes and kissed him: lips that promised, a tongue that teased.

"I don't think I can stand this much longer," she whispered. In brown skirts, a sleeveless bodice of palest yellow, green and brown over her clean chemise, her hair as bright and curly as always, she reminded him of a curious thrush, or an impertinent fox cub. Vixen, he smiled; yes, that suited her. Her crotch pressed against his, small breasts rested so close to his skin, and Ian realised that Betty Hancock knew exactly how to play him.

He buried his nose in her hair. "Stop, please stop, Betty."

"I'm not sure I want to," she said and kissed him once again.

Chapter 31

Matthew liked the mornings the best, and, in particular, these long winter mornings when someone else tended to the beasts, and he could dally in bed with his wife for a bit longer than he ever allowed himself in summer.

He rolled out of bed to coax the fire into renewed vigour, lit a candle and set it in the holder he had attached to the headboard, and laid back down to study his wife. She was awake, pretending to sleep, her eyelashes fluttering a bit too much and the corner of her mouth twitching.

"What?" Alex said drowsily. "Am I green all over?"

He laughed and tickled her with his hair. "Nay, not that I can see, but mightily strange all the same."

"Well, at least I'm not a frog, then," she replied, her eyes still closed.

He was transported back to a small cave on a Scottish moor, the first night they met. He'd stared at this woman with clothes that showed off every curve, hair so disturbingly short, and eyes that met his with a flare of indignant blue when she challengingly asked him what it was he was gawking at.

"It's the prince, not the princess, that's turned into a frog," he murmured.

"Be my guest," she laughed. "But I can't promise I'll kiss you back into manhood. I'm not too fond of frogs."

"Ah, no?" He nuzzled her neck, making her squeal like a lassie when he licked the skin just below her ear. She slapped at him, tried to hide under the pillows, but she was laughing, and, as if by chance, she inched her shift up high enough to bare her thighs, her buttocks.

He took hold of her braid and yanked – hard enough that she should know he would not be denied. Not that

278

she had any intention of denying him: he could see that in how she curved her body, in how invitingly she raised her posterior towards him. But she pretended, and for some moments they wrestled in the bed, a heaving silent fight that ended when he grabbed her by the nape and guided her down to his twitching cock. The candlelight gilded her hair; her hands cupped his balls. Teeth closed gently around him. He lay stock-still. Her mouth, her tongue, her teeth – her lips on his balls, his cock.

"Alex, I..." Whatever he had planned to say never got beyond an unformed thought. Instead, he sank his hands into her hair, and she released him, kissing his mouth instead. He didn't want her kisses, not right now. He took her with one strong thrust. As always, there was that long moment when neither of them moved, both of them savouring the sensation of being this close, joined to each other.

He dipped his head and brushed his nose against hers, thereby freeing them from their immobility. She raised her hips, he pushed into her. In the flaring light of the candle, her eyes shifted from cornflower blue to the deepest black, eyes that stared up at him with absolute trust. Her hands on his cheeks, she lifted herself off the bed sufficiently to kiss him – deeply. He increased his pace, she fell backwards, braced against the headboard and rocked to his rhythm. Every single drop of blood in his body was rushing downwards, filling his member with a throbbing, delicious ache. Her breath came in loud gasps that echoed his own. Almost there. His flesh merging with hers; his body fused to hers. He...she...oh Lord!

"It wasn't much of a success yesterday, was it?" Alex asked later, propped up against the pillows. Matthew had his head in her lap, and, had he been a cat, he would have been purring as her fingers stroked and tugged at his hair.

"I wouldn't say that. I think all but three enjoyed themselves."

"Four," Alex said.

"Five," he amended with a sigh, thinking it had been

a terrible evening. "It was a daft thing to do. Jenny would have gladly plunged a cleaver into Betty's head had she had one at hand."

"Why? Because she's in love with Ian?"

"Nay, because Ian's in love with her. And then there's the unfortunate coincidence that it was Betty who saw Jenny with Patrick."

"It would all have come out anyway."

"I think not, and nor does Jenny. It would have been a drearier marriage, but a marriage still."

"An unhappy marriage," Alex said with an edge.

"Aye, the magic was gone. All those years of childlessness…"

Alex shook her head. "That's not it. It's the sudden realisation that something has shifted in the other. It's difficult to dissimulate if you're regularly having sex with someone else."

"Oh?" Matthew sat up. "And you would know?"

Alex looked somewhat discomfited. "It's not as if we were married or anything, and we both saw other people. But I…well, I didn't much feel like…err, you know, bedding with others, while John, he would at times come back to me, and I could see in his eyes that he'd been sleeping with Diane – again." She squirmed. She rarely talked about her previous life in the future, and even less did she talk about that future man, John, or her best friend, Diane.

"Bastard!" Matthew hated the fact that John had been the first man in her life, and even more that the wee idiot had hurt her.

"That was ages ago." Alex burrowed back under her quilts.

"Nay, it isn't, it hasn't even happened yet." He looked at her. "You haven't happened yet, and still, here you are."

"Very creepy," Alex agreed and yawned. In a matter of moments, she was asleep and Matthew relaxed into drowsiness.

Christmas Day and the house lay silent around them, a warm peaceful silence. Today, he would, as always, read them the gospel according to Luke, and, as always, there would break out an amicable squabble between Ruth, himself and Mrs Parson as to the timing of the Flight to Egypt and the Slaying of the Innocents. And later, after a dinner of ham and roasted potatoes and mustard, Alex would bring out the Christmas cake, and the whole family would sit around the kitchen table. The whole family less two – no, three: Jacob and Daniel and wee Rachel, dead since many years back. He sent up a prayer that his lads be safe, smiled at the image of his wild Rachel decorously sitting on a cloud way up high, and rolled towards his wife for a nap.

"Sarah Graham!" Alex scowled. "Who let the dog into my kitchen?"

"He was cold." Sarah hugged the new addition to the canine Grahams.

"And now he's very, very stuffed seeing as he's eaten our Christmas ham," Alex told her.

The dog stretched its dark lips into what looked like a grin and collapsed onto its back, all four legs in the air.

"I'm sorry, I didn't think he'd touch it." Sarah scratched Viggo on his belly. "It isn't his fault," she protested when Alex opened the door and pointed the dog outside.

"Out! If you want to cuddle him then out you go as well. Once you've scrubbed the kitchen floor, of course."

"Scrub the floor?" Sarah looked down at the wooden planks. "It looks clean."

"He's eaten ham all over it, and there are some odd bits and pieces left dribbled all over the place. And, while you're at it, you can think up something else for Christmas dinner – and cook it." Alex grabbed at her cloak and banged the door behind her, choosing to turn a blind eye to the fact that Sarah stuck her tongue out at her.

"Nope," she said to Viggo, "you're not coming with me."

The dog ignored her, gambolling in the thin layer of snow. He was a very cute dog, Alex had to admit, laughing when he buried his snout in the snow and sneezed. Big and long-haired, Viggo looked like a cross between an Afghan hound and a wolf, although Matthew assured her that wasn't the case. Now, the huge dog ran circles around her, tongue hanging out like a pink tie against its dark grey coat.

Alex stepped over the low fencing that surrounded the little graveyard, brushed Magnus' headstone free of snow and cut a frozen rosebud from the bush in the corner to place on top.

"*Lilla Pappa*," she said, letting her fingers trace his name. No dates, just the name and the careful engraving of a bluebell that had taken Matthew hours and hours of patient chipping. Alex scrubbed at a patch of hairy moss and exhaled softly. None of the people who had known Magnus alive knew where he lay buried, and, even if they did, there'd be nothing left of the headstone in their time: it would just be an overgrown, cracked piece of stone.

"*Jag skall vandra, ensam utan spår,*" she murmured, and the Swedish hung heavy in her mouth. She rarely spoke it anymore – for the obvious reason that she had no one to speak it to. "Well, that's the way it is," she said to Viggo. "We're born, we live briefly, and then we die, and nothing is left of us, nothing at all…"

The dog sneezed again, not too interested.

"It's easier for you. You're too stupid to even comprehend your own mortality." She smiled down at her father's name. One of his more recurring gripes against God had been that He'd been cruel enough to make us all too aware of our own insignificant lifespan.

Around her, snow began to fall, small drifting flakes that quickly became an impenetrable curtain of white. Alex shivered inside her cloak, walked back down, and was crossing the yard when something furry and grey scurried away at her approach. She made a mental note to tell Matthew it was time to do some serious raccoon culling – preferably exterminate the entire family before they worked out how to get into their storage sheds, little bandits that they were.

The smoking shed was barely visible in all the snow, and

Alex decided she might just as well get her family something else to eat now that the dog had devoured the ham. She extended her stride, with Viggo a hopeful shadow, one ear flopping forward, the other standing straight up.

"No way," she said to the dog, "you stay outside. I'm not going to risk you with all my meat." She lifted off the heavy bar and stepped inside to lift down a leg of lamb. She was back outside, shoving the door closed, when the dog growled. Alex turned and then screamed.

"I told you," Alex gabbled to Matthew, "he's part wolf. Perhaps only a small part, but still. Or maybe he's one of those Russian wolf-hunting dogs, or is it bears they hunt? No, wolves; they bite them in the ears to hold them still and..." She was talking and talking, trying to stop her knees from shaking, and she looked Matthew firmly in the eye because she didn't dare to look at her right arm.

Two wolves, not raccoons, but wolves! Hell, she loved raccoons, they were almost like pets, but these huge beasts with yellow eyes that seemed to freeze her into immobility... okay, okay, she was exaggerating. Yes, they were big, but perhaps not that big, and Viggo had thrown himself at them, and they'd thrown themselves at her, or rather at the leg of lamb she was holding. She had whacked one of them in the head and the other had bit her. Bit her! Did wolves carry rabies? If they did, she was as good as dead. She sneaked a look at her mangled biceps and decided she might very well die anyway.

"Look at me." Matthew took hold of her unharmed arm. "Don't look at the bite." He anchored her trembling legs between his own and nodded to Ian, who sat down behind Alex and slipped his arms round her waist.

"I have to clean it," Mrs Parson said, "and it will hurt."

Alex nodded, her eyes never leaving Matthew.

"Talk to me," she said hoarsely, concentrating on the colour of his eyes. Green, gold, the odd dash of brown, but mostly a murky green, like when you dived into the river pool back at Hillview and opened your eyes to stare upwards at the sun-dappled surface. He brushed her nose with his own.

"Why in God's name didn't you just throw them the leg of lamb?"

"It's mine," Alex replied with far more bravado than she actually felt. "They can bloody well hunt something else. A huge big moose or a zebra or something."

"Zebra?" Ian laughed from behind her. "They live in Africa, Mama."

"Then they can emigrate." Alex wanted to cry or throw up or perhaps both. Agnes came over to the table from where she'd been busy at the hearth, and the kitchen filled with the scents of garlic and bee balm. Alex knew it was going to hurt like hell, and she didn't want it to.

"Bloody, fucking hell!" Alex gasped for breath, her chest heaving. "Shit, shit, shit." Her arm was on fire; she could smell the iron in her blood as it flowed down her arm to puddle on Sarah's recently scrubbed floor. Giving birth was a piece of cake compared to this!

Another burst of pain, and Alex couldn't help it: her hand closed like a vice round Matthew's fingers. More hot water, and Alex swore and cursed and cried, snot running from her nose. She could hear Agnes crying from somewhere behind her, and wanted to tell her to shut the fuck up, because as far as she knew it wasn't Agnes that was being cut, was it?

"How you go on," Mrs Parson sighed in a matter-of-fact tone that did a very bad job of disguising how upset she was.

Alex turned to glare at her.

"I must sew it. You know I have to, lass."

Alex nodded and peeked at the cleaned, gaping cuts.

"They were deep." Mrs Parson held her curved needle aloft.

"Bed," Matthew said once the arm had been sewn together and bandaged. He helped Alex to stand. She was wet all through with sweat, blood and spilled water.

"I stink," she whispered. "I don't want to stink."

"I'll wash you. Betty will bring me some hot water, won't you, lass, and then I'll wash you and put you to bed."

"I'm not very brave, am I?" she said as he supported her out of the kitchen.

"Brave enough to wallop a wolf with a leg of lamb."

Alex laughed against his shoulder. "That wasn't brave; that was just sheer stupidity."

He sat beside her afterwards and watched her sleep. Thank heavens for the thick cloak or there would have been no arm left; thank heavens for the dog or God knows what might have happened; and thank the Lord that he'd heard her scream and come running with his musket.

She'd looked right wild, blood streaming down her arm, the leg of lamb held high, and one wolf limping off while Viggo grappled the other one. Now, there was one dead wolf in his yard and an injured woman in his bed. He scrubbed his hands through his hair.

Alex woke in time for supper and, after a heated discussion with Matthew, she triumphantly left her bed to sit with her family at the table. Her younger sons were very impressed by their wolf-fighting Mama, and Alex told them about Tarzan, who lived in Africa and wrestled with crocodiles and lions and the like.

"Alone?" Sarah asked. "All alone?"

"He grew up with some monkeys, I think. Gorillas."

"But he can't live with them," Ruth said. "A wean live with wild animals…"

"Well, he did, and then he grew up and met this girl named Jane and they lived happily ever after."

"Jane?" Naomi laughed. "And she'd grown up there as well?"

"No. She came on a boat."

"Ah, that clarifies things." Naomi helped Tom to stand in her lap and bounced him up and down. "Who changed his clouts?"

"I suppose he didn't have any," Alex replied, although in all Tarzan movies she'd seen he was always most modestly covered.

"Could he talk?" Mark asked.

Alex sighed. "It's a story, right? All about this tragic shipwreck, and how the baby survives because some monkeys take care of him, and then one day he meets a girl and realises he isn't a monkey – although I suspect he's figured that one out before – and then he returns to civilisation, doesn't like it, and goes back to his monkeys. With Jane." She eyed them, all of them, from Adam sitting so that he could rest his head against her, to Ian with Maggie in his lap, and her chest tightened uncomfortably. "It wouldn't work, of course; the baby would have died. Human babies need human families." And then she was crying, because it had been so close, so goddamn close, and had the wolf bitten her higher up…

Once she calmed down, she cheered them all up by telling them the story of the Count of Monte Cristo. No gorillas, no woman called Jane, only a man whose life was torn apart by love and treachery. As Alex had forgotten most of the book, she concentrated on the betrayal and subsequent revenge, even if both Ruth and Naomi were disappointed to hear that Edmond never married Mercedes, and David loudly voiced that, if it were him, he would have run that nefarious Fernand through with a sword.

"Or shot him," Sarah said, glancing at the loaded musket that stood by the door.

As if on cue came the mournful sound of a wolf howl, and Alex shrank against Matthew.

"He mourns his mate," Matthew whispered, and tightened his hold on her shoulders.

Chapter 32

Charlotte Foster looked down at the small posy in her hand and dropped it into the gutter with a fleeting smile. A posy, and a hand-picked one at that... She took a hasty step to the right, shook her fist at Mrs Arnold, who smirked down at her with the upended chamber pot in her hand, and ducked into the storefront of Foster & Collin.

The small shop was full of people, and Charlotte curtsied repeatedly to the assembled goldsmiths. As a newly elected officer of the guild, Richard had become quite unbearable of late, a sizeable portion of his day given over to guild matters. She threw him a cautious look. Richard Collin was a solid man, as broad as he was tall, some would say, and quick with his hands when he wanted to be. She guessed him to be twenty years her senior, which left him fifteen years her departed mother's junior. How could he possibly have enjoyed bedding her, Charlotte mused, wrinkling her nose at the thought.

"Charlotte!" He'd seen her, his eyes narrowing in suspicion.

She opened her eyes wide and smiled. Richard smiled back, and Charlotte ducked her head before he should see the amusement in her eyes. Hetty was right: men were at times most gullible. That brought Jacob back to mind, the way his hand was so warm and big round hers, and how he had blushed when he handed her that sad little arrangement of flowers. Flowers! A girl like her required trinkets, a ring, perhaps an ivory comb, not some bluebells and a scattering of butterbur that he shyly told her he had picked for her. But he was a handsome lad, and the way his eyes rested on her made Charlotte Foster preen even more than usual.

She hurried into the room she lived in on her own now

that all three of her sisters were married, and after hanging up her cloak on a peg went over to sit by her looking glass, staring dreamily into her own blue eyes while fingering her swollen lips. Jacob was a good kisser, and should she want to, she had no doubts she could coax him into bedding her as well. But she didn't. She pulled out the drawer and studied the bunches of dried herbs he'd given her over the last few months, believing her story of debauchery and repeated rape.

Charlotte let her hand rustle through the dried heads of tansy and rue, and smiled. The day Richard Collin tried to bed her by force was the day he'd find himself without his balls. Her smile faltered somewhat. Richard was becoming quite insistent that they should wed, that she should sign her name to the marriage contracts so meticulously drawn up, and she was realist enough to understand he wasn't about to accept no for an answer. She could do worse, Hetty reminded her: Richard had all his hair and most of his teeth, and was a vigorous man with no legitimate children of his own. Charlotte felt a twinge of pity for Hetty, third wife to a man with seven children from his previous marriages. No wonder Hetty had no intention of giving him more, gratefully receiving the herbal supplies Charlotte procured through Jacob.

Charlotte rested her chin in her hand and frowned at her mirrored image. Now that the novelty of their secret meetings had worn off, Jacob Graham appeared as what he was: a poor apprentice with nothing to his name but some items of clothing and two books. His shoes were scuffed, his stockings were mended, as was his shirt, and no matter how often he washed, nor how much pumice he used, his fingers retained a greenish hue after hours working in that garden that he spoke so much about.

Charlotte yawned. She had no longing for the country, and his hesitant suggestion that mayhap she could one day walk with him to Chelsea had been met by two very raised brows. Walk? That far? But she was considering walking to Whitehall with him, fascinated by this uncle he spoke so warmly about. A rich man, she'd gathered, even a very rich man.

Charlotte studied her surroundings with pleasure. The bed in dark wood was hung with bed curtains of deep green; the floor was covered by a magnificent Turkish carpet Richard had bought off a Jew; and by the window stood the armchair he had commissioned for her fifteenth birthday, its leather upholstery decorated by golden fleur-de-lis. In the iron-bound chest that stood opposite to the window were most of her clothes – lace from Holland, rich velvets, and even a bodice in brocade – and in the pear wood desk at which she was sitting, lay her little hoard of jewellery. One string of pearls, some rings, a bracelet set with garnets, and the brooch her father had made to celebrate her birth. She picked at the brooch. This item in itself was worth more than all of Jacob Graham. She closed her eyes, and she could feel his lips on her cheek, her neck, hear his voice hitch when he whispered her name.

"I love her," Jacob said to Charles, sinking the mattock into the ground. The late April sun was boiling the back of his neck and bare shoulders, and an hour of work had covered his upper half in sweat.

Charles, a worldly-wise soon fifteen, made a derisive sound. "She'll never marry you."

"I know," Jacob said. "She'll never be allowed to, no matter how much she wants to."

"Perhaps you could run off together."

"Run off?" Jacob stopped mid-stroke and regarded his younger cousin. Every now and then, he considered that idea, but whenever he did, it struck him as incongruous – pretty, fragile Charlotte in Providence, so far from the bustle of London. Jacob went back to his digging, and Charles sat and watched, telling him this and that about his day at school.

"And then..." Whatever else Charlie had planned on telling Jacob was put on hold when Mr Castain showed up, waving three letters over his head.

"From home," he said, dropping the squares of thick, rustling paper on Jacob's discarded shirt.

Jacob wiped his hands on his breeches and picked up the letters, turning them over to study the unbroken seals. Mama's he could wait with, and there was one from Da, and one from Betty. Betty? Why would she write him again? Had she perhaps had a change of heart? He'd been remiss in posting his letters back in autumn, and so they would at best just be making it into Providence, which meant that, to all intents, he was still a married man. A married man with a permanent cock-stand for a girl he could never have, he sighed, his head invaded by that sweet smile he was sure Charlotte reserved only for him.

It shocked him. He read the letter once, he read it twice, he read Ian's long postscript three times, and then he plunked down to stare at absolutely nothing. Ian and Betty? But Betty was his! A wall of something he recognised as rage rose inside him and just as quickly collapsed, leaving him with a sensation of total abandonment.

"Jacob?" Charles shook his shoulder. "Jacob, what is it? Has someone died?"

"No," Jacob said in a breathless voice before surprising himself and Charlie by bursting into tears.

Charles decided Jacob's reaction merited a discussion with his father, and so it was that, an hour later, Jacob was seated in his uncle's study.

"At least he asked you first," Luke said, folding the letter along its creases.

"Aye," Jacob replied, confused by all these conflicting emotions that coursed through him.

"And you don't want her."

Jacob regarded Luke cautiously, belatedly recalling that Da had married a lass his uncle was very much in love with. "No."

Luke threw him the letter and wandered over to stand by the window, his hands clasped behind his back.

"I could have killed him for it, for taking what was mine and making it his."

"But she didn't say no, did she?"

"How could she? Alone with them, with my accursed father and my brother, and thinking me gone, perhaps even dead?"

"Hmm," Jacob replied. It did sound a terrible thing to do, to coerce a young girl into marriage after having thrown out her one true love. Somehow he couldn't quite see Da acting in such a way.

"But he paid," Luke said very softly. "By God, did he pay…"

Luke could still recall it perfectly: how he'd ridden home to Hillview, and out to greet him came Mam, his sister and his brother, the latter with his arm around Margaret's waist. He had fought down the urge to draw his sword then and there to make an end of Matthew Graham, and instead pulled back his lips into a stiff smile. Margaret's blue eyes had leapt to his, and that was all it took to reassure him that she still loved him, only him. With that little flame of hope burning inside his heart, he had dismounted and greeted his family after far too many years away from home.

At first, Margaret had tried to tell him no, not because she wanted to, but because she was wed and owed her obedience to Matthew. Luke had wheedled; he had begged. He had cornered her in the barn and in the dairy shed, followed her up the hillsides, and there, below a denuded rowan tree, she had finally kissed him one day, crying as she did.

From there, it was a quick return to their old habits: secret encounters on the moss; silent, needy embraces in the hayloft; hours spent in the woods. Afternoons when he would slip in like a silent ghost through the kitchen door and make his way upstairs to wait for her in bed, mornings when he'd hear Matthew hurry down the stairs and, moments later, Margaret would enter his room. For well over a year, this had gone on, until that afternoon when they froze at the unexpected sound of Matthew's voice below, and then his footsteps came up the stairs and the door was thrown open.

Luke closed his eyes at the memory of the devastated

expression on his brother's face when he saw them. But he had rejoiced in it at the time, laughing at Matthew. Luke rested his forehead against the glass. He was no longer aware of his nephew or his son. He was drowning in reminiscences of his beloved Margaret, and the far more uncomfortable recollections of how badly he had treated his brother, falsely accusing him of treason, raging when the sentence was commuted from hanging to imprisonment.

Three years later, Matthew returned home with a new wife, a wife that was a paler copy of his own Margaret. Luke didn't much like remembering what he had done to Alex. It was beyond doubt the single most cruel thing he had ever done, and to a woman who had never done him any harm. No wonder Matthew sliced off his nose, he thought, fingering the silver replacement he so rarely thought about any more. But it was all Matthew's fault, he reminded himself. Had Matthew not touched Margaret to begin with, none of this would have happened.

Luke made a huge effort to pull himself together, clearing his throat repeatedly. "It would seem your brother is wiser than mine was, and now it's only a matter of how you choose to reply."

"Choose to reply? I have no rights to her!" Jacob sounded angry.

"You didn't read it very thoroughly, did you? It says that unless you approve, your da won't allow them to wed."

"It does?" For a couple of heartbeats, Jacob was silent, brows pulled together in concentration. "Well then," he shrugged, "I shall give them my blessing." He looked about for paper and ink. "It must irk Ian," he grinned, "that his wee brother should have a say in who he weds."

Aye, Luke agreed, and felt a sudden longing for a lad he had last seen as a thirteen-year-old. Margaret had never truly forgiven him for giving up Ian. She had never understood how painted into a corner he had been by Matthew and their wily brother-in-law, Simon Melville. This last name made him smile. It would seem the tables were somewhat turned, and where once Matthew and

Simon had threatened him with exposure as a murderer, now he could do the same to wee Simon. Most interesting, that last correspondence he had received from Edinburgh, very interesting indeed. Conjecture, of course, no real proof, but gossip is a dangerous thing.

"So, what other news?" Luke asked.

"Lucy's getting married," Jacob said once he'd finished reading. "To Henry Jones, no less, and Mama says that's a relief as it definitely kills any hare-brained ideas that Ruth be wed to him." He laughed softly. "I don't think it much pleases Da to be called hare-brained."

"No, I imagine not. I wouldn't like it if my wife did it." Luke intercepted a sly glance between the boys and stifled a sigh. Luke Graham had no intention of marrying again, no matter the number of attractive widows his two procurers trotted up before him.

Very late that night, Luke added his own letter to the two Jacob had left on his desk for hasty delivery down to the docks. But Luke's letter was far shorter – and unsigned. He carefully inked Simon Melville's name and sat back with a satisfied smile. A little threat, enough to rock Simon Melville's boat, and even more by being anonymous. For now, that was enough, Luke reflected as he used his fingers to put out the candle – maybe it would always be enough.

Chapter 33

"He can," Adam repeated stubbornly. "He says my name."

"Really?" Alex said. "Not so that I can hear it."

"He whispers it." Adam caressed Hugin over his bright, black plumage.

"Ah." Alex smiled at her five-year-old and handed him a spade. "All that row, okay?"

Adam gave her a resigned look but started turning the long bed.

Alex sat back on her heels. Her youngest was no longer a baby, but a sturdy boy that pulled his own weight in the household. Hugin flew over to sit on Adam's shoulder, and Alex smiled at the two of them. She had serious doubts about the bird's vocal abilities, but none whatsoever about its relative intelligence.

"Up there with the pigs," she'd said to Matthew, making him laugh. Actually, Hugin spent a lot of time with the pigs, and so, in consequence, did Adam, the sow flapping her ears at him in warning when he got too close to her new babies, but otherwise tolerating him.

"I suspect she considers him one of her own," Alex also said to Matthew, and he had nodded and said that, yes, given the normal state of Adam's clothes and hands, that was probably a fair supposition.

It was the first week of April, a fine, bright day. This year, spring had taken a very long time coming before literally exploding, leaving all of them short-tempered in the unseasonal heat. Matthew and his elder sons were working themselves silly now that the fields were no longer waterlogged, and the rest of the household was coping with the chores they left undone, resulting in very long days. Alex massaged her back: three days of digging had left her muscles very sore.

Two loud voices drifted out from the dairy shed, and Alex didn't even have to check to know it was Ruth and Sarah, locked in their constant bickering. Those two were really getting on her nerves. Just the other day, Alex had surprised all — and, in particular, herself — by slapping the girls and telling them to leave the room. Since then, the continuous war was fought at a lower decibel, but was just as deadly, with the girls quarrelling over every ribbon, every garter, every single piece of clothing that wasn't clearly labelled with one or the other's name — which in practice meant every garment they collectively owned.

"You can always take away all their clothes," Matthew had suggested the other night when Alex complained.

"It will get better once their courses come," Mrs Parson said, grinning when Alex moaned that might still be years off. "Or you might consider staking them out in the forest and hope the Indians take them, no?"

"They wouldn't," Matthew had muttered. "Even Indians have a sense of self-preservation."

Alex stuck her head into the dairy, told Ruth to leave the skimming to Sarah, and to go and help Mrs Parson in the kitchen. It was touch and go which of the two girls looked the most upset by this distribution of chores, but they did as they were told, and with a chunk of cheese in one hand and a pitcher of milk in the other, Alex followed her eldest daughter to the house.

She sighed inwardly when she saw Peter Leslie ride into their yard, but arranged her features into a welcoming smile. Peter smiled back and dismounted.

"Alex." He bowed in greeting. "Is Matthew around?"

"He will be shortly," Alex replied. "It's dinner time."

Peter shone up, and Alex rolled her eyes at him.

"Come off it, you knew it was." She shooed him indoors and poured them both a mug of Mrs Chisholm's excellent cider, studying him surreptitiously. Ever since Constance had left for Virginia, Peter had been a frequent guest, and Alex suspected that he was very lonely. At home, Nathan and Ailish treated him with deference but no real warmth, Jenny had returned to Providence, and his two youngest children were strangers raised by the coloured woman assigned to wet-nurse them. No, his only family these days consisted of Thomas and Mary, so Alex supposed the poor man must at times be starved for conversation.

"Do you miss her?" Alex asked, making Peter look at her with surprise. "Constance," she clarified.

Peter took off his hairpiece and scratched at his head. "No, that marriage was a mistake." He replaced his false long curls and exhaled. "At times, I miss Elizabeth." He twisted at one of the pewter buttons on his coat cuff. "Ah well, she's best off dead. But I am blessed in my brother," Peter said with a faint smile.

Alex nodded. Thomas Leslie might be dull and unimaginative at times, but he was also steadfast and loyal, and very fond of his younger brother.

"And Mary," she teased.

Peter laughed softly. "Oh, yes…and Mary. It used to be I didn't understand what Thomas saw in her, but now I know. She's singularly sweet! Ineffective and vague, not the sharpest of intellects, but so restful to be with."

"Hmm," Alex said in a non-committal tone.

"I forgot." Peter dug his fingers into first one pocket, then the other, before extracting a letter and handing it to Alex. "It was sent on from Providence by Hancock – arrived with the first ship of the season."

She recognised the handwriting immediately: from Jacob. Alex held the thick square of paper in her hand, and what she really wanted to do was to leave the kitchen to read it, but instead she tucked it into her bodice with a mumbled thanks. It lay warm and promising against her chest all through dinner. It teased and murmured while she helped Agnes and Betty with the clearing up; it chafed in irritation at being left unread, screaming silently at her that she had to read it, and read it now. Alex couldn't agree more, and after ensuring things were as they should, she escaped outside to open it in peace.

★

Matthew heard her before he saw her, and turned to see a white-faced Alex thrash her way towards him, a crumpled paper in her hand. She stopped in front of him and held out the paper. Matthew's windpipe squeezed shut when he recognised Jacob's handwriting. He's injured, or ailing, mayhap even dying.

"Read," she croaked. And Matthew did, scanning yet another description of Jacob's days, his employer and the people he saw on a regular basis – including his uncle. Halfway through, Matthew raised his eyes to Alex. The tone of the letter was exuberant, not in any way alarming, and he couldn't understand why his wife was the colour of a dirty sheet.

"Go on," she said. Matthew turned the page, and there, just at the top, he found it. He swallowed audibly. No, this couldn't be right. He read it again.

> *I told you, did I not, of how Uncle Luke has a fondness for miniatures, collecting wee, bitty paintings that he keeps in his office. Pretty things for the most part: a tulip, puppies in a heap, lasses milking or sewing – a lot of lasses. Dutch, Uncle Luke says. And then there's this other wee painting that I saw some time ago. Uncle Luke is not much fond of it, but keeps it on account of it being painted by Aunt Margaret's mother, who disappeared when Margaret was but a wee bairn. Imagine that: a woman painter!*

By now, Matthew's skin was prickling with disquiet, and he wasn't sure he wanted to read the rest, but Alex's eyes insisted that he should.

> *Not a very good painting, all blues and greens whirling round and round, but most disconcerting, making my head ache and unsettling my stomach. To look at it was to be captured by it, and it seemed to me it sang – but that is but a fancy, brought on by how my guts cramped. No, personally I much prefer the lasses, and*

297

so, I think, does Uncle Luke. Not only painted lasses,
mind, but to say more would be to be indiscreet.

Sweat formed along Matthew's spine and in his elbow creases. His mind did strange leaps from one conclusion to another. A painting of swirling blues and greens, such as Alex's mother had painted and apparently littered the world with. Two sets of blue eyes under dark, well-defined brows, two women remarkably alike…

Impossible, it had to be impossible! But the painting! Dearest Lord, the painting! He had seen two of them before: squares of vibrant colour from which emanated the hushed, seductive whispers of a seashell, little pieces of art that had made his guts shrivel in fear. Both of them burnt to ashes, and now there was a third? This was the work of Mercedes, accursed witch that she was, and if so Alex and Margaret were sisters, born three hundred years apart to the same woman! And he, God help him, had married them both. It was enough to make him collapse to the ground, trying to stop the world around him from spinning.

"It can't be," he said. "It just can't!"

"It is," Alex said hoarsely. "No wonder we were so alike."

Matthew stared down at the letter again, willing the words to have changed, the description of that dangerous painting to be gone. Disconcerting…not a strong enough word for a painting that could send you helpless into another time.

"We must—"

"Yes, I know," she interrupted. "But I have no idea how to phrase it." If it had only been Luke, she wouldn't have bothered, she told him. For all she cared, he could drop right down into the twenty-first century and land in front of a bus or something, no matter how good he seemed to be to Jacob. Aye, he agreed, but now there were others to consider – in particular, their son – so somehow they had to warn them.

"I should have seen it," she said. "All those times when

I resented her for being so like me, and it never struck me!"

"And you find that strange?" Matthew took her hand and drew her down to sit beside him. "You had no reason to suspect she might be kin." He, who had at times seen them side by side, had not wanted to see the resemblance, made uncomfortable by the fact that they were so alike.

"No, it's kind of uncommon for sisters to be born with a three-hundred-year gap."

Matthew laughed nervously. A witch; twice he had married the daughter of a witch – the same witch. In his head, he raced through the Lord's Prayer. His windpipe shrank. Deliver me from evil, he repeated fervently, oh sweetest, dearest God, deliver me from evil!

"Be merciful to me and bless me and mine," he breathed. "Let Your countenance shine on me and keep me and mine safe."

Alex gave him a long look, but Matthew ducked his head, mumbling something about all of this being most confusing.

"Confusing?" Alex's voice was uncharacteristically shrill. "Bloody scary, that's what it is – and impossible! I wonder why Mercedes left," she went on, her eyes unseeing on the open fields before her. "What made her abandon her child?"

"Mayhap she had to."

Alex tugged at the grass. "Poor Mercedes, flitting from one time to another in a continuous attempt to find her way back to her own time. I hope she finally did and found some peace."

"Aye," Matthew replied, but more because she expected it of him than because he agreed. He was convinced Mercedes was one of those souls condemned to wander through the outer wards of hell, and he did something he hadn't done for many years: behind his back, he made the sign against the evil eye.

Matthew got to his feet and helped Alex up. "Walk?" He was too upset by all this to concentrate on work, and from the way her face lit up, it was obvious Alex was of like mind. They set off in the general direction of Forest Spring, walking in silence through the bright green of the maple woods.

Beneath the trees, the sunlight fell in slanting rays, and, with the exception of the background chatter of birds, it was blissfully quiet. Matthew inhaled, holding the air in his lungs for some seconds before exhaling. It helped: his mind emptied of all these confusing images of Margaret, Alex and Mercedes, of his Jacob staring for too long into a painting and disappearing from him forever. Instead, he rested his thumb on the inside of Alex's wrist, and he wasn't sure if it was her pulse or his own he picked up, but, whatever the case, the steady throbbing calmed him even further.

At the entrance to Forest Spring, they stopped for a moment to ensure they were alone, and then they drank at the well before sitting down with their backs against the weathered cabin wall.

"Why don't we do this more often?" Alex asked, extending her legs in front of her. "You and me, nature all around, and nothing else." She gave him one of those blue looks that could still make his cock stir. "It reminds me of that first time with you."

"Mmm," Matthew agreed, half closing his eyes.

"Not *the* first time," she corrected with a laugh. "But that whole first month. How we talked…"

"We still do," he said seriously.

"Yes, we do, don't we? But there's something about walking and talking at the same time… Besides, most of the time we talk, we're surrounded by an avid audience, right?"

"Audience? They don't listen much – they talk as well!"

"All the time," Alex sighed. She pulled her legs up and rested her chin against her knees. "We never discuss religion anymore. I can't remember when we last argued about the concept of predestination."

"Discuss religion with you? I thought we agreed that I was right and that you, as my meek and obedient wife, will follow where I lead."

"Hmph! A meek and obedient wife would have had you bored to tears in less than a day."

"Aye." He took her hand again. He twisted his head to look at her, smiling at how her hair had escaped her haphazard bun to fall in a wave along her cheek. She sat staring straight ahead, a long strand of grass between her teeth. "What are you thinking about?"

She turned her face in his direction, her mouth very soft. "The first time," she said huskily.

"Ah," he nodded and pulled her close. At last, his cock stretched, that took you a very long time.

"Four or five," Alex laughed a while later, trying to roll away from his tickling hands. "Or maybe even six – but definitely not once."

"I was young then," he mock growled.

"Yes, and it was ages since you'd had sex," she said, suddenly very serious. She sat up, half-naked, and looked down at him.

"A very long time," he agreed, just as serious. Three years in prison for something he hadn't done, and all on account of his accursed brother and false Margaret.

"Sister or not, I'll never forgive her for what she did to you."

"Brother or not, I don't think I can forgive him either," Matthew sank down to lie on his back. "I've tried, and he seems to have done well by Jacob, but I can't wipe the slate clean. He robbed me of my son, he stole away my freedom – twice – and what he did to you…" He shook his head, eyes tightly shut.

Alex lay down beside him and pillowed her head on his chest. "Yes, that was pretty bad. Still, life has done a pretty good job of punishing him, hasn't it?"

"You think? Rich and respected, two – no, three – homes, a likeable lad and two lasses…"

"And always alone. The single person he truly loved is no longer there for him, is she?"

He was silent for some moments, his hand stroking her scarred right arm. To not have her here with him, it was an unbearable thought. "No," he said, "that must be hell on earth."

"In Luke Graham's case, he might as well get used to it. After all, he's going to be spending all eternity in hell." She propped herself up on her elbows and looked teasingly at him. "Unless, of course, Luke has converted to Catholicism, in which case he can confess and repent and make it all the way to the rolling green meadows of heaven."

"Alex!"

"It's just a thought. Maybe I should include it as a suggestion in my letter regarding the painting." She laughed and kissed him on his nose. "Speaking of sin," she murmured and threw a leg over him.

"Not a sin." He smiled up at her, threading his fingers through her hair to make it stand like a dark halo around her. "More like a sacrament, aye? Heaven on earth, if you will."

And it was. Hands that knew exactly where to touch and how to fondle to make the other twist with pleasure, warm mouths, tongues that darted out to flutter teasingly over tautened skin, over moist and secret places. He rolled her over, kissed her eyes, her nose. She grabbed him by the ears, made impatient by all this foreplay.

Matthew chuckled, lifted her leg high, and in one swift movement came inside of her, gratified by her loud exhalation. He drove himself deep inside of her; she uttered an inarticulate sound telling him to please do it again, and do it fast. So he did.

"Promise?" she said as they walked back.

"Promise," he replied, smiling tenderly at her.

"A long walk once a week, right?"

"Every Sunday, lass. You and I and no one else."

"Good, especially seeing as tomorrow is Sunday."

"Insatiable," he groaned.

"...and the lucky man is...you!" She stuck her tongue out, making her astoundingly like Sarah at her most enervating. Young and wild, she looked, walking barefoot with her hair undone.

Matthew plucked an early columbine and handed it to her with a very formal bow. "I love you."

"I sincerely hope so," she laughed back. "After such an afternoon, who wouldn't?" She stopped and stood on her toes to smooth back his hair from his forehead. "I love you too."

Chapter 34

Simon winked and handed Betty a sheaf of papers. A free woman again — at least until her father found out. Well, she wasn't going to tell him, not after their latest acrimonious exchange along the lines that soon the two years of grace were up, and after that Father had every intention of seeing her wed — quickly.

"He won't like me for this," Simon said, "but you should consider getting with child before you tell him."

Betty's cheeks heated uncomfortably. A rounded belly would go a long way in convincing Father to agree to a match with Ian Graham — not much else would, given Jacob's behaviour.

"I'll shame him twice."

Simon shrugged. "It happens — and you didn't set out to, did you?"

Betty folded the documents together, slid them into her petticoat pocket, and danced out of the room. Jacob had signed the annulment with quite the flourish, leading her to believe he had been relieved rather than aggrieved. Now it was all done, their marriage vows declared null and void through these documents. She wasn't going to tell Ian, not yet. Instead, she went in search of her mother, finding her in the little parlour.

Betty stopped for a moment in the doorway. Mother had taken a long time to recover after her latest ordeal in the birthing chamber, and even now, with little Harry close to a year, a grey tinge clung to Mother's skin. On account of all those sleepless nights watching over Harry, Betty sighed, thinking that her baby brother was not long for this earth, no matter how much effort Mother expended on keeping him here. She went over to sit on the low stool at her mother's feet.

"There you are," Mother smiled. "I was just wondering where you were."

"I was with Uncle Simon." Betty gnawed at her lip. She wanted to tell her mother about Ian and the fizzy feeling that soared through her every time he looked at her, but she wasn't sure she dared to. Would Mother not go immediately to Father, and then what?

"No letter from Jacob?"

"Not as such," Betty replied with a little shrug.

Mother let her embroidery drop to her lap and gave Betty a searching look. Betty pretended great interest in a spot on her skirts, not wanting her mother to see the huge smile that she felt on her face. Mother stroked Betty's hair, the hand lingering for a while on Betty's head.

"I don't want to know, but I'm very glad for you, child."

With a little sound, Betty pillowed her head in Mother's lap. "Thank you," Betty whispered into the folds of Mother's skirts.

"…but that was only to be expected," Thomas said, twisting in his saddle to look at Matthew.

"Not by the Piscataway," Matthew said, wiping at his face to clear it of some of the driving rain. "They hoped for something more out of the original treaty." A waste of time, this latest meeting regarding the militia, with more animosity directed at Robert Chisholm for being a papist than at the Iroquois. He threw his Catholic neighbour a look, but Robert looked as unperturbed today as he'd done throughout the meeting. Not that Matthew was fooled by Robert's impassive exterior. He knew the younger man well enough to know he'd had to struggle to hold onto his temper on several occasions, foremost when Edward Farrell was at his most provocative.

"We can't risk lives to defend Indian against Indian," Thomas protested, "and it's best to remain neutral in their indigenous squabbles." He pulled his cloak closer, muttering something about it being spring, not winter.

Matthew hemmed: in this, he had to concede Thomas

had the right of it. Besides, there was very little a white militia could do to support the Piscataway.

"I saw Philip Burley yesterday." Thomas gave Matthew a quick look.

"Aye, so did I." Matthew spat to the side. By the time he'd called out the constables to arrest the bastard, he'd been gone.

"Took to the water," Thomas said when Matthew recounted this. "Swims like a fish, that one." He shook his head, making his long, greasy hair bounce. "Fool to come here! There's a price on his head, and yet he has the effrontery to stroll down Main Street."

"He didn't know that until he got here," Matthew said. "I dare say he'll blame me for having been outlawed."

"Probably." Thomas frowned. "About time, if you ask me. Those brothers should have hanged years ago!"

"As I hear it, Walter Burley remains in custody," Robert Chisholm put in. "Why they haven't hanged him yet is something of a mystery."

"Mystery?" Thomas snorted. "The Burleys are well connected in Virginia. Besides, the girl has changed her story. Now, she no longer recalls who it was that raped her, saying that she fears she may have identified the wrong man."

"Has she, do you think?" Robert asked.

"No," Matthew said. "But Walter Burley has very persuasive brothers, doesn't he?"

"Poor wench." Thomas sighed.

"What do you think of the new minister?" Matthew asked to change the subject. He looked back to ensure Betty and Agnes were keeping up, and nodded at his new field hand, John Mason. He bit back a smile at the thought of Agnes: meant to stay behind in Providence now that her contract had expired, she had been afflicted by a bout of panic and decided she preferred to return with the master to Graham's Garden – helped along, Matthew suspected, by John Mason's golden locks.

"Somewhat dour," Thomas replied.

Robert chuckled. "All your ministers are dour. Your churches are dour, your rites and sermons are dour."

Thomas' face acquired a bright red hue. "Papistry is nothing but—"

Matthew placed an arm on his sleeve and shook his head. "Nay, Thomas, leave him be. Robert is but teasing. I liked the man and I didn't find him dour, rather the reverse."

Minister Allerton reminded him of Sandy Peden, his dear friend and minister, with dark grey eyes and a thinning head of what must once have been reddish hair. Not when he spoke, because Minister Allerton had never set foot outside his native Boston until this new assignment had been given him, and he spoke with an accent quite different from anything Matthew had ever heard before. But he had enjoyed the sermon on the Good Samaritan, and he had liked it when the minister congratulated him on his fine son, Daniel.

"You know my lad?" Matthew had asked.

"Oh, I've had the pleasure of teaching him for well over a year, and that is one very bright boy. Most devout as well," Allerton continued, smiling in a way that made his eyes twinkle. "Not always the most well behaved, and he has a disturbing effect on the younger female population – which he well knows."

"He's almost fifteen," Matthew had said, "and lads like lasses."

"Oh yes. And your son, I think, very much likes a certain Miss Temperance Allerton."

"Ah. Your lass?"

Minister Allerton had beamed proudly. "Yes, my eldest."

"He's never even mentioned a Temperance in his letters," Alex laughed when Matthew told her all this a couple of days later. "Temperance...poor child!" She slipped her arms round his waist and scrubbed her cheek against his shirt. He held her to his heart for a couple of seconds before going back to his unpacking.

"He's a lad," Matthew said in a teasing tone. "We don't

tell you everything. And if the daughter is anything like the father, I would say he has chosen wisely." He kept his back to her while he fiddled with his leather satchels.

"Chosen? As you said, he's a lad. Besides, you just told me Minister Allerton has almost no hair and resembles Sandy. Poor girl, I tell you, poor, poor girl."

Matthew chuckled. "When have you ever seen a lass with no hair?"

"It happens, and what is it you're hiding?"

In response, Matthew brought out nine coloured glass panes: six red and three green.

"Oh!" Alex knelt and picked up one of the red panes. "They're beautiful!" She twisted it this way and that, sending coloured light to dance on the whitewashed walls of their bedroom.

"For our room," he said, delighted by her reaction. "I thought it would make a nice pattern on the floor and the sheets."

Any further inspection of her gift was precluded by Ruth, who fell into the room, followed by an equally excited Sarah.

"Jenny..." Ruth gasped.

"...and Patrick!" Sarah filled in, her eyes round with amazement.

"Here?" Alex got to her feet.

From outside came Ian's voice, raised in anger, curses flowing from his mouth in a surprising and uncharacteristic flow that had Matthew raising his brows.

"Here apparently," he said and rushed down the stairs.

"Ian! No!" Da's voice cut through the red curtain of rage that had invaded Ian's brain. Strong arms took hold of him, and he was pulled back, with Mama and Betty standing themselves between him and Patrick, who was getting to his feet helped by Jenny who had dismounted.

"You could have injured him!" she snapped at Ian.

"Do you expect me to care?" Ian snarled. He shook himself loose from Da's restraining hold, and crossed his arms to stop himself from shoving Mama aside to hit Patrick again, or was it Jenny he really wanted to hurt?

"Why are you here?" Ian demanded. "And why did you bring your fancy man along?"

"My wife and I..." Patrick began.

"Wife?" Ian looked from Jenny to Patrick. "You're married?"

Jenny nodded in confirmation, her eyes on the ground while she fidgeted with her cap.

"Once a whore always a whore," Mark said, giving Patrick a belligerent look. "But seeing as she comes reasonably well dowered, I don't think you particularly care."

Jenny flushed a painful red, and, to his irritation, Ian felt sorry for her.

"Mark!" Mama frowned and indicated the very interested group of children who were following the conversation. "Now, assuming we're all done with the pleasantries, why are you here?"

"I want to see my children." Jenny looked directly at Ian and cleared her throat. "Please?"

Ian was very tempted to say no, but on his nape rested Da's eyes, and, even more, Malcolm was pressed tight against his side, craning his head back to look at him. Ian drew a thumb down his son's nose. "Go on, lad," he said.

Malcolm shifted from foot to foot, but remained where he was.

Ian couldn't help it. He raised his chin to meet Jenny's eyes in triumph. See, he taunted, he's already lost to you. But the apparent pain in her face shamed him, and he crouched down, smiling at Malcolm.

"It's alright, son. She's your mother, aye?"

Malcolm took a hesitant step in Jenny's direction, he took two, he took three, and then he was in her arms and she was crying in his hair.

"Any particular reason for this impromptu visit?" Da asked.

Patrick threw him a cautious look. "We're here to make our farewells. We leave for Carolina within the month."

"Carolina?" Ian asked.

"To the south," Patrick said.

"I know where it is," Ian snapped, "and it's very far away from here."

"Far enough." Patrick nodded with obvious relief, eyes straying to the assembled children.

Ian's face tightened to the point of being painful as he watched Patrick study Maggie, who was standing to the side, fingers sunk in Viggo's shaggy coat. Ostentatiously, he walked over to his lass and swung her up to sit on his arm. Maggie made a series of warbling sounds, gripped his shirt, and hid her face against him.

"May I?" Jenny held out her hands. Ian nodded and handed Maggie over. His wee Maggie did not much like to be carried in the first place, not now that she could stand and take the odd step, and even less to be held by someone she didn't know. She stiffened in Jenny's arms, brows pulled together in a ferocious frown. When Jenny attempted to kiss her, she opened her mouth and bawled. Quickly, Jenny returned her to Ian, retaining a hold on one small, bare foot.

"She looks very healthy." She stroked the soft skin.

"She is, somewhat of a temper on her, but very healthy." Now that Ian understood this was a final visit, he was feeling more generous, and so he smiled and caught Jenny's eye. "Like her mother."

"And her grandmother," Jenny whispered back. She studied Maggie's little face, eyes darting back and forth between Ian and Patrick.

"Much like me in other things," Ian said with a clear warning in his tone.

"Yes." Jenny let go of the squirming foot.

Betty waited until she was certain Ian had settled his children for the night before sneaking down to his cabin on soundless feet. The evening was warm enough that a shawl was excessive over her shift, but she tugged it tighter round her shoulders and swallowed so loudly it almost made her giggle. She had seen the way Ian's gaze had locked on

Jenny's waist when she sat up on her horse, and, after some scrutinising of her own, had understood that Jenny was with child – again.

All the way up the lane, Ian had followed his former wife and her new husband with his eyes, and Betty had seen him afflicted by doubts and uncertainties when he looked from Patrick to Maggie and back. It would have been easy to laugh it all off. Little Maggie had no doubts as to who was her father, and with her dark hair and light eyes she looked very much a Graham. Except that her hair grew in a widow's peak – just like Patrick's – and her lower lip jutted out – just like Patrick's.

Betty decided not to knock. The well-oiled latch lifted easily, and Betty slipped inside a room that was dark after the lingering dusk outside. She had never been here this time of the night: Ian's and her love trysts had mostly happened in the hayloft or out in the woods. She could hear her own pulse; loud and red it swished through her head. Her stomach was a mass of writhing things, her knees were beginning to wobble, and her mouth… She opened it and breathed in short, audible gulps. This was unseemly. A woman should not come like this to a man.

She groped behind her back for the latch, and for a moment considered escaping back outside, before something happened that was irreversible, but she knew she wouldn't, not now that she had worked up the courage to come. Besides, he needed her, she sensed that, especially tonight after seeing his ex-wife ride away with the man that had put horns on him. She felt a forceful cramp in her privates, and blushed in the dark. If he needed her, she wanted him, her body yearning for his touch.

"Betty?" Ian sat up in bed. "Is that you, lass?"

She closed the door fully, and now all she could make out was the white of the bed linen, a blob of light in the dusk. She dropped her shawl to the floor, tugged her shift over her head, and before her nerve failed her, she walked towards the bed.

"What…?" He didn't get to say more. She kissed him,

and his arms came up around her, so warm against her goose-fleshed skin.

"Betty..." he groaned when her hands slid in under his shirt. "We mustn't. I've promised Da."

"I don't care," she told him, and soon he wouldn't either, of that she was quite sure, her fingers caressing the soft heaviness of his balls. "I'm no longer married," she said between kissing him, "and so I come to you..." She raised herself on her arms to look at him, a dark shape no more. "If you want me," she said uncertainly.

"Oh, I do, very much I do." He rolled them over, bent his head to nuzzle her throat, and Betty's toes curled together. Betty inhaled loudly when his cock nudged at her. Go on, she told him with her hands, please go on. She wriggled even closer, and finally he was there, where she wanted him to be. She laughed out loud.

"I must talk to your father," Ian said next morning. They were alone in the stable, each of them sitting by a cow.

"Not yet." Betty walked around with a sensation of disembodiment, her legs extraordinarily heavy while the rest of her was a weightless blur. She sniffed and blushed. She could smell him on her, everywhere on her, and she liked it so much she hadn't washed properly this morning. A slight shift on the milking stool relieved the heat that flared between her legs...wanton, she chided herself. Betty Hancock, you're wanton.

"Now," Ian insisted, smacking the cow out of the way to see her.

"No." She intended to take no risks, and if that meant forcing her father's hand then so be it. "We wait." They had until her eighteenth birthday, and she fervently prayed that she might conceive before then.

Chapter 35

Jacob rounded the corner of Watling Street and Bread Street in such a hurry that he crashed into the couple coming the other way. Only by his quick reactions did he save them all from landing sprawled in the unappetising gutter.

"My apologies," he stuttered. "I'm so sorry, sir, mistress." He helped the woman straighten up and was surprised to find himself face to face with Helen – Mistress Cooke.

"Inconsiderate fool!" the man huffed, rubbing at a smudge on his breeches.

"I'm that sorry," Jacob repeated, "but my master has sent me with a hasty delivery to one of the seafaring ships." With his head, he gestured towards the waterfront. After yet another quick bow, Jacob took off, and not one word had he said to Helen.

He had placed an arm around her waist to stop her from tumbling to the ground, and he frowned, trying to grasp what it was that was bothering him. It struck him just as he reached the Customs House, half out of breath after his run. Her belly... Jacob swallowed rapidly and shook his head. Fat, he tried, dear Helen had gained weight. A lot of fat to be in one place, a cynical corner of his brain laughed.

On his way back, Jacob counted. Helen had been married since late September, and for her to be heavy with child in May was in no way surprising – if it hadn't been for those reassurances of hers that she didn't want a child with her elderly husband. Jacob licked his lips. It had been a very long and intense night back in September, and... nay, of course not! He increased his pace, in a hurry to get back to Master Castain. His head buzzed with all the information he was presently revising for his examination the coming month.

Jacob had scarcely slept of late, working far into the light evenings, and spending a further few hours studying with Master Castain, who seemed as nervous as Jacob was. He stopped for a moment and gazed up at the May sky. These long evenings were something very special, purple round the edges with all the shades of blue one could imagine. Well, when it didn't rain, of course, which it had done quite a lot the last few weeks. Fortunately, Jacob smiled, thinking back to a most agreeable hour a week or so ago, spent in the protection of one of the arches of St Saviour's in Southwark with Charlotte on his lap.

He adjusted his breeches over his privates. Charlotte had a very competent hand, and when Jacob was in one of his darker moods, he couldn't help but reflect over where she had learnt such skills. Maybe he should ask her, he mused; he could do that tomorrow. A smile spread over his face at the thought of tomorrow — he hoped she would like the ribbon he had bought her.

"Where have you been?" Richard cornered Charlotte with his bulk.

"Out," she said.

The slap left her reeling. "Where?" The three apprentices in the workroom kept their eyes on the work at hand.

"In church."

The next slap threw her back against the wall.

"Try again," he said, "and the truth might be a better option."

Charlotte's throat dried up. Richard gripped her by the arm and she was half carried, half dragged up the stairs to the private quarters.

"That country lad needs a lesson," Richard said once he had beaten the truth out of Charlotte. Every single meeting she had listed, from that first time she smiled at him in St Mary-le-Bow to this latest evening stroll beyond the Tower. The red ribbon had been torn to pieces, and Richard prowled the room, glaring alternately at her, alternately at the stained glass panes in the long low window that faced the street.

Charlotte sidled away from him. No one had ever hit her before, not like this, and she didn't like the way Richard was looking at her. He blocked her way out of the room and invited her to sit, smirking at her obvious discomfort.

"The contracts, it's time you sign them."

Her hands were shaking where they lay in her lap. "The contracts?" She attempted an innocent gaze.

Richard gave her an amused look. "No, no, little Charlotte. That may work with a callow youth not yet eighteen, but it won't work with me – not this time. So, the contracts, you'll sign them tonight."

"Tonight?" Charlotte swallowed. "But I'm not yet sixteen."

"Ah, but I'm thirty-eight, and I can't wait to bed my beautiful, blooming bride." His fingers traced a patch of reddened skin on her face. "It's difficult, isn't it? To believe you have the upper hand and suddenly realise you don't." He leaned forward and wound a tendril of her hair round one of his fingers. "I chose to wait, Charlotte. But now I choose to wait no longer."

Charlotte wet her lips. "I'll sign them."

"Oh, but of course you will." He toyed some more with her hair, dragged a finger down her cheek, smiling when she flinched. "Tonight, before witnesses." He took her by the arm and propelled her to her room. "I'll be back in some hours, and I expect to find you radiant." He kissed her cheek and all of her trembled. "Wear the brocade bodice," he said as he closed the door behind her. To her surprise, she heard a bolt grate into place on the outside, and when she turned to angrily draw her own bolts, she found them gone. Charlotte Foster felt very frightened and very alone.

Luke listened in silence as a most aggravated Richard Collin expounded on Jacob's deviousness, detailing meeting after meeting between Jacob and the fair Charlotte. The goldsmith couldn't sit still, pacing the room as he talked, his big hands fisting whenever he spat out Jacob's name.

Luke poured Richard yet another glass of wine. "Silly

lad! I have repeatedly warned him off."

"To no avail." Richard threw himself into a chair. "Do you think he's bedded her?"

Luke considered the question. There was no question that Jacob very much wanted to bed her, but Luke doubted that she had allowed it to go that far. And, to give Jacob his due, he was so besotted he'd insist on wedding her first.

"No," Luke said.

Richard stood and tweaked his dark coat into place. "Seven, then, and don't be late."

"Oh, no," Luke promised, "I'll be punctual, most punctual."

"I'll keep it in mind," Richard said in lieu of farewell.

"Keep what in mind?"

"That he's your nephew." Richard let the door swing shut behind him.

Luke opened the door. "Richard!" He waited until the goldsmith had turned his way. "I avenge my own. Best you don't forget that, aye?"

"...and what about garlic?" Master Castain said, holding up the door to let Jacob through.

"Ah well, garlic..." Jacob took a deep breath to launch into a description of all the uses of this versatile little onion, but was cut off by a beefy hand that came down over his mouth. Jacob struggled, and someone clobbered him over the head. Vaguely, he heard Master Castain's loud protests, how the door to the shop squeaked open, and the master was pushed inside before the key turned, twice.

Jacob was pulled to his feet. Dazed, he was led through streets full of people, people who stopped what they were doing to gawk before hastily returning to their tasks. He had by now regained his senses and tried to fight himself free. A decisive yank, and he had one arm free, but three against one were uneven odds, even more so when something sharp dug into his lower back.

"Come along nicely, or else..." The blade dug that bit deeper, and Jacob's inhalation whistled down his windpipe.

Sweet Lord, but that hurt! He rose on his toes in a vain attempt to evade the knife's tip, and tried to control the loud thumping in his head that he recognised as his racing heartbeat.

They marched him past St Mary-le-Bow, took a left down Friday Street, and well before they reached Maiden's Lane, Jacob knew where they were going, his stomach tightening into a hard knot at the sight of Richard Collin's house. When he was led into the secluded yard and tied spreadeagled to the fence, he had to swallow hard not to cry.

He didn't like the glint in Richard Collin's eyes, nor did he like the look of those hands. And then pain exploded in his face, in his chest, in his abdomen, as Richard proceeded to beat him from top to toe. He almost fainted when Richard broke his nose. A foot was brought down on his toes, and he yelled out loud. His head snapped back when a punch was driven into his chin, a blow on his ear had his head ringing, and all the time blood was flowing from his nose, dripping from his bitten lip. An eyebrow burst, and Jacob sagged in his ropes, crying for Da. He heard Richard's heavy breathing; a hand grabbed hold of his hair and forced his head back. Jacob could barely see.

"Enough?" Richard asked.

"Enough for what?" Jacob managed to say, his tongue probing his teeth.

"Enough that you never approach my wife-to-be again."

"Your wife-to-be?" Jacob coughed. "So it's no longer enough to abuse her? Now you have to force her to marry you as well?"

"Abuse her? Is that what she's been telling you? That I make free of her on a nightly basis?" Richard leaned very close, but Jacob only saw him in a haze. "I've never touched her, you fool, and I hope for your sake that you haven't either." He straightened up and kicked Jacob in the balls. Jacob couldn't scream, he couldn't breathe – all he could do was register the excruciating pain that had his privates howling in agony.

After that last kick, Richard snapped instructions, and

317

Jacob was sluiced in bucket after bucket of water. Someone crudely reset his nose, which almost hurt as much as the original break, and then he was led off to where Richard was waiting.

"Had I wanted to truly maim you, I would have crushed your hands," Richard said, "but I promised that this time I wouldn't. However if I ever – ever – find you anywhere close to Charlotte again, I will. Understood?"

Jacob fisted his hands. Yes, he understood. Without his hands, he was doomed to poverty, unable to work at anything but the most menial of tasks. His brain was incapable of processing everything that was happening to him, but one thing kept echoing round and round, and that was Richard's cold assurance that he had never touched Charlotte. Jacob tried to clear his mind. If not, then why all the herbal remedies? Why all these detailed stories of evenings spent behind her bolted door while her inebriated stepfather pounded at it?

He concentrated on studying his ten whole fingers. He had no idea why he was here, looking like a dishevelled ruffian, or who Richard had promised not to maim him for life. Charlotte, of course, he smiled, seeing a weeping Charlotte on her knees, begging for him. It heartened him, this image of his distraught love, her fair hair undone, her blue eyes looking pleadingly at her stepfather.

"Come with me," Richard said, and for all that he could scarcely walk, Jacob shuffled after him. He shivered in his wet clothes, his face was a throbbing mess, and at least one tooth was missing. He wondered if he had swallowed it as he had no memory of spitting it out.

He was dragged up a flight of stairs and led into a dark-panelled room, where he was pushed to sit on a stool. Jacob took shallow breaths and leaned back against the wall. He very much wanted something to drink, and then he wanted someone to tuck him into bed and promise him all this hurt would soon be over. Mama...he gritted his tender jaw in an effort not to cry. Instead, he wiggled his toes and a shaft of pain shot up his leg.

There was a commotion by the door, several male voices talking and laughing at once. Gingerly, Jacob opened one swollen eye and, to his consternation, the first person he saw was his uncle. He closed his eyes, hoping thereby to remain invisible. A careful peek indicated that hadn't worked very well, because here came Luke, eyes blazing in an uncommonly pale face. Luke was intercepted by two of Richard's men, and from the ensuing argument, Jacob gathered that his uncle intended to rip their hearts out unless they allowed him access to his nephew. The men were adamant, and with a glowering look that should have reduced both of them to smouldering ashes, Luke retired to stand on the opposite side of the room, his eyes never leaving Jacob.

Jacob wanted to reassure him, tell Luke he was alright, but everything hurt too much, and so he just opened his mouth a couple of times, blearily taking in his lavish surroundings. There was a table placed centrally in the room, and Jacob counted to twenty candle holders, all with burning candles, which seemed excessive given that summer daylight still lingered outside the long small-paned window. St George and the dragon, Jacob concluded after having studied the stained glass for some time. Dark polished floors, walls that were decorated with tapestries, several small tables that held goblets and flasks of wine – this room was grander than Uncle Luke's parlour. He fidgeted. He needed to pee and his balls hurt.

"Ah, quite the blushing bride-to-be," Richard said when he came to fetch Charlotte. She tried out a smile and straightened her spine. In the tight brocade bodice, her breasts rose high and round. Richard extended his hand. She glided over the floor, fully aware of how fetching she looked with her unbound hair falling down her back. Her heart was beating like a trapped bird, and when his fingers clasped hers, she could hear a golden fetter close around her wrist.

She entered the parlour on Richard's arm, and the first person she saw was Jacob, a shivering, befuddled Jacob that gawked at her as if she'd been an angel come to earth. Richard made a warning sound, and Charlotte swept by Jacob without as much as a glance.

"My dear, you must of course greet our guests," Richard said, indicating the men who were standing near the centre of the room. Charlotte smiled and swept them a deep curtsey. She knew one of the men was Jacob's uncle, and a quick inspection made it very clear who that was, his bright eyes regarding her with such dislike she wanted to sink through the floor.

After some minutes of polite remarks, Richard steered her across the room to where Jacob was sitting hunched on his stool. Charlotte was inundated with shame for what had been done to him. He didn't deserve this, not for loving her and giving her flowers and holding her hand.

"Do you know who this is?" Richard asked.

Jacob's head jerked back, something green and dangerous moving in his eyes.

Charlotte cleared her throat and made a number of looking Jacob up and down. "No," she said, "but I'd assume he's an apprentice given his scruffy appearance."

Jacob slumped at her words.

"What has he done?" Charlotte asked, parroting the lines she'd been told to say.

"Done? Oh, he's played at Icarus, my dear. Flown far too near the sun and singed his wings." Richard chuckled at his own joke and led Charlotte to stand in the middle of the room, just by the table. She wiped her sweaty hand on her skirts and sneaked a look at Jacob, who was sitting with his head lowered. She looked the other way, and there were those intense green eyes framed by hair the colour of a fox pelt.

Richard proceeded to explain why they were here, declaring how glad it made him that his sweet ward, his precious Charlotte, had at last found it in her heart to accept his offer of marriage. Precious Charlotte simpered and tried to look as happy as a bride-to-be should look. He held out the dripping quill, and it seemed to her that the door to her gilded cage slammed permanently shut when she signed her name to the contracts on the table. She stood very still when Richard kissed her on the mouth, and then she was excused, curtseying deeply before fleeing the room.

Luke refused the wine and the sweetmeats, grabbed Richard by the elbow, and propelled him to stand by the window. "I told you I avenge my own."

Richard threw Jacob a disinterested look. "He's not badly hurt. A broken nose is no great loss." He looked at Luke's silver nose and smiled.

Luke increased the pressure to the point that Richard uttered a muted yelp. "You touch him again, Master Collin, and you'll have more than a broken nose to worry about." Luke leaned forward so that his mouth was very close to Richard's ear. "And yon lass... Her eldest sister was a slut, the second one as well, and as I hear it wee Hetty is also generous with her favours. Marrying them doesn't stop it." He could see that struck home, and with an infinitesimal bow, he released his host and went to take his nephew home.

Jacob could barely stand, leaning heavily on Luke as they made slow progress down the stairs.

"My foot..." he mumbled through his bruised and battered mouth. "And my nose..." Once in the carriage he wept, silent tears coursing down his cheeks. Luke could do nothing but clasp his arm, but that made Jacob inhale loudly, so Luke let go, patting Jacob's thigh instead.

Getting Jacob inside required two footmen, every single step accompanied by a strangled gasp from Jacob. Luke shushed and helped him undress; he himself lowered Jacob into the bath, saw to his bruises and shallow cuts. He had his barber-surgeon sent for and held Jacob's hand while the toes were set, after which he put him to bed, patting the clean linen sheets into place round Jacob's body. He smoothed at the heavy fringe, sweeping all that hair away from his nephew's pale and battered face.

"Da," Jacob murmured. Luke sat beside him for a long time, wondering how this nephew of his had so effectively managed to capture his heart.

★

Charlotte heard the bolt draw back and sat up in bed. She had hoped he wouldn't come, that with the signing of the contracts she had bought herself a period of grace. Richard entered the room and stood for some time by the door, regarding her.

"I hear you've been telling these most unflattering tales about me, about how I rape you, night after night." He sauntered towards the bed, undoing the buttons of his coat.

"I have never—"

He put a finger to her lips. "Don't lie, Charlotte." He had by now undone his breeches and Charlotte stared with trepidation at his swollen member, poking its way out through the cloth. "And after tonight, it will anyway all be true." He pushed her down and she didn't protest or fight. This was her soon-to-be husband, the man who controlled all her worldly goods, and her body was his to use as he pleased. It was a very long night for Charlotte Foster.

Chapter 36

"I hate snakes. I really, really hate them." Alex threw an apologetic glance at her husband, but remained on the table, the huge iron frying pan in her hand.

"It's not venomous," David said. "It's a corn snake – pretty, isn't it?"

Objectively, it probably was: a soft brownish yellow decorated with deep red blotches, but Alex was in no mood to see it. "I don't care what it is, or if it shits gold. Just get it out of here!"

David lifted the snake off the floor. "You've hurt it."

"Tough. It shouldn't be in here to begin with, should it?" She glared at her eight-year-old.

"I had to put it somewhere," David said. "If I leave it outside, Adam's corbie goes for it."

"Good. I'm all on Hugin's side, and if I see it again, well then – wham!" She brought the frying pan down hard on the tabletop, making David and Matthew jump. With a last reproachful look, David took his pet outside.

"Are you planning on staying up there for long?" Matthew asked.

"Can you guarantee there are no more snakes?"

"Here? Aye. Outside, no." He helped her down from the table and took the frying pan from her. "Four rattlesnakes, lass. That's all we've killed in the years we've been here."

"But we've seen more," Alex said with a grimace. "And, speaking of snakes, what's this I hear about Constance showing up at Leslie's Crossing?"

Matthew just shook his head. "Come for her bairns, she says, and she has her father with her to back her up."

"That won't help, will it? And, besides, Peter and Constance are still married."

"Unfortunately." Mrs Parson entered the kitchen on tiptoe. "No snakes?"

"No, not anymore." Alex said.

A shaft of sunlight struck Mrs Parson full in the face, and the old woman squinted, raising her hand to shield her eyes. As always, she was dressed in black, her collar, cap and cuffs starched into perfection. The hair was a silky white with very little grey in it, and, at times, all of her creaked when she moved. But her black eyes remained the same: inquisitive and intelligent, they assessed the world around her as quickly now as they had always done.

"Still alive, am I?" Mrs Parson asked with an edge, making Alex start.

"I think so, and if not, you're a scarily solid ghost."

Mrs Parson laughed and sat down in her chair. "So, wee Constance, when did she arrive?"

"Yesterday," Thomas replied from the door, allowing Mary to enter before him. "What happened here?" he asked, taking in the thrown benches, the shattered clay pitcher and the blond dents in the dark floor.

"Snake," Alex said, "a huge thing all over my kitchen floor."

"Three feet at the most," Matthew corrected her, righting the furniture. "A corn snake."

Thomas put on his most serious face. "Oh, one of those dangerous snakes."

Mary set her basket on the table and uncovered several meat pies. "We decided we could dine with you. Our Adam and Judith are with the girls."

"That bad?" Alex said.

Mary rolled her eyes. "And we live in a separate house. What it must be like for Ailish and Nathan, I can't imagine."

"Throw them out." Alex placed mugs and plates on the table.

"Oh, he will," Thomas said. "Constance is presently committing the gravest mistake in her life. My brother has quite a vindictive streak in him when roused, and he didn't appreciate being called an old farting fool by his wife." He sighed, nodding his thanks when Agnes served him some beer. "No, I fear it will be a long time before she sees her sons again – and nor will he grant her a divorce. No grounds."

"He can do that? Refuse to divorce her, maintain her on what he considers reasonable, and deny her access to her children?" Alex actually felt sorry for Constance – for like a microsecond.

"Yes," Thomas said, "of course he can. Nor will it help her to appeal to the ministers."

"So, where will she go?" Alex discreetly spat out a piece of gristle.

"Back to her father to ease his old age," Matthew said sarcastically, "and not until Peter dies will she be free to marry elsewhere."

"And we live a long time in our family." Thomas grinned before digging into his second helping of pie.

"I brought you something, Matthew," Thomas said once he'd finished eating. He produced a book from his coat pocket. A new book... It made Alex's fingers itch. Not once since she had left the twenty-first century behind had she seen a book in such condition, the pages crisp and unturned, the leather back unbroken.

"What is it?" she asked, kicking in the general direction of Matthew to make him hand the book over.

"Ouuf!" With a dark look at Alex, Thomas bent down to rub his shin.

Matthew opened the book to read the flyleaf. "The Pilgrim's Progress," Matthew read out loud.

"Oh!" Alex leaned over the table. "I had this when I was a child!" Not in this version, obviously: a heavy book in grey covers with several colour plates – in particular, she remembered the picture of Atheist, almost toppling over with mirth as he derided Christian.

"You did?" Thomas laughed. "I think not, Alex. Not unless you are much, much younger than you look. This book is not yet three years old."

For a moment, Alex was tempted to tell him the whole story, from when Christian sets out from his house, pointed in the direction of the wicket gate by the Evangelist, and how he strays from his path due to all the characters he meets. Mr Worldly Wiseman, Help and Hopeful with whom he crossed the River of Death...

"Alex?"

"Hmm?" She returned with a mental thud to find Matthew regarding her. She stretched out her hands to caress the dark red leather. "It must have been the cover that triggered a memory. More beer, anyone?"

"It's just..." Alex shook her head, slipping her hand into Matthew's. "I suddenly realised how often I had read it, and I have no idea where I got it from. Definitely not the kind of book Magnus or Mercedes would have given me." They were sauntering towards the river for some time on their own.

"As I hear it, Master Bunyan is an impressive preacher. Mayhap he spun a tale you liked."

She nodded, her eyes lost in the blue of the summer sky. "He dies. He leaves his family, driven by this great need to deliver himself from sin, to find God, and he does, and he's so happy, but all I could think of was his wife and his boys, left all alone without him."

Matthew's lips curved into an exceedingly sweet smile. "I don't plan on leaving you." He raised their braided hands and kissed them.

"Never?" she quavered.

"Not until I die, and not even then, I think."

"I don't want you to die," she said through a constricted throat.

"Aye...it's easier to contemplate the thought of dying than that of being left behind."

Alex couldn't reply; she just nodded.

"Ah, lass, come here, aye?" He gathered her close and she buried her nose into his shirt and inhaled, drawing in the warm, reassuring scent of her man. He kissed the top of her head; she clung to him. Matthew nuzzled her neck. "I'm still here," he said, his exhalations tickling her. "And there's plenty of life in me still." A big, warm hand slid down her back, his other hand followed suit, and she was being held impossibly close, all of her squashed against him.

A couple of heartbeats later, she was on the ground. He was shoving her skirts out of the way, and she was tugging at his breeches. A wordless, intense coupling, a reconfirmation that he was virile and here with her, would be for many, many more years. Alex lost herself in the here and now, relishing his strength, his weight, the sound of his heavy breathing, how he groaned her name when he came.

Afterwards, she held him, tightening her hold when he made as if to roll off.

"No," she said, "not yet. I need…"

Matthew subsided and, for the coming minutes, she stroked his back, his arms, his head. When he snorted her in the neck, she giggled. He did it again, and she laughed, laughing even more when he tickled her.

"Better?" he said as he helped her to her feet. Alex smiled and nodded – but it wasn't, not really, because now that he asked, the suffocating realisation that one day he might die and leave her all alone was back.

Alex was sitting in the graveyard, shredding a white rose to pieces, when Ian came to find her.

"Mama?"

"Mmm?" She laughed when he held up a bruised thumb.

"Will you blow on it?"

She blew and he sat down beside her. "Can you bend it?" she asked, nodding when he bent his thumb up and down. "You'll live."

"What is it?" He studied her narrowly.

"I don't know." She gave him an embarrassed smile and went back to her rose shredding. "I guess I'm just having one of those days when mortality hangs heavy."

She kept on seeing herself standing to the side while they buried Matthew, and just the thought had fear clawing at the inside of her chest. To wake alone, go to sleep alone, live out day after day alone… Alone amidst all their children, every single one of them a painful reminder of him. So she had come to sit here, beside Magnus, and she wasn't sure that had helped at all, because all she could hear was her father's sarcastic laughter whenever the concept of afterlife was discussed.

Ian heard her out, not saying anything, but his arm was a comforting weight around her shoulders, and it was so much easier to talk to him of how afraid it made her to imagine a world without Matthew than it was to speak to Matthew of it. She refused to mention the Burley brothers, but their threatening presence hung heavy all the same, and Ian tightened his hold on her shoulders, a brief, one-armed hug.

It grew dark around them, a fragrant summer night laced with honeysuckle and the blooming mock oranges that stood like sentinels around the graveyard. Before them, the ground fell away in a gentle slope towards the main house, and, further away, the river was a band of light grey, bordered by the darkness of the woods. Alex reclined against Ian, and for some time they sat in silence.

"She's with child," Ian said, and she could hear the joy fizzing through him.

"That was quick."

"You knew?" He sounded unsurprised, more resigned.

"Let's just say that Betty has been coming in very late – or should I say early?"

"Does Da know?"

That came out much more apprehensive, Alex noted.

"He isn't blind. The two of you have been going around as bright as fireflies the last four or five weeks."

"Ah." Ian fiddled with his belt. "Is he upset?"

Alex snorted. Matthew had won his bet, hadn't he?

"Bet?" Ian sounded confused.

Alex patted his hand. "It makes us both very glad. However, it's not exactly going to make William Hancock a happy bunny, is it?"

★

328

Alex found all this haste somewhat excessive, but Matthew and Ian were adamant: the wedding must take place before Betty began to show – for her sake. So, off they went to Providence, armed to their teeth and with Dandelion at their heels. Once in Providence, Matthew shooed Ian and Betty off to talk to Minister Walker, before taking Alex by the arm and setting off in search of William.

"No." William set his mouth in an implacable line and shook his head. "Absolutely not." He half turned towards Esther for support but she kept her eyes on Harry, her shoulders rigid with reproof. "I have other suitors for Betty, some of them most advantageous."

"For her or for you?" Alex heard Matthew sigh, and she didn't need to look at him to know he was looking at her with mingled pride and exasperation.

"For her, of course," William retorted, his cheeks going a purplish pink.

"But she wants to marry Ian," Alex said.

"And before that she wanted to marry Jacob!" he flared.

"Actually," Alex said, "you wanted her to marry Jacob. They just brought things forward a bit."

By now, Matthew had managed to get his hand in through the side slit in her skirt and pinched her, hard. Alex muffled a yelp and Esther's eyes flew to meet hers with concern.

"I'm afraid matters have proceeded beyond the point where they can be stopped by a parental no." Matthew got to his feet, uncoiled himself to his full height, and went over to stand close to William, overtopping the lawyer by several inches. "The lass is carrying my grandchild, and I won't have it born a bastard or, even worse, raised by a man no blood kin to it."

"Slut!" William hissed.

"She loves him," Matthew said, "and she knew you wouldn't consent unless you had to."

"I can still say no," Hancock threatened.

"Aye, you can. But it'll be a wee bit difficult to explain that to the ministers. In particular now that Betty and Ian have admitted their sin and expressed their wish to do the only right thing: wed." Matthew placed a tentative hand on William's shoulder. "It's not a bad start to a marriage, to know you love each other."

"No," William grudgingly admitted. "I suppose it isn't." His eyes drifted over to Esther, a shadow of a smile playing over his lips.

Betty Hancock spent the last night as a formally unwed woman in the room she had for so many years shared with two of her older sisters. The room was hot and uncomfortable, reminding her of that night almost two years ago when she and Jacob… Betty backed away from the memories of a heavy fair fringe, eyes framed by thick lashes and a long mouth.

She opened the small window and stared up at the clouded sky. Hot and rain, not the best of combinations, and especially not tonight, when what she wanted was a star-studded sky and a crescent moon to gaze at. Jacob had written a very nice letter, and Ian had twisted like a hooked worm at Jacob's stiltedly worded blessing. Scamp, she smiled, she had no doubts he'd taken great pains to come up with the exact wording, making sure his big brother felt properly indebted to him – for life.

"God bless you, Jacob," she whispered to the June night.

Next afternoon, sweat beaded Betty's upper lip, her chest, her lower back. Her thighs were slippery with it, and a quick look at Ian showed he was sweating as much as she was. She half laughed, converting it to a discreet cough. How could she possibly be this nervous? He tightened his grip on her hand, and from the way his fingers trembled, she knew he was as affected as she was. She was barely aware of the people around them, of Minister Walker in front of them. All she concentrated on was his strong comforting hand that was holding on so hard to hers. And then it was over, and she was Betty Graham – for real.

The wedding was celebrated in her father's house. Five

elder sisters and their spouses, an assortment of nephews and nieces, as well as a number of family friends had the little house bursting at the seams. Mother had made miracles when it came to the food, and there was ham and salted dried lamb, there were baked fowl and, in pride of place, a dish heaped with jellied fish.

A few hours later, Betty retreated to a corner. The room was still full of people and, over by the door, Father and Matthew were standing to the side, talking intently. Mother was laughing at something Minister Walker was saying, and Kate Jones floated by, gravitating towards the men. Simon Melville was dancing, and Betty couldn't stop herself from giggling as this oh so round man capered about the room, as elegant as a doe in flight. Betty adjusted her borrowed skirts, fingers lingering on the light green silk.

"You look beautiful," Mother said, making Betty smile. "So do you."

Mother shrugged, saying that weddings required an effort. Betty nodded, taking in the silver buckles that adorned Father's shoes, Mother's dark blue bodice, and Ian's new breeches. Everyone was in their best – well, with the exception of Alex, who was standing to the side in her everyday clothes, her shawl wrapped round her shoulders. Betty frowned. Alex looked sad – and hurt. Betty was on the point of going over to talk to her when Ian pulled her into a dance, and when next Betty looked, Alex was no longer there.

"Now?" Betty looked at her husband. Husband; she tasted the word and suppressed a grin.

"Now." Ian said something to his father, who gave an imperceptible nod, and then he took Betty by the hand and escaped out of the house, rushing her through the empty, sun-baked streets of Providence.

"Oh, Ian..." Betty could barely speak. The room was decorated with fragrant herbs and meadow flowers, from the door all the way to the bed. He undressed her, garment by garment, and all the time he hummed, a sound of deep joy that made her skin pucker and her knees – well, they seemed to have permanently given up.

331

Chapter 37

"Alex! It's hot enough as it is without you plastering yourself to me." Matthew rolled over onto his back to glower at her.

"I'm not. It's just an uncommonly narrow bed, okay?" As if to underline her words, she shoved at him, her eyes a frosty blue.

"And my back hurts," he complained, "and my head aches something fearful."

"Poor you," Alex said witheringly. "That's what you get when you over-imbibe."

"It was a wedding feast, and the ale was very good."

"Mrs Malone's, I suppose? After all, you would know, right?"

"Aye." Matthew stretched. Ah Jesus, his back! "Will you…?" He placed a hand on his aching muscles.

"No way! But, hey, why don't you ask Kate – or Mrs Malone." With that, she was out of bed, pulling on her clothes.

He sighed. She hadn't forgiven him for yesterday, even if she had tried to not let it show too much at the wedding itself. The pretty bodice she had preened in lay thrown in a corner, and he wasn't quite sure how to go about this. He had other concerns, far more urgent than his wife's trampled vanity, but Matthew hadn't liked how hurt she had looked, or how she had stood in the corner of the Hancock parlour, her far too warm shawl crossed tightly over her plain, everyday wear.

"Did you enjoy yourself, then?" he asked, which, from the look she gave him, was not the best of openings.

"No," she replied coldly. "I felt the poor cousin from the country."

Matthew squirmed. He had lost his temper when she'd

called him a straight-laced idiot, and had retaliated by telling her no wife of his would go about dressed like a whore. Alex's eyes had gone very round, an expression of absolute hurt flitting over her face, before she turned her back on him to change. All afternoon and most of the evening, she'd stood to the side, her normally so vivacious self submerged into a grey mouse – because of his excessive prudery as she'd put it, before telling him the only reason she was going was because of Ian. And even worse, somewhere halfway through, she'd just left, not even bothering to tell him – nor had he noticed, not at first.

"You looked very pretty – you always do," he said, trying out a smile.

Alex raised her brows. "Don't lie, okay? I looked by far the oldest and drabbest woman in that room. I hope that was the effect you wanted to achieve. It sure helped boost my self-esteem." She finished dressing in icy silence, braided her hair as harshly as she had done yesterday, picked up her straw hat, and left the room without a backward glance.

Matthew groaned and sank back against the pillows. She had been so proud of that new bodice, but all he could see were her breasts rising far too prominently above it, and he didn't want anyone – anyone, you hear? – to see her like that except himself.

He exhaled and got out of bed, making for the small window. He drummed his fingers against the windowsill, and reverted to the dark concerns with which he had woken.

According to William, Walter Burley had been released a few weeks ago. From what William had heard, the brothers had left Jamestown, to a large extent due to the irate kin of the poor lass. The question, of course, was whether they'd come back here or not. Not, William had insisted, reminding Matthew that they'd been outlawed by the elders.

Matthew wasn't quite as convinced. He nibbled at a torn nail and frowned at nothing in particular. How unfortunate it hadn't been Philip's throat he slit all those years ago, he reflected. Somehow, he suspected it was the eldest brother that carried the largest grudge against him.

★

Alex shook loose her hair the moment she left the inn, produced one of her hairpins, and swept it up into its more normal soft bun before replacing her hat. She'd behaved like a truculent child yesterday, protesting at his prudery by making sure all of her looked its worst. Even Simon had commented, wondering if she was practising for the part of a future widow.

She set her teeth at that. Old – there were days when all of her felt old, and when she put on that beautiful red bodice yesterday, she had seen herself in the mirror and she had actually smiled because she was quite pretty, her breasts still round and relatively high, and her skin a becoming pink – thanks to rigorous use of her homemade body scrub and oils. When she'd turned to show Matthew, he had walked his eyes up and down her body in frank admiration before telling her she was going nowhere like that – not his wife, to display herself like that before the elders of his kirk. Stupid man! All the other wives had been on display, all other women had shown some expanse of chest skin, albeit not as daring as Kate Jones in that gorgeous olive gown of hers. And Matthew, goddamn him, had looked and gawked, but her, his wife, he gave no opportunity to compete. Plaster herself to him indeed… Arsehole!

Her black mood abated somewhat during her quick walk to Joan's home. She'd been wrong in her previous comment to Matthew: the drabbest woman in the room yesterday had been Joan, not so much due to her clothing, which if sedate had not been entirely prim, but because of how gaunt and grey she looked.

Alex bit at her lip. She'd caught the flying glances between Joan and Simon, and so much was clear to her that something had them worried. Lucy? Alex thought not. The girl looked as sleek and well-fed as a cat in cream, and it was probably all to the best that she and Henry were to be wed within the year.

Joan led her out to sit in the small backyard, and Lucy brought out tea with the help of Ruth, who was staying in

Providence with her cousin for some weeks. Initial caution had transformed into a wary acceptance, and the two girls soon had their heads bent over the chessboard.

"She's very quick," Joan said to Alex, indicating Ruth. "Less than three days, and she has already picked up quite a lot of Lucy's hand signs."

"Mmm." Alex regarded her sister-in-law levelly. So far, they had discussed the wedding, little Harry Hancock's declining health, Kate Jones' somewhat daring gown, the weather, and the state of Joan's leek and cabbage bed. "What is it?"

Joan arranged her features in an expression of mild surprise.

"Oh, stop that! It just makes you look a total idiot."

Ruth raised her head at Alex's irritated tone, but after a few seconds went back to the game.

"I miss home," Joan said.

"All of us miss home – more or less, of course, but nonetheless." Alex leaned forward, inspecting Joan minutely. There was a grey tinge to her skin, hollows under her eyes, and her normally so full long mouth – a feature she shared with her brother – was thinned into a gash. "Is it the pain?" To her consternation, Joan began to cry, a silent weeping that resulted in slow heavy tears. "Joan, honey…" Alex whispered so as not to alert Ruth, whose ears seemed to have grown to the size of an elephant's. "…let's get you inside, okay?"

"Better?" Alex sat down on the side of the bed.

Joan nodded and closed her eyes, taking yet another drag at the half-smoked joint. It made Alex feel like a drug runner, to supply Joan with the tight rolls of hemp leaves, but they did seem to help.

"It's getting worse, isn't it?" Alex took Joan's hand.

"Aye," Joan said, avoiding meeting her eyes.

Hmm. Something other than the illness was gnawing at her sister-in-law, and Alex was willing to gamble a small fortune on that it all had to do with their hasty departure from Scotland.

Joan cleared her throat. "Would you...would you be kind enough and fetch Simon for me?"

"Of course. Now?"

"Now."

Alex burst into Simon's office, still out of breath after her short but speedy sprint, and came to an abrupt stop at the sight of Matthew. He was sitting side by side with Simon, his head lowered over some documents that Simon quickly covered at Alex's entrance.

"Joan asked me to fetch you."

"Is she poorly?" Simon grabbed at his coat, a look of panic in his light eyes.

"Not more than normal, but she wanted you."

"Lock the door, aye?" Simon threw a large key in the direction of Matthew, and flew out of the room.

"How bad is it?" Matthew asked once they were alone.

Alex was tempted to ignore him, but Joan was his sister. "Bad. She's dying. Bit by bit, whatever it is she has is eating its way through her. Unfortunately, I fear it's going to take a very long time." Alex shook her head. "But that's not really it. Something else is driving her half-mad with fear, but she just won't tell."

"Aye." Matthew replaced the few documents left scattered on the desktop in the drawer, locked it, and dropped the small key into its hiding place in the single china vase that decorated the sparse room. "It's driving Simon mad too."

"It is? You know what it is?" She really had no intention of talking to him, ever again.

"Murder, our wee Simon is a murderer. And someone, apparently, knows." He picked up the single paper he had left out and handed it to Alex. She frowned at the handwriting: very stiff, as if someone had made an effort to disguise their hand.

It isnae easy tae end someone's life. A blow tae the heid, many blows tae the heid, and they lie deid in the mud. Ye thought ye wurnae seen, but ye wir, darting oot from beyond St Giles tae hurry hame tae yer wife

336

*an yer deef lassie. Ultimately, naebody evades the lang
arm o the law, Master Melville, naebody...*

"Oh dear." Alex read it again, folded it together and gave it
back to Matthew. Simon? She had major problems seeing
him bashing someone over the head to the point of killing
them.

"They threatened his lass. One of the aldermen's cousins
told Simon that comely deaf lasses would fetch quite the
price on the right market, and so..."

Alex took a shaky breath. "So, he killed this cousin and
they took the first boat out?"

Matthew nodded and shredded the paper into pieces.

"Strange," he said once he was done. "Written in Scots
but, according to Simon, it came from London." He turned
to face Alex with a tight little smile. "And who in London
do you know that speaks Scots and probably knows where
Simon lives?" He waited, watching her as she thought this
through.

"Luke," she said after a long while, "but surely he
wouldn't—"

"You think not? And who was it that so neatly clipped
Luke's wings and deprived him not only of Ian—"

"Whom he no longer wanted," Alex interrupted.

"...of Ian, but more importantly of a very large sum of
money?" Matthew finished. "Simon is adamant that there
were no witnesses, and, if so, this is nothing but mischief.
Nasty mischief, but nothing more than that."

"Enough to hurry poor Joan into an even more
premature grave," Alex muttered. God! How she hoped
her letter had made her dratted brother-in-law curious
enough to lose himself in the painting and land at the feet of
Neanderthals or something.

Once he'd locked the door, Matthew offered her his arm.
Alex shook her head. She was perfectly capable of walking
on her own, thank you very much. After all, she had walked
all the way back to the inn alone yesterday, hadn't she?

"Alex," Matthew sighed. "I'm sorry, aye? But I don't

like it when you wander around half-dressed to be gawked at by other men. It makes me jealous."

"So, instead it was me that had to be jealous and feel ugly and unattractive."

"Ugly?" Matthew shook his head. "You're never ugly, Alex."

"Really? Is that why you spent so much of yesterday staring down Kate Jones' cleavage instead of standing by my side?"

"I didn't!"

"Yes, you did. Every single woman in the room you looked at – all of them except me."

"You were angry with me," he mumbled, "and I did look at you – from time to time."

"Huh." She didn't say anything more for the remainder of their short walk.

"I had looked forward to yesterday," she said, following him to their room. "It isn't as if we do much partying, is it? And you took it all away from me." She was being ridiculous, petty, childish, but she just couldn't help it. "I want to go home, as soon as possible."

She retrieved the discarded bodice and caressed the deep red, running her fingers over her own excellent needlework. Red on red, she had embroidered the alternating panes with clambering vines, and all along the lacings there ran a line of small, small daisies.

"Won't you wear it now?" Matthew said.

"Whatever for? I wanted to look pretty and young, make you proud of me, but…" She threw the garment on the bed. "I'll cut it down to something for Ruth or Sarah."

Matthew winced at her tone and tried to take her hand. She shifted away. He exhaled – loudly – and made for the door.

"You haven't forgotten that we are to have dinner with Minister Allerton, have you?"

"No, as far as I know, I'm not demented." She preceded him out of the room and sailed down the stairs.

Alex wasn't exactly mollified when they ran into Kate.

"Feeling better today?" she asked Alex before smiling radiantly at Matthew.

"Better?" Alex shook her head. "I haven't been ill."

"Oh…I thought that since you left before the dancing yesterday… Pity, given what a good dancer your husband is." Again, Kate smiled at him, receiving a weak smile in return.

"Yes, he is, isn't he?" Alex purred, throwing mental daggers at Matthew.

Kate gave her an interested look and, with a slight wave, ducked into the nearby bakery.

Alex said not one word to Matthew as they made their way up the street to the little eating house. It made him nervous; she could see it in how he kept on glancing her way. They found the minister waiting outside, a nice-looking man with gentle eyes and hair the colour of carrots. He smiled at Alex and told her just how much he'd been looking forward to meeting her, given that Daniel spoke so warmly and so often of her.

"He does?" Alex said, feeling a burst of pride.

"Now, now, Mrs Graham. You know he does – what son would not boast of a mother such as you?"

Well, that compliment definitely settled things for Alex, and for the rest of their meal, she concentrated her attention on the minister, totally cold-shouldering her husband. Instead, she leaned forward to meet Julian Allerton's eyes; she laughed and talked and flirted quite blatantly with him. The poor man didn't quite know how to handle this, eyes leaping nervously from her to Matthew, but if anything that made her intensify her attack.

"Is she pretty, your wife?" Alex asked.

"I think so," the minister said, smiling. "Actually, most men find her pretty," he added with some pride.

"And you don't mind?"

"Mind? How mind?"

"That other men admire her."

The minister laughed and said that he most certainly didn't – rather the reverse.

"Ah." Alex threw Matthew a barbed look. "But I suppose she's always modestly dressed, right? In black or dark grey, like you."

"Black? My Hope in black? I think not. She likes colours, does my wife – and silks." Minister Allerton lowered his voice. "Some would call her vain."

"And is she?" Alex asked.

"Vain? Yes, of course she is – but a woman as handsome as my wife is entitled to a certain vanity." The minister's face softened into a little smile.

Alex went on to say how glad she was to hear that some men took pride in their wives instead of begrudging them what little pleasures they might have. At this, Matthew's foot came down on her toes – hard. She retaliated by kicking his shin, had the satisfaction of hearing his hissing intake of breath, but otherwise pretended he didn't exist and returned to her conversation with the minister.

Minister Allerton looked quite relieved when she initiated a discussion about the ministry instead.

"When did you know for sure?" she asked, and Minister Allerton smiled.

"I was eighteen, nineteen perhaps?" He patted her hand. "Daniel will know, or he will not. And if he doesn't know then the teachers responsible for his spiritual well-being will urge him to wait or perhaps do other things in life. Be a teacher or such." He smoothed back his sparse hair to lay flat against his pate and gave her a serious look. "Will you be disappointed in him if he's not ordained?"

"Disappointed? Me?" She swallowed back on a gust of laughter. "No, I won't. I just want him to be content with the choices he makes."

"Content?" He tilted his head. "Not happy?"

"Content is good enough – and it's a definite prerequisite to being happy now and then." With that, she stood up. After a quick curtsey in the minister's direction, she grabbed the basket she had placed below the table and hurried off.

★

Matthew wasn't quite sure if he was mostly angered or humiliated by his wife's behaviour. He kept his eyes on her as she made her way through the small room, head held high. By the door, she stopped for a moment to exchange some words with Minister Walker and William. It irked him to see her smile and laugh, to see how she for an instant leaned forward to say something to the minister, one hand resting as if by chance on William's arm. And then she was off, as light-footed as a wench, and not one word, not one look, had she exchanged with him.

"May I be forward enough to suggest it would seem you have displeased your wife in some way?" Minister Allerton said before serving himself an extra slice of cheese.

"I already know that," Matthew said. "What I don't know is how to make it better."

Chapter 38

"Are you planning on milking this much longer?" Matthew asked a few mornings later, his hand closing around her wrist and thereby hindering her from leaving the bed. Two days of icy silence, of eyes that stared blankly through him, were quite enough. And last evening... It had cut him to the quick to have her sitting as far away from him as possible, laughing and talking with Simon and William, but the moment he joined them, she'd stood and walked off.

"Milk what? That you made me dress like a nun, or that you had the gall to dance with other 'half-dressed' women while I was back here alone?"

"Both, I imagine," he said, refusing to let go despite her irritated tugging.

"Jerk," she hissed.

"I've tried to apologise."

"Not for dancing with Kate – her and her tits that were more or less hanging out."

"Alex!" Matthew laughed. "That they were not!" He pinned her down, eyes locked into hers. "I promise there will be an occasion for you to wear that pretty bodice of yours, and on that occasion I will dance only with you. And your breasts, should they wish to join in."

"Dream on! When I want to dance, I'll dance with a man that properly appreciates me." She shoved at him, and when that didn't help, she took a firm hold of his hair and yanked, hard. "Let me go, you oaf."

"Stop pulling my hair," he growled. "And you'll not be dancing with any other men but me."

"Hypocrite! So it's okay for you to drool all over Kate Jones' breasts, but I'm not allowed to do the same, am I?"

"What? Drool over Kate's bosom?" He winced when she tugged at his hair again.

"You know what I mean! And let me go, I…"

He kissed her. She spluttered and bit his lip. He returned the favour, swallowing her indignant yelp.

"Listen to me." He grabbed her wrists and forced her to let go of his hair. She scowled. "I'm sorry," he said. "I was wrong to do as I did, spoiling the wedding for you."

"Huh."

He brushed his nose against hers. "I don't like it, when we argue."

"Me neither." She gave him a sharp look. "So, when is this occasion?"

"Very, very soon, so you best begin to practise. Dancing with me is exhausting, aye?"

"I can keep up," she said, her mouth softening perceptibly.

He gave a silent word of thanks to Minister Allerton for his brilliant idea and kissed her.

"Don't push it," she murmured when they came up for breath.

"Oh, aye? Do you want me to stop?"

"Umm…" She shook her head.

"Nay, I thought not."

A loud banging on the door had them breaking apart, and when Matthew recognised the voice, he rushed for the door. A panting Ruth stood on the other side, her hair still in night braids.

"Harry," she stuttered, "wee Harry is dead, and I'm to get Betty."

"Dear Lord." Matthew closed his eyes: poor Esther, poor William.

"When?" Alex asked.

Ruth had no idea. She had just done as she'd been told: run to fetch Betty, and tell her parents.

"I suppose it's something of a relief for little Harry," Alex said. "He had a hard time of it the other day, didn't he?"

Matthew nodded. The laddie had struggled for breath

343

through most of the wedding, clinging like a limpet to his mother.

"But nor for the mother – or the father." His eyes found hers, and they shared a moment of silence, recalling a beautiful, angry girl-child running to the defence of her father – and her death. "Rachel," Matthew breathed, "our wee Rachel…"

Betty smoothed down a waving lock on the small head, adjusted the brand new smock so that it lay as it should, and beckoned to her father.

"He looks at peace, I think," she said, smiling down at little Harry, who did look at rest, his feather lashes shading the thin cheeks, the mouth slightly open as if he were about to say something. Her father sobbed and stroked Harry over the cheek with his forefinger.

"Another little angel for God," he said.

Betty nodded, thinking that taking six from the same family was excessive, and that wasn't counting the four Mother hadn't borne to full term. She fussed with the baby shawl Mother had insisted he be covered with, folding it to lie close to the little body. It had always been a matter of time before Harry died, constantly ill since the day he was born. Even had he grown up, what would have become of him? Sweet little Harry was not like other children, his tongue somewhat too big for his mouth, his eyes so strangely slanted. But he had been a happy boy, a child that attempted to smile even as he struggled to drag air into his lungs, and now he was dead.

Mother lay prostrate upstairs, and had it not been because it was unseemly to display grief at the death of a child – little Harry was, after all, reunited with his heavenly Father – Betty suspected her father would have gladly joined her, much more shaken by this expected death than she'd thought he would be.

"She sleeps – at last," Joan said, coming down from where she'd been sitting with Mother. From the kitchen came Willie's voice, high and plaintive, and then Alex's lower voice was there to shush. A moment later, Alex opened the door with her hip before entering with a laden tray that she set down on the table furthest from the little coffin.

"Food – and beer," she said.

Betty's throat and eyes filled with tears. Her brother was dead, and the room that two days ago had been the scene of her wedding now held a wake. With a small sound, she exited the room, needing a few minutes of solitude.

"I must," Betty said a few days later. She didn't want to. She wanted to ride back home with Ian, but she couldn't leave her parents to cope on their own, not for some weeks.

Ian kissed her nose. "We have a lifetime before us, young and healthy, the both of us."

"A lifetime?" Betty leaned her head against his chest. "That's relative. Harry had a lifetime as well – a very short one." She blinked away her tears. It must be the pregnancy that was making her this maudlin, just as it was making her over-tender and nauseous. Ravenously hungry, she would fry up eggs, and then she couldn't eat them, her whole stomach flipping at the sight of those quivering yolks.

"A long lifetime." Ian smoothed back her hair, no longer imprisoned in a tight braid but collected in a soft bun at the back of her head like he wanted it.

They were all rather subdued when they set off, very early on a Tuesday morning, but by the time it was Thursday, and home was only a few hours away, they were in a considerably better mood, however uncomfortable the previous night had been – rainy and cold. The only irritant was Matthew's horse, because poor Moses had developed an inflammation in one of his hooves.

"You ride on." Matthew sighed and got off. "He's gone lame again."

"Ride on?" Alex shook her head. "I'm not about to leave you all alone here. We can walk together."

"We're only hours from home; go on with you." Matthew pointed at Dandelion. "I keep the dog with me; you take the mule."

"I'm not sure..." Alex dismounted. "What about Indians? Or the Burleys?"

"The Burleys?" He managed a little laugh. "Why would they be here?"

"Stranger things have happened," she muttered, "and we know for a fact they're not in Jamestown, don't we?"

"I very much doubt they're anywhere close," Matthew said, "and, as to the Indians, we haven't seen any since spring, have we?"

"Nay, we haven't." Ian scanned the forest around them. "I can ride on ahead and you can come walking."

"Alex can go with you. Have supper ready for me when I come in."

"Hmph," Alex snorted. "I think I'll walk instead." But she threw a hasty look to the west, because she was in a hurry to get home and make sure all her children were alive, not dead like poor little Harry.

"Go on, lass, I'll be fine, aye?" Matthew helped her back into the saddle and smacked the horse into a trot.

Ian and Alex had just forded a shallow stream when Alex drew her horse to a halt. "Are you sure he'll be alright?" She looked back in the direction they had come.

"Aye. He has both pistols and musket."

Alex chewed her lip. This was a bad idea: to leave Matthew alone. "I'm not sure. Maybe we should go back."

"Mama," Ian groaned, "we've covered a mile or so already."

"So, we uncover it."

"We ride on," he insisted. "He has the dog – you know how frightening he can be."

Alex chuckled. Dandelion was as huge as his sire, dear dead Narcissus, and just as protective of his family.

"We should have named him Fang or something." She grinned.

"Or Yellow Devil," Ian suggested, nudging his horse on. He made an exasperated sound when Alex refused to budge, sawing at the reins to turn her mount.

"I'm riding back, but you go ahead, okay?"

★

It was the dog. If it hadn't been for how Dandelion stiffened, Matthew would have become aware of them too late. A deep rumble emanated from Dandelion, hackles sprouting in a yellow crest along his back and shoulders. Matthew whipped up one pistol in one hand, musket in the other, frowning as he scanned the woods.

There: silent shapes moving like pack wolves through the undergrowth. He recognised them with a flare of fear. When the four men stepped into sight, one of them a huge man Matthew had never seen before, Matthew leaped for cover.

Dressed like Indians, hair braided the Indian way, the Burley brothers and their unknown companion could easily been mistaken for natives – at a distance. Close up, those light grey eyes gave them away for what they were: white men with souls the colour and consistency of pitch.

"Well, well, Mr Graham. Imagine running into you like this." Philip Burley grinned, eyes never leaving Matthew's guns.

"Aye, I imagine it's a right surprise."

"Surprise? No, not really – we've been following you since some hours back. However, we didn't expect to find you alone. Fortunate – for us." Philip's voice heaved with threat.

"Alone?" Matthew held back the snarling dog with a clipped command.

"Four against one," Philip said.

"And two of you at least will die – as you should, outlaws that you are."

"Ah, yes. Something else we have to thank you for, isn't it?" Philip took a step towards him.

"Thank me? You've brought the weight of the law down on yourselves without any help from me."

"Is that so? That's not how I hear it. I hear how a certain Mr Graham has presented evidence that paints the three of us as ogres, men without morals or hearts."

"I've told nothing but the truth," Matthew said.

"Absolutely." Philip inclined his head in a little bow.

"And we will prove you right. Prepare to die, Graham, slowly and painfully."

Matthew levelled his pistol and fired. With a little 'eh', Stephen clapped his hands to his thigh and sank to the ground.

The shot almost made Alex fall off her horse.

"Matthew!" Alex thumped her heels into her surprised mount, leaned forward over the mare's neck, and yelled her on. Ian thundered by, half standing in the stirrups, musket in one hand, and Alex used the free ends of the reins to whip her mare into galloping even faster.

Another shot rang out, and now there was the distinctive sound of Dandelion's barking, threaded through with Matthew's raised voice. Indians, Alex thought. Oh my God, I'm going to find him dead and scalped.

The woods thinned as she got closer to the sounds. Light filtered through the foliage, leaves rustled in the wind, and the moss squelched under her mare's hooves. Ian was by now well ahead. Alex gripped her pistol, trying to remember if it was loaded or not, and tried to make her mare fly.

She wasn't quite sure what happened next. Ian barged into a small clearing, and three men in Indian garb turned to see him bearing down on them. Holy Matilda, it was them, the Burleys! One of them was down, lying curled together on the moss.

A shot rang out. Matthew threw himself to the ground, yelling something unintelligible. The dog lunged, a yellow massive shape that threw itself at the man crawling on the ground. Philip – yes, she was sure it was Philip, his dark hair falling in a signatory lock over one eye – raised his musket at Ian. She heard Matthew scream a warning. Ian rode on, his barrel pointing straight at Philip. A shot – no, two shots – rang out. In slow motion, Ian tumbled from his saddle to land on the ground with a sickening crunch. Matthew screamed his son's name, and Alex rode straight into the men still standing, shrieking like a Viking berserk.

She was too frightened to think. With her pistol in one

hand, she launched herself off the horse, bringing Philip to the ground. Bloody hell, that hurt! Philip shoved at her and she whacked him over the head with the pistol. She was on her feet, and Matthew was screaming, the dog was barking, one of the horses neighed, while Ian lay still and silent on the moss. Her son! She ran towards him.

Someone grabbed hold of her skirts. Alex almost fell, but succeeded in remaining on her feet. She pulled free, intent on getting to Ian. So still. Was he dead? Out of the corner of her eye, she saw Walter fire. Matthew stumbled backwards, and Walter cheered. Oh God, was he wounded? But, no, she heard Matthew call her name, there was a whooshing sound behind her, and, at the last moment, she flung herself to the side. Philip cursed and came after, lifting his musket as a club.

She had no time for this; she had to help Ian. Without really knowing how, she'd bunched her skirts, baring her legs. Philip's brows rose, eyes nailed to her limbs. Keep on gawking, mister! She rose on her toes, swivelled and slammed her leg into Philip's side, causing him to double up and gasp.

Stephen – she assumed it was Stephen, not seeing much more than his bleeding backside – screamed and tried to shield his head from Dandelion. Walter kicked at the dog, yelling for Philip to come and help. Matthew discharged his musket, and Walter staggered. The fourth man was already limping away, and Alex aimed her pistol at Philip.

Two light eyes stared at her. His tongue flickered over his lips, and he took a shuffling step backwards. She came after.

"Die," she said and squeezed the trigger. Nothing happened. Philip sneered and advanced, the steel of his knife glinting in the sun.

"Philip!" Walter screamed, pressing his hand to his bleeding side. Dandelion was back, worrying at Stephen's leg like a terrier. Philip cursed and hurried to his brothers' aid. Matthew fired, Stephen howled, his brothers heaved him up and fled, leaving a thick smear of blood in their wake. Dandelion bounded after, barking wildly. Yes, the dog was right: they should probably set off in pursuit and finish the bastards off once and for all, but all Alex could think of was Ian, his hand immobile and pale against the dark mulch of the ground.

Matthew rushed towards Ian. His sleeve was dark with blood, and he grunted as he fell to his knees by his son.

"Are you alright?" Alex knelt beside him.

"Ian," he said in reply, "oh Lord, Ian!" He made as if to lift Ian up, injured arm or not.

"No, wait. He landed badly on his back." She placed a hand on Ian's cheek, keeping her eyes from the spreading dark red stain on his shirt. "Ian?"

Ian's eyelids fluttered open.

"Does it hurt?" she asked.

Ian managed to nod.

"Well, thank heavens for that," Alex said, making Matthew glare at her.

"Thank heavens?"

"It means he can feel something. If it didn't hurt, his spine would have been broken." She didn't like the way he was lying and to carry him back like this… "Go and get help. We need a door or something to carry him on, and quilts."

"Go? I can't leave you here!" He threw a wild look at their surroundings as if expecting the damned Burleys to reappear at any moment.

"Matthew! Go! You can ride much faster than I can, and I'll be alright. They're wounded and won't be coming back. And, if they do, I'll castrate them for damaging my son." She put a hand on Dandelion's collar. "He stays with me but for God's sake, ride and ride now."

Matthew stood indecisive for a further few seconds, looked down at his bleeding, very still son, and, with a curt nod, sat up on Ian's chestnut gelding and spurred it away.

Ian lay listening to the receding sounds of horse and rider before opening his eyes.

"Mama…" Ian whispered, trying to blink her into

focus. His side was on fire, and he recalled being hit, and then…God! His back!

"Be quiet," Mama said. "Can you move your toes?"

He made a huge effort, near on swooning with the pain. She gave him an encouraging nod. "Good. Your fingers?"

He dragged them across the moss. But his whole back throbbed, and he was convinced there was something hard pushing into his spine. Tentatively, he shifted to his right. Pain flew up his side and banded his chest, making him gulp for air. She stopped him from trying again by placing a hand on his arm.

"I don't dare to move you," she said, stepping out of her petticoats. She rolled them together and fashioned a pillow for him, lifting his head carefully. Then she squatted down to inspect his side.

Ian lay staring up at the patches of sky visible above the high chestnuts and sycamores. Blue sky, tree crowns silhouetted against it… It was all spinning; slowly but irrevocably, the trees danced around him, and he was aware of a growing nausea. Her hands were soft and competent, so warm against his skin.

"Will I die?" he asked.

"Someday," she replied with a hitch to her voice, "but not today."

But mayhap tomorrow, or the day after, unless Mrs Parson was good with gunshot wounds. The ball had lodged itself inside of him; he could feel it when she probed. He gasped, was relieved when she told him it would do for now – at least she had staunched the blood. Instead, she covered him with the blankets that the two horses left behind carried, and then she just sat there and held his hand.

He shivered, having to grit his teeth to stop them from chattering. "So cold," he said.

"Shock," she muttered, and, to his consternation, she stood and undressed, calling for Dandelion to come and lie close on his uninjured side.

"What are you doing?" Ian croaked.

"I have to keep you warm."

It wasn't that he hadn't seen her naked before – of course he had, if nothing else during all those baths when he was still a lad – but he was very conscious of the fact that he was a man, and she, for all that she was his mama, was a woman. She piled her discarded clothes on top of the blankets and lay down as close as possible. He was horribly cold and she was wonderfully warm, and her breasts were very soft. Soft and round, he reflected drowsily, and it was nice to have her holding him like this. He closed his eyes, safe in the knowledge that she was here.

By the time Matthew made it back with Mark, Alex was stiff with cold, but at least Ian was moderately warm, his breathing regular if shallow. Inch by careful inch, they slid him to lie flat on the door they had brought with them, and Alex packed him in a mountain of quilts, all the while talking soothingly to him.

Ian groped for her hand.

"Will I die, Mama?" he asked again in a trickle of a voice.

"Someday," she said through tears, "but not today."

Chapter 39

Jacob sat back on his heels and surveyed the garden. He had done it! Not by himself, of course, but to a very large part the Apothecaries' Garden was the product of his efforts. He filled his hand with well-turned soil and let it dribble through his fingers. Rich, loamy and dark, the soil brought forth plants of exceptional quality, and in one corner stood Jacob's own contribution to what, according to Master Castain, was destined to become the foremost herbal garden in the world.

Jacob wandered over to inspect the squash plants and was joined by Master Castain, who was fascinated by these fast-growing new additions to his collection.

"So you eat the fruit?" Master Castain said as he always did.

Jacob nodded. According to Mama, you did.

"Have you found a berth to Maryland?" Master Castain asked as they strolled towards the small cottage the master used as office and summer abode.

"Aye. With Captain Miles. Fitting, isn't it?" He chuckled at the thought. It was Captain Miles' generous gift two years ago that would pay his way back home.

"You could stay," Master Castain said in a light voice.

Jacob shook his head. "I want to go home."

Ever since that terrible evening at Richard Collin's, the dazzle had gone out of London for Jacob, and several days of bedridden pain hadn't much helped. He fingered his nose: would they recognise him when they saw him, or had he changed too much? He frowned down at his hands: still fully functional as was most of him, but the clap to his ear had left him with a recurring ringing, and the broken toes had healed badly, so now Jacob walked with a constant twinge.

Only once since his ordeal had he seen Charlotte. She had come to an abrupt standstill and raised her hand in a tentative wave. Jacob had wheeled and left, his heart hammering against his ribs.

"Why did she lie?" he had asked his uncle repeatedly during the time he spent in bed. "Why fill me with these terrible stories?"

Luke had tilted his head. "And if she had told you she was happy and content?"

Jacob had stared up at the ceiling considering this. "Then I wouldn't have cared for her," he finally admitted.

Luke ruffled his hair. "You needed to be the hero, and you cast her as your Dulcinea."

That had rankled. Jacob had never shared Mark's or Mama's fascination with Don Quijote, finding the aged bachelor ludicrous and gullible, and here he was, as gullible himself.

"In one thing, your da and myself have been much alike," Luke had gone on, "and that's in our choice of women. Both of us have loved women who have loved us as wholeheartedly back."

"Choice?" Jacob had said bitterly. "More a question of being fortunate."

Luke had regarded him for a long time. "Aye, you're right. It wasn't choice; it was fate." His face softened, making him look very young. "I knew it, aye? From the moment I first saw Margaret – and I was only six."

Jacob found that most incredible, but kept that to himself. He fell asleep while Luke told him of long gone days at Hillview, days spent running through the meadows with Margaret at his side.

Over the last few weeks, Jacob had spent what time he could with his uncle and cousins, regaling them with one story after the other about his life and family back home.

"It seems so much more exciting there than here," Charlie said after Jacob had recounted how narrowly he had escaped being abducted some years back.

"You could come with me." Jacob looked his cousin up and down with a teasing smile. "Not like that, mind. Velvet doesn't do very well in the woods."

Luke squashed that idea in the bud, informing both son and nephew that Charles had obligations and duties here, in England.

"And no," he added, "neither Marie nor Joan will be going either." Jacob rolled his eyes at his very bonny girl cousins, making them giggle.

"She looks much like mother," Charles had informed Jacob the first time he had met Marie. If so, Jacob concluded with a flash of disloyalty, Margaret was much, much more beautiful than Mama. In response to his open admiration, Charles had led him into Luke's bedroom, and there Jacob had stared at this unknown aunt, exquisitely captured by Peter Lely himself.

"We'll never find a wife to replace her," Jacob informed Charles in a reverential voice.

"No," Charles said, sounding very pleased.

Jacob remained in front of the portrait for an extended period of time, staring at this entrancing woman, her perfect skin highlighted by ivory silks, the blue in her eyes underlined by the green of her ribbons. All he could see was Mama: in the shape of the face, and the slant of the eyes, in the way those dark eyebrows arched, and in the slight curl of her mouth. It was most disconcerting, and there was no one he could comment it with. Even more disconcerting was the day the letter arrived.

"A letter for you." Master Castain handed Jacob the thick square. "Read it later," he said in an irritated voice when it would seem Jacob was going to tear it open immediately. "We have an illustrious visitor to prepare for."

Jacob made a face. Preparing for an illustrious visitor meant he, Jacob, had to scurry over the exhibition beds and ensure it all looked perfect, while Ned chased the gardening lads to shear the grass of the paths as short as they could get it. Then they were expected to melt into the background as Master Castain in his best velvet coat expounded on the various plants to a patron at best capable of recognising lemon balm, at worst only there because he had to be.

It was evening by the time Jacob remembered he had a letter to read, and eagerly he opened it to find it contained but a short note for him, and a sealed letter to be delivered to Uncle Luke. For all that he was now a man rather than a lad, Jacob was beside himself with curiosity. His mama write to Uncle Luke? He read his own letter twice only to find it contained very little news – except for the fact that the new field hand, John Mason (who, his mother informed him in fact was a mason, from a long line of masons down on the south coast somewhere, and wasn't that interesting? No, Jacob thought impatiently) was giving Agnes the eye, and about time it was that this nice young woman found herself a man, no matter that she had the intellect of a confused hen.

It wasn't until the next day that Jacob had the opportunity of delivering the letter to Luke.

"What does she say?" Jacob asked, forcing himself to remain seated when what he wanted to do was rush over and snatch the letter from Luke's hand.

"I imagine that should she have wanted you to know, she would have told you," Luke replied in a teasing tone, but a deep crease between his brows indicated he was concerned by what he had just read.

Luke folded the letter and stood up, wandering over to stare out at the June twilight. How could Alex know anything at all about a painting he kept hidden from public view? He read the short paragraph again. *Destroy it*, he read, *and never look for too long or too deep into its swirling midst.* Why not? Luke was most intrigued. *Please do not let my son look too close, nor any of your own children unless you wish to see them disappear before your eyes.* Luke felt a ripple of disquiet move up his spine. Black magic... Margaret's mother... And once again, how did his sister-in-law come to know?

"Uncle Luke?" Jacob's face was very close to his own.

"I think we need to do some experimenting, dear nephew. Wait here."

Luke returned a half hour or so later, with the kitchen lad in tow. At their entrance, Jacob rose from the window bench.

"Now," Luke said to the kitchen lad. "When I tell you to, I want you to look very closely at the painting."

The laddie blinked. Two large brandies had him somewhat unsteady on his feet, and, in his hand, he clutched the golden guinea Luke had given him. Jacob stood a few feet away, looking green around the gills.

Luke frowned. "Ready? Keep your eye on the lad, and if anything happens to him, grab him."

"And if something happens to me?" Jacob asked.

"I'm right here." Luke cocked his head at his nephew. Jacob was not only pale, he was sweating profusely, eyes firmly averted from the wee painting.

"Right then, lad, look and look deep," Luke said.

The kitchen boy stepped up close to the table, staring down at the painting. At first, nothing happened, and Luke was on the point of discontinuing this disappointing little exercise when the painting began to sing, a hushed humming that made Luke sway where he stood. From a white point at its centre, bright light gushed forth, and the kitchen lad uttered a muted 'oh', extending first one, then the other hand towards the dazzling light.

Dear God! Luke's stomach heaved violently. The lad's arms were gone, and now his head, his torso were fading as well. The laddie screamed and tried to back away, but it would seem the painting had him in a vice, dragging the hapless bairn into invisibility. Jacob grabbed hold of the lad's breeches and pulled.

"Help me!"

Luke rushed forward to take hold of a foot. Together, they threw themselves backwards and the lad shrieked like a gutted pig. For a sickening moment, Luke feared they'd not be able to hold him, so strong was the force that was attempting to swallow him.

One concerted heave, and the lad landed on the floor, his eyes squished closed.

"God in heaven..." Jacob was shaking all over, staring from the picture to the lad who was now curled together, holding his head between his hands.

"Most fortuitous that you grabbed him when you did." Luke attempted to sound calm.

"Aye, there was very little left of him." Jacob sank down to sit against the wall. "Please..." he said, indicating the painting. "Please cover it."

Luke did, and Jacob slumped, breathing heavily.

The lad struggled to sit. "Me head," he groaned, "it hurts fair to kill me." His face, his neck, what was visible of his hands and arms – all of him was covered in large, black bruises.

"More brandy." Luke rang for one of the footmen and instructed him to ply the lad with brandy until he fell asleep.

"He..." Jacob coughed. "Did you see? He...Oh Lord, what is this?"

"I'm not sure." Luke wrapped the painting in an old shawl and returned it to its drawer. The canvas hummed with life, and Luke slammed the drawer closed. This was witchcraft: black, dangerous magic. He made a note to himself to ensure the lad was kept well and truly drunk for a couple of days before being sent off to the Oxford house.

"Burn it!" Jacob whispered. "You can't keep something like that!"

"I won't, of course I won't. Dear Lord, what if one of my children were to come upon it?"

Jacob nodded, reclining against the wall with his eyes closed. "How could Mama know?"

"That, I fear, is something you must ask your mother."

"Aye, I suppose it is," Jacob said.

They never spoke of it again.

The day Jacob did his final examinations, Luke presented him with a new set of clothes. In sober, well-cut broadcloth, new silk stockings, new shirt and a cravat to match, Jacob felt most conspicuous. In particular, it was the shoes with their two-inch heels and impressive rosettes that had him moving with exaggerated caution, very aware that he overtopped every single man around him – including his uncle.

Afterwards, as a newly confirmed apothecary, Jacob invited Master Castain to supper, and, by the time they returned home, the short summer night was nearly over, the sky a delicate shade of pink. They stood for a long time by the river, watching the anchored ships.

"I'll miss you," Master Castain said.

"And I you," Jacob replied.

"If…" Master Castain coughed a couple of times, found a handkerchief to wipe himself fastidiously around the nose and mouth, and cleared his throat. "If you ever need it, there's a place for you here, with us." His only child was not yet twelve, he added, but with time she would inherit a profitable business.

Jacob laughed. "Wed little Isabelle? I think not, master. She scares me as it is."

Master Castain joined in his laughter. Isabelle was a headstrong child, he admitted with quite some pride.

"I must go home," Jacob continued, watching as one of the ships on the river unfurled its sails.

"And it helps, of course, to return an educated man," Master Castain said with a hint of bitterness.

Jacob clapped him on the shoulder. "I'll plant a herbal garden of my own one day, and I'll name it after you."

"Me?" Master Castain flushed with pleasure.

Jacob wasn't quite sure what to say, but Helen looked at him with such open pleading in her eyes that he finally gave a small nod.

"Not much of a godfather," he said. "It's not as if I'll be able to contribute to her upkeep or such."

"Keep her we can do ourselves." Helen smiled at the babe in her arms. "Here." She handed him the child.

Jacob had held weans most of his life, and automatically he adjusted his hold so that the head was supported by his arm. A pretty enough child, he supposed, with fair, long lashes and a generous mouth. "What will you name her?"

"Rachel." Helen met his surprised look calmly. "For her father's sister."

"Oh." Had he ever told her of his dead sister? He suspected he had. Still, Rachel was a common enough name, wasn't it? A mere coincidence, no more. He stared down at the sleeping wean, quelling an urge to undo the laced cap and see if she had any hair.

"I'll never forget you, Jacob Graham." Helen smiled, reclaiming her daughter.

"I don't think I'll forget you either."

She laughed and ducked her head. "No," she said in a sultry voice. "I don't think you will."

As he stood to leave, she took hold of his coat lapel, and stood on her toes to give him a kiss. "Thank you," she said, "for everything."

Luke insisted on accompanying Jacob down to the docks, standing to the side as the man Jacob told him was the captain greeted Jacob with a hug.

"You've grown," the captain said, craning back to meet Jacob's eyes.

"Nay, I haven't." Jacob grinned. "You've shrunk." He beckoned for Luke to join them, so he did, noting how the captain's face tightened as he approached.

Luke frowned. As far as he knew, he had never laid eyes on this man before, but from the way the captain was staring at him, it would seem the captain had the advantage of knowing exactly who he was.

"This is Captain Miles," Jacob introduced, "long since a friend of the family."

"Aye," Captain Miles said, "ever since I had the pleasure of helping Mrs Graham on her voyage to find and reclaim her abducted husband."

"Ah." Luke didn't extend his hand, but kept them as clasped behind his back as the captain kept his own.

"Terrible," Captain Miles went on. "An innocent man be carried off as an indentured servant."

"Hmm," Luke mumbled. It was Margaret's fault that particular scheme to permanently rid this world of brother Matthew had failed. It had taken years for him to forgive Margaret for helping Alex finance her rescue mission. Even now, twenty years later and with a nephew before him he would never have known had it not been for the success of that expedition, a nasty coil of resentment shifted inside of him. It was best if they never met again, his brother and him, he reflected. Too much anger, far too much. And yet... Luke looked at his nephew and hoped that Matthew would understand that what he had done for Jacob, he had really done for him – his lost brother.

"I already know all that," Jacob said, bringing Luke tumbling back to the present.

"You do?" Luke said.

Jacob hitched his shoulders. "They don't talk about it, not much, but enough that we all know how our dastardly uncle had Da clobbered over his head and carried off to slavery."

Luke squirmed, making Captain Miles grin.

"And still you wanted to meet me?" Luke asked, ruefully recognising that he wanted this young man to like him, even love him.

Jacob regarded him out of eyes that were uncomfortably like Matthew's. "As I said, it wouldn't be polite not to." With that, he swept Luke into a long embrace, and Luke wrapped his arms around him and held him hard, so very hard.

Chapter 40

"Oh, for God's sake, Ian, what do you expect?" Alex glared at him. "Seriously, you're the worst patient I've ever had."

"Talk about the pot calling the kettle black," Mrs Parson said, shoving Alex out of the way to inspect the healing wound.

Ian had been unconscious when they brought him in, and that was, in retrospect, a blessing. It had taken hours to clean out his gaping side wound, and then they'd had to open it again a few days later, pus spurting out of an abscess the size of an egg. But now the wound had closed, with Ian complaining more about the itch than the pain.

Mrs Parson prodded at the pink scar tissue and straightened up. "You stay in bed, at least the week out."

Ian groaned, but subsided against his pillows.

"I don't think I'd want to live if I can't move," Ian confided to Matthew one evening. He shifted his legs, a spasm of relief flying across his face at the verification that they seemed to be working.

"Mmm," Matthew replied, moving his stool so that he sat very close to Ian. At Alex's insistence, Ian was in the big house. At Ian's insistence, he was in the parlour so that he could see his family going by.

Ian craned his neck to look at the overcast sky. "Raining?" he asked.

"Not yet, but it will – soon enough." Not too much, Matthew hoped, not this close to harvest. He studied his son for a while, and took a big breath. Alex insisted he had to be told, now. "You'll find it difficult to move at first." Constant pain, Mrs Parson had predicted after seeing Ian's lacerated back. Strong experienced fingers had dug their way along his spinal knobs, the crease between her brows growing deeper and deeper the closer to the pelvic area she got.

"I imagine so," Ian said. "After four weeks flat on my back, I don't think my legs will easily recall how to walk."

"It may be that you'll never walk as you once did." Matthew's heart shrank to the size of a walnut at the expression on Ian's face.

"How do you mean?"

Matthew clasped Ian's hand. "The damage to the back is severe, Ian."

His son closed his eyes and turned his face away.

"He says he'll never walk again," Betty said to Alex. "That's not what you told me."

Alex sighed from the other side of the raspberry canes. "Honestly, I don't know. None of us knows. I think he'll walk. After all, he can move his legs and feet, but I also think he'll find it painful at times." As far as they could ascertain, two of his vertebrae had been damaged, and Alex suspected such injuries never fully healed – at least not on their own.

"No full days on the fields," Betty said.

"No, probably not." Alex switched baskets, filling the next one with blurring speed. "Swimming might be a good start."

"Swimming?" Betty poked her head through the canes. "Why would that be useful?"

"Because you float, and there's no weight to press down on the spine as you move." She gave her daughter-in-law a thoughtful look. "Let's try, this afternoon."

Minister Allerton said he thought swimming was an excellent idea. When Betty had received news of Ian's injury, the minister had offered to accompany her and Ruth home. Once at Graham's Garden, he had been invited to stay and done so, an interested and supportive observer of everything Alex and Mrs Parson did. He bombarded them with questions, clearly very impressed by how clean everything was kept – knife blades held in fire and dropped into boiling water, bandages boiled and dried before they were used.

Even if Alex was at times tempted to stuff his mouth, mostly she enjoyed his company and unfailing optimism.

"I can help carry him." He was still in his prime, the minister told her, not yet thirty-five. He flexed his arms and straightened up to his middling height.

"I think he'll prefer to walk," Alex said.

"Walk?" Mrs Parson said. "That's a fair bit, Alex."

"I don't propose that he walk all the way down there today, but he must make a start."

"There are moments when I'm right grateful you're not my real mother, and this is one of them," Ian hissed through gritted teeth. He was covered in sweat, his legs trembling after having crossed the yard on his own two feet, with Betty propping up one side and Alex the other.

"Bullshit." Alex grinned, helping him to sit on the stool that David was carrying for them. Bad idea: he whitened with pain. "Lie down instead." She spread her shawl for him in the grass. "On your front." She pulled his shirt out of his breeches before tugging them down to bare his buttocks.

"Mama!"

Alex ignored him and beckoned Betty over.

"Oil," she said. "That, and warm hands."

She showed Betty how to massage the rigid small muscles along his spine, how to work her way down to the gluteus. Under their hands, Ian at first relaxed; then began to fidget in a way that made Alex smile.

"Everything else on him is in working order," she said to Betty before getting off her knees. She winked and motioned for David to come with her and leave them alone. "Call me when you need us, okay?"

"Witch," Ian murmured from where he had his head pillowed on his arms. "She planned this, didn't she?"

Betty looked about and had to laugh. Alex definitely had, ensuring Ian had made it all the way to her primitive bower, a mass of mock oranges and rose brambles left to grow as wild as they wished, but very secluded. Betty kept her hands on Ian's sun-warmed back, moving them in a way that made Ian groan. Clumsily, he rolled over to look at her.

"Everything else is in working order," he mimicked with a smile. "I don't want to know how she knows that."

"But it is." Betty closed her hand round his cock.

"Aye," he said, and his eyes widened at what she was doing to him.

"Betty," he moaned, and his fingers twisted into her hair.

"See?" Alex said, watching Ian bob up and down by the river shore. "Just what he needs."

Matthew snorted from where he stood beside her. "There are other things he needs more."

"And he has had them as well."

Ian had looked blissfully content when Betty had called for them, had even allowed Matthew and the minister to carry him down to the river for his bath and swim.

"He *is* nice," Alex said, nodding in the direction of the minister, who stood close to the water's edge shouting encouragements to Ian.

"You shouldn't sound so surprised," Matthew chided. "Are you implying most ministers are not?"

"Prigs, most of them, inflated, bigoted, and surprisingly ignorant."

"Alex!"

"Richard Campbell, need I say more?"

"Hmm," Matthew replied, his cheeks shading into an uncharacteristic pink. Well, they should – after all he'd sided with that obnoxious minister against her.

It was a bright-eyed Ian who joined them for supper that evening, even if he had to excuse himself halfway through.

"You okay?" Alex asked, half rising from the table.

"Aye." Ian motioned for her to sit down. "I just need to lie down." Slowly, he made his way from the kitchen, the cane thumping against the floorboards.

All the same, Alex hurried through her meal, delegated the cleaning up to the girls, and went to find Ian. He was lying very still, his jaw clenched, and it took Alex some time to work through his back. Once she was done, she helped him into a clean shirt and busied herself plumping up his pillows, smoothing down quilts and sheets. Ian was nearly asleep when she kissed him on the brow and tiptoed for the door.

"Mama?"

Alex stopped at the door to look back at Ian, a dark blob against his pillow.

"Yes?"

"I move back to my cabin tomorrow," he said in a voice that left no room for discussion. "Betty will manage."

"Oh, I'm sure she will." Alex made to turn away, but his voice stopped her yet again.

"Mama?"

"Mmm?"

"Thank you." It came out very gravelly.

"You're welcome, son."

For a man who had never before spent more than his nights in bed, the sudden immobility was a chafing fetter. Ian woke and began the automatic roll out of bed, only to be painfully reminded of the fact that any movements now had to be considered and planned. The wall opposite his bed became dented as he vented his frustration by throwing whatever he had at hand to fly unerringly across the room.

"At least both your aim and your arm are good," Betty said when he crashed yet another earthenware mug. "But maybe you could throw something that doesn't break?" He glared at her, but when she used a piece of coal to draw what he thought was a cow, but she sulkily informed him was a catamount on the wall for him to aim at, his lips twitched into a smile.

He tired easily. The walk across the yard to the stable was enough that he had to catch his breath, but once there, among the animals, he was comforted, because these were things he still could do, even if it all took much longer than it used to. Pain became his constant companion: at times, a dull, throbbing ache; at other, short, sharp twinges that had him doubling over. But he refused to let the pain rule him, and so he curried, he milked, he shooed the beasts out to graze once he was done, he fed the piglets and the sow, and spent hours verbalising his frustration to the pigs. The sow twitched her ears now and then, occasionally stuck an inquiring snout into his crotch or nibbled at his wooden cane, but Ian was sure she understood.

It was hell at times. Ian swore and cursed; he cried when no one saw, hating this body of his for no longer moving as fluidly as it once had done. He did the strange exercises Mama had set him, lying on his front while he lifted arms and legs, ignoring the warning twinges when he overdid it. Stubbornly, he extended his walks, waving away offers of help, and there were days when Betty would have to go out to look for him and find him half lying, half sitting, incapable of moving as much as a toe.

He resented them all sometimes: from Da, who so casually bent to swing Maggie up to sit on his hip, to Mark, a carbon copy of himself as he used to be, agile and strong. But it was getting better, and the day he struggled all the way to the river by himself, Ian whooped with joy. For a long time, he stayed in the water, swimming lazily back and forth and relishing the fact that it didn't hurt – not at first. Afterwards, he barely made it out, and when Betty found him, he was shivering with cold in the grass, unable to crawl to where he had left his clothes.

"Don't overdo it," Mama warned one afternoon, coming to sit beside him under the oak.

"I have to. I must be back on my feet." He nodded his head at the ripe fields. "The harvest is in full swing."

"And you'll not take part," Alex said, "not this year." She helped him to stand and handed him the cane. "You have many years before you. Either you recognise your limitations and live a good life within them, or you ignore them and push yourself so hard you permanently damage yourself."

"I'm already a cripple," he said bitterly.

"Ian…" Mama took a firm grip of his arm. "You've been up and about three weeks, no more. And look at you:

you stand, you walk, you can sit, have sex with your wife."

Ian was somewhat flustered, but nodded a grudging agreement.

"This'll take a long time to mend," she continued, "and it will never mend entirely, but it will get better – much better. Will you ever be able to work four weeks in a row from dawn to twilight harvesting? Probably not. Will you be able to work at all? Probably yes."

"Probably yes," he reminded himself later that evening. "Probably yes, probably yes."

"Yes what?" Betty yawned beside him.

"Nothing," he replied. "Don't mind me, love. I was just thinking aloud." He rolled over on his front, shoving the pillow out of the way. "Will you please?" He fell asleep under her hands, a cloud of peppermint scent around them both.

It had been a strange homecoming for Daniel: none of the happy loud welcome of last year, even if Mama hugged him until he thought his bones would break. And then there was Ian, a pale, strained version of the brother he remembered, and Da, who looked haunted.

On top of this, Daniel was very confused to find Minister Allerton at Graham's Garden, and even more when the minister stated his intention to stay and help through the harvest now that the eldest Graham son was injured.

"But you're not a farming man!" Daniel blurted. The Allertons he had met were merchants, and the minister's brother was a prominent man in the Boston community.

"We all are to begin with," Minister Allerton said cheerily. "*When Adam delved and Eve span, who was then a gentleman*, as John Ball said."

"For which he was hung, drawn and quartered," Mama pointed out.

"Yes, unfortunately." Minister Allerton looked grave. "But then, very many men have met with a similar fate for similar reasons. Besides, he was right: all men are born equal in the eyes of Our Lord. It's the life he leads that should distinguish a man, not his ancestors."

"I totally agree," Mama said, "which is why I have major issues with all this predestination stuff."

"Stuff?" Minister Allerton raised a brow.

Daniel shifted from foot to foot, throwing a pleading glance at his da. Could he please nip this discussion in the bud?

"All that blather about how some men – and a smattering of women, I suppose – are offered grace depending on God's whim, not their actions, while the rest sink into perdition…" Mama shook her head. "Strikes me as a most unjust God."

"God is unjust," Minister Allerton said, "at least from a narrow human perspective. We can never attempt to comprehend his infinite mercy and wisdom – which is why we must assume he knows best. As is stated in the Holy Writ: *Trust in the Lord with all thine heart and lean not unto thine own understanding.*"

"Huh," Mama snorted, "then what's the point? If already at birth it's predestined whether you will go to heaven or hell, why bother?"

"Firstly, because you never know to whom God will extend grace," the minister said, "and secondly because even if God has chosen you as one of the saved, you must prove yourself worthy."

Mama mulled this over for some time. "No, sorry. I still can't accept it. That means that your actions can only count against you, never for you, so once damned, always damned, no matter how saintly a life you lead." She stood to fetch the pies from the pantry, and Daniel took the opportunity to steer the conversation elsewhere.

"You mustn't mind what Mama says," Daniel said to the minister after dinner. "She can be somewhat frivolous at times."

"Frivolous?" Minister Allerton gave him a stern look. "What a disparaging comment to make."

"She doesn't really know much about matters of faith, and you must keep in mind that she's Swedish."

"She's a woman with doubts – all of us have them at

times. Her arguments against predestination have been raised many times before, by men both wise and learned. One doesn't wave away doubts as being misinformed. One strives to convince instead." The minister's mouth set, and Daniel groaned quietly. This could become a very long month.

Some days later, Daniel was sitting in the long slope just above the kitchen garden, swamped by the sensation that he was no longer part of this life: he was a visitor, as much an outsider as the exhausted minister. The grey wood of the buildings, the fields that shone golden in the setting sun, and the glittering band of the river – it was all part of a world that he had stepped out of.

All day, Daniel had been longing for home and it had been a disagreeable insight to realise that he was home – these were his people, this was his place. Except that it wasn't, not anymore. Now, it was Boston he thought of as home; it was with Temperance Allerton, not Ruth, that he shared his hopes for the future, his everyday concerns.

He heard Ian's shuffling progress behind him and closed his eyes. To see his big brother so damaged cut him to the quick, and even more it galled him that everyone else seemed to consider things were still the same, that Ian was unchanged, despite the fact that he had to walk with a cane. Ian stopped beside him, but where before he would have dropped to sit, that was no longer possible, so instead Daniel stood, making Ian smile wryly.

"Does it still feel like home?" Ian asked, surprising Daniel.

"No."

Ian just nodded, as if this was to be expected. "But, when you're there, don't you miss it?"

Daniel considered this for some moments. "Yes, I do."

"And Ruth?"

Daniel nodded. Very much he missed her, but she didn't seem to miss him much, did she?

Ian smiled down at him, still a couple of inches taller. "Much more than she lets on."

"Does it hurt much?" Daniel asked as they made their way back down.

"Aye." Ian turned to face him, and in his unshielded gaze Daniel saw just how much it hurt, and what effort went into concealing it. "But I could have been dead," Ian said with a little shrug that conveyed how weak a comfort he found this.

Daniel dug his bare toe into the grass. "That would have killed her."

"Who? Betty?" Ian smiled.

Daniel gave his head an irritated shake. "Mama, of course."

"Mama?" Ian sounded very surprised.

"She loves you best. We all know that." Daniel smiled at the dumbfounded expression on his brother's face. "We don't mind, aye? And she can't help it, can she?"

Ian cleared his throat, looking like quite the daftie with his mouth hanging open.

Daniel grinned and went to find Ruth.

Chapter 41

"Something's going on." Alex turned suspicious eyes on Mark, Daniel and Ian in turn, only to be met by three blank faces. She let her eyes travel over to Minister Allerton, who put on his best bemused face. "None of you will ever win an Oscar," she said, biting back a laugh at their confused expressions. Well, if they weren't telling, nor was she. She had already tried Mrs Parson, only to be met by a satisfied little cackle, and Naomi had blinked and widened her eyes, assuring Alex she had no idea.

"All of you," she said wagging her finger at the four present. "You're all in on it."

She cornered Agnes in the dairy shed, and after spending close to half an hour discussing the cheese, she casually let drop that her birthday was in five days.

"Aye, we all know that." Agnes concentrated on pouring the cream into the churn.

"You do?"

Agnes fitted the wooden lid and took hold of the churn-staff.

"Aye," she said, before becoming as close-lipped as the others.

Alex rolled her eyes and went to look for Betty whom she found in the kitchen garden.

"I hate surprises," Alex confided to Betty. "I really, really hate them. So I hope Matthew isn't planning something. Not that there's any reason he should. After all, forty-nine is a very unimportant birthday, isn't it?"

Betty's bright eyes twinkled. "I have no idea, Mama Alex. Mayhap you should ask Da?"

"Huh," Alex snorted, "minx." She stalked off, leaving Betty to harvest the corncobs all by herself.

Even the children were in on it — not the youngest, obviously — and Adam quickly changed the subject by taking her by the hand to inspect his latest patient.

Alex almost threw up. "It's cruel to leave him alive," she said, picking up the deformed kitten. "Its back is broken."

Hugin leaned in a bit too close, a gleam of interest in his black eyes that had nothing to do with the diagnosis. Alex flapped her hand at him, and the raven hopped out of reach, clattering its beak at her.

"So was Ian's," Adam said.

"No, honey, it wasn't. If it had been, he wouldn't be walking. He hurt his back badly, but he didn't break it. But this…" She held up the mewling kitten. "…this back is cleanly broke. See? Its hind legs just hang."

"So, what do I do?" Adam used his finger to caress the little head.

"We end its suffering."

"Is that what you would have done to Ian?" Adam asked in a small voice.

"God, no!" But he would have wanted us to, she thought.

"…and then of course I had to kill it," Alex said with a grimace, when she recounted the incident to Matthew.

"How?" Matthew asked.

"I wrung its neck." Alex shuddered. One sharp crack and the little animal was dead. She helped Matthew unharness the oxen, and gave him a concerned look. "How are you?"

In the whirlwind of the last few weeks, they had barely spoken. First, Alex had been entirely focused on Ian, then the harvest had begun in earnest, and Matthew worked and worked, with Mark and John Mason his constant shadows. Minister Allerton and Daniel had done their fair share, as had David, but the brunt of it fell on Matthew, and he had worked from well before dawn to late into the evenings, stopping only to eat and sleep.

"Tired." He felt old, he muttered, his body protested at being used this way, his knees and back ached, and his shoulders had stiffened into a permanent band of pain.

"You should have told me," she said.

Matthew shrugged. She had enough to do with her own harvesting, keeping them all fed, and on top of that minding and chiding Ian.

"Men! Come here, you." She extended her hand to him.

"Better?" she asked an hour or so later, smiling down at him.

"Mmm." He was almost asleep in the hot water, his body relaxed. She washed him, singing softly under her breath. He smiled as she sang about summer breezes and how deep her love was.

"I like that," he said, humming along with the chorus.

"You do?" She splashed water in his direction. "I used to dance very, very slow dances to this."

"Did you now?" His eyes cracked open. "You've never danced a slow dance with me."

"You've never asked me to, have you?"

"…but when I ask you to…" he said, his eyes fully open.

"…well, then I will," she promised and pushed his head under water to rinse his hair.

Once he was clean, she dried him, patting her way down his body. She slowed her hand over his crotch, running a tentative finger down his penis. It twitched in response. Alex stroked it again, thinking that she couldn't quite remember when they'd last made proper love. Since Ian's accident, there hadn't been time for more than the odd, urgent coupling, often just as they were drifting off to sleep. But now…

"Lie down," she said, pointing at the bench. He was naked, she was dressed, and when he made as if to undress her, she shook her head. Not yet, not until he was quivering with need.

She kissed her way up his legs, all the way from his toes to his groin. Her hand on his member, a fleeting kiss to its tip, and he groaned. Alex smiled and concentrated her efforts on his eyes, his beautiful mouth, his neck. A series of swift kisses down his sternum, her cheek resting against his belly while her hand fondled and teased, and he exhaled, sinking his hand into her hair.

"For pity's sake, woman," he said, sounding very hoarse.

Alex slid upwards to kiss his mouth. For a long, long time, they kissed. He rolled her over, smoothing the hair off her face. She gripped his ears, pulling his mouth down to hers. He shoved her skirts out of the way and plunged into her.

"I needed that," he said afterwards.

"So did I." Alex gave him a brief kiss. "Massage? I think you need that too, right?"

It was as she was working out the tensions in his back that he began to cry. Not a noisy, sobbing weeping, but a low, heart-rending sound, and Alex stopped what she was doing and leaned her cheek against his back.

Matthew hid his face against the bunched linen below him and wept, and she cried with him, for the young man who would never again run unhampered through the woods, or walk for hours behind the plough, safe in the strength of his own body.

"It won't be that bad." Alex wiped at her eyes. "He can already walk without his cane for short stretches."

"But he could never walk on the moors like you and I did," Matthew said, "and I was older then than he is now."

Alex didn't reply. She stroked him over his head until he fell asleep, sitting cross-legged beside him as he slept.

"Now," Alex said, prodding Ian's side a bit too hard. "Tell me what is going on."

"Mama!" he protested, laughing. "Will you resort to torturing a weakened man?"

"You bet, and it's much easier to torture someone who's already lying down." She peered at the healed scar, her hands soft when she inspected his flank. "That doesn't hurt at all, does it?"

Ian shook his head.

She indicated that he should roll over, and dipped into her home-made heat rub, consisting mainly of mints, goose grease and camphor. She massaged him until his whole back was bright red, added yet another layer of her grease, and covered him with a quilt to ensure he held the heat.

"So what is it?" she asked.

He pretended to snore.

"What if I don't like it? At least if you give me a hint, I can pretend to like it."

"Like what?" Ian asked, opening his eyes. He smiled at her irritated noise. "You're imagining things."

"Of course, which is why Mark suddenly just had to ride over to the Chisholms' for beer."

"Thirsty work, harvest," Ian said, and just like that, his mood plunged.

Alex saw it in his eyes and sighed. How often did she have to tell him to be patient?

He glared at her, eyes an intense green, and pointedly turned the other way.

"It's up to you. Either you choose to see the glass as half-full or half-empty." She patted him on the back and left the room.

Minister Allerton made his way over to where Ian was sitting on the little bench in the graveyard and sat down beside him, holding out a stone bottle.

"Beer?"

"Hmph," Ian said, but took the bottle anyway. "She sent you, didn't she?" he asked, wiping his mouth with his hand.

"Who?" Minister Allerton opened his eyes disingenuously.

"Mama." Who else?

"She isn't your real mother, is she?" the minister sidestepped.

"In everything that counts, she is."

"Something of a mother bear, most protective of her young."

Ian smiled despite himself at the likeness, and nodded an agreement.

Minister Allerton raised the bottle to his mouth and drank.

376

"Who's that?" he asked, indicating Magnus' headstone.

"That? Oh, that's Offa. Mama's father."

"Ah." The minister sat beside him for some time before turning to face him. "She's right, your mother: you can view what happened to you as a terrible misfortune or as a miraculous deliverance." He stood up and nodded his head in the direction of the gravestone. "There could have been one more – one with your name on it. But there isn't, is there?"

"Am I being very difficult?" Ian asked Betty later that night. She looked up from where she was knitting him a pair of stockings, and the light from the candle beside her fell like a soft golden glow over her face.

"No more than can be expected," she said after some consideration.

"I don't want to be difficult. At all," he snapped, and then smiled ruefully at himself.

She folded together the stockings, went over to check on the sleeping bairns, and came to join him in bed.

"Back rub?"

Ian shook his head and patted the bed beside him.

She knew how he liked things by now, and pulled off her shift to stand naked before him. When she turned to extinguish the candle, he could see how her belly was beginning to round. She crawled in to lie beside him and took his hand, placing it on her stomach.

"I felt him today," she said in an awed voice. "And it was like holding a trapped moth in my cupped hands. A flutter of life in my womb..." She turned towards him and kissed him on the mouth, one of her very slow and teasing kisses. At times, Ian wondered how someone as inexperienced as Betty could kiss like that – hot breath escaping through open lips, her tongue flicking so expertly against his.

"He'll know his father," Betty said as she broke away. "And he'll have many, many brothers and sisters. That's a good thing, isn't it?"

"A very good thing," he repeated in a voice that barely carried. He kissed her again, tasted the raspberries they'd had for supper on her breath, and drew in the scent of roses and lavender that clung to her skin. He smiled. She had bathed and oiled herself for him.

"How many?" he asked later, lying flat on his back.

"How many what?" Her voice drifted down from above him.

"Brothers and sisters," he clarified with an effort. His cock pulsated inside of her, brimming with life and strength.

"As many as you want, but perhaps not more than ten."

"No more than ten," he agreed breathlessly.

Alex saw Ian emerge from his cabin next morning, and she knew that something had shifted for him. She took Matthew's hand and turned him to watch Ian stretching on his door stoop. In only his shirt, his dark hair messy, Ian raised his arms high over his head and extended himself to well over seven feet, gracious as a giant cat. Unaware of his audience, he took a careful, shuffling step off the stone stoop and lifted his shirt to piss, his face raised to the rising sun. He was smiling, a huge face-breaking smile. Someone said something to him and he laughed, shaking himself thoroughly. Betty appeared at the door, naked as the day she was born, and Alex had to grin at Matthew's little hiss.

"She's his wife, and I'm not wearing much more, am I?" She smiled fondly in the direction of Betty and Ian, and slipped her arms round Matthew's waist.

"I love you," she said to his chest hairs.

He kissed her hair. "I adore you."

"And if you don't tell me this minute what it is you're planning behind my back, I might just…" She cupped her hand around his balls.

"You might what?"

"Do this," she grinned, very pleased by his surprised gasp.

Chapter 42

He woke her with a kiss, told her to put something on, and led her out to the kitchen. Alex just gaped. At Jacob, at Matthew, and back at Jacob.

"How—" Before she could say anything more, her son had crossed the floor and swept her into his arms. God, he was big, bigger even than his father, and blond and good-looking and whole and safe and… Alex couldn't stop crying, her hands flying over him.

"A beard?" she asked, fingers examining the thickened bridge of his nose.

"I couldn't shave up in the woods." Jacob scratched at his patchily covered cheeks.

"Up in the woods?" Alex whirled towards her husband. "Why you—" She flew at him, but she was laughing, and allowed him to draw her close and kiss her.

"Happy birthday, lass," he said. "I couldn't think of something you would want more."

"How long has he been home?" Alex asked, kissing him back.

"A week." Jacob sighed theatrically. "Living like a savage in the woods."

"Nay, you haven't," Matthew retorted. "You've been sleeping in style in the hayloft."

"And you've all known," Alex said.

"Aye, well, he isn't invisible, is he?" Matthew's voice was loaded with pride. No, he definitely wasn't. The half-grown boy had returned a man.

"Have you seen Betty?" Alex asked bluntly, making both son and husband grin.

Jacob nodded, twisting somewhat as he muttered that it had been a bit awkward at first, to see a girl he had for some years considered as his future wife so besotted with his brother and already with child. "She's happy," he said, "and she deserves to be."

"And you?" Alex raised a hand to the unfamiliar bearded cheek. Hazel eyes softened and looked down at her, and in the back of them Alex saw pain and humiliation, heartbreak and a tentativeness she had never seen there before.

"I'm home," Jacob sidestepped.

Alex was confined to her parlour for the rest of the morning, with Mary Leslie as her watchdog. From the kitchen floated enticing smells of baking hams and pies and bread, and out in the yard she could hear loud voices calling instructions, laughter and the occasional muffled curse as her family went about setting up their surprise. Not much of a surprise, she smiled to herself, listening distractedly while Mary told her the latest news from Boston.

"...and Harriet believes the girl is as taken as he is," Mary finished.

"Ah," Alex said.

"Alex!" Mary laughed. "You haven't been listening, have you?"

"No," Alex admitted.

"I was talking about Daniel, him and that girl of his."

"Girl of his? Oh, you must mean Temperance!"

Mary nodded. "A very nice girl according to Harriet, and quite the catch on account of her mother. Hope Allerton is the only daughter to a draper, and the business is worth a substantial amount of money."

"It is?" To Alex, all of this just meant one thing: her son might marry and settle so far away from her she would but see him rarely, and as to any grandchildren...

Mary sighed in agreement. Only once had she seen Harriet in the last five years, and as for the two girls left behind in England, the once so regular letters had dried up to become a dutiful annual epistle.

"I suppose Boston is better than England," Alex said, "but it's so uncertain to have them gone, isn't it? Anything can happen to them, and we'll never know until it's too late."

"Yes," Mary replied shortly.

Too late, Alex remembered that Mary had recently lost one daughter to childbirth down in Virginia, only to find out in a stilted letter from her bereaved son-in-law. Alex covered Mary's hand with her own.

All of them gawked: Ian, Mark, Jacob, Daniel – even David stared at his mama in her dark red bodice. Not that she noticed, because all she cared for was the look in Matthew's eyes. She twirled, adjusted her laces, and smiled at him, a slow smile that she accompanied with a fluttering of eyelashes that made him laugh rather than pant. Still, when he took her hand, his fingertips caressed the inside of her wrist, and his eyes had gone a very golden shade of green, making something stir inside of her. She leaned towards him, a brush, no more, of her daringly exposed chest against his shirt.

"We have guests," Mark reminded them.

"Many guests," Ian nodded, and all the present Graham children burst out laughing at the way their mother rolled her eyes.

"Ouff!" Alex sat down with a thud on a stool, and flapped her hands in an attempt to cool her overheated cheeks. The barn was full of people, dancing, eating, drinking copious quantities of beer. Luckily, the Chisholms had brought some extra beer and cider with them, but what had seemed a mountain of food was now reduced to a couple of pies and a half-eaten loaf.

Alex grinned at the sight of Mrs Parson dancing with Peter Leslie, and turned to face her son. "She's seventy-one. You wouldn't believe it, would you?"

Jacob shook his head. "It will be him that keels over first."

As if he had heard him, Peter held up his hands in an apologetic gesture and dragged himself over to where the drink was.

"Was she pretty?" Alex asked.

Jacob's mouth curved into a reluctant smile. "I thought

so, but then I thought a lot about her that later proved to be false." He met her eyes. "Later, I'll tell you all of it later."

"Of course you will," she said, and he nodded in defeat.

"Should he be dancing?" he asked instead, pointing at Ian, who was on the dance floor.

"No, but if he's willing to take the pain that comes tomorrow, well, that's his business." She stood up and extended her hand to him. "One more, Jacob, seeing as your father has escaped outside."

"Mama," he groaned, but got to his feet anyway.

"Nowhere close, not anymore," Matthew said to Peter and Thomas Leslie. He had looked, God how he had looked, those first few weeks after the attack. Mark and he had scoured the woods, and had they found them, the Burley brothers would no longer be walking the world. Where before the Burleys had mostly woken fear in him, now it was hatred and rage that flowed through his veins when he thought of them. He cleared his throat. One day...

"They make dangerous enemies," Thomas warned, regarding Matthew through a thin veil of pipe smoke.

"So do I, and I won't forgive them for damaging my son."

"Mmm," Peter nodded, "terrible..."

Matthew felt it unnecessary to comment.

"Will you help me find them?" Matthew asked, directing himself to Thomas, who nodded.

"And what will you do if you find them?" Peter asked.

"If?" Matthew shook his head. "There's no if. It's a when." He closed his hand round the piece of bread in his hand and watched it disintegrate. "And when I do..." His voice trailed off into heavy silence.

Any further conversation was interrupted by Alex, appearing rosy and warm in the barn door.

"You promised you were going to dance with me, Mr Graham," she said, and came to take his hand.

"I did? As I recall, what I said was that, if I danced, it would only be with you."

"Same thing," she said and tugged at him. "You also made some very cocky remarks about dancing me off my feet. So far a lot of words and no action, if you see what I mean."

"No action?" His mouth was very close to her ear.

"No action," she repeated, and pulled him back with her into the barn.

Matthew danced her off her feet. When she pleaded for mercy, he shook his head, leading her out into every dance. They twirled, they stamped, they weaved through complicated patterns with the other dancers, but all the while his eyes were glued to hers. She was lifted in the air, she was held close enough that he could feel the rise of her breasts against his chest, and only when she threatened to sit down where she stood, did he take pity on her and lead her off the dance floor.

"You said how you would dance a slow dance for me," Matthew murmured some time later, handing her a cup of cider.

"Not for, with, and I'm ready whenever you are." She drained her cup, set it down and walked with swinging skirts in the direction of the woods. He followed, smiling when he saw that she'd taken off her shoes and stockings, walking barefoot through the grass. She held out her arms to him, winding them hard around his neck.

She sang in his ear, the same song she'd sung him in the bath about summer breezes and touching in the pouring rain, and he tightened his arms around her and kissed her, trying to show her just how deep his love was. Forehead to forehead, they slowly turned, singing the chorus together.

From where he was standing a few feet into the forest, Qaachow watched Matthew and Alex slow their dance to stillness, saw him take her hand and lead her towards the house. He motioned for his men to remain where they were, and stepped out of the wooded fringe that surrounded the central buildings of the farm. When he was a boy, not that long ago, all of this had been forest, oaks and maples and sycamores standing never-ending round him, and now it was all gone. His land was gone, his people were gone, the spirits of the deep woods had fled further north and further west, and soon nothing would be left to show his people had ever been.

From the barn spilled the sound of white man's music; in the door he saw the shapes of white men's bodies, skin that shone fair in the light of lanterns. In the yard, a group of children ran and played, boys mostly, but here and there he caught the long braids of a girl.

We should have driven them off, he thought bitterly, our ancestors should have thrown them back into the sea whence they came. Even now, it was perhaps not too late. Kill all the men, take the children and women with them, and make them forget who they were and where they came from.

Qaachow sighed and turned away from the sounds of dancing and enjoyment, gliding back into the invisibility of the trees. He stood there a while longer, and now his eyes were riveted on the boy – his foster son. Tall like his father, dark of hair, and with a fluidity in his movements that made Qaachow smile with pleasure. White Bear leaped high in the air and landed with the ball in a firm grip, ducked to avoid his elder brother and, with a whooping sound, threw the ball to another child. Soon, Qaachow mouthed soundlessly, I will come for you soon.

"Alex?" Matthew groped for her hand.

"Mmm?" She braided her fingers round his.

"I love you," he said to the dark, overcome by an urgent need to tell her what she surely knew anyway. "So very much do I love you."

She raised herself on an elbow and kissed his cheek. "I know," she said, nestling back down against his chest.

He waited and waited, and thought she might have fallen asleep.

"I love you too," she breathed against his skin. "I always have, and always will."

384

"Always?" His fingers brushed through her hair.

"Since before I was born," she replied, giggling at her own jest.

"Alex?"

She didn't reply, and, from the sound of her breathing, she had fallen asleep.

Matthew cradled her to him and kissed the top of her head. "I don't think I'd want to live without you," he said out loud, his cheeks heating. "I don't think I could."

Alex opened one eye and smiled. Me neither, she thought drowsily, me neither, Matthew Graham.

★ ★ ★

"A package?" Simon turned it over. "Who'd send me something from London?"

"Unless you open it, you won't find out, will you?" Joan offered him her scissors to cut the string. She laughed at his hesitation. "It won't bite you."

"Oh, aye? And how do you know?" he said, but he smiled at her as he said it. He sneaked her a look from under his lashes. Whatever it was Alex had suggested she take, it helped, even if at times the sweetish smell was rather cloying. There was a tinge of pink in Joan's previously so grey cheeks, and her mouth that for years had been set in a line had relaxed back into its natural fullness.

Simon Melville wasn't a fool. He knew his wife was dying – she'd been doing that for the last five or six years – but now it seemed these last few years would not be one long agonising journey, and for that he was hugely grateful.

He unwrapped the last of the packing around the object. "Dear God," he whispered, almost throwing the small square from him. He had seen something similar to this once before, and he knew what they could do. Joan leaned over his shoulder to look, a shocked exclamation escaping her. A painting: swirling greens and blues, a heaving mass of colour that entrapped your eyes and enticed you to look deeper, lose yourself in it.

"How?" she said. "And why to you?"

"I don't know." He nudged the painting. "Do you...do you think it's the same?"

Joan swayed, gripped his arm and sat down on a stool, eyes tightly shut. "Yes," she groaned. "Dearest Lord, take it away, destroy it!"

"Joan?" Simon gave her a gentle shake. In response, she moaned, a weak mewling no more.

"Joan!" He grabbed at her when she slipped off her stool.

Lucy started from where she'd been reading by the window, oblivious to their conversation. Her eyes flew to her parents, and she rushed towards them.

"Here." Simon rewrapped the painting with one hand, the other arm supporting Joan. He handed it to Lucy and waited until she was looking at him.

"Burn it," he said slowly. "Burn it, aye?" He jerked his head in the direction of the empty hearth. Lucy nodded, took the package and made for the kitchen where there always was a fire.

But Lucy didn't burn it. She couldn't – not when for the first time in her life, she heard sounds, wonderful magical sounds.

The Graham Saga continues in:

Revenge and Retribution

The sun had just cleared the eastern forest when they set off next morning: six horses, two loaded mules, and seven people. Thomas Leslie took the lead, with his armed manservant riding just behind him. For practical reasons, Alex was riding pillion behind Matthew, while Daniel rode the roan she'd ridden down, and, given the general bustle of departure, it took Matthew some time to realise his wife seemed out of sorts, uncharacteristically quiet and distracted. She didn't join in the banter between Ian and Daniel, she expressed a vague "Hmm?" when Betty asked her something, and to Matthew she didn't say a word, a silent warmth at his back no more.

"What is it?" he finally asked.

"Bad night." She tightened her hold round his waist.

She'd tell him in her own good time what it was that was preying on her mind, so instead Matthew concentrated on the way his stallion moved beneath him. Aaron was in many ways a throwback to his sire, but where Moses had been a singularly docile horse, Aaron was far more hot-blooded, capable of taking a leap to the side in an attempt to dislodge his rider – or get closer to the mare.

"You've had her already, you wee daftie," Matthew said, slapping Aaron on the neck. "She's with your get."

"Do you think he knows?" Alex sounded very amused.

"What? That he's served her or that she's with foal?"

"Both, I suppose."

Matthew thought about that for a moment. "I hope, for his sake, he recalls the serving of her. It's not much more than a dozen times a year for him. But as to the foal…nay, he doesn't know."

"Oh." Alex fell silent for a while. "Do you think he's alright?" she asked with a hitch to her voice.

"Who?" Matthew did a swift count through his head – all their bairns were, as far as he knew, safe.

"Isaac," she whispered.

"Ah…" No wonder she'd been tossing through the night. She'd been dreaming of her lost life, of her people in the hazy future, foremost amongst them her future son – this no doubt brought on by the discussion they'd had about that accursed little painting. He shifted in the saddle. Thinking about this made him right queasy: his wife a time traveller, her mother a gifted painter that painted portals through time, and wee Isaac seemed to have inherited his grandmother's magical gifts. After all, it was one of Isaac's paintings that Magnus Lind, Alex's father, had used as a time portal all those years ago, appearing one day much the worse for wear in yon thorny thicket back home.

Matthew strangled a nervous laugh: first his wife, then her father. And as to those paintings… Ungodly, such paintings could only be created with the help of potent magic – black magic. Matthew tightened his hold on the reins and uttered a brief prayer to God, begging him to protect them all – and especially his wife – from evil. He coughed a couple of times.

"What do you think?" he said.

"I'm not sure. I never miss him, not truly. Yes, I think of him, wish him well in his life and all that, but he's no hole in my heart. What if I am a hole in his?"

Matthew reached back to squeeze her thigh. "He was but a lad when you disappeared from his life. Aye, surely there are nights when he dreams of you, moments when you are a vaguely remembered shade, but a hole in his life that you are not. Man is too resilient for that."

She didn't reply, but he felt her relax, and after a few minutes of silence she changed the subject by asking him what he thought of Lionel Smith, pompous shit that she found him.

It was nearly noon before they stopped for a break – and by then Alex had been fidgeting for some time. She more

388

or less fell off the horse and made for the closest screen of shrubs. Alex hiked up her skirts and crouched. She cocked her head to where her men were busy lighting a fire in the glade, grinned when Daniel loudly complained about the state of his buttocks, tore off some moss to wipe herself with, and rose.

"Mrs Graham, what an unexpected surprise."

The voice froze Alex to the spot, but with an effort she turned, only to find herself a scant yard or so from Philip Burley. Still with that messy dark hair that fell forward over his face in an endearing manner that contrasted entirely with his ice-cold eyes, still with a certain flair to him, albeit that he was dishevelled and dirty. Alex opened her mouth to yell, but all that came out was a squeak.

"Down to witness the hanging of my dear brother?" Philip continued, his voice far too low to carry to her companions. Low, but laden with rage.

"Good riddance," Alex managed to say. She whirled, screaming like a train whistle.

Things happened so fast, Alex's vision blurred. The ground came rushing towards her, her face was pressed into the mulch by Philip's tackle. She heard Matthew roar, set her hands to the ground and heaved. Up. Philip grabbed at her skirts, Alex kicked like a mule, and here came Matthew, bounding towards them. Philip scrambled to his feet, and Alex crawled away on hands and knees.

In Matthew's hand flashed a sword, Philip levelled a pistol but had no opportunity to fire it before Matthew brought his blade down, sending the gun to twirl through the air and land in a distant bush.

Men. From all over, men swarmed, and there was Walter Burley, fighting his way towards Matthew with an intent look on his face. He was brought up short by Dandelion, over a hundred pounds of enraged dog throwing himself at Walter. A howl, a long howl that ended in a whine. Walter brandished his bloodied knife and cheered, a sound cut abruptly short when Thomas Leslie charged him. A hand grabbed at Alex; she tore herself free and backed away, looking for some kind of weapon, anything to defend herself with. And there was Matthew – everywhere was Matthew: kicking her assailant to the ground, fending off Philip's sword, swinging round to punch Walter, grinding an elbow into yet another man, and all the while he was yelling out commands to his sons and Thomas.

Like a deadly whirlwind was Matthew Graham, and beware to anyone coming between him and the man he was screaming at, spittle flying in the air as he advanced, step by step, towards Philip, a Philip who seemed surprisingly taken aback, retreating towards the woods. Matthew lunged, Philip fell back, using a stout branch to defend himself. Again, and Philip took yet another step backwards. Alex intercepted a swift glance between the Burley brothers, and she didn't like the smirk on Philip's face. Matthew charged, Philip turned and fled with a triumphant Matthew at his heels.

"No..." Alex croaked. A dull crack, and Matthew staggered, a giant of a man appearing from where he'd been hiding, brandishing a cudgel. Walter Burley whooped, doing a few dance steps. Alex didn't stop to think. She launched herself at him, landing knees first on his chest. There was a whoosh when the air was expelled from his body, and then he went limp.

She picked up Walter's pistol from where he'd dropped it and turned to find her husband locked in a fight with two men, while Thomas, his man and her sons were kept at bay by seven. Philip Burley yelled when Matthew succeeded in sinking his dirk into his right arm. For an instant, it seemed as if Matthew was about to tear himself free from the unknown huge man, but there was Philip, whacking Matthew over the head again. Matthew's knees buckled under him and Alex fired into the air.

"I'll cut his throat!" she screamed, holding Walter's lolling head by his hair. "I'll do it now!" Her hand was shaking so badly she at first couldn't get to her knife through the side slit of her skirt, but then her fingers closed on the familiar handle and she pulled it free.

"Let him go!" Philip Burley glared at her. "Let go of him, you fool of a woman, or I'll gut your husband like a pig."

Matthew tottered, blood running in miniature rivulets over the left side of his face.

"An impasse, it would seem," Alex said, struggling to keep her voice steady. "You let my husband go, and I'll let your brother live. For now." She increased the pressure of her blade on Walter's skin, making him gargle.

Philip sneered and glanced down at his bleeding arm. "You stand no chance, Mrs Graham. We are ten to your six."

"Seven," someone said. A shot rang out, and the large man helping Philip to hold Matthew dropped like a stone to the ground, shot through his back. "And now you are but nine."

Burley's men shifted, trying to find the sharpshooter. Thomas' hand flew out and one of the men fell to his knees, gripping at the hilt of a knife that stuck out from his thigh. A collective muttering ran through the six men left standing, their eyes sliding towards the relative safety of the woods. Alex's hand was slick on the handle of her knife and, to compensate, she tightened her hold on Walter's hair, pulling so hard the man squealed.

Philip scowled: at Matthew, at Alex, and at the woods. With a swift movement, he levelled a pistol at Matthew's head.

"If any more of my men are hurt, I'll kill him," he shouted, scanning the surrounding trees. He jerked his head in the direction of the forest, and his men helped their wounded comrade to stand, closing ranks around him. Ian and Daniel closed in on Philip, who was dragging Matthew with him as a shield.

"My brother," he said to Alex. "Release my brother, and I'll release your husband."

Ian raised his musket and aimed it at Walter.

"Do as he says, Mama. And if Da isn't released before the count of three, then Walter Burley is no more."

Walter's breath came in loud hisses, his pulse leaping erratically against her hand. At less than ten feet, Ian would never miss. Daniel aimed his weapon at Philip.

"Nor is Philip Burley," he vowed, but the barrel trembled a bit too much.

Alex let go of Walter's hair and stepped back, watching as he lurched to his feet. At least one broken rib and, if she was lucky, maybe two or three. Walter Burley wheezed, wrapping his arms hard around his midriff.

He lifted strange light eyes to Alex. "You'll pay," he spat through colourless lips.

"You can always try, and next time I'll squash your balls instead." It took a superhuman effort to retain eye contact with those eerie grey eyes, but she did, stiffening her spine with resolve.

"One," Ian counted. "Two…" Matthew was pushed to land at Daniel's feet, and Ian swung the muzzle of his musket towards Philip and the band of renegades. "Three," he said and fired, as did Daniel.

For a Historical Note and more information about
Matthew and Alex, please visit Anna Belfrage's
website at www.annabelfrage.com

CPSIA information can be obtained
at www.ICGtesting.com
Printed in the USA
LVOW11s0121310117
522686LV00002B/182/P